A KING OF CRIMSON DREAMS

DAUGHTERS OF CHAOS SERIES
BOOK 3

MINA B. CASTILLO

DELPHINUS STAR PUBLISHING LLC

"Well do I know that though cowards quit the field, a hero, whether he wound or be wounded, must stand firm and hold his own."

— HOMER. *THE ILIAD*. TRANSLATED BY SAMUEL BUTLER, 1898.

A KING OF CRIMSON DREAMS

DAUGHTERS OF CHAOS SERIES

By: Mina B. Castillo

Formerly writing as Mina Brower.

A King of Crimson Dreams is a work of fiction. The story, all names, characters, and incidents portrayed in this book are fictitious and are products of the author's imagination. Resemblance with actual persons (living or deceased), places, buildings, and products is entirely coincidental.

Author name formerly: Mina Brower

Published in the United States by Delphinus Star Publishing LLC.
Paperback ISBN 979-8-9912482-7-3
Ebook ISBN 979-8-9912482-6-6

Visit authorminacastillo.com to learn more about the author and her upcoming books.

Editors: Megan Carver at Thorns N' Roses; Nadara Merrill at Nay's Notations; and Lisa Ulrich at Melissa Smith Editing

Fight consultation by New York Combat Stage and Screen and Thorns N' Roses

Cover graphics from Canva

To my readers:
There is strength in allowing others to help you.

1

RENNA

Fiery burgundy eyes bored into mine, almost paralyzing me.

I was staring into the eyes of an executioner. Who claimed to be my mate.

And was on a mission to kill Sethos.

If it weren't for Khellios wrapping his arms around my waist, tugging me away from the man in front of me, I would have been frozen on the spot. Unable to form words as Aeroth, the personification of the Astral, looked upon me with an expression as if I was nothing. As if his presence in my life had not just shifted my axis.

I recalled Aeroth's words moments before:

"I need to tell you who I am . . . and what I suspect I am . . . to you."

No.

I refused to believe him.

I stopped walking and opened my mouth to refute Aeroth's lie.

"Renna, *please* cooperate," I heard Khellios plead. "You are injured and need medical attention . . ."

Not breaking my stare from Aeroth, I shook my head in

answer to Khellios. I needed to speak with Aeroth. My injuries could wait.

"*No?*" Khellios asked me and, in the next breath, bent down and swept me up in his arms, pressing me against his chest as he began walking away.

"Put me down!" I yelled, thrashing against Khellios.

"No!" he argued back. "You don't know what is good for you—"

And then blinding agony wracked my body, and I screamed.

The sensation of pain spread from my temples; it felt like a pole had been shot into my temples and lanced straight through from one end to another, spreading pain down into my eyes, sinuses, and the rest of my body.

I writhed in Khellios's arms so violently he almost dropped me.

"Renna! What is wrong with her?" he yelled, panic in his voice.

"It hurts!" I screamed, feeling as if a searing fire blazed within me, clinging to the marrow inside my bones.

The blonde woman in silver armor who had been with Khellios rushed to him and I.

"We must take her to the infirmary," she ordered and urgently waved people toward her.

"*No,*" Khellios barked. "Cylas is at the infirmary with Demira and Illona. It's not the time for Renna to meet them."

My mind almost froze at the names of my half sisters, but another wave of pain hit me and I wailed, pushing my head against Khellios's chest. I closed my eyes.

"You cannot control that!" the woman roared at him.

"And you don't know anything! Prepare her a cabin," Khellios snapped at her. "The medic mages can see to her there. Her wounds . . . I don't like this, Elrie."

"This is *my* star craft, you stubborn fucking tyrant. Stop telling me what to do!"

"And she is *my* responsibility!" Khellios yelled.

But I wasn't his responsibility, and I hated that he spoke for me. I opened my mouth to say so, but a shot of pain wracked my body once more, making me cry out.

"Follow me," Elrie said through gritted teeth.

We moved after her, all the while the flock of people still surrounded us. I closed my eyes as tears streamed down my face and their loud, anxious voices filled the air.

What was wrong with me? I was fine just a few moments ago . . .

Before I left Aeroth's side.

We moved some more until the voices around me died down, and I opened my eyes to see we were in a cabin bedroom. The interior was all gray with sleek gray walls with mounted long tube-like lamps giving a soft glow to the room, honeycomb panels on the ceiling revealing piping, and one singular cabin window showing the starry landscape outside as we traveled through space. Three red couches by the window and a small table decorated the rest of the space. The room felt lifeless and sterile, as if I were in a laboratory and was the specimen.

A door quietly closed behind us.

"What do you need?" Khellios asked as he held me, almost sobbing himself. "Ren, I can't bear to see you like this. What has Sethos done to you?"

"Put her down," Elrie said, her soft tone rising above his anguish as she pulled gray sheets back from a bed in the middle of the room. Like the other red accents in the room, the headboard was also red and curved like a half circle.

Khellios set me down on the bed gently, and I immediately curled up in a ball.

"Bring the medic mages," he growled to Elrie. "*Now.*"

Elrie stepped up to Khellios, her chest almost touching his. "Do *not* speak like that to me," she gritted. "Not now, not *ever*."

Khellios's chest heaved as if he was barely containing his rage.

A knock at the door sounded, and Elrie moved from Khellios to presumably open the door. I closed my eyes again as sounds of shuffling feet filled the room. Khellios then spoke to whoever had entered.

"She's suffered visible injuries." Khellios paused. "Her leg . . . It's . . . The open wound there."

"Take a deep breath," Elrie said to him, her voice soothing.

"Where was she?" a male spoke.

Squinting, I noticed three cloaked figures standing next to Khellios in front of me. Heavy hoods cast shadows across their faces, but a bit of light caught the left side—the half that had been replaced by a white and silver robotic prototype. It extended from their forehead down to the neck, including their left eye. Were they robotic beings?

"She just portaled in from Daya," Khellios replied.

One of the figures stepped forward. The other two each held an almost transparent tablet with red glowing script that they seemed to be taking notes on.

"What is she?" it asked Khellios while inspecting me with a detached, clinical gaze.

"Half god, half siren," Khellios answered.

His quick response about my lineage only reminded me of how easily he had lied to me. He took me from my university campus, all the while knowing exactly who I was. Rage boiled inside my gut, mixing with the raw pain I felt.

The being who spoke to Khellios stepped closer to the bed, leaning over as he said, "With your permission," he said, looking at me, "I'd like to conduct a medical scan."

"Do it," Khellios barked.

The being straightened and, with pursed lips, looked at Khellios.

"I was not asking *you*, God of the Moon and Stars," he replied before returning his gaze to me. "I was asking the patient for consent."

I clenched my jaw and nodded as tears continued to run tracks down my cheeks.

The being nodded back once in acknowledgment and leaned over again. His robotic eye turned red, and a wide horizontal laser began to scan my body. The scan was painless.

"Patient is approximately twenty-seven or twenty-eight mortal years. Magic is fully integrated in her body . . ."

Memories of arriving in Daya and the magic's manifestation flooded my mind. Sethos had been there when my magic had fully integrated into my bloodstream.

I curled my hands on the bedsheet to keep myself from screaming in anger at how powerless I felt in that moment. I wanted nothing more than to throttle and make Sethos hurt for the pain he caused. But I also knew without a shadow of a doubt that my father's magic changed Sethos. I watched as his demeanor changed over the time I knew him.

Khellios knelt next to me, grasped one of my hands, and kissed the back of my hand. "I will kill Sethos, Renna. I swear to you. He will answer for what he's done."

Fear gripped me. Like Aeroth, Khellios's threats to end Sethos's life sent me into a panic. Sethos needed to be stopped, not killed.

I shook my head. "*No*," I whimpered, tears streaming down my face. "Am-Re's magic has poisoned him, Khel."

"That is precisely why he needs to be killed."

The mage spoke. "I ask that you allow me to continue my assessment."

Khellios nodded and stepped back to stand next to Elrie.

"Patient has multiple lacerations throughout her body," the mage continued. "The injuries lead me to believe they were created with weapons and magic." He paused and frowned, looking me up and down. "She is also experiencing a different pain that is attributed to—"

"You are taking too long! You are a medic mage. *Cure her!*"

The laser stopped. The mage straightened its posture once more and turned its entire body to Khellios.

"We have never met the patient before and need to understand what type of treatment her body will accept," the mage replied, trying and failing to keep his tone even.

"Khellios," Elrie spoke from behind me, but I didn't have the strength to turn to see her. "We should leave them to care for her."

"I'm not leaving her side anymore."

"They are trusted medic mages sent by my father—a man you respect! You cannot keep interfering in their assessment."

"Do you not see her pain?" He gestured to me. "Look at her! She is *broken*!"

Despite the agony I felt, I glared at Khellios, forcing myself to speak through clenched teeth. "Sethos did not break me. Now get out," I bit.

"But Renna—"

"*Get out!*" I screamed, instantly whimpering as another shot of pain ricocheted through me. I squeezed my eyes shut.

Elrie and Khellios exchanged a few quick words with the mages before they stepped outside. Khellios assured me he would be right outside the door.

Soon, the room was quiet again except for the mage, who continued his assessment. My lips trembled as I waited for a diagnosis.

"What I was trying to tell the God of the Moon and Stars is your extreme bodily aches are not caused by your wounds. But before we get into that, what may I call you?" the mage asked politely.

"Renna," I winced as my vision blurred with tears.

"Renna," the mage repeated calmly. "Firstly, I want you to know the magic running in your veins is slowly regenerating, which is *good.* You used a lot of magic in the altercation that resulted in your wounds, I am presuming?"

I nodded.

The mage turned to the other two mages, who stood just behind him, and spoke. "Her magical reserves are low, which impedes her self-healing. The separation pain is also adding to her discomfort. We will need to address that hastily." They nodded as the mage turned back to me. "You will have full access to your magic in about two days, if not sooner."

"What are you talking about? You're saying words I don't understand," I asked, trying to breathe through the discomfort.

"By nature, magic grants us all the ability to self-heal, but you used a lot of it. When that happens, it slows your healing. You need plenty of rest while your magic regenerates. We will prescribe to you a tonic to help you sleep and to speed up wound healing. As I mentioned, you are also experiencing additional pain not related to the physical wounds. The separation pain—"

I interrupted him. "*What?* What is separation pain?"

The mage pursed his lips and folded his arms across his chest. "This is about your mate."

I felt blood drain from my face.

Am-Re kept me in the dark for much of my life about the supernatural world, feeding me bits and pieces of information about other beings. He never shared anything about mates. I concluded it was because Am-Re never expected me to live long enough to meet mine, not after he trained me with enough magic to harvest like an animal fattened for slaughter.

However, Sethos had done the honors of regaling what a mate was—and in frightening detail.

Sethos shared that a mate was a connection between fae. The connection was described to me as a manner for Source to promote procreation between fae. Sethos's distaste for the bond made it sound like it was almost forced intimacy . . . In my mind, it had sounded like rape.

Panic began to settle into my body, making me feel like someone was gripping my lungs. I tried to push off from the bed to stand.

"I need to leave," I croaked.

The mage gently pushed me back down and offered me a small smile. "You need to rest. A mate is nothing to fear. All species of fae were designed to have a mate. When the match activates for the first time, there is a bonding period. If the bonding period is disrupted, it results in separation pain."

I frowned and tried shaking my head, but pain shot through me, making my head ache even worse.

"You need to have your mate close by to ease this pain," he concluded.

I remained silent as his words sank into me.

Aeroth.

Had he been telling the truth?

"Do you know where your mate is?" the mage asked.

I blinked at the three mages, not knowing what to say.

"You must have just recently come into physical contact with your mate. That is how the bond activates."

My eyebrows raised.

Aeroth had touched my hand.

"You didn't know?" The mage's tone was as if he were surprised.

I shook my head and winced again at the movement.

"Would you like me to explain mate bonds?"

"Y-yes," I muttered, reclining back and closing my eyes.

"A mate bond was designed to promote procreation among fae species. The goal was to diversify and strengthen the fae as a whole. The fae have mates specifically outside of their origin species. Source believed faes procreating with their own species weakened the genus. Therefore, a forest sprite would not have a mate with a forest sprite. A mountain elf would not have a mate with a mountain elf. And so on."

My mother had been a sea siren fae. That made me part fae.

What was Aeroth?

"When a mate bond is established, there is a one-year period known as The Settling. This one-year period forces mates into close proximity with the hope of procreation. Physical separation from your mate during this time creates separation pain."

This was a nightmare. I would be forced to be by a stranger for a year?

Why would Source think anyone would rejoice at that?

I clenched my teeth to prevent a moan of pain escaping my lips. "And after that year is up?" I asked, breathless.

"The separation pain will end. However, you will always have a strong desire to be by your mate."

No, no, no . . .

I had lived under my father's tyranny for twelve years. And then under Sethos's manipulation. Men only brought cruelty. The thought of a mate under these circumstances was deeply limiting to me.

Another shot of pain cracked through the middle of my head, and I moaned loudly.

"How is this possible?" I gritted.

"Finding a mate is rare. You must make contact with their skin to know for certain."

"For certain? Is there another way to know?"

"In a way. Mates get flashes of each other throughout their

lives. The souls seeking each other form a brief mental connection, creating an image. But these never come with a warning, and many fae discount them as nonsensical thoughts. Dreams."

"This cannot be happening."

"I apologize for the shock this has caused," he offered, his voice gentler. "We will try our best to keep you comfortable. As I said, we will make you a tincture to help you sleep and to speed up your healing. For the separation pain, I would suggest you summon your mate to alleviate these symptoms. Closer proximity to them will be enough to make you feel better."

Aeroth.

He was my . . .

I could not find the words to even say it.

After everything I had been through to fight for my own freedom, now I had no choice. There had to be a way to get out of the bond.

I curled my fists and asked, "Is there any way to relieve the pain without being by my mate?"

The mage paused before answering. "Some mates devise creative ways to circumvent the separation bond, but it can backfire." I opened my eyes at his tone to see him frown and shake his head. "There is no straight answer to your question, and as a medic, I highly discourage fighting this bond as it's clearly causing you immense pain."

I was practically vibrating from anger. "I don't accept this."

"Does the God of the Moon and Stars know who your mate is? Perhaps he can help us locate or summon—"

"Please don't tell Khellios." My heart was racing. Khellios would go ballistic if he knew. He was so overprotective.

The mage nodded. "Of course. There is patient-medic confidentiality. Would you like us to fetch your mate?" he asked politely.

Another wave of pain rushed through me, and I curled into a ball on my side.

I hated this. And even though I didn't want to put my trust in any man, especially after everything I had gone through, I'd do anything to alleviate the pain.

I squeezed my eyes shut and fisted my hands against my chest, curling tighter.

"His name is Aeroth," I said through clenched teeth.

The mages collectively gasped and were silent for a few moments thereafter. I opened one eye and saw them standing motionless, looking at me with their jaws open.

"*Aeroth?* You mean the King of the Astral?" the mage confirmed, blinking several times.

"Are you certain?"

"*Yes!*" I yelled, more anger threatening to spill from inside me. "How common is the name Aeroth?"

The mage opened his mouth to speak, but I cut him off.

"He's on this craft. Besides him, don't let Khellios or anyone else in this room. Now please go!" I covered my face with my hands to block out the light. My sinuses felt like they were exploding, and my teeth ached.

"We will inform him at once. He is likely also experiencing pain and no doubt eager to be by your side," the mage said rapidly before I heard them exit.

A mate was a Source-created bond that took away my right to choose a partner. I'd been forced into a situation I did not want.

Especially not with him.

2

AEROTH

I sped through the white hallways of Elrie's craft, my boots echoing against the polished black floors.

Toward her.

Renna.

Fate had a cruel sense of humor pairing me with the one woman hellbent on saving the man I was sworn to kill.

A man who'd harmed her, and now I wanted to destroy him more than ever before. I wanted to scream from frustration. If Sethos had only been in Daya when I got there, I would have killed him.

Simmering dark red blood lined the inner edges of my eyes, and I saw red dots in my vision.

I froze, knowing what the red dots in my vision meant.

Signs of bloodlust.

I *never* wanted to go back to that period of my life. I paused and closed my eyes, shaking my head side to side as if that would clear it. But I knew better.

Bloodlust was a natural, animalistic response when one's blood kin or chosen kin was threatened. Not every Naaviri fae suffered from bloodlust, but it had kept the species alive as someone with bloodlust descended into madness to protect one's kin.

I had not experienced bloodlust in years . . . Why would it appear now?

My family was safe, to my immediate knowledge.

And Renna meant nothing to me. I barely knew her.

But she was my mate. Was my body, on a base level, recognizing her as kin?

I reached for the dangling necklace buried under my clothes. I held the dainty ring in my palm, clutching it as I tried to calm my breathing.

Trudging to the nearest wall, I put my free hand out on the cool surface to hold me steady. I wanted to crumple on the floor and scream as the pain moved through me in torturous waves.

I squeezed my eyes shut as more red dots filled my vision.

If I allowed bloodlust to take over, my vision would diminish, forcing my body to rely more heavily on smell and sound to detect the living. I could already hear the sound of their heartbeats . . .

I needed to get to Renna.

It had been excruciating to watch Khellios take her away, to hear her screams. But I could not intervene at that time. How would Renna have felt if I—a stranger—ripped her from the arms of her friend to soothe our separation pain?

I moved so my side was now leaning on the wall and massaged my right temple with my free hand while the other gripped the ring.

Breathe.

Breathe.

This was a disaster.

The last thing I needed in my life was a *mate*.

There had only ever been one woman for me. I would have given anything for her to have been my mate.

"King of the Astral," a male spoke.

I dropped my hands and steeled against my aching body to stand up straight, hating how the red dots blurred my vision. But a king never showed vulnerability. I had learned that the hard way.

Turning, I saw three medic mages standing before me. The humanoid beings stemmed from the Arcturian Galaxy.

They waited for me to speak.

My voice strained as I began, clenching my fists against the pain. "I should have guessed Princess Elrie had Arcturian medics on her craft. This craft is like a floating city. You nomads are . . ." I took a deep breath and clenched my teeth as a wave of pain shot through me, "a long way from home."

The one who spoke bowed his head.

"We have an urgent matter to discuss, Your Majesty."

My body tensed as a jolt of pain shot through me, but still I kept as still as possible. Years of military training had taught me control. "*Yes*?"

"Your mate is on this craft. You must go to her." He inclined his head. "She is in pain. I am sure you know of whom I speak?"

I nodded and ground out, "Renna."

The mage hesitated and frowned.

"*What?*" I snapped, as a cramping spasm ran through my body, tightening all my muscles.

"As Arcturians, we do not support any violence or conflict. You must know the God of the Moon and the Stars hovers outside your mate's room with deep worry over her state." The mage paused. "Your mate has banned entry to any but . . . you. But I fear the God of the Moon and the Stars may be upset to see you enter her room. It may cause further discomfort to her. Commotion of any kind will interfere with her overall recovery."

I did not blame Khellios for his reaction at being banned

from Renna. He had torn the universe apart in search of her. Across lifetimes, millennia.

I respected that.

But none of Khellios's wants mattered now; a deep conflict settled within me. In a way, I felt loyal to him for confiding in me that he loved her. I also felt loyal to Renna and the pain she was experiencing.

"Your Majesty," the mage said politely. "You have the ability to bypass time and space with the mere wave of a hand, opening up pockets of reality as the Astral ruler. May I suggest entering her room through the Astral Plane to avoid being seen through the hallway?"

I crossed my arms, considering the best course of action.

Source created three forms of travel: the first was Astral projection. Astral projection was when the living body remained in one place while the spirit or soul of a person detached and traveled to the Astral Plane. This could occur during sleep, meditation, or altered mental states such as trances.

The Astral Plane was a mirrored alternate reality where the souls could rest. Some visited the Astral in dreamtime to visit their childhood homes or places they loved. It allowed the soul to heal and gain perspective. A peaceful spirit was a fundamental right of every living person, and the Astral Plane provided that. As the ruler of that plane, I had no need to Astral project, as souls came into my sphere.

The second form of traveling was through portaling. Traveling through a portal, the body reorganized from solid form to floating cells and then rematerialized back into a solid body upon arrival. With practice, portaling was painless. Some even reported it as exhilarating. I thought it bothersome to have my body reorganized and put back together.

The third form of travel was exclusive to the rulers of the Astral and was the one I preferred. As the current ruler, I had the power to command reality to open a door from wherever I was, go through the Astral as a type of intermediary hallway or wormhole, and then exit where I desired in the real world. It was an instant travel method that was as fast as the blink of an eye. My body remained intact, and there were no side effects for me.

"Sire?" the medic asked, rousing me from my thoughts. "You must go to her."

"Has she asked for me?" I demanded. "I will not enter her room without her consent."

The law of the universes discouraged using a portal or the Astral to travel to a person without their consent. It broke universal privacy laws, as one could travel to another during deeply intimate times.

"She asked for you," the mage confirmed.

I sighed in relief. In order to travel to someone, one had to imagine their essence and form a connection to a portal or, in my case, use the Astral to travel.

I closed my eyes briefly and brought an image of Renna to my mind. Her brown curly hair. Her eyes, in pain . . . just like they had been in Daya. Her face bruised from where she had been injured. The blood on her arms and legs . . .

Anger at Sethos boiled inside me, and I opened my eyes.

Red dots blurred my vision.

Bloodlust.

I took in another deep breath.

I couldn't put her in danger. If I allowed bloodlust to take over, my baser animal instincts would overpower me, transforming every cell. It would change me from a logical man to a beast that relied on scent and sound to detect living beings. It would drive me to catch prey or destroy others in close proximity to my loved ones—my kin.

"Do you require medical attention, Your Majesty?" the mage asked, his tone hesitating. "You look unwell . . ."

A frown pulled at my lips, knowing he was not referring to the separation pain.

I could not tell him of the bloodlust. News would spread that the King of the Astral had succumbed again . . .

"Just separation pain," I growled, daring him to speak further. "I shall go to her."

The mage quickly bowed his head. "Of course."

The mages stepped around me in a circle to create a physical barrier with their bodies as I waved my hand to open a doorway into the Astral to prevent any passerby from getting too close.

A door into deep space opened before us in the hallway, a sparkling nebula of stars shining from the celestial plane. Black tendrils of space beckoned me toward the door, and an instant chill filled the air. Ice crystals formed on the ground and ceiling where the doorway to the Astral door touched.

Only a ruler of the Astral Plane could enter the Astral this way. Anyone else would freeze and shatter to death.

Without thinking twice, I cracked my neck to the side and walked into the Astral to travel to her room.

Renna needed me.

And I needed her.

3

RENNA

A bright white light exploded in my cabin, forcing me to cover my face with my hands.

Through parted fingers, I watched the glare fade to a luminescent black neon glow. The light morphed into what looked like a rectangular doorway, a bit like a portal. Tiny silver glittering dots like thousands of diamonds dotted the blackness, and I realized they were stars.

A figured cloaked in black stars stepped forth, and I was reminded of when Sethos visited me in my university dorm all those months ago. He had been able to travel using the Astral as well through my dreams . . .

But I knew instantly this was not Sethos. Where Sethos had been lithe and athletic, this figure was much taller and broader—as if he were made of chiseled muscle.

And although this felt like a nightmare, it was very much real. Because there was only one person who would come from the void of space to me.

The figure before me lifted the cloak of night off his body to reveal himself: Aeroth.

The cloak hung around his shoulders, turning into dark

shadows at the hem. His red eyes glittered as he stepped fully into the room.

The pain that rocked my body slowly subsided, but my shock still forced me to push myself as far as I could from him.

"Stay where you are," I said quickly.

"If I had a choice in the matter, that is exactly what I would do," he said coolly. "I didn't ask for *this*."

He walked toward the bed in slow, calculated steps.

"You're an asshole," I roared.

"I would return the insult, but a gentleman does not insult a lady."

"Stay back!" I yelled. He continued advancing. "I mean it!" I shoved myself to stand on the bed while slowly backing up toward the wall.

"It seems like we find ourselves in a unique situation, princess."

"Don't 'princess' me," I snarled. "There's nothing more insulting than a man using that term in a derogatory manner. I'm a grown woman, and I have a name."

He stopped at the foot of the bed, crossed his arms, and tilted his head as if he was bored. "Is the pain gone?"

My pain abating at Aeroth's presence was the last shred of confirmation I needed to know the mate bond between us was real.

It was sickening.

"Almost," I said with gritted teeth. "So . . . aren't you disappointed?"

"About?" he asked with narrowed eyes.

I lifted my chin. "What I said to you before. I will fight you so Sethos may live."

"Ah, *yes*. The man who left you for dead in the forest. I gave my word to the Galactic Federation that I would kill him. Being at odds with each other should make for an interesting year as the mate bond settles."

Before I could respond, my foot suddenly reached the end of the bed, and I fell backward. But I never made it to the ground.

Aeroth looked down at me as he held me in his arms, and for a fraction of a breath, I found myself locked in his gaze. Aeroth's gaze moved down my face until it settled on my lips, and as if my rational brain had caught up, I realized my position and pushed off him to stand.

"You're welcome," he said icily as he took a step away from me.

I noticed my pain from the mate separation was completely gone. All that remained was the aches from my wounds created by Sethos—the seen and unseen.

I glared at him, refusing to say thank you.

"So, what now?" I snapped. Aeroth crossed his arms once more. When he didn't answer, I narrowed my eyes. "I'm to be by your side as you murder Sethos?"

He raised his eyebrows. "No one is asking you to save him. He doesn't deserve it. He sure as shit didn't give two fucks about you."

My lips trembled, and I clenched my teeth to control the emotions that were threatening to spill from me. Sethos had cared for me, once. He had killed my father in retaliation for the abuse I suffered and guarded me for seven years while I was at university—even if he plotted to use me in the end. My history and time with Sethos would always be complicated.

"You are *no one* to speak to me in this way. Do you not believe someone can be reformed? That someone can get treatment for trauma? You know nothing about how he became what he is. Do you not believe in restorative justice?"

"*For him?*"

"He absorbed my father's magic. It transformed him into

something else. Combine *that* with his deep pain from abuse and personal tragedy. I will not let you kill him!"

"For fucks sake, Renna!" He raised his palms up. "He was a career soldier for Am-Re. He has killed many. He is not innocent. He is planning a carnage."

"And are you without fault? Last I checked, he has *not* attacked Taria yet. There is time to stop him."

"To what end? So you can get back together with him to continue whatever *arrangement* you had? Khellios shared that you were not his prisoner."

"How dare you—"

"Is that what this is about? You wanting to save him. Are you both together?"

I scoffed. "And what would it be to you?"

I knew Sethos was not good for me. Romantically, I could *never* take him back. I owed that to myself. I had made that decision while I lay on the forest floor of Daya in the cell he created for me.

Aeroth narrowed his eyes to slits, his tone low as he said, "I draw the line at supporting abuse—especially against women. So if this is some ploy to get back together with him—"

"I wouldn't need your permission!"

"Clearly. So fuck whoever you want, but the fact remains that I am sworn to kill him. I hope you keep your memories, because there won't be anything left of him."

Aeroth spun to face my cabin window. His response took me aback, and I blinked several times.

"Do you think you can just come into my life and start dictating what I'm supposed to do?"

He turned and opened his mouth to respond, but I cut him off.

"Do you think this is easy?" I yelled. "I've had every major choice taken from me, and now I find myself with a mate bond I never asked for. There is a man out there who needs serious intervention. And while I don't know the best solution to help him, helping him is *my* choice."

"He lied to you. Beat you. *Wounded you.*" He said the last phrase with a growl. "And imprisoned you. And you dare come to his aid?"

"My dynamic with Sethos is none of your concern!"

A bitter chuckle escaped from Aeroth's lips.

"It's very much my business," he said as he sauntered closer. "He is the man I have been tasked with killing. My honor and reputation are on the line. You, on the other hand, have this ridiculous goal of being a martyr and saving him."

I curled my fists. "Of all people to be tied to you . . . there has to be a way to dissolve this bond."

An uneasiness spread within me as Aeroth stared for a few moments.

"Unfortunately for the both of us, mate bonds are for life. But there may be a way to somewhat circumvent the mate separation rules."

My heart raced. I didn't care about the potential risks involved in finding a loophole to work around the bond.

"Tell me. I hope you know I don't want this bond. I reject it."

Aeroth narrowed his eyes. "And do you think *I* want it? This is an inconvenience to me. I am King of the Astral. I don't have time for a mate bond, much less with a woman who clearly needs her priorities checked."

His words stung, but at least I had his honesty. And I couldn't be angry at his rejection of the bond because I, too, wanted nothing to do with it.

In that, at least, we had an agreement.

I took a deep breath. I needed to focus. "How are we able to bend the rules?"

Aeroth gestured between us. "We need to carry a part of each other."

I frowned. "What do you mean?"

"We need to trick our bodies into thinking we are together. Luckily for you, I am a Naaviri. My kind have a way to stay close to our partners."

"What type of fae is a Naaviri?"

"We mainly sustain ourselves off blood."

My eyes widened; his words stopped me in my tracks.

"And while that may sound disgusting to you and many people, Naaviri exchange blood to remain close to their partners. I *have* heard of Naaviri exchanging blood to help with mate separation during The Settling."

The thumping of my racing heart filled my ears. "I . . . I am not giving you my blood."

"Do you have a better idea? Because otherwise we'll need to remain together. Every hour of every day for an entire year."

I shook my head. "There must be another way—"

"There isn't."

"Well, I refuse."

Aeroth sighed and ran his hands over his face. "Renna, I am not your enemy in this situation. I'm trying to help you by not forcing you to be tethered to me. This bond is not something I want either."

"You may not be my enemy, but you are a rude fucking asshole. You make jokes when I want to help someone who is a danger to themselves and others. And you mocked the abuse I suffered."

Aeroth blinked and shook his head, as if what he was hearing was ludicrous.

"So apologies if I'm not ecstatic at the thought of sharing my blood with you," I snapped.

Deep down, I knew exchanging blood with Aeroth was the

only solution for now. It was a take-it-or-leave-it situation. Besides, space apart from Aeroth could allow me to plan a way to help Sethos.

And to have some privacy.

"I'm sorry," Aeroth said then, his voice low. "I should not have treated you that way. It was never my intent to hurt you—"

"Well, you did. Don't mock someone else's experience with violence."

"I understand."

I narrowed my eyes and stepped up to him. His view of me going back to Sethos was demoralizing. Going back to Sethos romantically would make me feel weak. It was important for me to clarify to Aeroth.

"And not that it's any of your business, but I will never go back to him in that way. Me helping Sethos is a personal debt. And out of a duty I feel to the people of Taria and the gods there. I only want to try and stop Sethos from attacking."

Aeroth observed me in silence for a few moments and then hung his head low as if he was processing my words. When he looked back up at me, he said, "I'm sorry."

I put my hands on my hips. "If we truly are going to be stuck with each other, then you need to understand right now that I will never allow you to disrespect me like you did. I will call you out every fucking time. I am not powerless. I can defend myself."

He nodded. "I understand. I was not myself when I spoke before. My mother and sister would be ashamed. I'm sorry my words hurt you—I'm sorry *I* hurt you."

His apology and words seemed sincere, and I was surprised because I was expecting him to argue with me or try and dismiss my feelings again. I was unused to an apology like Aeroth's. My body tensed and jaw clenched; I didn't know what to do.

"What would you like to do...?" he asked.

I lifted my eyebrows and narrowed my eyes. "*Right now?*"

He nodded.

"I want to get away from you." I knew I was being blunt and rude, but I was done walking on eggshells for people. Never again.

After a brief pause, I said, "Let's exchange blood. If it gets me away from you, I'm willing to try it."

He remained expressionless as he responded. "Very well. Blood needs to be extracted from either the carotid artery in the neck or the femoral artery in the inner thigh."

"Extracted *how*?"

"I have fangs that extend when I feed. My fangs act like needles to puncture skin, but my saliva has a slight numbing effect. You won't feel the puncture after I bite you."

I shook my head. This was all too much. I had thought there would be a medic mage to help exchange blood with needles and blood bags. "Why can't you use my arm like medics do for lab work?"

"It would take longer to drink from you, and your arm would be sore for a day or two. Depending on how often we have to exchange blood, I'd rather you have your arms strong if you need to defend yourself."

"And my thigh? Would my thigh be sore and prevent me from combat?"

He lowered his chin as if giving my question some thought. "The thigh heals much faster. There is more muscle there."

The thought of Aeroth biting me in my thigh was far too intimate for me.

"The medic mages on board know of our bond. Just have them do the blood transfusion. I don't want you biting into my skin."

Aeroth nodded. "Very well. Stay here to continue resting, your wounds need to close. I will go and locate the mages. But know while I am gone, you and I will experience separation pain."

I hugged my arms and sat down on the bed. The anticipation of the pain was awful, but I had just met Aeroth; having him bite into my skin did not seem like the most reasonable thing to do.

At least he is respecting your boundaries . . . my brain reminded me.

I almost rolled my eyes at my internal thoughts. As if women deserved the bare minimum.

"Hurry," I replied.

He nodded, and with a wave of his arm, a type of doorway revealing the cosmos opened in my cabin and he stepped through.

The pain was almost immediate, forcing me down on the bed, curled on my side.

4

RENNA

I looked down at the catheters and tubes nestled in the crook of my arm and shivered.

The medic mage next to me eyed my severe facial expression warily, as if expecting me to throw up.

I had never been squeamish about blood, but I was disgusted that this was my reality.

Aeroth shifted next to me, and I turned to look at him. He also had two catheters for the blood transfusion sticking out of his arm. I quickly averted my eyes and closed them, taking a deep breath.

We were both seated with our backs against my headboard as the three medic mages moved around us to ensure the transfusion went well.

When the mages arrived, they were noticeably confused at my desire to have the transfusion done this way. They commented that many fae enjoyed drinking blood straight from their mate. They tried to convince me it would be faster if Aeroth and I drank from each other, but with a quick command from Aeroth, they set us up for the transfusion.

After a while, I finally murmured a *Thank you* to Aeroth. He just ignored me. I knew he disliked this as much as I did. That was at least something else we had in common.

"I may not always be able to provide a medic mage for you," he said after a while.

I knew what he was trying to convey: There would be occasions where we would have to drink from each other, and I would need to be prepared for that.

"And after a year . . . we will lead separate lives?"

I opened my eyes when he remained silent once more and caught him staring straight ahead as if he was lost in his own thoughts.

"Yes. With a few distance limitations."

Aeroth continued. "Mates who reject a bond can lead fulfilling lives with other partners and families, but they tend to either settle in the same community as their rejected mate or the next city or town over. I cannot tell you the *exact* distance of when separation pain would hit—it's trial and error."

I frowned. "What happens if a mate has a partner or spouse and family before meeting their mate?"

"I would imagine they make do and wait it out a year. Perhaps the mate fits within that established family unit or partnership . . ."

"The whole dynamic of mates is so strange to me. I'm nearing thirty. To think about being forced—"

"The transfusion is complete," the medic mage interrupted. "Since your bodies are new to The Settling period and you haven't exchanged blood before, we don't know how much blood is needed to prevent pain separation. You may need more soon."

I wanted to curse.

The mage looked to me and lowered his chin. "This is why methods to subvert The Settling are risky."

I rolled my eyes. "So you've said."

The mages began to take off the tubes while Aeroth and I remained silent.

So many thoughts ran through my mind. What I needed to do to help Sethos and how to best protect Taria. How to help protect the land that had sheltered me and the people in it. But I also wanted to stop Sethos from destroying the land and himself.

How could I do both?

I looked to the mages, who were busy applying bandages to our arms. I wondered, would medics know how to help a person consumed by foreign chaotic magic?

"I need your guidance," I asked the mage who had been leading all interactions thus far.

The mage looked up, its red robotic eyeball shifting to my person, as if trying to assess if there was anything else the matter.

Aeroth shifted in bed to face me.

"Yes?" the mage asked, folding its hands in its front.

I sat up straighter and continued. "If someone has absorbed the magic of another, how would they get rid of that magic?"

Aeroth cursed under his breath.

The mage stood still for a moment before answering. "We do not support violence of any kind," the mage began. "The information I share does not condone any violent acts."

I opened my mouth to say I was proposing helping someone, not injuring them, but the mage put his palm up to stop me.

"Absorbing magic of another is a violation of Source law. If one drains and absorbs the magic of another completely, the act could kill the person being drained. This is because magic melds into the blood of each supernatural, and taking someone's magic essentially drains them of life."

I nodded.

"When magic is absorbed, the acquired magic becomes part of the new host's blood. To get rid of the particular magic the new host absorbed, someone would need to drain the magic from them. The act of draining magic is dangerous, as the risk of death is also present. One would have to ensure the magic in question is separated from the host's blood, so the correct magic is extracted. Not many survive this process."

I sat frozen for several moments, not knowing what to say.

I would have to capture Sethos somehow and subdue him enough to drain his magic. I doubted he would let me do this freely, since he was determined to have his revenge.

I could not capture him on my own . . .

I looked to Aeroth, a hard line on his lips as he gazed back at me.

Would he help me?

Aeroth sighed and shook his head. He stood, running his hands over his face. My heart fell into my stomach. How was I supposed to move forward?

As we were bandaged, Aeroth refused to look at me again. Did he anticipate me asking him for help?

"If that will be all . . . we can take our leave?" the lead mage asked.

"Yes," Aeroth agreed before he finally locked eyes with me. "Please be available tomorrow. The lady will require you again for another transfusion."

The medic mage nodded to me and bowed his head. "Anything for the King and his consor—"

"That will be all," Aeroth cut him off.

When we were alone, I locked my arms over my chest.

"Was he about to call me your *consort*?"

Aeroth's eyebrows furrowed. "I would imagine. But you and I are not pursuing that type of relationship."

I gestured with my hand for him to elaborate. "Which would be?"

His lips set in a firm line, and he gave me a forced smile before answering.

"Marriage."

I laughed. "*Right.*"

"Many mates marry," he said while shrugging.

"Why would he assume *I* would marry *you*?"

Aeroth scoffed and ran his hands through his hair.

"Don't you want to hear what powers you would gain by ascending as Queen of the Astral Plane? Many women would jump at the opportunity."

I rolled my eyes and put my hands up to cut him off. "Many would consider freedom powerful too."

His eyes slowly dropped from my eyes to my lips. "I wouldn't be forcing you to marry me, of that you can be sure."

I laughed. "You flatter yourself if you think I'd beg to remain at your side."

He smiled, and his gaze trailed back to mine. "I like a challenge."

I got closer and narrowed my eyes. "Get over yourself."

"I don't like you."

It was my turn to smile. "The feeling is mutual." I took several steps back. "So what is next? You're here to kill Sethos?"

He frowned. "I am on this star craft as a guest with other fae monarchs. We all have been tasked with dealing—"

"*Killing*—"

"—Sethos."

We stared at each other for a moment before he spoke again.

"Finding you was never part of my plan," he said and crossed his arms. "In fact, you're a hinderance to everything."

I pointed to him. "You're rude."

"And what about you? You've done nothing but attack me, yet I've done nothing wrong. This mate bond is not my fault, Renna."

I bit the inside of my cheek. I felt like a caged animal.

"May I ask what your exact plan is?" he finally asked.

"I need to stop Sethos," I stated. "I need to get to Taria."

He lowered his chin. "Then we do have something in common."

Shaking my head, I scoffed at the thought. "We have very different goals, Aeroth. I am not your friend."

He nodded and looked away from me. "Understood. This just keeps getting worse."

I rolled my eyes.

"And here I was going to offer to take you there . . ."

My head whipped to him. Would he truly help me portal there? With my limited magic at the moment, I didn't think I could portal on my own.

However, my rational brain knew I would have to change my attitude to convince him to help me.

"The mage told me my magic would likely be fully replenished in the next day or so. I would portal on my own, but if you got me there sooner . . ."

Aeroth turned to look at me, an amused grin cut across his face. "Oh, I'm sorry, are you asking me for help?"

I pursed my lips. "You won't have to kill Sethos if I can get through to him—"

"It's not that simple, Renna."

"What do you mean? I need to speak with him to stop this. Surely you wouldn't deny me the opportunity to speak with him?"

"It's not about letting you speak to him. A mate bond is complex. It's not just the separation pain that poses an issue—"

I put my palms up and said, "What else is there to know?"

He tilted his head. "Two things. If you *just* let me talk—"

I stepped up to him and put my hands on my hips.

"You are taking *too* long."

"And you have *no* patience." He stepped up toward me.

"I am done being patient!" My chest was heaving.

We were now nose to nose.

"So tell me everything you need to tell me *now*!" I yelled. I was grasping at anything to feel in control, to keep me from emotionally spiraling.

Aeroth paused and took a deep breath before answering.

"You cannot die."

I shook my head and felt the tension rise in my chest.

"Sethos would *not* kill me—"

Aeroth massaged his temples and began to pace the room.

"You are not listening to me, Renna. Have you forgotten how he left you in Daya?"

I walked to Aeroth and stood in front of him.

"I just want to talk to him! Why can't you understand—"

"Will you *please* let me explain?"

I narrowed my eyes.

"Do you know what happens when a mate *dies*?" he asked.

"*Sorry, no.* My father did not educate me on the particulars of having a mate when he was abusing me."

Aeroth's eyes suddenly flared a bright red, and his face darkened, practically turning burgundy with rage.

My eyes widened, and I stepped back, surprised at the sudden transformation.

His dark, deep voice filled the room. "What did you say?"

5

AEROTH

Anger flared in my body when Renna mentioned her past.

Despite the innate savagery in my Naaviri blood, I had a strict code to never harm women or children. And it didn't matter how infuriating a woman could be, I had never lifted a hand to one.

I watched my father, King of the Astral, abuse my mother. I watched the light fade from her eyes, and as a child, I could not stop him. He later abused my stepmother. Her silver sea fae locks used to glow like moonlight. Over time, they dulled from the savagery he showed her. I was glad she left him.

Then, when my father moved onto my sister Cressida, who was a child and helpless, patricide had been the only thing on my mind. I was a man then, able to protect those I loved.

And so, I killed my father.

I was the only ruler in my lineage to have taken the throne by force, and I would do it again.

Hearing Renna speak of her father's abuse did something to me.

Khellios had shared what Cylas had told him about Am-Re's

return, and I wanted nothing more than to find Am-Re and kill him properly—and that was before I knew his daughter was my mate.

I laughed bitterly at the thought of killing Am-Re.

At the sound, Renna set even more distance between us.

Her anxious eyes darted up and down my body, as if she was deciding if I was a danger to her. As a Naaviri, my species was a danger to many. But I never wanted her to fear me.

I wasn't like my father, nor hers.

Or Sethos.

How I longed for the moment he and I were face-to-face. He would regret the moment he ever set a hand on her. I closed my eyes and took in several deep breaths to rein in my fury.

"Aeroth . . . ?" Renna asked. "What's going on?"

I forced myself to remember the last thing I had told Renna before murderous thoughts overtook me.

Breathe.

I had asked her if she knew what happened when a mate died.

Breathe.

Trying to school my features to be as passive as possible, I opened my mouth to explain, but she cut me off.

"What the hell was that?" she demanded with hands on her hips, ordering me to respond like a queen making demands.

No one spoke to me like she did. Gods she was infuriating.

"Nothing," I replied, then clarified. "Nothing to do with you."

It was the truth. But Renna furrowed her brow, taking me in with caution.

"I remembered someone from my past who liked to raise their hands at others," I explained. "You talking about being abused was . . . triggering."

Renna's mouth opened in a silent *O*, and she looked down to the floor. She twisted her lips to the side in a tight line, as if she didn't know what to say.

After all, what did you say to someone who saw or experienced abuse?

Renna's voice was quiet when she asked, "What happens if a mate dies?"

Right. Our conversation.

"When you form a mate bond, if the mate dies, it causes excruciating pain. The pain never stops. The bereaved mate usually takes their life shortly after. No one can live with that pain."

Renna's shocked expression said more than words could.

"This doesn't make any sense. I was killed in my past lifetime. Yet you live."

"That is because the mate bond had not been activated."

"This is all insane," she breathed, massaging her temples.

"Quite," I replied. "So as much as I respect your decisions, letting you simply walk across a battlefield to talk to Sethos is not a true option. It's not that simple."

"For *you*," she growled.

My body tensed at being put on the spot.

"Why should I care if you take your life from pain?" she asked.

"I not only rule the Astral Plane, I *am* the Astral Plane. My death would be complicated. I have no heirs, and my sister, who is the spare, does not want to rule. When the Astral ruler dies, the heir needs to ascend within moments to ensure safety and continuity of the plane," I spat, barely able to control my irritation. "So, I will respect my sister's wishes and stay alive as long as I can so that my offspring can one day ascend to the throne."

Renna was silent for several moments and eventually moved away from me to stare out the cabin window.

"I don't know what to do," she said quietly.

Although I didn't know Renna yet, the disappointment in her voice reminded me of my mother's voice. Of my sister, Cressida . . .

And of Isidra.

I could never forget her eternal judgmental stare . . . But I didn't like to think about the woman I had once loved. Isidra's memory was too painful.

"I'm sorry, Renna—"

Renna spun, and the anger and grief in her eyes rendered me immobile.

"I could have been fine being paired with a mate if he had even a shred of mercy in him!"

"Renna—"

"I don't condone what Sethos did. Or what he plans to do. All I ask is for one last attempt to make him realize how wrong he is."

Renna's determination echoed Isidra's urgency to help me when my world had turned upside down. Even after I succumbed to bloodlust many years before, Isidra had never given up on me.

A vision of Isidra handing me her baby son wrapped in a bundle of blue blankets as she died flashed in my mind.

Against my better judgment, I cautiously asked Renna, "Would Sethos even let us drain your father's magic from him?"

"I don't know!" she said, covering her face. "You know I don't do it out of some romantic notion I have for him." She dropped her hands and heaved a great sigh. "Any feelings I had for him like that died. I want to intervene out of a moral obligation for saving me twice from my father. For keeping me safe for many years. I know he hurt me. I will never forgive him for that. It's just . . . complicated."

Another vision of Isidra passed through my mind, and feelings of guilt filled me.

"What is the second thing I need to know?" Renna asked.

"Khellios informed us his enclave and the witches from his

land have moved the dimension of Taria from the planet Andora."

She frowned, her despair turning to near-rage as she practically yelled, "To where?"

"Taria is a dimension, so it has the ability to merely float on its own in space. It doesn't need a planet. For example, my own kingdom, Eniraath, floats in the Astral Plane. I believe the gods initially located Taria within Andora for sentimental reasons so the dimension could be next to their old city," I replied evenly.

"How is it possible to move a dimension?"

"I could not tell you. Moving a dimension involves witchcraft—something I have no gifts in."

"You have to help me portal there," Renna said and moved forward to hold my hands. "I don't have the energy to portal. *Please.*"

I knew Khellios would object to Renna going to Taria. His goal was to keep her safe from Sethos. I shook my head, gazing down at her hands over mine.

"Renna . . ."

She gave my hands a squeeze. "Haven't you ever wished you could have saved someone before?"

Her words gutted me. Flashes of Isidra's strained breathing and the sound of a baby's wail filled my mind. Isidra had taught me about mercy.

I could not save her. But she would have insisted I help Renna, to give her the opportunity to at least speak to Sethos.

I finally met her eyes. "You speaking to him does not guarantee he will live."

"But I have to try. Every soul is worthy of redemption."

Not mine.

Never mine.

I didn't know what the logistics behind facilitating a conversation would look like, but like Renna, Isidra had fought for me when I had shut everyone else out.

Perhaps I could honor Isidra's memory by trying to emulate her humanity. Perhaps this was the way I could let her ghost rest, to end the torment and guilt.

I squeezed my eyes shut.

I saw blood in my memories.

Blood everywhere.

Breathe.

Breathe.

"I can help you speak to him."

"*Will* you?"

Her tone forced me to look at her. Her eyes were red and glassy from unshed tears, and her palms were open, facing up. She was pleading. Begging for someone to help her. I didn't know how to respond to women getting emotional. My first instinct was to rage at the cause of their sadness, but this time, I was one of the contributing factors.

"I will try to help you."

"Thank you, Aeroth," she sighed, the relief plain in her voice.

I wanted to open my arms and embrace her.

Instead, I cleared my throat.

"I would rather you not resent me for the rest of our lives," I told her. "I would also rather ensure your safety so you don't go on a whim and get yourself—*and me*—killed in the process. We would have to plan it."

"I understand. But we need to leave today."

I groaned. "We cannot simply show up and thwart ongoing military strategy, Renna. We need to be strategic. The monarchs are not expected in Taria until the battle commences. The monarchs and I have planned our arrival, and I have coordinated a defensive strategy with the monarchs with military experience.

If I arrive in Taria before the battle against Sethos and Am-Re begins, I will lose the respect of my peers."

My method of attack involved weaving in and out of the Astral Plane to surround and attack a foe. They could never reach me in time before I disappeared from their view and emerged behind them. The monarchs and I planned to isolate Sethos so I could strike a final blow.

"I cannot wait that long," she insisted. "We need to prevent the battle from *starting*."

I realized I was still holding her hands and dropped them quickly, placing them on my hips and taking a step back. Once she was healed, Renna didn't need me to portal. She only had to wait for her magic to fully regenerate. If she traveled on her own, it could be deadly.

Me going with her was the lesser of two evils.

So, I would help Renna speak with him—even if her efforts were futile.

The question was, how would we get Renna to Taria without angering everyone around us? My loyalty to the Federation's cause would be questioned if I came face-to-face with Sethos and didn't kill him.

I began to pace again. "Perhaps I could suggest a trip to Taria before battle to meet the other gods and soldiers . . ."

"Yes!" she exclaimed, rushing over to me. She grabbed hold of my arm, her touch making my clothes and skin hot. I knew it wasn't magic . . . just my body responding to her closeness. Moving back, I continued pacing to release myself from her hold.

Renna began biting her nails. "I could say that I snuck into your portal and that you had no option but to follow me around Taria to ensure my safety . . ."

I doubted anyone would believe I did not notice someone using my portal. Her suggestion was childish, but I kept silent.

"*Please.*" She ran her now shaking hands through her hair.

"Sethos and my father could arrive at any moment. I can't wait for my magic to regenerate."

I had a commitment to the Galactic Federation and to the monarchs who accompanied me on this journey to kill Sethos. Sparing his life went against the honor I had pledged. But if I could save a life . . .

I pinched the bridge of my nose and closed my eyes. I took a deep breath.

"You have the power to help me. Please, Aeroth. *Help me.*"

Why did she have to be my mate? Why her?

Why *now*?

"Let me speak with Khellios about me traveling there. Then we can make a plan." She nodded, but based on her conversation with the mages, I was compelled to ask, "And what will happen if Sethos refuses to speak with you?"

Renna wrung her fingers. "We'll have to capture him," she said.

A bitter laugh escaped me.

"No. You ask too much."

"If he refuses to listen to reason, then we have to drain his magic!" she said, coming closer to me. "He is not in his right mind, Aeroth!"

What had I gotten myself into?

"*Please,*" she said, barely above a whisper. "I cannot do it alone. If my life means that much to you—"

My eyes snapped open, and I grabbed her by the shoulders.

"If your life means that much to me? You are my mate! Have you heard nothing of what I have just shared?"

"Then help me do this," she said, shrugging herself from my grip.

I took another deep breath. Isidra would tell me to save Sethos. Her humanity was my moral compass.

I shook my head.

"I will help you speak with him," I told her. "*That's it.* I cannot guarantee anything else."

Renna sighed and slowly strode away from me, stopping to stare out the cabin window.

"I am leaving to speak to Khellios about leaving for Taria," I informed her, unsure of what else I could say to comfort her. I felt like a traitor to my peers for helping my mate. I felt like a traitor to my mate for not abandoning plans made with my peers. Letting people down made me feel like a failure. Guilt burrowed its way into my body, painfully curling itself around my heart and lungs. It was hard to breathe.

"I trust you will be alright in my absence?" I managed, feeling out of breath.

"Yes," she replied. Her voice was cold.

I massaged my temples. Life with Renna would not be easy if we were at odds at every moment.

"I suppose we will see each other again once the transfusion effects begin to wane, whenever that is," I added.

She just ignored me. So, without another word, I opened a portal and made my way to the star craft command room.

6

RENNA

My heart was speeding like I had just run for my life, making my breath ragged. My mind raced too, trying to process everything that had just happened.

Aeroth was going to help me.

I didn't know if my conversation with Sethos would occur, but I had hope. So far, I only had one plan to save Sethos—or at least, try to. But I couldn't rely on just one plan. I had learned to be self-reliant, and that meant making backup plans.

My first instinct was to search for Khellios and ask to travel with him to Taria to await Sethos.

I changed into the clothing left for me on a chair. My outfit included a dark gray top and pants. Everything fit me somewhat loose, but I was grateful to change out of my torn clothing from Daya. The top had brass buttons along the front, with light gray piping on the hem, arms, and neck. On the left side of the jacket was an embroidered badge of a planet surrounded by stars with a star craft. I ran my hands over the embroidery and wondered if this was a symbol for Elrie's crew. The pants were the same shade as the top with the same piping down the side of the legs. Luckily my boots were still good, so I opted to keep them on after a change of socks.

I carefully dressed over the injuries on my body. Unfortunately, the effects of Aeroth's blood did not speed up my healing, and my body was still sore. Thankfully, my magic was restoring itself quickly, and now that I wasn't in unbearable separation pain, I was able to call on my magic to begin forming scabs on my scratches and other wounds.

The layout of Elrie's star craft was much like Khellios's home. The walls and ceiling were stark white, with soft white rectangular panel lighting above. There wasn't any art on the walls, but upon close inspection, I noticed the wall was made of a honeycomb pattern. The material had the slightest silver outline, giving some subtle texture to the room.

The black and polished floors provided a sharp contrast. My feet echoed with each step as I walked away from my cabin room, unsure where I was going.

As I continued down the hallway, small groups of two or three uniformed people walked past me. They wore uniforms like mine that varied from gray, black, and navy blue.

Their skin varied in color from lighter pink shades to dark brown to blue and even purple skin with webbing. Some even had red skin with green eyes. I was mesmerized by their neon hair, and by their tall stature; I found myself gawking as I passed them. Guessing at a distance, they were around the same height as Khellios and the rest of the gods.

My walk around the star craft came to a halt when large floor-to-ceiling windows revealing space greeted me. The room brightened in hues of warm orange and gold as we passed a nebula. The stardust from the ongoing celestial event—the birth of new stars—was hypnotic. Nestled in the middle of the nebula were bursts of deep blues, cobalt, and aquamarine, all moving in circles as if weaving together small orbs.

"I wish I could stop time so that I could watch you like this forever," a smooth, familiar voice said behind me.

My body shivered as a slow smile broke across my lips. I turned to find Cylas standing with his hands in his pants pockets, a lazy smile on his lips. My skin flushed.

Cylas was unbelievably attractive, and somehow I was always affected being near him.

"Hi," I said, my voice coming out quieter than intended.

Cylas walked closer to step out of the way of a group of armored women walking past us, pushing a cart filled with helmets and guns.

"Women in uniform," Cylas drawled, his eyes following the women. "Looks like I found my calling."

I snorted a laugh and covered my mouth. Cylas turned to me, his wicked grin deepening.

"What?" he said, looking down at my lips and back up to my face.

"What calling would that be?" I asked.

"Finding a job on this craft doing whatever," he chuckled. "The women look lonely."

"How charitable of you." I laughed. "What if they don't prefer men?"

Cylas stepped closer to me and pushed a strand of my curls behind my ear. "I'm everybody's type. I'm my own category of being."

I rolled my eyes. "You and Misha would be quite a pair."

He bit his lip. "You, the Goddess of Lust, *and I*, would be quite a thing."

My skin broke out in goosebumps at the potential image of the three of us together. Misha was beautiful—even I had been drawn to her when I met her at the nightclub.

"Aren't you convalescent?" I asked Cylas, recalling his injuries in Vasarys. "Are you serious?"

He smiled and moved his wrists up to show me. The blackened skin from the Alaric Chains was completely gone. "I've never been more serious in my life. The medic mages sped up my healing, and my own magic helped."

I felt my face heat. The mention of me being involved with Cylas sent a delicious shiver down my spine, and I almost forgot the slight pain from my wounds.

Cylas leaned down to whisper in my ear. "I missed seeing you blush, Ren baby."

I squeezed my thighs together and moved to look at him. He'd always had an effect on me—perhaps anyone that ever crossed his path.

"Ren baby?" I said, giving him a gentle shove. "*Really?*"

He shrugged. "I can't give you a nickname now? You're gone for almost four months with a villainous asshole, and now you emerge from his lair all serious?"

I knew Cylas meant well and was trying to lighten the mood, but his words still stung.

"Speaking of," I said, clearing my throat. "We need to talk about what he's done. I know Aeroth is planning on . . ." I took a deep breath. "Killing him."

Cylas sighed. "And I'm guessing from your *tone*," he said with a grimace, massaging his temples, "you plan on helping Sethos? Even though you know he deserves to be completely taken out—"

"It's . . ." I started, but paused to collect my thoughts. "It's . . . complicated, Cylas. I need you to help me. Aeroth is willing to help me speak with him, but I feel like we'll need backup. If I can just get Sethos to see things differently, I think I can stop this war."

Cylas stared at me for a few moments before speaking.

"I hate wars, Renna. I hate death. It destroys life, my creations

. . . but what you are asking for . . ." He sighed. "It's not that simple."

The same response as Aeroth.

Before I could respond, hurried footsteps approached.

"Renna."

Khellios stood in the hallway alone, breath heaving, his eyes searching my face.

"Khellios."

"I wanted to be the first one you spoke to." He shook his head and ran his hands over his face. "The mages prohibited me from entering your cabin. I stood outside, *waiting*—"

"Yes, but, Khellios—"

"I moved away for *one moment*, and came back to find your door was open and you were gone." He stepped closer, reaching to touch my arms, but stopped short.

"Khellios," I said gently and put my hands on his forearms. I squeezed. "I'm okay."

"No." He shrugged from my grasp and looked at the scratches and bruises still marring my face. "You're not."

A group of crew members walked past, their eyes wide as they stared at the three of us, murmuring to each other.

"Perhaps we move this doomed romantic reunion somewhere else?" Cylas suggested.

Khellios glared at Cylas.

"Or not," Cylas added. "By all means," he gestured around us, "continue in the hallway."

"We need to talk," Khellios said, looking back to me.

I nodded. "I agree."

"There's a library room up ahead. It should be private."

"Literally, what I *just* suggested," Cylas added.

"Cylas," Khellios snapped. "*Enough.*"

"I didn't say anything!"

I turned to face Cylas. "You and I still have some unfinished business," I reminded him. "I'll find you afterward?"

"Sure thing, Ren baby," Cylas drawled, that easy smile making a return. "In the meantime, I'll go find the delicious commander woman in armor running craft operations. Blonde isn't a usual pick for me, but I cannot resist—"

Khellios cut in and took a step toward Cylas. "Stay away from Elrie," he growled.

Cylas put his hands up. "How did you know I was talking about Elrie? I didn't know you had a thing for her. Do you find her delicious as well?"

Khellios stepped closer to Cylas.

"I *don't* have a thing for her," Khellios snapped. "I just . . ." he paused. "Stay away from her." He pointed a finger in his direction. "I mean it, Cylas."

Cylas smirked and saluted Khellios. "Got it, old man. I'll stay away from the woman you do *not* have a thing for, because why would you care otherwise?"

I quickly grabbed Khellios's arm and moved him with me down the hallway.

"Don't pay attention to him," I murmured to Khellios. "Cylas likes to provoke people."

"Cylas is an idiot," Khellios snapped.

I kept my mouth shut, walking with Khellios until we stopped at two glass sliding doors. Following his lead, we walked inside the empty entryway.

The library was two stories high, with bookshelves lining the walls. They framed the massive floor-to-ceiling windows, which revealed our journey through space. At the moment, we were passing by a solar system with several blue and green planets.

The rest of the room had sleek red leather couches set up around silver steel lounge tables, creating little conversation areas. Khellios and I sat on one of the couches overlooking the cosmos.

"From what I can see," he said softly, looking at my hands, "some wounds are almost closed. But you still sound very tired."

A dull ache had begun to form throughout my body, and my heart dropped. I wondered if it was the separation pain returning. Had Aeroth's blood worn off already?

I closed my eyes to focus on my breathing.

"You should rest," Khellios stated.

I shifted in my seat. "I'm okay for now."

Khellios sighed and looked out at the stars. "I missed you," he said dryly.

"I missed you too." Despite how everything had unfolded in Taria, I did care for Khellios. Very much.

"What happened in Daya, Ren?"

My body tensed.

I fell for a man who had plotted to lie and had manipulated me for months.

He slept in my bed.

I gave myself to him.

Repeatedly.

Flashes of my body moving against Sethos's flooded my mind, and I sat forward with my head between my hands. More flashes of Sethos and I overwhelmed my system, and I almost screamed from frustration.

I felt stupid. Used. Horribly used.

I stood and ran my hands through my hair.

"He hurt you. That much is clear," Khellios said gently.

I nodded and turned to look at him, my back to the windows. Sadness replaced my anger as I saw Khellios's eyes glassed over with unshed tears.

"I cannot stand to see you in pain, Renna."

"My body is healing. My magic is speeding things up too."

"I'm sorry I was so against you using magic. Perhaps if I encouraged you to use it, you would have been better protected from Sethos."

His apology settled between us, reminding me of the gentle side of Khellios, one people rarely got to see. Khellios was all hard edges on the outside, always wearing a tough armor of control. But I knew he could be gentle and loving. I had almost fallen for him . . .

I could have loved him. Madly. Deeply.

But just because we had been in a relationship before did not mean we should be in a relationship again. And in this lifetime, the timing for us to come together was off. I was a different person from when he had first met me so many years before. And I knew he had changed too.

I shifted on my feet, weighing my response before I responded. "While I don't agree with your reasons for preventing me from using magic, I do understand."

Khellios leaned forward, pressing his forearms on his thighs. He laced his fingers together and looked at his hands.

"Elrie reminds me about my control issues," he said with a sad smile. "It drives her nuts."

I tilted my head to the side. "Your need to control drives me crazy too."

When Khellios looked up at me, we locked eyes for a long moment and I saw love and fear and rage.

Khellios pushed to stand, walked toward me, and gently grabbed my hands.

"You wanted honesty from me," he said. "I'm sorry I did not give that to you. When you were in Daya, I went to the Witch District in Taria and spoke with Merida, the Head Witch. I asked her to explain how Sethos located you and if you were safe with him . . . From my conversation with her, as I understand it . . ." Khellios paused. "You were not his prisoner."

I took my hands back from his hold and hugged my arms. I felt my stomach roll, dreading the questions that were coming.

I took a deep breath before answering. "I was not his prisoner. Not in the beginning."

"I—" He shook his head. "I do not understand. He is *vile*, Renna."

I bit the inside of my cheek. I knew I didn't have to answer any of his questions, but the weight of this conversation with Khellios felt like closing a chapter that had barely begun. I could almost anticipate him asking for another opportunity, and I wanted him to know that after everything in Daya, I was not ready to be in a relationship with anybody.

"Sethos entered my life almost eight years ago."

Khellios's eyes widened.

"He found me when I was living in one of the human slums in Andora. He followed Am-Re to where I was living. Am-Re was posing as my mentor at the time. Am-Re was . . ." I shook my head. "He was abusive. He provoked magic in me. I know I never shared that part of my life with you."

Khellios nodded. "Merida shared about Am-Re's mentorship."

I was grateful to the witch for at least saving me from that painful conversation.

"Sethos saw the abuse," I continued. "He killed Am-Re shortly thereafter and wove his way into my everyday life." I shook my head, looking down to my feet. "I . . . I can't even—"

My lips trembled recalling those days, and Khellios reached out, placing his arms around me for comfort.

"I feel so stupid," I said, my voice breaking. "That I allowed myself to trust Sethos. You're not going to look at me the same way if you know what I did."

"But none of this is your fault, Renna," he growled. "You being born with Am-Re's magic is not your fault. Your father is at fault because he began *everything*."

I uncurled my hands from my arms to wipe the tears from my eyes, and words rushed from me, and we both sat down on the couch. I started to tell him about the day I left home for university, after Sethos killed Am-Re. Recounting the story of how Sethos had entered my life felt like hours.

Khellios sat in silence next to me, his arms tightly crossed on his chest.

"Fucking hell," he murmured when I was done.

There was silence.

"Sethos loves you." A statement, not a question. "In a very fucked up way. It's toxic, Renna. It's unhealthy. You must see that."

I was silent.

He turned to me, studying me for a moment before reaching for my hand.

"How could he look at a woman like you and not give up the world?"

I squeezed his hand. "I begged him, pleaded with him to change—"

"You love him."

My eyes glassed over.

"I don't want to." My voice was barely audible. "I'm not in love with him, but I love who he was before everything broke down. There are different kinds of love."

Khellios blinked a few times and looked to the window.

"There are," he said after a while.

"I don't think I'll ever know what my exact feeling toward Sethos will be. How do I even begin to fully process this?"

He chuckled sadly. "I am the wrong person to talk to about processing relationships and feelings." My heart broke for him and the history we had. Standing, he continued. "I don't think

Sethos will ever be the man who you need him to be. Or who you deserve."

I grabbed Khellios's arm.

"Please help me speak to him. I know if I can just speak with Sethos, I can make him see—"

Khellios's gentle features sharpened into hard lines, and he snatched his arm back as if I had burned him.

"I cannot."

I shot up from the couch. "Yes, you *can*. I want to go to Taria when you leave. I can help prevent the attack by speaking to Sethos."

"He refused to listen to you in Daya. He won't listen to you now. I cannot let you near him. He chose his path. He scorned you, even when you confessed your love to him. He won't change, Renna. Make peace with it."

He started to walk away, but I grabbed his hands, forcing him to look at me. "I cannot give up on him. This magic destroyed him. *Please.*"

Khellios gently removed my grasp and shook his head.

"I will not. In fact, you must know the shield of Taria is now magically protected to only allow gods and other war allies in. You would not be able to enter if you tried to portal in. I am glad for that."

A wave of panic moved through me.

"*Why?*" I yelled.

"I will not have you in a place where he is. I refuse to lose you again!"

My jaw dropped. "There is nothing to lose!" I spat. "*I am not yours to lose!*"

Khellios grabbed my shoulders, shaking me slightly. "And don't you think it kills me?"

"Let me go!"

Khellios released me and turned away. "I wanted you for so long," he said. "So fucking long."

"I know that."

"No," he murmured as he turned. "You don't know."

I crossed my arms.

"Your death and the death of others when Old Xhor fell . . ." he shook his head. "It haunts me. I wanted more time with you. A chance. But I cannot force you, and now I'm left with these feelings for you. For us. Of who we were. Of who I was. All I can do now is protect you. And I will cling to that."

Khellios mentioning the fall of Old Xhor only reminded me of the tragedy of Isyos.

"It's grief, Khellios."

"Don't you think I know that?" he snapped.

"Having me at your side will not make these feelings of guilt go away."

I was tired of Khellios's singular mentality of believing his feelings were the only ones that mattered. He had played a role in Sethos's journey, and I had seen it torment Sethos daily.

I lifted my chin and squared my shoulders. "Sethos mourns too. His grief changed him. You would know."

Khellios narrowed his eyes. "What are you saying?"

"*You* attacked Isyos. In the attack, you killed Sethos's mother. And countless others. People he loved."

"I—" Khellios frowned, trying to find the words. "I . . . I didn't know."

"How could you, Khellios? You think a person just"—I snapped my finger in his face—"becomes a monster overnight? You and the other gods contributed to Sethos's pain."

Khellios remained silent as I continued.

"You made a monster out of a child, and he grew up with revenge on his mind for hundreds of years. The rage that lives inside him won't let him move forward either."

Khellios simply stared at me, his eyebrows furrowed and his hands on his hips as if he could not believe my words.

"Tell me why you attacked Isyos."

He immediately backed away from me, putting his palms up, creating a wide berth between us.

"Renna, I didn't know civilians lived in Isyos. You have to believe me. I would never—"

I shook my head. "How could you, a god, not *know*?"

"We attacked Isyos with Arios's command as leader of our enclave. He told us Am-Re was using the planet as his base. We knew there were criminals there, but we did not understand the extent of the population. I would *never* kill civilians."

"Yet you did."

I moved away from him.

"Renna—"

"You both grieve, Khellios! Can't you see that?"

"I am not the one set on killing for revenge! I know what the gods and I did was wrong. I would not repeat it. There is a difference to me and—"

"I am not saying you are the same. I would never." I stepped toward Khellios and grabbed his hands. "I'm just saying you both experienced loss. You had a support system around you to help you overcome your grief. Sethos has nobody. He needs help."

"You know nothing of my grief. But know I do regret what happened on Isyos. But no amount of regret will ever make me have sympathy for his actions now."

"I don't want anyone in Taria to die. We have an opportunity to stop this! You and I can help end this conflict."

Khellios shook his head.

"This will end when Sethos is dead. This war is about more than him. In fact, we expect Am-Re will be on the battlefield. There have been reports of him possessing bodies . . . We know he is weak and hope to use that in our favor." Khellios drew me in closer. "Don't ask me to help you, Renna. *I don't want Sethos to kill you.*"

I pulled away from him and said, "Sethos will not kill me!"

"And what happened to you in Daya?" he roared. "You have to see this from my side." He jabbed a finger to his chest. "Put yourself in *my shoes.*"

"*Your shoes?* Your overprotectiveness—"

"Renna," he pleaded and strode toward me so we were now almost touching. "Do you forget how he hurt you? How he locked you up?"

"I will never forget—"

"Then you are delusional."

My jaw dropped. "Don't insult me! By letting this war happen, you're letting people *die.*"

Khellios pointed at me. "Do *not* pretend you know *anything* about war just because you now have control of your power."

Fury boiled inside me at his tone.

"You're all making a mistake," I said.

"I don't think so. I think *you* are making a mistake in putting your faith in a man who is beyond help. And who certainly does not deserve you. To have you risk your life for him?" Khellios shook his head. "You may never return my love, Renna. I can live with that. But do not ask me to live through your death again when I now have the power to prevent it."

His words stung. Not because they were offensive, but because of the weight they carried and how they made me second-guess my actions.

I turned from him to sink back down on the couch, resting my head in my palms.

"You said there are different kinds of love," Khellios began after a few minutes. "You are not in love with Sethos, but you love him enough to risk your life to save him."

I glanced up at Khellios. My heart raced as his words settled into my system.

"The day we found you, Aeroth asked if I was in love with you. And I have love for you, Renna. Perhaps the type of love I feel for you has changed over time without me realizing it. But know this: Out of my love for you, I must make difficult decisions to protect you. I will *never* risk your life. And that is why, for as long as I live, I will ensure you never see Sethos again."

The words hit me like a wall. My heart dropped into my stomach, but before I could respond, Khellios portaled out of the room, leaving no space for me to argue back.

My plans for helping Sethos were gone. I was living in a nightmare.

7

RENNA

I sped through the hallways in search of Aeroth.

We had to find a different way to get to Sethos.

Just then, my vision blurred and my body started aching. I knew intuitively it was the separation effects.

"*Fuck . . .*" I cursed as I held onto a wall. The expression earned me a few stares from crew members walking past. I clenched my teeth and pushed myself off to keep walking.

A pang of pain hit me, stopping me in my tracks.

Renna.

It was Aeroth's voice as I remembered it from the Astral. I froze and looked around, my eyes dashing side to side. The only other time Aeroth had spoken through my mind was when we interacted in the Astral.

Perhaps I had imagined his voice due to my need to see him?

Where are you? Aeroth asked.

I froze again and spun around, my heart now racing. I could not have imagined Aeroth's voice a second time . . .

Was this part of the mate bond? If so, I hated it.

But maybe I could speak back to Aeroth and he would be able to hear me?

In that moment, I saw Cylas walk down the curved hallway, and my heart leaped.

He was busy talking to a young woman with ebony skin and long silver hair topped by a crown. Her elaborate blue dress made her look like a queen.

A second woman approached Cylas then. She was dressed in a green dress and had long black hair with a silver white streak toward the front of her face . . .

I squinted.

I had seen her before. I paused to take a deep breath.

Where have I seen her before?

The woman turned to look my way, and the second I locked eyes with her intense violet stare, every cell in my body froze.

It was the woman from my vision all those nights ago in Daya. The woman who had warned me about Am-Re's return in a dream.

'He comes for the Heir of Darkness and Ruin.'

My heart almost stopped beating as I processed her warning and the unbelievable fact that she was *real*. I took a step in their direction when someone grabbed my right arm, pulling me into a room.

I didn't even have time to scream. A hard chest pushed against my body, shoving me into a crammed space.

The second the separation pain melted away, I knew it was Aeroth. That, and by his scent of musk and oud.

"What the fuck was that?" I yelled at him.

We were in a dim-lit small utility closet of sorts with a large square machine with buttons at the end. It was wide enough for two and overall big enough for no more than five people.

"You didn't answer me," he gritted out.

"Was I supposed to?" I yelled. "What even was that?"

Aeroth opened his mouth to speak, but I cut in, jabbing a

finger in his solid chest. It hurt, but I was too angry to acknowledge the pain.

"And how *dare you* grab me like that," I snapped. "You can't just pull me around wherever you wish."

"We need to exchange blood."

"Why were you inside my mind? How fucking dare you do that, have you no sense of privacy?"

"Renna—"

"I'm pretty sure you broke some sort of universal law regarding boundaries—"

"Strongborn—"

"You don't get to come into my life and—"

Aeroth grabbed my arms and tightened his grip slightly, forcing me to meet his gaze, his words rushing out. "Strongborn. I'm sorry. I was in a meeting with the representatives from—"

I shrugged him off and crossed my arms. "You just did it again."

Aeroth closed his eyes and pinched the bridge of his nose. He took a deep breath out before opening his eyes and straightening his posture.

"I'm sorry. I will not do it again."

My eyes narrowed. "Do what?"

"Speak to you in the way I did, through the Astral."

My eyes grew. "And?"

"Or grab or pull you or touch you in that manner." He frowned. "Without your consent," he added quickly.

I shook my head. "You spoke to me through the Astral Plane? But we aren't in the Astral."

He put his palms up. "I don't understand it myself. When you were crossing to Daya and asking for help in the Astral Plane, I heard your voice distinctly. Over all voices. Souls talk in the Astral, so it can all blur together. But when I realized I was able to speak with you, I could not believe it. You were the first soul who actually heard me."

"Is it because of the mate bond?"

Aeroth shifted on his feet, and his brows furrowed as if he was deep in thought.

"Perhaps because you and I were created for each other, and I was destined to be King of the Astral, Source enabled us to communicate this way. I have never heard of this kind of telepathy."

I wondered whether I could speak back to him with my mind, but something about the urgent way he spoke about his meeting made me pause.

"Is everything alright with your meeting?" I asked.

Aeroth crossed his arms. "I do not know. I had to step away because of the pain."

"Is there news from Taria?"

"No, but we now have two representatives from the Galactic Federation aboard. They brought guards with them. It's not a good sign."

Aeroth had mentioned the Galactic Federation before. The name seemed imposing and reminded me of the Planetary Council. Except the Planetary Council was a group of humans that governed the three human planets on Andromeda Galaxy.

"What is the Galactic Federation?" I asked.

"The Federation is a cross-universe governmental body of multidimensional beings with the goal of enabling lasting peace between all seven universes. They are a council made of eleven species."

"And they asked you to kill Sethos."

He nodded. "They ensure war does not break out across the universes. Myself and the fae monarchs stepping in is their way of containing the conflict to only the fae species."

"And the god enclaves," I reminded him.

"Yes."

My heart sped up at the thought of them arriving on Elrie's craft with guards.

"What do they want?" I asked. "Haven't you already agreed to help them?"

"I had to leave the room before they explained why they arrived." He crossed his arms. "I don't like that they're here."

"You need to go back to that meeting."

"Yes. I don't like that the Federation is here—and armed. And I apologize for grabbing you in that manner. I panicked."

From his posture and tone, I knew he was sincere. "I accept your apology. Now let's summon the medic mages."

"I instructed them to meet us in your cabin after I left the meeting. They should be heading to your cabin now. I suggest we portal to your room to wait for them. Unless you'd rather walk out of this closet together?"

I laughed. "Walk out of this closet with you?" I rolled my eyes. "People will talk. No thank you. Let's portal to my cabin."

"Shall we?" he asked and extended his hand.

I forced a smile and placed my hand in his. "Yes. It's so nice when you ask—"

In the blink of an eye, we'd landed in my cabin.

Once my feet were on the ground, I took my hand back and moved across the room from him to create space. I wasn't uncomfortable around him. He just . . . unnerved me.

"The medic mages should arrive soon." His light tone made it seem he was completely oblivious to my anger and anxiety. He sat down casually on one of the couch seats, and his carefree demeanor sent me over the edge.

I'd learned to expect men to betray me or have a self-motivated agenda. What was his goal?

He looked comically large in his armor, especially on the small couch. My annoyance at his presence began to build inside me, but I couldn't ask him to leave. Not yet, at least. We were tethered, after all.

"Do you always wear your armor?" I asked, tilting my head. He lifted his eyebrows and looked down at his chest for a few moments.

"Is that a problem?"

"We are inside. Not on a battlefield. You look ridiculous."

Aeroth shrugged. "Keeps me alive."

I laughed, the sound bitter.

However, Aeroth's armor looked impressive. I had no doubt I would choose the same for battle. I hadn't truly paid attention to what he wore before, since the shock of our bond made me hyperfocus on our dynamic and nothing else. His armor was pitch-black and worn in some places where old scratches marred the surface. There were a few dents on his arms, and the suspicious red stain on the bottom of his chest plate made me shiver.

This was not the pristine armor of a man dressed for pageantry. Aeroth's armor had likely seen combat, and he didn't care who noticed.

Before I could ask him about his armor, someone knocked on the cabin door.

I froze.

Was it Khellios?

"Renna?" Cylas called through the door.

I met Aeroth's eyes, my heart pounding in my ears. His pursed lips and raised eyebrow clearly showed he was not amused.

"Well this is awkward," he said.

"Leave!" I snarled at him.

"You mean leave so you can be shrouded in pain for your rendezvous with your other lover?"

My eyes narrowed. "It's not that type of meeting. Cylas is a friend."

"Who calls on you this late in the night?"

"This isn't precisely a normal type of day, is it?" I snapped.

"Where do you want me to go?"

I shrugged.

"Renna, are you in?" Cylas asked and knocked again.

I gripped my hair, unsure what to do.

"Why are you so nervous for him to see me here?" Aeroth asked, crossing his arms.

"Because it's late! I don't want him asking questions. You and I have nothing to do with each other, and if he sees you here—"

He lowered his chin. "You and I have everything to do with each other."

My jaw dropped, and I blinked, not knowing what to respond to *that*.

"*Just go!*" I hissed. "I'm still trying to figure out this mate bond, and I don't need a third party's input. People will find out soon enough, but not tonight."

I looked around the room for places to hide, but he was so tall and large that I could not fathom where he could go.

My eyes settled on the armoire in the corner.

"I am *not* going in there!" he whispered.

"Well no, because you're so strangely large!"

He lifted his eyebrows. "That's not the usual descriptor women give me—"

"Aeroth!"

He smirked and said, "The *strange* part. Now the large part—"

I quickly spun toward the cabin bathroom, turning away to prevent him from seeing me blush at the thought of what he might be describing.

"You're going to have me hide in the bathroom, aren't you?"

I snapped my finger at him, pointing inside the small room. "Get to it!"

"You can't be serious."

"*Get in the bathroom!*"

Aeroth narrowed his eyes at me.

"Renna, are you alright?" Cylas asked. "I can hear the sound of your voice. I'm coming in."

"*Wait!* One second!"

"What's going on?" he asked through the door.

"*I uh . . .*" I squeezed my eyes shut to think. "I'm getting dressed."

When I opened my eyes again, Aeroth was staring back at me, unimpressed.

"Well don't get dressed on my account," Cylas drawled.

Aeroth's eyes grew, and his face became red with something akin to rage. "You expect me to be in the bathroom while you two—"

"Nothing will happen, that's just how Cylas speaks! Get in the fucking bathroom, Aeroth!"

He lifted an eyebrow. "*Or what?*"

I almost screamed in frustration. "Please?"

Aeroth rolled his eyes and brushed past me into the bathroom. The second he closed the door, I sped to the cabin's main door to open it.

Cylas had his arms crossed. An intense stare and a severe frown were unusual on Cylas, and it made me uneasy.

"Cylas? What's going on?"

Cylas shook his head and walked into the cabin.

"You can't be in here," I said, still holding the door open.

"Close the door, Renna."

I scoffed.

"We need to talk. Two agents from the Galactic Federation have arrived."

My muscles clenched at the mention of the Federation, and I hugged my arms against a shiver.

"What do they want?" I asked while closing the door.

"The Federation sent the two agents to collect you and your half sisters. They are now also on this craft."

My mouth dropped.

"Why? And how do they know I'm here?"

"Khellios. And the presence of the fae monarchs on the craft. They all have kept the Federation updated on their progress with Sethos."

My eyes widened. I could not believe the audacity of Khellios speaking about honesty a few moments ago and not even mentioning he had arranged for me to be escorted from the craft.

"Are you joking? I'm not going with anybody!"

"I wish I was joking, Ren baby."

I massaged my temples and paced the room.

"And where are they planning to take us?"

"Back to the Galactic Federation headquarters. The Federation deems you and your sisters a high risk for the success of the campaign against Sethos."

"So I'm supposed to, what—go with them? I've done this before, Cylas. I was taken to Taria because I didn't know how to fight and use magic. I'm capable. I'm not hiding anymore."

He sighed and rubbed his eyes.

"I thought you'd say that," he said and dropped his hands. "Stubbornness runs in the family."

"What do you mean?"

"Your sisters also refuse to go."

"Where are they now?"

"Demira and Khellios just met with the Federation reps. Illona stayed behind, and I kept her company. Khellios wants you to meet the representatives tomorrow, but he's giving you a night's rest. He told them you are badly injured."

"If the Federation asks me to go with them, I'm not going."

"And where will you go?"

I stopped pacing and looked at him.

"I need to get to Taria."

"The shield around Taria will not grant you entry. You cannot get in," he put his palms out. "There's not much you can do. The Federation reps plan to take you and your sisters to headquarters tomorrow."

My heart pounded almost painfully. I sat down on my bed and put a hand on my chest.

"You should sleep. I can help you brainstorm tomorrow as to what to do. Maybe I can join you three at the Federation headquarters to keep you company?"

I shook my head. I wasn't going anywhere with the representatives.

"I'll see you tomorrow, Cylas." I stood and gestured to the door. "Please leave. I need to think."

Cylas nodded and headed to the door.

"I want to meet my sisters tomorrow . . . before I speak to the people from the Federation."

"Alright. I'll arrange it."

"When I refuse to go with the representatives . . . will you help me?"

Cylas stared at me for a long moment. "I would do anything for you, Renna. Anything."

Cylas's words were reassuring, but uneasiness tingled through my skin, overpowering all other feelings.

"Even if gods must comply with the Federation?" I asked.

Cylas smirked and strode back, stopping right in front of me.

"Don't women love an outlaw?"

I tried to smile.

"Good night, Ren baby," he said with a smile and leaned in. He kissed me on my cheek gently before turning to leave. While his reassurance should have made me feel better, it only made me shiver.

Cylas shut the door quietly, and Aeroth burst out of the bathroom.

"'*Ren baby*'?" Aeroth demanded.

I groaned and walked back to my bed, sitting down and resting back on the headboard.

"You eavesdropped?" I snapped as the mild separation pain dissipated.

"I was quite literally in the other room."

I closed my eyes to keep from rolling them.

"So what do I do?" I asked him. "I don't want to go to the Galactic Federation. I won't be forced."

"No one will force you to do anything—that I vow to you. I will go to see the representatives now and find out what I can."

But he couldn't leave the room. Not without us exchanging blood.

And the medic mages had not arrived.

"So will we drink from each other?" I asked him.

Aeroth tilted his head. "Only if you allow it. I know you don't want to be forced into situations. I respect that. However, my ability to investigate may help you."

I nodded, and for some reason I could not make sense of, I moved to the side to make space for him.

Aeroth sat along the edge of the bed as if it were the most natural thing in the world.

"You're sure?" he asked.

"Do we have a choice? I'd rather you find out what is going on."

"Just to be clear, you were vehemently against this type of blood exchange earlier today. I won't have you later say that I tried to force you or take advantage of you."

I lifted my chin and pursed my lips. "My freedom is more important."

"Alright," he said. He rose from the bed to stand and began to take off his cape.

Aeroth's black cape appeared to be made of velvet or some thicker material. My eyes traveled down the length of the cape and saw a slight shimmering shadow gathered at the bottom of the cape, as if it were black and gray smoke mixed with stars. The familiarity with Sethos's cape settled deep within me, and I shook my head to clear my thoughts.

"Everything alright?"

I zipped my head up to meet Aeroth's gaze. He held the cape over his arm.

"Yes," I said and scratched my neck.

"Is me undressing making you uncomfortable?"

I shook my head. "No, I just . . ." I frowned, not knowing what to say as I glanced back to his cape.

"Is it my cape that bothers you?" he asked, holding it up.

"N-no . . ." I cleared my throat. "It reminded me of someone, that's all."

He chuckled, tossed his cape on the bed, and started to take off his armor.

"I'm certain you haven't seen a cloak like that before. Mine is made of the Astral Plane itself," he said.

I played with the bed cover underneath me, not knowing how to respond.

Sethos had Astral projected to me in my dream wearing a cape dotted with stars. His cape had been different in that it didn't have the same smoke and shadows like Aeroth's cape, but still, the similarity was eerie.

"The cape doesn't enable you to Astral travel . . . Right?" I tried to sound as casual as possible.

He shook his head. "No, but it provides my physical human body with protection from things like solar flares and other radiation."

"There isn't any solar radiation inside the craft."

"No, but I can travel through the Astral at a moment's notice. I have it with me at all times out of habit."

"How did you acquire one? Did you conjure one?"

"The priestesses in my kingdom weave cloaks like this for all astral heirs."

I nodded, trying to push Sethos from my mind.

"I'm sorry I was rude," I said quietly as he took off his gauntlets, reminding me of my earlier comment ridiculing him.

Aeroth nodded once and sat on the bed and began to unclasp his shin plates.

"I know this is not easy, Renna. I'm sorry."

A silence settled between us as he continued to take off his armor. I was at a loss for what to say. Aeroth was being kind, and I didn't know how to feel about it.

"So how does this blood exchange work?" I asked, trying to change the subject.

"The ideal places to feed from are either your neck or thigh. We already went over why your arm would not be an ideal place."

"So what do I do?" I asked, my throat feeling dry.

He gestured to the collar of my high-neck shirt. "You would have to take off your shirt so I could access your neck. Or your pants, so I could access one of your thighs."

I took a deep breath. I had to do this. My freedom was at risk.

"The neck is fine," I said quickly and whipped off my shirt without thinking twice. "Let's get this over with."

I then diverted my eyes as I sat in front of him with nothing but my pants and an ill-fitting brassiere. Elrie had left it for me, not knowing I needed something bigger.

When Aeroth did not move or speak, I peeked at him from my peripheral.

"What?" I asked him.

In that moment, the left strap of the brassiere fell, threatening to expose my left breast. Aeroth's mouth was slightly ajar, and his gaze was on my chest. His stare made my skin hot, and I cleared my throat and quickly pulled the strap up.

"Get on with it!" I snapped. "Surely you've seen other female breasts before?"

He almost choked on a cough before answering. "Yes."

"Well?"

In that moment, the medic mages opened my cabin door and walked in.

They froze and stared wide-eyed at us, and in a blink of an eye, Aeroth stood directly in front of me, blocking my body from their view.

"King Aeroth," they said almost in unison and bowed their heads. "We did not mean to intrude on an intimate moment. If this is not a good time—"

Aeroth growled.

"There is no intimate moment. And you're late. *Turn around*," he gritted to the mages.

I glanced around his shoulder and saw them turn to face the cabin door, which was now closed.

Aeroth turned to me. "Are you okay? I'm sorry they surprised us like that."

His concern for me felt odd. It felt genuine, and I didn't know what to make of it. With Sethos, I had sometimes felt anxiety if I did anything wrong. With Khellios, his concern for me sometimes felt like I had to continuously thank him for everything he'd done.

It was strange to have someone genuinely concerned for my well-being with no expectation of anything in return.

"Yes," I replied.

Aeroth nodded and turned to give me privacy. "Let me know when you're dressed."

I quickly put my shirt on and pulled the sleeves up to the

inside of my elbow so the medic mages could put the catheter in my arm.

After I arranged myself so I was sitting against the headboard, I said, "I'm good."

Aeroth turned and sat next to me against the headboard as well. He narrowed his eyes to where the mages stood.

"You may turn," he said in a deadly tone. "And knock next time. Don't *ever* let this happen again."

The mages turned slowly and moved around us, never meeting our eyes.

"You Arcturians may preach peace, but I don't adhere to such teachings. I don't take kindly to disrespect against my own."

My jaw dropped slightly at him considering me one of his own. I couldn't help the small thrill that ran through me at seeing someone stand up for me.

The main medic mage from before spoke without lifting his eyes. "Certainly, King Aeroth. We meant no disrespect."

Aeroth clenched his jaw and barked, "Get on with it."

The mages almost jumped and began to work. I closed my eyes and let the transfusion happen without another word, feeling strangely safe with an almost complete stranger.

8

CYLAS

It was a quiet night throughout Elrie's craft.

I walked through the craft with a glass of ambrosia in hand, passing fewer than ten people on my way to my cabin.

Gods didn't need sleep—it was somewhat of a luxury we allowed ourselves. And while I never turned down the indulgence and chose to sleep every night, my mind would not turn off.

I was worried for Renna. And her sisters. Even Demira. The powers they had were palpable, you could feel it like a forcefield around them.

And since Am-Re was alive, even in a weakened state, that made his daughters a liability, practically walking chaos. If Am-Re got a hold of any of them, he would drain them of their power in an instant to slowly restore his energy—especially Renna.

What worried me most was how long the Federation would detain Renna and her sisters at the Federation headquarters. The Federation's representative had a strange interest in Renna, asking about her as if she were a specimen. It made me uneasy . . .

No other offspring had ever replicated a parent god's power. It was unusual. Would she be subjected to testing against her will?

When I opened the door to my cabin, my mood immediately dampened.

There were many things I thoroughly enjoyed in life. Having women in my bedroom was at the top of the list.

However, seeing the angry faces of Demira and Illona was not a pleasant surprise.

I sighed.

"Get the fuck out of my room," I chided, closing the door behind me.

"We go from one cell to the next, Cylas," Demira gritted out. "You need to help us."

Ignoring them, I began to walk around my cabin getting ready to sleep. I didn't even look up at her when I answered. "I don't need to do anything, especially for you. Or did you forget that time you tried to kill me?"

"Cylas," Illona began.

I groaned internally at the sound of her voice. It was gentle and low, smooth as silk.

"That *is* my name," I answered, not daring to look into her ice-blue eyes. They tended to suck me right in, and I didn't like it. I felt captive under her gaze, and it was unsettling.

"Please help us."

I took off my shirt, and Demira yelped, quickly turning the other way with her arms crossed.

"Have you no decency?" she yelled over her shoulder.

"I'm in my own room, it's late, and I'm getting ready for bed. If you don't like it, *leave*."

Illona stepped toward me.

"We need to speak with you," she said, her eyes never leaving mine.

"Isn't that what we're doing?" I asked, a smirk forming on my lips.

Her eyes were beautiful, and I found myself lost in them. They were the same color as the deep Nordaluns Sea. I wondered if they changed color when in ecstasy, and realized I'd started leaning closer to her.

"I'm not going to the Galactic Federation," Demira cut in. "Neither is Illona. They were assholes to me when I met with them. Especially the short one."

I tore my gaze away from Illona and looked to Demira. "I'm sure they're not too pleased to be sent by the Federation to babysit someone like *you*," I quipped.

Demira spun around, her violet eyes glowing with fury.

"*Babysit?*" she snapped. "Now that Sethos is gone, *I* am regent of Vasarys. I don't need anyone to babysit me. My only goal is to return to Vasarys and get rid of anything that threatens my rule."

I crossed my arms.

"Oh sure, let's go to the villainous kingdom where Sethos and Am-Re will eventually return," I quipped. "You know, Sethos and your father would kill you in an instant if you opposed their rule," I replied.

"I want to meet Renna," Illona interjected, her voice firm but quiet. "The Ancestors have told me a lot about her in the last few hours."

I nodded. "She wants to meet you too—"

"We're not going to the Federation, Cylas," Demira gritted. "You need to help us."

I pinched the bridge of my nose. I had vowed to help Renna, and now her sisters were asking for help.

I looked to Illona, who looked at me with a hopeful stare, and something in my chest stirred. I recalled how she rushed toward me in Vasarys when I had been handcuffed. She had draped her body over mine as she fought to help me. No other being had ever spoken up or tried to help me the way she had.

I would help her in a heartbeat.

There was something about Illona that just . . .

Demira cleared her throat.

"Hello?" she snapped. "I just asked you to help us."

I tore my eyes from Illona to look at Demira. "Why should I care? You handcuffed me in Vasarys with no problems before. I'm sure there is something you can think of in that murderous brain of yours."

Demira lifted her chin and flashed a satisfied smile.

"I *have* thought of a few things," she fired back.

"Besides, how do you suppose we thwart them?" I asked her. "Where would you go afterward? You've been under house arrest in Vasarys for hundreds of years. You wouldn't survive one day in the wild."

Demira's expression contorted into a fiery red, but before she could open her mouth, Illona placed a hand on her shoulder and spoke instead.

"We are going to Taria," Illona said.

I laughed.

"The enclave blocked you both and Renna from accessing Taria. The shield will not let you in."

Demira tilted her head to the side. "There is a solution for that."

I frowned.

"Demira has recurring visions of riding into Taria on the back of a Metidon," Illona shared.

I blinked in surprise.

Metidons were massive, feathered winged serpent beasts. Their feathers ranged from pale blue to icy white, and they were sometimes iridescent. It made them difficult to spot in both the daytime and nighttime since they blended in with the sky and clouds.

The creatures also breathed ice in powerful, invisible blasts, spewing it from the sky. It could strike foes without them knowing. To find oneself at the mercy of the beasts was deadly.

Most importantly, Metidons were the first feathered winged beasts created by Source and had the most concentration of pure Source magic and could withstand any magic . . . A Metidon would be able to break through the shield around Taria.

"Is this a joke?" I asked them both. "Metidons are deadly. And you have no business going to Taria. Find another kingdom. Marry . . . or something. Move on."

Illona's pale eyes turned a dark, stormy blue.

"That's sexist," she stated. "Take it back."

I clenched my jaw. I was getting used to Demira's incessant, annoying voice and demands each passing day. But Illona? She was reserved. Quiet. Reasonable.

And any ire from her felt . . . *wrong*.

I didn't like that she was upset—especially toward me.

I crossed my arms and looked to the ground. "I'm sorry."

"Apology accepted," she replied, and I glanced up to catch a slight tug on the corner of her lips.

I stared at that corner until Demira spoke once more.

"It's no joke, Cylas," Demira stated. "Your allies are going to Taria to deal with Sethos. You know my father will follow on the battlefield. He will find a way. Especially if his magic is controlling Sethos. It will create a connection to locate Sethos."

"Do you *wish* to die?" I asked Demira.

"I'm not getting left behind while the outcome of my father and Sethos gets decided by *your kind*," she said, crossing her arms. "I have too much to lose. Khellios, the gods, and their allies are only fighting for Taria. I fight for my freedom and Vasarys. I'm going on behalf of my people."

If I liked Demira at all, I would be impressed with her bravery. But as it were, I could not stand her.

"And you think Metidons will agree to help you sway the outcome of this battle?" I mocked.

She lowered her chin and took a step toward me. "Yes. I have to trust my vision."

If she was right and the Metidons agreed to help her . . .

I ran my hands through my hair.

Having the Metidons in battle would be invaluable. Metidons played a pivotal role in the Galactic Wars. The universes found long-lasting peace because of their involvement.

I wanted peace for Taria.

I hated wars.

I hated destruction.

I hated death.

Perhaps the Metidons would be a good solution . . .

The problem was, after the Wars, I could not remember the last time I had seen one. As God of the Planets, I could not feel their presence on one of my planets.

"And pray tell, where are the Metidons?" I asked Demira, tilting my head. "Surely your vision told you?"

"I don't know," she responded. "Their location was not shown to me."

Illona spoke. "You are the Creator God. The God of the Planets. We hoped you would be able to know of their location . . ."

I shook my head.

"They're not on any planet. They must be in a dimension. The Galactic Federation protects their location."

Demira cursed and began pacing. "The Federation cannot know we are looking for Metidons. And you cannot tell Khellios. They will all know why we plan on using them."

"So how do you expect to begin your search?" I asked, more curious than judgmental.

"*You* will portal us out of here to Konah Universe. I know Metidons originate from there."

I laughed and shook my head. "*You* cannot make demands of *me*."

Demira smiled and walked so close we were almost nose to nose.

"Laugh all you want, but you are the key to getting us out of here. Because in my vision, there was a woman seated next to me riding a second Metidon." She began to list off each point as she lifted a finger. "She has tan skin . . . brown curly hair . . ."

My heart rate began to increase.

". . . hazel eyes . . . and is about this tall." She gestured to the middle of my chest.

I frowned as an ominous feeling began to roil in the pit of my stomach.

"That could be anyone," I argued.

"Except that it's *not*," Demira snapped. "I saw her on this ship for the first time earlier today. And you know what I realized? I have seen her in other visions as well. I just never knew who she was. She resembles Illona and I."

I swallowed the hard lump in my throat.

It was Renna.

Renna was my weakness—I would always protect her. But I could not trust Demira and Illona with Renna's safety. They had been under house arrest for most of their lives. They knew nothing of traveling the universe.

If Demira's vision was correct, then Renna would surely join in their search, and they would somehow thwart the Federation's command as they traveled to the headquarters.

They would also ride Metidons, and the thought of Renna near one of the beasts made my body tremble.

This was a disaster.

"So," Demira said, taking a slight step back to stand in front of me. "You will help us escape this star craft because if I'm correct, Renna is in my vision and we have places to be."

9

ILLONA

I frowned in my sleep as a low buzzing sound slowly began to build in my ear. Demira and I had stayed up late planning our trip to find the Metidons with Cylas, and I was exhausted.

But no matter how much I tossed and turned, the buzzing noise—an indicator of a nearby spirit—would not cease.

Except it was never any random spirit. For me, the buzzing sound was always my Ancestors.

Go away, I said internally.

They usually respected my sleep time and left me unbothered. But not tonight. Curse the gift of speaking to the dead. A gift too lowly to be considered significant by my father, yet disruptive as a tempest for me.

Speaking to the dead was a result of having Golden Fire magic. The magic allowed me to create life like plants, but I also had the power to resurrect animals and pull people back from near death. As a result, I was also deeply connected to the realm of the undead.

When I asked the Ancestors about what to do about our

impending trip to the Federation, they insisted I remain with Demira no matter what happened. They gave me no indication about whether the trip to the Federation headquarters would occur or if Demira's vision about the Metidons would come to pass.

Remain with Demira, they said over and over again.

The buzzing sound continued, and I groaned. It was a combination of murmurs from tens of thousands of Ancestors who were speaking at the same time. I could tune into each individual one if I wanted to, but not tonight.

Demira shifted uncomfortably next to me in the large bed, almost shoving me as if to quiet me as she too tried to sleep. The night felt so still, but the buzzing continued. I turned and faced the other way, covering my head with the blankets. I just needed a few hours of silence to not think about anything.

I squeezed my eyes shut and tried to focus on pleasant images in my mind's eye to get the Ancestors to quiet, but the sound persisted.

Wake up, a familiar voice said.

My eyes opened.

It was the voice of a female ancestor I called Appah. She was a wise, old woman with long braids and white hair who had lived thousands of years ago. She had an attachment to me and looked after me like a grandmother. Appah tended to not communicate as often as the other ghosts in my mind, but her voice was one I listened to the most.

I sat up in bed and looked around. The Ancestors usually appeared in my mind's eye, but I saw nothing.

Get up and get your sister, Appah spoke into the night.

What's happening? I asked.

Hurry, Appah said with no other explanation.

My body began to shiver, and I reached around to nudge Demira.

"Dee," I said, calling to Demira in the nickname I had given her when I was a child. "Wake up."

Demira groaned and waved a hand to get me to be quiet. I knelt on the bed and shook her gently.

"Dee, we have to get up."

"Illona," Demira whispered sleepily. "Go to sleep."

"We have to get up."

Demira only pulled the blankets higher, shifting away from me to the end of the bed.

Pack your things, Appah said.

This was not normal.

Thump. Thump. Thump.

I heard the quick footsteps of someone running outside our room.

Then came the shouts.

My heart stopped as I looked to the door, expecting someone to barge in.

"Demira, wake up!" I yelled and shook her until she woke. She shot up in bed, disoriented.

"What's happening?" she asked.

Suddenly the star craft shook, and the electricity flickered.

"Get dressed!" I said and began reaching for my own clothes. We both changed from our pajamas rapidly into the long pants and long-sleeve shirts we had arrived in. I sat down and quickly pulled up my boots.

Demira was already done by the time I finished, and she stood by the door, a dagger in hand. It was the only weapon she had been able to bring.

"Stand back," Demira said, her voice stone cold and eyes trained on the door.

More shouts came from outside, and then the lights went out.

A chill went down my spine as the temperature of the craft plunged.

A crack sounded behind me, and I turned my head to see a fracture slowly expanding along the window in the cabin.

"We need to get out," I urged. "The pressure of the cabin will expel us—"

"Shh!" Demira said, and I whipped back to see her put a finger to her mouth, her eyes still focused on the door.

That's when the wail of alarm sirens began to go off, and the cabin was filled with red blinking lights.

My breath clouded as it left my lips, and I could not remember the last time I had felt this cold. The frigid air had a sense of desperation and deep grief, as if nothing good could ever happen again.

That's when the door of our cabin opened.

Demira lunged forward to slash at our intruder, but the figure grabbed her wrist before she could land a blow, squeezing hard. Demira dropped her blade instantly.

Green eyes met mine.

"Are you trying to kill me again?" Cylas demanded.

"What the fuck is going on?" Demira screamed.

"Sethos sent an army of mages to attack us. They boarded this craft and blew an engine."

"*What?*"

"We need to go," Cylas said to me. "We're meeting in the command room to evacuate. Let's go." Then he looked to Demira. "Your vision to avoid the Federation and find those Metidons might actually come to fruition."

10

RENNA

The blaring of sirens and red flashing lights startled me awake, so much so that I fell out of bed.

"Aeroth?" I called out, looking around the room. "Aeroth?" I tried again, hoping he was in the bathroom.

Nothing.

Then the star craft shook, as if it had been hit by something. I pushed off the ground to stand and ran to the bathroom but fell over as the star craft began to tilt on its side. Furniture from the cabin began to slide my way.

"No, no, no!" I said, holding onto the bathroom doorframe. I looked down and saw my boots at the far corner of the bathroom, along with the clothes I had chucked on the floor before bed. If I let go of the door frame, I would slide toward my items, but I wasn't sure how I would leave the room.

Suddenly a sharp and piercing noise filled the air, like steel was being ripped in half. The electricity shut off, plunging the room into darkness, other than the light filtering in from the cabin window.

The sirens fell silent.

And screams began to ring out.

The star craft slowly tilted back to level, and I sprang into action. I sprinted to the corner, where I knew my things were, and dressed rapidly.

Once done, I closed my eyes and called forth my Black Fire, praying that I had restored enough magic to use it. The inside of my chest began to warm, and I felt my magic stir inside it like gentle waves. I visualized the black, shimmering, swirling magic and couldn't help but smile.

My magic did not feel as strong as it usually did, but it was there, and I felt a thrill of happiness flood my bones.

I directed the magic to move from my center up my shoulders and down my arms. When the magic then channeled down to my palms and fingertips, my skin tingled, and I visualized black flames hovering over my skin.

I opened my eyes.

Black Fire danced just above my palms, glowing in the dark.

I moved my palms and fingers experimentally to see if the flames would diminish, but the glow remained.

"Thank you," I whispered to my magic. "Don't fail me now."

I willed the Black Fire in my right hand to morph into a black dagger, the flames there slowly shifting into the blade. I disliked how sluggish my magic was in creating the weapon, but I was grateful my magic was working at all. When the dagger materialized into solid form in my right palm, I gripped it and moved it around. The hilt was cold and smooth to the touch. A light dagger, but I felt confident holding a weapon once more, grateful for the training I had.

Next, I willed the fire in my left hand to morph into a bow, with a quiver full of arrows at my back. Once the magic transformed into what I needed, I inched toward the door and considered my next move.

As a general rule, I knew star crafts were seldom attacked because of the artillery used to fend off foes. And given the size of this craft, only someone with a death wish would attempt a confrontation. Deep down, I knew there was only one person who would attempt such a feat: either my father or Sethos.

My father was looking for me, but I knew he was weak and would likely not survive a counterattack. Sethos, however, had unchecked powers. He had to be behind this.

But if Sethos was on Elrie's craft, I could have an opportunity to see him. He had to be stopped. I could use my magic to try and stop him.

Unlike my father and Sethos, I would use my powers for good.

The craft shook again, and more screams rang out.

"I'm not afraid, I'm not afraid," I whispered over and over again in the dark, letting the dim light of the Black Fire dagger guide me to the door. When I opened it, people ran past from the left.

"I'm not afraid," I repeated to myself again.

Another person in my position would say I had two choices: Either go right with the others and escape or go left and face the threat head-on.

But I knew I had only one choice.

I took a deep breath and began to push against the flow of people, running toward the left. The light emanating from my Black Fire dagger and quiver made me glow in the darkness, and people luckily gave me a wide berth as I ran in the opposite direction.

Two hands then gripped my shoulders and spun me around.

Aeroth's red eyes glowed in the dark.

"What are you doing?" he demanded.

"What does it look like?" I spat back. "People are in danger and I'm going to help!"

I shrugged off his hold and turned to continue running, but Aeroth grabbed my right arm again.

"Wait!" I yelled and moved against him to free myself. "*Stop!*"

Aeroth stopped and spun again to face me.

"There is nothing to run to, Strongborn," he said and began to drag me in the same direction as the rest of the moving bodies. "I was just there. The mercenaries fighting off the attack—they're dead. Sethos sent a fleet of mages to attack. Someone gave them our exact location. They fired magic into the craft and created a large hole in the bottom of the craft. Things are now being sucked into space. Now the engine is losing pressure, and we will need to evacuate immediately."

"But we need to help!"

"We killed off the first wave of mages, but the last mage confessed there are more crafts coming our way with the instruction to take you and your sisters."

A feeling of dread shocked my body.

"And the gods on this craft?" I asked. "The monarchs? Can they not fight back? Surely they—*you*—are more powerful than mages."

"It's not worth staying to fight the next wave or fix the craft. This craft is damaged beyond repair. We must evacuate."

I nodded, unable to speak. I called back my Black Fire weapons, and they disappeared from my hands.

"We are meeting with your sisters and the others in the command room." Aeroth looked to the people in the hallway. "The people you see running past us are headed for evacuation pods at the front of the craft."

"This is my fault." My voice was barely a whisper. "I trusted Sethos in the first place . . ." I swallowed a lump in my throat and wiped my eyes. "And because of it, he's looking for me. I put these people in danger."

Aeroth shook his head and pulled me into his arms, his embrace crushing me to his chest.

"I need you strong, Renna," he said. "Can you do that for me?"

I nodded against him.

Aeroth looked down at me. “Do not let his memory weaken you.”

I gulped and nodded again.

“Let’s go,” Aeroth said and grabbed my hand.

We ran down the hallway to the command room.

11

RENNA

The command room was a blur as people were mobilizing to evacuate. Emergency lights on the ground provided little light. Aeroth and I walked toward a small conference room encased in glazed glass walls. I could make out two or three people inside the room.

"You will stay in there," he said brusquely as we walked. "Don't fight me on this."

"Yes," I said, nodding.

Aeroth stopped before he opened the door and turned to me.

"Do not leave this craft without me."

I searched his eyes. "Where would I go?"

"*Do not,*" he reiterated, ignoring my question, "leave this craft without me. We should be evacuating shortly."

"Alright," I replied. "I won't leave without you."

Seemingly satisfied with my answer, Aeroth gestured for me to enter the room, and I stepped past him and turned to face him.

"I'll be back," he assured me again.

When he closed the door and walked away, the mate bond began to pull at me immediately, and I took a deep breath. I had to be okay being apart from him for a few moments.

"Well, well, well . . ." a female said behind me.

I spun, and my heart paused.

I recognized the woman in question instantly. It was Demira.

She looked me up and down, her eyes cold and sharp. "The firstborn arrives. *Renna*, right?" She grimaced and raised her eyebrows. "Should I bow?"

Illona stood next to her with a neutral expression.

I took in Demira's angry eyes, pursed lips, and the white strands of hair that framed the left side of her face.

Sethos had shared how much Demira hated me. He had warned me that if given the chance, Demira would try to kill me for two reasons.

The first reason was that my death in the first lifetime had resulted in Demira's birth and her mother's death in childbirth.

Unbeknownst to Am-Re at the time, my conception in my first lifetime had stripped him of some of his magic and weakened him. Later on, Am-Re learned the only way to recuperate his magic was to train me and make me stronger so he could kill me and harvest my magic for himself.

I'd escaped him and joined forces with his enemies—the Celestial Enclave. When he killed me out of revenge for my treason, he set out to have more children with the goal that they too be born with magic that he could harvest. Demira was born out of that attempt, and her mother died in childbirth. Demira blamed me for her misfortune.

The second reason Demira hated me and would likely kill me was that I was a threat to her claim to rule Vasarys.

Sethos explained that Demira wanted Vasarys's throne above all else. He believed Demira had plotted to assassinate him to depose him from the throne. He reasoned that because I had been born with all of my father's magic, the people in Vasarys would look to me as the true heir and forever ban Demira's claim.

However, Demira didn't know that I didn't want the throne of Vasarys. I didn't want anything to do with my father's homeland.

"I heard you dislike me," I stated.

Demira merely pursed her lip in a frown.

"Renna," Illona said, her voice gentle. Her eyes were warm as she looked me over. "I've thought about meeting you so many times."

My body tensed at her words. Although her tone was friendly, I was wary of her as well. Sethos had mentioned he liked Illona, but that Demira controlled her.

"I don't know what to say," I said to them both truthfully.

Demira laughed, the sound bitter. "How about nothing?"

Illona looked to her and frowned, as if silently scolding her. Demira only rolled her eyes in response.

I had longed for family all my life, and now that they stood in front of me, I felt sick to my stomach with grief and anger. Grief because I doubted I would ever have a real relationship with these women. They blamed me for their misfortunes, and in a way, I sympathized with them. The anger was at my father for having poisoned my siblings against me.

A ragged breath left my lips as my chest closed in.

"I'll leave," I said, inclining my head to both of them. I looked to Illona specifically. "It was nice meeting you."

I knew I was acting cowardly, but my skin itched and I wanted nothing more than to escape their stares.

"Wait!" Illona pleaded. "Please. We need to stay together."

I frowned.

"We're all evacuating," I replied. "I can wait outside until I leave."

She shook her head. "You don't understand. We need you," Illona said to me and turned to Demira. "*Tell her.*"

Demira stared daggers at me, and I looked to Illona again.

"Listen, I'm wasting time. I know the Federation is looking for me, but I'm not going with them. I need to get to Taria. Hopefully I can slip by—"

"You can't go," Demira stated.

"Excuse me?" I snapped. "And why the fuck not? You can't tell me what to do."

"Because," Demira replied, her voice still cold, "we're not going to the Federation either. They cannot force us to go."

I crossed my arms and tilted my head. "And what does that have to do with me?"

"We are also going to Taria," Demira stated.

My heart began to race.

"How?" I asked, shaking my head. "The shield around Taria is restricted."

Demira lifted an eyebrow. "Metidons," she replied, as if the answer was simple.

"Oh . . ." I wasn't sure what Metidons were. My cheeks flushed as I nodded, pretending like I knew what she meant.

"They are ice-breathing feathered winged serpents," Illona offered lightly, her deep eyes observing me.

"Konah Universe is rumored to have a planet with Metidons," Demira continued. "We are going to find them."

"I'm not understanding . . ." I narrowed my eyes.

"I saw you," Demira began, "in a vision—"

"One she's had *multiple* times," Illona emphasized.

I looked to Demira, who nodded.

"In my vision, there were hundreds of Metidons flying behind me toward Taria. It's a vision that won't leave me. You were in my vision, riding alongside me." She scanned me thoughtfully, her mouth pursing. Her eyes snapped to mine. "The Metidons are our way into Taria. You have to come with us to Konah Universe."

The possibility of finding another way to enter the land of the gods gave me chills, but I wasn't sure what to do. The women in front of me disliked me, or at least Demira did. And because of their hatred for Sethos, I was unsure what they would think when I told them I meant to help him through an intervention.

I hugged my arms and shifted on my feet. "You are forgetting the shield of Taria," I reminded Demira. "We can't get through it."

She scowled and took one step toward me.

"*Metidons,*" Demira began, her voice painfully slow, as if she were talking to a child, "are the *only* beings that magic does not work on. We can break through Taria's shield with them."

"But we ourselves are blocked from entering. How could that work?" I asked.

Her lips curled.

"Metidons have a protective barrier around them. Think of it like a hovering invisible shield that wraps around their bodies. If you get close enough, the barrier around a Metidon envelops you as well."

My heart stopped.

"So the magic that would prevent us from entering Taria—"

"We would be able to get in," Demira said. "But we need the Metidons."

My jaw dropped at her words. This was my way into Taria. The possibility of being able to go to Taria seemed clear, and excitement thrummed through my body.

That excitement, however, was quickly quashed when I started to wonder why Demira and Illona wanted to go there. I knew Sethos despised them.

A chill ran through my spine, and I shifted on my feet.

"Why are you going to Taria?" I asked her.

Demira crossed her arms. "I'm going to make sure Vasarys stays safe."

I frowned. "But the war is not about Vasarys."

She tilted her head. "As long as Father and Sethos live, Vasarys will never be safe."

"You mean to kill him?" I asked her. "Sethos?"

She laughed. "Wouldn't you?"

I opened my mouth to speak, but she cut me off.

"My father kept us under house arrest. And Sethos was no different. I hate Sethos for his treatment of us, and I hate him even more for not killing Father properly."

I held my hands together to prevent them from shaking.

Sethos had wronged so many people. I doubted I would have a chance to speak with him properly before someone killed him.

"Come with us," Illona said to me. "The vision is clear. Demira speaks the truth. You must enter Taria on the back of Metidon. That is how it must be."

I looked at the women uneasily. We were family, but they were strangers.

Strangers who hated Sethos.

"We have very different goals," I began, my voice shaking. "I mean to speak with Sethos to stop him from—from attacking Taria."

Demira chuckled bitterly, but I expected the reaction.

No one believed I could save him.

Aeroth believes in you, my mind reminded me.

"And why would Sethos listen to *you*?" Demira asked.

"I know him, there is good in him," I began but was cut off by Demira's boisterous mocking laughter.

"We know him too," she gritted. "Do not tell me you support him!"

I shook my head. "I do not support what he's become. I want him to stop. Am-Re's magic is destroying him."

The women grew silent and looked to each other. I wondered if they, too, had noticed a change in him as Sethos allowed my father's magic to consume him. As Am-Re's daughters, both Demira and Illona had shared a home with my father and Sethos. They had to have noticed him descend into the madness that covered him like a shroud now.

"Demira, I'm sorry, but I can't go with you to find the Metidons," I told them, "If you kill Sethos before I get the chance to speak with him, there's no point in me going with you."

"And how else do you plan to get into Taria?" Demira snapped.

I grew quiet.

"We have different goals," I told Demira. "I need to speak with him before anyone attempts to kill him. I need to prevent this war."

Demira opened her mouth as if to argue, but Illona placed her hand on Demira's shoulder and stepped forward.

"Renna," she said, her voice gentle. "Do you know what my gift is? I wield Golden Fire. One of the things it does is it pulls beings back from the edges of death."

I nodded.

"My magic means I am almost always near that middle part of the veil." She put her right hand up vertically as if to demonstrate a barrier or wall. "I can hear them, Renna."

I lowered my chin. "Who?"

"The Ancestors. The dead."

I swallowed.

"And what does that have to do with me?" I asked her.

"The Ancestors decree you will go with us. They are never wrong. But visions must be followed for them to come true," Illona added. "We can get to the Metidons, but we need you there to make the vision true. You have to come. Your absence would invalidate the vision."

I closed my eyes and massaged my temples.

Their offer was tempting.

I knew Aeroth had offered to help me, but after being let down by so many males in my life, there was a part of me—perhaps my prideful side—that resented having a man help me. I wanted to solve this situation on my own, and I hated having to ask a male for assistance.

Somehow, having women at my side—even if they did not like me—seemed like the better way forward. I didn't have to befriend them to find the Metidons. I only had to stay cordial and work together to locate the beasts.

"We need you," Illona said.

"And I would love nothing more than to find a way into Taria. But I need assurance. If we are successful in getting Metidons and going to Taria, what is to stop Demira from killing Sethos before I can speak with him?"

Illona wrung her fingers and looked to her sister.

Demira narrowed her eyes and stepped forward. "Do you plan on claiming Vasarys as your own since you are the eldest?"

I shook my head. "I could never live there. I want to be far from anything Am-Re represents. After this conflict is done, I plan on going somewhere far from all of this."

"I want Vasarys," she gritted, eyeing me warily.

I shrugged my shoulders. "So take it. I make no claims over it. I don't have the stomach or personality for politics or ruling."

Demira was silent but continued to bore her eyes into me as if trying to call my bluff.

"Swear it," she demanded, her voice like ice. "If you swear you will not take Vasarys for yourself, I will not kill Sethos."

I blinked. "Is my word not enough?"

She scoffed and put her palm out. Purple Fire enveloped her hand, materializing into a dagger. She sliced her palm, and blood oozed from the cut.

"You need assurances, and so do I. A blood oath," Demira said, shoving her palm toward me.

I looked to Illona. "Is this necessary?" I asked her and then looked to Demira. "I just said I don't want Vasarys."

Demira's faced contorted into a sneer. "I have wanted to rule over Vasarys all my life. And I will not allow any opportunity for it to be taken from me."

I looked to her hand.

"What does a blood oath signify?" I asked her.

"A blood oath binds us magically so that we can never go back on our word. If you try and renege on the oath, your body will undergo immeasurable pain. You will wish for death."

A shiver ran through my body. The idea of my body undergoing even more pain was something I didn't want to risk, but I also knew I would never make a claim over Vasarys.

"Renna," Illona said. "Please. You must come with us to Konah."

If a blood oath was the price I needed to pay to have an opportunity to speak to Sethos on my own terms, then I would take it.

I wanted to be the one to solve this problem.

Not Aeroth.

Me.

I quickly grabbed Demira's dagger and sliced my palm.

I winced as the cut burned momentarily, and in an instant, Demira gripped my palm.

"I vow to not kill Sethos if you do not take Vasarys," she said to me.

"I vow to not make a claim over or take Vasarys."

Demira studied my eyes as if waiting for me to add more to my vow, or to make my vow contingent on her not killing Sethos, but I stayed silent.

Perhaps hearing my definite vow to not take the kingdom from her shifted something inside her, because she smiled slightly. It was so brief I barely registered it, and in a moment, she dropped my palm and cleared her throat.

I instructed my magic to heal my palm, and I internally groaned over the energy it would cost me, since my magic was still regenerating. Even though I wished I could instruct my magic to heal the rest of my injuries, I knew I had to bide my time.

"If you won't kill Sethos, what do you want for him?" I asked.

"I want him arrested," Demira glowered. "I want him tried by a tribunal for his cruelty. I want him imprisoned. I want him moved out of my fucking way."

"I see."

Demira aggressively stalked toward me, standing so close that we were practically nose to nose.

"Is it true you have the power of Darkness?" she asked me, her eyes studying mine. "Are my visions of you true?"

I frowned. "I don't know what you have seen."

"I have seen a version of you wield death. Shadows. *Darkness.* Screams and wails cry out from under your palms. You cover the skies with black."

I clasped my hands to keep them from shaking.

"I'm not like Am-Re," I told her, steeling my voice so that I sounded more in control than I felt. "I will never be like him."

"But if you are threatened?" she asked me and lifted an eyebrow. "What then?"

I froze.

What then?

I had been training in self-defense to ensure I was never captured in battle, to fight my father's dretani and Am-Re himself.

I had also vowed to never let anyone abuse me again.

My body tensed at the memories of my childhood and what it felt like to have my father's hands wrapped around my neck as I struggled for air, my eyes shooting to my foster mom, begging her silently to help me.

Never again would I be at the mercy of anyone's fists.

I unclasped my hands and clenched them into fists at my sides.

"I will use Darkness for self-defense if I need to defend myself or others," I reiterated. "I will never let anyone hurt me again."

Demira nodded, and the corners of her eyes slightly crinkled.

"*Good,*" she said and lifted her chin. "We may need your skill if the Federation tries to take us to their headquarters."

I frowned. "Would they be violent in their attempt to take us?"

She shrugged. "I guess we will see."

My heart thundered, and my palms became clammy.

"I'm glad you decided to come with us," Demira said, and she gestured to the door that was now opening. "Because it's too late to back out now."

I looked to the door and saw Cylas, Khellios, and Aeroth step inside.

Khellios wore gleaming, golden armor sporting his sigil. He'd tucked a helmet under his arm, one with a golden crown of laurel leaves atop it. A white, gleaming cape that glowed like moonlight draped over his shoulders. And a sword the size of half his body was sheathed at his left side with a hilt encrusted with emeralds and moonstones.

Khellios was like a god personified: magnificent. He was splendor and awe itself.

Aeroth's midnight-gray armor was a sharp contrast to Khellios's. His armor was dented and, in some areas, looked to have dried blood. Unlike Khellios, who glowed in a resplendent white cape, Aeroth's black cape almost sucked in the darkness around us, as if he were a black hole. The shadows that licked the hem of his cape and feet made his figure all the more ominous, like a prince of death. And in many ways, he was.

Then my eyes landed on Cylas. Unlike the other two men in the room, Cylas wore his black leather jacket with his usual black pants and boots. He looked positively unbothered about the emergency outside. If it had been any other time, I could have laughed.

Cylas flashed me one of his smirks, and Khellios cleared his throat.

"Renna. Representatives from the Galactic Federation are here to escort you to safety. You must go with them to wait out the battle against Sethos."

I blinked. Memories of Khellios telling me I had no option but to go to Taria for safety to escape the dangers on my university campus came back. I had been helpless then without a true understanding of my magic. With no family to fall back on to make an educated decision.

I looked to my half sisters.

Illona nodded to me, and warmth filled my chest.

My sisters would likely never see me as their true family, but we had a common goal and that made me brave enough.

I faced Khellios. "I'm not going."

He shook his head slowly. "You don't understand the risks."

"Khellios—"

"You do not understand, Renna. I will *not* accept your answer."

Khellios was acting like an overbearing parent. He loved me, but his hovering was suffocating me.

"You're making a mistake," he pressed.

I scoffed. "And that is *my* mistake to make."

"And what am I to tell the Galactic Federation?" Khellios challenged, his voice louder and more patronizing. I really wanted to throw something at him.

"I don't give a shit what you tell them. I didn't know they existed until very recently, and I don't consider them as having any power over me. I'm not going with them."

"The Galactic Federation has jurisdiction over every supernatural being. You are a supernatural being."

Demira walked to stand next to me. "Illona and I aren't going either, Khellios. And don't even try to force us."

Illona now stood at Demira's side. "Tell them you lost track of us with the evacuation," Illona suggested.

"This is ridiculous. The Galactic Federation offers you safety, shelter, warm beds, food—and where will you all be?" Khellios asked the three of us.

"I will take them to one of the newer planets in the Stallias Universe," Cylas said, stepping up. He looked at the three of us with a neutral expression and then looked to Khellios. "I discussed this with all three of them already. Plus, this way I will remain by Renna's side to ensure she is protected. Something I vow to do."

The lie flew off Cylas's lips so easily I almost believed him, wondering if we actually had discussed something.

Aeroth spoke then. "I, too, offer my protection to all three of them. You asked me to help you locate Renna before. I can ensure she stays safe by monitoring their location."

Khellios remained silent as he stared at everyone, his jaw clenched and fists curled.

Then the star craft completely lost power and shook, as if it had been hit by something.

Demira immediately conjured light, brightening the room.

"That's our cue to go," Cylas said. But before we could move, the door to the conference room yanked open and Elrie appeared.

"Khellios, I need you out here!" she yelled. "More mages have attacked. The lower levels are now compromised. I need to get my crew out immediately."

"I need a moment," Khellios responded. Elrie cursed and left the doorway to go back out to the command room.

Khellios turned to me, and the look he gave me was a mixture of grief and terror. His eyes were glassy with unshed tears.

"Renna, I vowed to defend you with my life all those years ago. I failed and have lived with the consequences of my actions ever since."

I shook my head. "It's not your fault—"

He walked toward me and grabbed my hands, gently pulling me to the corner of the room.

"You and Old Xhor were ripped away from me before. I will do everything I can in this lifetime to ensure Taria and you are safe from harm. This is my chance to fix all that I could not do then."

"Khellios—"

"If I fall," Khellios paused.

I squeezed his hands. "Please don't speak like that."

"*If I fall,* I am appointing you as sole heir of all my possessions. Do with them what you want. My life is yours."

"Khellios," I shook my head again, "don't speak as if you will die—"

"Sethos sent his soldiers to attack a star craft he knew contained *gods*. He is reckless and bold. You have to understand that even if his mages die, he is sending a message. He is confident. And that is dangerous."

I wanted to scream from rage at Sethos's actions and the helplessness I felt in that moment.

"We are not immune to death, Renna. It *can* happen. Sethos killed Am-Re's physical body. By now he must understand how to kill a god's soul. It could be me next."

"But many will join the battle."

"Listen to me, *please*. If you hear that Taria has fallen, then we have failed and I may already be dead. Do not come and look for the remnants of Taria."

I shook my head. "Do not ask that of me."

"Renna," he said and ran a hand through my hair. He cupped my jaw. "If I fall, I need you to head to Planet Lishea in the Milky Way Galaxy. Go see the oracle of the gods, Hellia. I have sent her a message. She knows to expect you and will protect you."

"I can help defend Taria with my magic, Khellios. Please let me join you!"

As if he didn't hear my words, Khellios continued. "There are caves underneath Hellia's lair where you may hide while you figure out what to do."

My eyes began to water.

"Khellios, stop thinking like you won't survive . . ." I whispered as my voice broke. "How would I even get to Lishea? I have never even heard of that place—"

"I will take you."

I turned to see Aeroth behind me, stepping forward. He nodded to Khellios.

"Promise me you will honor my wishes," Khellios pleaded with me.

I clenched my jaw to stop my emotions from tumbling out of me and nodded once more.

"Say it," Khellios's voice was hard. "Tell me that you will keep this promise."

"I promise."

In that moment, all the disagreements and fights we had left my mind.

Khellios loved me.

In his own way—but he loved me. And I loved him in my own way as well. He would forever be a part of my story.

I wrapped my arms around him, and he did the same.

"I will always hold love for you, Khellios," I said against his neck. "*Always.*"

He pulled away to look at me. "And I will always love you, Renna."

I pulled him to me and placed my forehead against his.

"You need to live, Khellios," I whispered. "You have so much left to live for."

Khellios did not respond but nodded against me.

"Stay vigilant," he instructed. "Stay safe. Stay close to Cylas. And Aeroth. I know they will lay down their lives for you."

"I will."

Khellios pulled away from me and cupped my cheek. I held his hand there with one of my own.

"It has been the greatest honor of my life to get to love you twice, Renna."

My lips quivered. "This is not goodbye," I insisted as tears began to fall from my cheeks.

"It's never a goodbye." He smiled sadly. "Not from me."

I nodded and wiped tears with my shirt sleeve.

Khellios looked behind me to Aeroth before glancing back at me.

"You're worth loving," Khellios whispered to me, his eyes searching mine. He kissed my forehead with such tenderness that my heart felt like it was being torn in half. "Find someone who deserves you."

My vision blurred with tears again as Khellios moved from me, and I spun to watch him walk away. He stopped in front of Aeroth, and they exchanged a stoic look. Neither said anything, but Aeroth nodded once and, after a few seconds, Khellios nodded back to him and walked away.

Khellios did not look back but stopped at the door and looked to Cylas.

"Leave *now*," he told Cylas, his voice gruff, and then opened the door and slipped out into the chaos.

12

RENNA

Our evacuation from Elrie's craft happened almost immediately after Khellios left the conference room. We could not risk the mages or Federation representatives finding us.

"Where are we really going?" Demira asked.

Cylas ignored her and waved a hand to open a portal.

The green smoke danced along the edges of the portal, mimicking Cylas's magic. In the middle of the portal was a swirl of dark blue and green, dotted with twinkling lights that shimmered like stars.

Cylas looked to Demira.

"How certain is your vision?" he asked her.

Demira lifted her chin as if daring Cylas to challenge her words. "I've been having the same vision for months," she replied.

"And you are confident Renna is in it?" Cylas asked her.

She nodded. "*Yes.*"

"What's going on?" Aeroth asked.

"I see you're late to the party," Cylas drawled, his tone dripping in condescension.

“Don’t be rude,” I told Cylas, stepping next to Aeroth. He cast me a curious look, as if my intervention was unexpected.

I wanted to tell him to not think anything of it, that it was really my anger toward Cylas that made me speak up.

“I don’t have time to explain,” Cylas told Aeroth, then leaned toward me and grabbed my hand, drawing me away from Aeroth. “We can exchange pleasantries when we arrive at our destination.”

And within a few moments, we all walked through the portal.

13

RENNA

We landed in a flash on a beach covered in jagged, small rocks, next to a large lake surrounded by dense trees.

Three moons bathed the night sky in a soft glow, and I wondered why their illumination wasn't brighter.

Cylas steadied me and Illona as we gathered our footing.

Demira slowly rose from the ground and dusted off her clothing.

Aeroth stood off to the side with a scowl, looking around the dense landscape.

"Where are we?" Demira asked, looking around.

"Elinoor," Cylas replied.

"The Planet Elinoor is in Konah Universe, not Stallias Universe," Aeroth remarked, stepping toward us. I watched him approach Cylas. "You lied to Khellios."

"Wow, you are clever," Cylas said coolly. "Do you want the Federation to find Renna and her sisters? You know Khellios is honorable to a fault. He would never lie to them about our whereabouts."

I crossed my arms. "Why are we here?" I asked.

"That is a *great* question," Aeroth replied while looking at Cylas. "You had better explain what we are doing here. The planets in this universe are practically deserted. There is no shelter here."

"People live here," Cylas argued. "In cave systems, and they may have the information we need about Metidons."

Aeroth narrowed his eyes and opened his mouth as if he were about to say something.

Demira walked toward Aeroth and cut in. "I can explain. I've had several visions of riding into Taria on a Metidon . . . with Renna." She inclined her head my way.

Aeroth spun to face me. His jaw was clenched, and a vein on his forehead protruded.

"*Metidons?*"

"It's the only way I can get into Taria."

"Did I not say that I would help you? Besides, there are no physical traces of Metidons," he scolded and turned to everyone else. "This is a waste of time. A fool's errand."

"Not true," Cylas barked and knelt to touch the ground.

Green and white magic emerged from Cylas's palm like glittering smoke, and he closed his eyes. I wondered if he was trying to locate them as he also ruled flora and fauna.

"I rode into battle with Metidons during the Galactic Wars," Aeroth seethed. "I'm telling you, *they are gone*."

I scratched the back of my neck and shifted on my feet as the tension between the men became more apparent.

"The only chance to find the Metidons is through the descendants of the riders," Cylas said as he closed his eyes. "And the last I heard . . ." He paused and opened one eyes to scan the tree line. "The descendants resettled here."

"Here, *where*?" Demira asked.

I looked to Illona, wondering why she had been so quiet, and saw her staring off toward the forest. Illona lifted her hand and pointed to the trees to her right.

"There is a population of people that way."

Cylas pursed his lips and stood, staring at her.

"And pray," Cylas said, tilting his head and crossing his arms. "What magic do you claim to have that could possibly tell you that? I am the God of Creation. The God of the Planets. The God of Flora and Fauna. I feel life on each planet. You are merely half fae, half god."

Illona jutted her chin up and crossed her arms as well.

"To start, I, too, have the power of life. I wield Golden Fire."

Cylas laughed and shook his head.

Illona's cheeks turned a dark red hue, and her eyebrows gathered. "And while I cannot pretend to have powers like yours, I can breathe life back into souls—"

"Golden Fire would not tell you the location of other people."

"Of course not," Illona paused. "The Ancestors do. And they are pointing us in that direction." She jutted her chin to the right again.

"And I'm supposed to just *trust you*?"

Illona's eyes darkened.

"And what is your plan?" Illona asked, her tone cool. "Are you trying to find the Ancestors of the Metidons through talking to garden beds?"

"Excuse me?" Cylas snapped.

Demira cursed under her breath and strode toward Illona, pinning her gaze on Cylas. Purple Fire flickered from her left palm as if to warn him. When Demira reached Illona, she grabbed Illona's hand, and both women began walking off in the direction Illona indicated.

"Illona has some nerve," Cylas said to me.

"We heard that!" Demira said over her shoulder.

"*I* am the God of Creation," he gritted under his breath as we watched Demira and Illona continue their march. "My magic is far better—"

"Would *you* have figured out the location of the population here?" I asked him, my eyebrows raised.

"Eventually," he murmured, his jaw tensed.

"I would think as a god of life, locating other living things would be relatively easy."

He shook his head.

"Source gave us very specific powers that correspond to very specific things. I like to think it was its way of creating balance, so no one god could ever become more than Source. While I have the power to create planets, as well as the plants and animals on them, I feel the imprint of all life on my planets. Imprints generally help me in eventually locating a person. I can tell you for a fact that Elinoor is inhabited by people. I feel their energy."

"And how would you have located people on Elinoor?" I asked, still unimpressed.

"I was scanning for vegetation likely planted by people. That would indicate they could be settled near there."

"We should go with them," Aeroth interrupted, gesturing to Demira and Illona, now disappearing through the tree line. "Women shouldn't walk alone in the forest."

I frowned.

"Are you saying women cannot take care of themselves?"

He closed his eyes and took a deep breath, pinching the bridge of his nose. "No. Stop assuming you know what I'm thinking."

"Because that's what it sounded like you meant."

"Why don't you ask me what I'm thinking first?"

I narrowed my eyes. "I did!"

"*Question* . . ." Cylas cut in.

"*What!*" Aeroth and I said at the same time, whipping our heads to Cylas. His eyes widened.

"Can you give Aeroth and I a moment?" I scratched the back of my neck.

"And leave you with a blood-sucking Naaviri you barely know? I don't give a shit that he's a king. He is what he is."

"You're unpleasant," Aeroth said to him, looking him up and down.

"And I'm starting to not like you at all," Cylas countered, turning to me and grabbing my hand. "I'm not leaving you with a strange man, Renna. Let's follow Demira and Illona together."

I wiggled my hand free from Cylas.

"Both of you, stop it," I said. "I need to speak to Aeroth in private. Cylas, please join Demira and Illona, and I will join you momentarily."

"*Why?*" Cylas asked.

I groaned. "Cylas—"

Cylas crossed his arms. "Anything you have to say to him, you can say it with me around."

"Aeroth will not hurt me."

Cylas laughed. "You're so sure?"

"*Yes!*"

"Tell me *one* good reason why."

"Because Aeroth is my mate!"

Silence settled around me. Cylas blinked several times.

"*What?* You cannot be serious!" he finally yelled, launching himself at Aeroth, but I stepped in the middle.

"I am." I sighed. "Aeroth and I are handling it."

"You heard the lady," Aeroth said. "*Leave us.*"

"You being her mate does not change the fact that you barely know her," Cylas seethed.

"Are you suggesting I would hurt her?" Aeroth snapped.

Cylas was silent, his eyes full of resentment.

"I don't trust Naaviri."

"And I don't trust you." Aeroth glared at him.

"Wise man," Cylas growled and then looked to me. "Don't take long. Call out to me if you need me."

I nodded and watched him leave.

Once he'd disappeared through the brush, I spun to face Aeroth.

"Do you think women are weak?" I asked him.

"No." He shifted between his feet. "My mother raised me to be chivalrous to women. Seeing women walk into forests they do not know, when I am here and capable of providing combat assistance, went against my upbringing."

"What if Demira and Illona are very good swordswomen?"

"Renna," he sighed. "Coming here was not a good plan."

I looked to the sky, not knowing what to say.

"I'm not confident in this plan," Aeroth said while scanning the tree line. "I know you want to travel to Taria but, Renna, even if you do find Metidons—they are not friendly. They take a long time to bond with their riders."

I bit my lip as I weighed my options.

He shook his head and continued. "When I rode them into battle during the Galactic Wars, we had to train with them for months at our camp to even get them to obey us. They are stubborn beasts."

I couldn't wait months for a Metidon to bond with me, but this was the best option I had. My hope was the Metidons would be reasonable to our request for help. No one else could take me to Taria.

"I have to believe and hope in Demira's vision," I said, my voice quiet.

Aeroth frowned, and he ran his hand through his hair. "I respect that sentiment. But hope is not enough."

"Hope is all I have."

"If Metidons have not been ridden in ages, then they must be almost feral, untamed. It's dangerous. Please think this through."

"What else am I supposed to do?" I challenged. "This is my way into Taria."

He blinked, and his eyes became darker. It wasn't the look of worry on his face but of anger. He opened his mouth as if he wanted to say something but paused.

"Heavens damn Sethos for putting you in this position," Aeroth finally gritted out.

I shrugged. "This is the reality of the situation, Aeroth."

Aeroth simply stared at me, his lips pressed in a tight line.

"You can go at any time," I reminded him. "You don't truly need to be here if we meet up regularly to exchange blood. Think about the other fae monarchs. Won't they wonder where you are?"

"I told them I would help Khellios evacuate."

"Now you know where I am. Cylas will keep me safe."

Aeroth clenched his jaw and put his hands on his hips, his eyes sliding to where Cylas and my half sisters had left.

"I can protect myself," I stated.

"Yes. Of that I have no doubt," he said, returning his eyes to me. "But this is a strange planet, you don't know the terrain, and I don't have faith in Cylas keeping three women—*people*—alive." He corrected. "And I need *you* specifically to stay alive."

I rolled my eyes.

"Of course. How could I forget?" I laughed. "This is all about you and your rule as king."

Aeroth's face became red, and his eyes narrowed. I patted his shoulder.

"Don't worry," I said, leaning in. "I don't plan on dying."

I turned around and walked away before he could respond.

14

RENNA

Aeroth and I walked silently into the dark forest, following Cylas. He walked a good distance ahead of us, but Cylas was illuminated by a silver aura guiding our way.

I shivered. Elinoor was cold. Like Daya, Elinoor was heavily forested. The chill in the air made me almost melancholy for the desert heat of Andora. I longed to feel the sun on my skin.

Like in Daya, the forest in Elinoor was also brimming with bioluminescent foliage. The trees here had wide trunks that extended all the way to the sky. Dense canopies blocked off all light. Fog also covered the ground.

As we walked through the darkness, I kept my eyes on the ground to avoid tripping over tree roots. I was grateful for the bioluminescent plants on the ground helping to provide some light.

We had been walking quite some time, and the lack of sleep was beginning to wear me out. My thighs were aching. A few moments later, we reached a clearing where Cylas stood, looking between Aeroth and I with a scowl.

"You okay?" Cylas asked me. "You took too long."

"I'm fine. The forest is dark and hard to walk through. And I'm walking slow because I'm tired. Also, Aeroth didn't kill me."

Cylas grunted.

"Any more questions?" I asked him.

Cylas rolled his eyes and turned around.

Beyond him was a purple shield in the shape of a dome that covered most of the clearing. It looked similar to the one Sethos created around the fortress in Daya. The perimeter of the shield had stones with runes on them, glowing with purple light.

There was a large bonfire in the middle of the shield, surrounded by five sleek, white sleeping pods that resembled a half-egg shape with a bed and pillow in each. The beds were covered in dark blankets, and I almost cried at the thought of climbing into one of them to sleep.

Demira and Illona stood by the bonfire with blankets wrapped around them.

"Well your murderous sister Demira conjured individual sleeping pods for us," Cylas stated. "I dislike her, but I must say Violet Fire and the ability to conjure physical objects is hot."

In that moment, Demira turned to face us as if she had heard Cylas. He winked at her, and her eyes glowed violet in the darkness, sending a chill through my body.

Cylas leaned over to whisper, "She's scary as fuck, but I'd be turned on if she hadn't tried to kill me."

Demira pursed her lips, and I could swear she'd heard that too. She reached up to touch the top of the violet dome. The stones around the perimeter where we stood extinguished, and a doorway formed.

I swallowed a laugh and rolled my eyes at Cylas as we stepped over the rocks to join Demira and Illona.

"We are too exposed," Aeroth commented as we walked, scanning the perimeter. "I don't like this."

"Nobody knows we are here," Cylas argued. "These woods are deserted."

"We shouldn't seek attention."

"Well I'm not sleeping on the ground in a tent," Cylas countered. "So I will enjoy catching up on some sleep in one of those pods."

"Gods don't need sleep."

"But gods enjoy pleasure. And sleeping is one of them."

Aeroth scoffed. "Then I will keep watch," Aeroth growled.

Cylas shrugged. "Suit yourself," he said and walked ahead of us.

The thought of sleep summoned a hundred questions about tonight's sleeping arrangements with respect to Aeroth and I. The pods were side by side, but still a good distance from each other. Aeroth and I would be apart.

"What will we do?" I whispered to him. "The pods are spread too far apart. Will we need to exchange blood?"

He regarded me for a few moments. "No. You will sleep, and I will sit by the bonfire next to your pod to keep watch."

"Don't you sleep?" I asked gently.

Aeroth shook his head. "No. I rule the Astral. The Astral is always open, and I feel the millions of souls traveling through my realm. Quieting my mind to sleep is not easy."

Aeroth was not a god, but many of his qualities—like a lack of sleep—were very godlike. He reminded me of Khellios in that way and his duty to his celestial bodies.

"Did you sleep before you became king?"

"Yes." Aeroth nodded. "When I became one with the Astral, the chemical makeup of my body changed. My body doesn't need to sleep anymore."

"Would you *like* to sleep?" I inquired.

He shrugged.

Just then, Illona interrupted our conversation when she approached to offer us two metal plates of food with silverware. I saw the plate was heaped with cooked rice and steamed vegetables.

"Where did all of this come from?" I asked Illona.

"The food is from Cylas," she said, gesturing to him. He stood eating by the bonfire.

"Don't expect meat on your plates," he called out from where he stood. "I'm not going to kill the animals I create. And I already cleared them from this area in case any of you *think* of killing them for food." He stared at Aeroth saying the last comment.

Aeroth merely stared back, his jaw visibly clenched.

"Where did the plate and silverware come from?" I asked Illona.

"Demira's Violet Magic. It allows her to conjure physical objects."

The pods were impressive, and having plates for our meal when my stomach was growling was even more enticing.

"What else can Demira's magic do?" I asked.

Illona's voice lowered. "A great deal more if given the chance. Living with our father and then Sethos was difficult for her. They placed magical wards around Vasarys so that everyone's magic was suppressed."

Aeroth cursed and shook his head.

I thought of Sethos's dome around Daya's fortress and how it suppressed my ability to portal. It still made me furious thinking of his violation, of limiting someone's free will. At the same time, I thought of mortal government systems and their limitations on citizens to ensure people would not challenge those in charge. Mortal governments and magical ones were not so different after all.

"I'm sorry you both lived through that," I said, my voice quiet.

"I respect you," Illona quipped. "Wanting to try and stop Sethos is noble."

I shook my head. "Why? He was terrible to you."

Illona hugged her arms. "He wasn't always like that."

I blinked as I processed her words. Her statement gave me hope that perhaps Sethos could change.

My heart surged at the possibility.

"Eat your food and we can talk about Sethos later," she said with a small smile. "I suspect we will have many days to talk everything through on this trip."

I wondered if she knew something we didn't about how long it would take us to find Metidons.

"And you also need to sleep," Aeroth said while looking at me.

"Yes," I acknowledged, nodding.

"I do too," Illona added. "Hopefully I will be allowed to sleep today."

Her statement was odd, but I did not know her well to ask for clarification. The thought of me not knowing my sister made my chest feel heavy. Am-Re robbed me of the opportunity to know her and have her as family. I did not doubt it was he who poisoned my sisters against me by urging them to hate me.

The heavy feeling remained as Aeroth, and I followed Illona to the bonfire, each of us taking a seat on tree stumps placed around the fire.

Everyone was quiet as we ate, either staring at our plates or looking into the fire or tree line. I was too tired to even attempt conversation. Luckily the food was warm and savory, and for only being grains and vegetables, surprisingly filling.

When Cylas was finished with his food, he stood up and stretched.

"It's incredibly rude to stretch when people are eating," Demira gritted, her piercing eyes looking him up and down.

"Demira?" Cylas asked.

She lifted an eyebrow in question.

"Shut up," Cylas snipped.

Demira laughed and stood. "Make me," she challenged him.

Cylas smiled and crossed his arms. "I will decline for fear of my bodily safety."

"That was one time!" she yelled.

"One time of trying to kill someone is one too many," he shot back.

Their back and forth was exhausting, and I rose.

"I'm headed to bed," I told the group. "See you all in the morning."

Illona rose next to me. "I'll do the same." She looked to Demira. "Please remember Cylas is not our enemy."

Cylas clapped. "*Thank you!* There is one sensible sister amongst this group."

I pursed my lips at Cylas, and his skin turned pink. Rolling my eyes, I placed my plate of food down on the grass and headed for the closest sleeping pod by where Aeroth was seated.

The pod had a mattress wide enough for one person and was covered in navy blue bedding with a thick, soft blanket. I wrapped it around myself as I climbed into bed. The mattress was a dream to sit on. It was the perfect amount of sturdy but also softly molded to my body.

Illona walked to stand next to me.

"The pod has a button that slides a cover top so you are truly enclosed and can get a good night's rest." She pointed to a white button next to a space by my pillow. "Press this when you're settled in, and the pod will close. Demira designed the inside of the cover to have little tiny lights like stars, so it's not completely dark. Press the button again when you want to open the pod."

"I can't believe she conjured these so quickly."

Illona smiled. "We cannot see the stars in Vasarys. The skies are a perpetual haze of red fog. Demira conjured these back at the palace in Vasarys so we could pretend to lie under the stars."

Her words made my chest tighten. "Sethos never let you leave Vasarys? Truly?" I asked.

Illona shook her head, and she paused. She looked beyond me to the forest as if she were recalling a memory. "He changed," she said. "He was not always that way. Pain changes people."

A chaotic mixture of relief and grief began to claw its way to my already tight chest, threatening to cleave it in half. Relief at hearing someone else believed in the possibility of redemption for Sethos and grief at knowing how much his pain had transformed him into something monstrous.

Illona offered me a small smile. "The Ancestors won't show me what happens to him after we reach the Metidons. Perhaps you really can sway him to change."

I didn't know what to say. All I could do was nod.

I could not lose hope.

Every soul had a chance at redemption.

Illona cleared her throat. "Get some rest."

"Yes. Thank you," I said.

Illona offered me another smile. "Good night."

When Illona turned to walk away, I found Aeroth's eyes on me. He was still seated on the tree stump, eating his food. I was happy the proximity bond was not an issue at the moment. He could easily stride to me in four or five wide steps.

He nodded to me as if wishing me good night and turned around to resume eating.

After taking my shoes off and placing them on the ledge at the foot of the bed, I settled under the covers and pressed the button Illona had shown me.

Tiny lights began to glow as the pod closed, and a sense of calm settled inside me. The quiet of the pod and twinkling stars reminded me of being in the Astral, the tranquility I had found there with Sethos and Aeroth.

Illona's words to me tonight had been a gift. And the chance to fulfill Demira's vision of finding the Metidons so we could enter Taria filled me with hope.

I had to believe in that moment that everything would be alright.

15

RENNA

I startled awake, hitting my head on the ceiling of the pod. Curling to the side as a dull soreness concentrated on the top of my skull, I rubbed my head and whimpered. I instructed my healing magic to move through me and up to my head, and a rush of cold magic followed, soothing the affected spot instantly.

"You okay, Strongborn?"

It was Aeroth.

Hearing his voice so close made my heartbeat race.

"Yes . . ."

"What happened?"

I sighed. "I sat up too quickly and hit my head. I was startled, that's all."

"Do you need anything?"

"No. My healing magic is taking care of it."

"Well . . ." he paused. "Call out if you need anything."

I waited for a moment. He sounded very close. Had everyone heard me startle awake?

"*Where are you?*" I asked him.

"Outside your pod."

His words caused a pleasant tingling sensation to spread through my body, and I couldn't help but smile. Had he stayed there all night like he had promised?

"How long have I been sleeping?" I asked.

"It's almost daybreak."

My jaw dropped.

"Did you manage to sleep?" I asked, hopeful.

"To sleep, I need to quiet my mind. You snore. Your snoring kept me awake and vigilant," he commented, and by his light tone, I could imagine him holding back a laugh.

"You're rude," I said, trying to pretend offense.

"And you prevented me from sleeping."

I laughed. "Sorry?"

"You're not the first woman to prevent me from sleep."

I turned pink, and Aeroth cleared his throat.

"Do you need to do anything morning-related?" he asked, his voice a little hesitant.

I narrowed my eyes, confused by his question.

"You know . . ." he said and paused. "Take care of any body functions?"

My eyes grew, and the sensation to use the bathroom immediately rushed through me.

"Yes!" I said and pressed the button to open the pod.

When it opened, I saw Aeroth standing next to the pod, rubbing his head.

"What happened to you?" I asked, unwrapping myself from the blanket I still had around me, and hopped off the mattress to the grass below.

"You opened the pod cover too fast. It hit my head."

"Wait," I began. "Were you sitting against my pod?"

"Yes. Like I told you I would be."

My eyebrows raised. "The whole night?" I bit my cheek to prevent myself from smiling. He had stayed true to his word.

He protected you. Trust him, my brain quipped.

I wanted to ponder his good deed, but the urge to use the restroom occupied my thoughts. I looked to the perimeter, knowing I would have to go behind a tree and simply take care of business.

Aeroth stood.

"I have to come with you," Aeroth said. "So lead the way."

"*No.*"

"Renna." Aeroth shook his head. "This is the way it is. Do you want to be in pain while you go to the bathroom?"

"I don't want to be in pain, but I also don't want to be by you when I go to the bathroom."

The need to exchange blood with him became blatantly apparent. I would have no privacy to bathe or use the bathroom in peace.

But there was no time to discuss that now.

We both headed to the perimeter, and I noticed the shield was down.

Aeroth must have seen my surprised face because he spoke up. "Demira woke up earlier and went to take care of her needs. She kept the shield down afterward, knowing you all would wake up wanting to do the same."

I nodded and sped into the forest for some of the most embarrassing moments of my life.

NOTHING BONDS you to a person more than being in the same vicinity as them when you take a piss.

"We need to exchange blood," I blurted out as we walked back to the camp perimeter.

"I figured you would say that," Aeroth said, walking with his hands behind his back.

"And I need to bathe," I added. "And I would prefer to do it without you."

He raised his eyebrows but maintained his eyesight straight ahead. "There is a first for everything."

I frowned. I was sure his comment referred to other women. "Don't flatter yourself," I snapped. "And don't even think I would invite you to watch."

Aeroth shrugged with a cocky smirk on his face. "Suit yourself."

My skin flushed with heat.

"So you've had a lot of women," I said, and instantly regretted it.

He laughed.

"Is that a question?" he asked.

My skin was flushed, and even though I knew I shouldn't care, I kept digging myself into a deep hole of bad decisions as I pressed on. "Should it be?" I asked.

Why did I care?

"Do you think I've been with a lot of women?" he asked.

I bit the inside of my cheek as my stomach did somersaults.

"You . . ." I paused and cleared my throat. I peeked at him up and down. "You seem like the type."

He chuckled. "The type to do what?"

Aeroth looked sideways at me for a moment, then returned his gaze straight forward.

I lifted my chin.

"The type of man who would—"

"Have a lot of women?" he offered.

I shrugged.

"Would that be a problem?" he asked.

I crossed my arms and looked forward as well as I answered, "Well, seeing as we're stuck together, I don't want to be around your . . . romantic situations."

"You mean when I fuck?"

I almost stumbled forward at his words. My eyes widened, and my lips parted.

I looked to him and said, "You don't have to be so crass. I barely know you."

"And yet I feel like I am starting to know you very well." Aeroth put a hand out in front of him. "For starters," he put a finger down, "you are extremely stubborn."

I opened my mouth to protest, but he cut me off.

"It doesn't take a stranger to learn that. Second," he put a second finger down, "in the likelihood of combat, I'm going to have to work extra hard to keep us both alive because you seem to like danger."

"That is unfair—"

"Must I remind you how I stopped you from running toward the squadron of mages that attacked Elrie's ship?"

"So I was supposed to do nothing?" I snapped. "I'm not the type of woman who sits back and lets things happen to her."

Aeroth raised an eyebrow while looking down at my lips. His brazen look made my skin grow hot, and I looked away to focus forward once more.

"*Third,*" another finger was put down, "You snore. Horribly so."

"Are you kidding me—"

"And quite frankly, I am glad you rejected our bond as sleeping next to you would be unbearable."

I slowly turned my head to look at him. He had the biggest grin on his face, and his skin was flushed.

"You are a very dislikable person," I said, narrowing my eyes.

He put his hand on his chest. "You wound me."

"And you're not very kingly at all."

He snorted a laugh. "I'll renounce my crown since you're *clearly* an expert on the matter."

I rolled my eyes.

"Fourthly," he continued.

"*Fourth.*"

"Excuse me?"

"You said '*fourthly,*' which is grammatically incorrect. It's first, second, third, and *fourth*—not fourthly. Fourth would be the next number."

He grumbled under his breath, and I smiled.

"We would never work out, as you clearly would grow jealous of the hordes of women I keep," he said.

I stopped walking.

"Are you serious right now? *I'm not jealous*—"

A triumphant smile appeared on his face. "Not now, perhaps."

"And I never *will* be jealous."

He pursed his lips. "You did get a little confrontational about my many—"

I put a hand up. "*Don't* say another word! I don't care about your romantic entanglements."

"Who said anything about romance?"

I sighed and, rolling my eyes, I said, "*Aeroth*—"

"You don't need romance to fuck."

I could feel my entire body tingle at that word, and I covered my face with my palms to bring my emotions under control.

"Well, that's unfortunate." Aeroth's voice was now stern, as if all the humor had been sucked out of his tone.

I dropped my hands to look at him.

Aeroth was scanning the forest around us. "You don't pay attention to your surroundings in the woods, do you?" he asked me.

"What?"

After that moment, everything moved rapidly.

I watched as an arrow flew through a bush toward me.

Aeroth's hand snatched it so fast I barely registered it had happened until I saw it snap in half at our feet.

Just as quickly, three silver-armor-clad individuals stepped out from the shadows of the trees. They advanced toward us with calculated, almost mechanical steps. They wore helmets with shiny, red face shields and large backpacks with various compartments.

Two of the attackers held crossbows with blue honeycomb-like shields in front of them, as if to protect themselves from counterattack. The third had a large triple-barrel laser gun pointed at us.

Aeroth shoved me in the direction of the camp.

"Go and tell the others!" he demanded as the attackers surrounded us.

"No!" I yelled, summoning a Black Fire bow and quiver full of arrows. I stood next to him with my weapon drawn. "I'm stuck with you, remember?"

I immediately commanded my magic to erect a protective shield around Aeroth and me. The shield emanated from my chest, where my magic was stored. The translucent dome of protection moved with me. Since the dome was visible, the attackers stopped advancing.

"Mercenaries," Aeroth called out. I could not see his face as he'd put his back to me, but his tone was deadly. "What do you want?"

The attacker with the gun cocked the weapon. "Stand down. You don't ask the questions here," he said. His voice sounded almost artificial, robotic. The voice was definitely not from a living person.

Aeroth scoffed. "Esterons."

I frowned, unsure what the word meant.

"They are artificial mercenaries," Aeroth continued in a low tone so only I could hear. "It's all machine."

"How do you know?"

"The way it moves. And its speech. These Esterons look expensive from their armor. Their owner must be wealthy."

"What can they do?"

"Wield weapons. The backpacks they have allow them to levitate. We are lucky there are tree canopies above us that limit their movements. You never want one to shoot at you from the sky."

"Can they practice magic?" I started thinking of ways I could protect myself.

"No," Aeroth replied. "They're machines."

One thing Sethos had taught me during our grueling training sessions was to always think ahead during a fight. It was vital to have a backup weapon or plan. You never wanted to be caught idle.

And so, I called back Black Fire bow and arrow and allowed my palms to be unencumbered and summoned my electrical magic.

Electricity quickly coursed up from my center, around my shoulders, down my arms, and to my palms. Green and black magic crackled between my fingers.

Aeroth must have felt my magic because he turned his back slightly.

"Hold," he said to me, but my eyes shot to the attacker closest to me with the crossbow who advanced a step, and I raised my palms. On instinct, I fired my magic at it.

I watched as my green and black currents moved like lightning, shooting at the Esteron's helmet and disappearing inside. Closing my eyes, I willed my magic to burn and sever all machinery inside the Esteron. Within moments, the artificial mercenary began convulsing and toppled backward.

Seeing their artificial comrade fall, the other two charged at us.

The Esteron with the laser gun was fired at my shield, and

although my shield protected us, I could still feel some of the force from the laser. I cried out and held my chest. Another laser shot was fired, and I recoiled, falling backward.

"Godsdam it, Renna!" Aeroth cried out, putting an arm around me to support me. "I told you to hold! You stubborn woman!"

"Do you have a better plan?" I yelled. "It's better to use magic than fight them hand to hand."

"Stay in your shield," he gritted out, and with a wave of a hand, he opened up a doorway into the Astral and was gone.

My jaw dropped open as I stared at where he had just been.

Was he coming back?

Not wanting to wait, I pushed to stand and called forth my electric magic again.

In that moment, Aeroth materialized behind the Esteron with the laser gun, and with a swift movement, produced a Black Fire sword, slicing the Esteron in half.

Aeroth disappeared instantly like a shadow and then swiftly reappeared behind the remaining Esteron. With one quick strike, he cleaved the machine in half from head to toe. Once all three Esterons lay unmoving, I called back my shield and stood speechless, looking at Aeroth.

His face was furious, eyes red and glowing. Merciless. His chest heaved as he looked down at our foes.

This was the type of killing skills he had been hired for.

My eyes moved to the Black Fire sword in his hand. A silver glow outlined the weapon, making it look almost like it was glowing silver and black neon. The only other person I had ever seen wield Black Fire had been Sethos.

"*You have Black Fire too?*" I whispered.

Black Fire was magic granted only to supernatural fae who engaged in war. Although I had never engaged in war, I had Black Fire as a result of the chaotic and war-like magic from Am-Re. It made sense that Aeroth would have Black Fire as well since he was always clad in armor and had fought in past wars.

Aeroth smirked. "We do have something in common after all."

I rolled my eyes and laughed. "Being able to wield weapons of war isn't something to bond over."

"You know what our newfound connection does do?" he asked.

I pursed my lips. "*What?*"

"Gives you an advantage over the hordes of women in my harem. I can finally connect with a woman on something of substance, not just—"

"*Aeroth!*" I yelled, cutting him off.

He cleared his throat. "Right."

"We should go to camp," I reminded him and crossed my arms.

"We should." I could tell from the way his lip barely curled that he was fighting back a smirk, and I wanted to yell at him again.

Instead, I lifted my eyebrows and gestured with my arms toward camp. "Then let's go!"

"Lead the way," he said, "my comrade in Black Fire—"

"*Stop.*"

Aeroth leaned his head back and laughed, and I couldn't help but stare and fight the small smile forming on my lips.

16

RENNA

Our camp was overrun when we arrived.

Illona stood in the middle of the dome by the bonfire, tears streaking her face, watching Cylas and Demira outside of the shield fighting off more attackers on foot while another fired shots from a hovertror circling by air to break the shield. The attackers here were people as many had no helmets and I could see their faces.

I knew from experience that holding a shield up was draining, and Demira was not only holding a shield up but also trying to fight by using her Violet Fire. As flames emerged from her hands, she fashioned weapon after weapon to fight the attackers off. But she seemed uncoordinated, as if she had never used a weapon before.

Aeroth and I sprang into action.

I raised my Black Fire bow and fired an arrow at the hovertror rider, but missed.

The rider looked our way, and he smiled slowly. "I can't kill you, but I'll have a lot of fun torturing you, little bitch," he shouted and raced toward us with a crazed look in his eyes.

I put my protective shield up and cocked another arrow.

Just as I was ready to release the bow, Aeroth appeared in the sky next to him and lunged forward, swinging a Black Fire sword in a swift horizontal motion to cut the rider in the stomach. The blow forced the rider to fly from his seat to the ground, and the hovertror crashed into my protective shield, the impact pushing me to fall back.

"Renna!" Aeroth yelled and appeared at my side, kneeling beside my protective shield. "Are you okay?" he asked. His hands moved to my shield, lying flat against it.

"Yes," I called out, my chest heaving.

Demira then cried out, and we both turned to look at her and Cylas.

Demira was on the ground, awkwardly clashing swords with a female attacker trying to cut Demira down. Cylas's head kept swinging back from his own fight to look at Demira, who was now being approached by two more mercenaries.

I stood, and Aeroth and I both ran toward Demira.

Cylas swung his sword up to strike at the soldier he was fighting, but in that moment, Demira screamed again from her own fight. Cylas turned to look at her, and the soldier he was fighting took the opportunity and lunged forward to strike him.

Terror gripped me, and I stopped in my tracks. "*Cylas!*" I screamed.

Cylas froze for a moment and turned his body back just in time before the mercenary's sword made contact with his torso.

In a flash, Cylas transformed into water, and the mercenary attacking him jumped back, confused.

Cylas instantly materialized into his physical form behind the attacker and kicked him in the back. The impact sent the soldier flying through the clearing.

"Cylas should have killed him," Aeroth said to me.

Cylas turned to face us from a distance and winked at me.

"I'm the Creator God, Ren baby," Cylas called out with a grin.

"I can transform into any element or natural object on my planets."

An arrow flew past Cylas's ear, and he jumped, and his skin turned bright red, as if embarrassed.

"He should stick to creating trees," Aeroth murmured to me. "He's no good in a fight."

Cylas was a god. Why could he not do something with his magic to banish all the mercenaries?

Were they sent by Sethos?

Or worse . . . my father?

When we finally closed in on the scene, two attackers turned to face Aeroth and I. They slowly stalked toward us, double axes in each hand.

"Renna," Aeroth said calmly. "Go inside the camp shield with Illona and stay there."

"No!"

In that moment, the two mercenaries sprinted toward us. I erected my shield as Aeroth ran toward the attackers to fight them off.

One of the two swung his axe at Aeroth, but when it made contact with Aeroth's armor, it bounced off. Whatever his armor was made from was strong enough to withstand an otherwise killing blow. Aeroth spun and slashed at her stomach, forcing her to fall back.

Steadying my bow, I grabbed an arrow, nocking it and pointing at the woman. I called on my Black Fire power, lacing the arrow with crackling energy.

In my mind I began to speak to the magic in my arrow, I watched as it glowed brighter as if it could hear me.

Poison.

Venom.

Death.

Don't miss.

Hit true.

I released the arrow, and it swooshed through the air. At the last moment, I called on Darkness and ordered it to follow the arrow. A strand of Darkness wove through the air and encircled the arrowhead.

When it struck, it lodged in the attacker's helmet. I watched as black liquid spurted from her head.

A deep satisfaction emerged through me.

Aeroth spun to face me.

"You killed her."

I grabbed another arrow and nocked it, aiming for the second attacker who rushed at Aeroth. I whispered in my mind to the arrow.

Poison.

Pain.

Death.

Boils.

Darkness.

I released again, and it sped through the air, hitting the attacker in the chest.

Aeroth watched as the attacker stumbled and began screaming.

The attacker took off their helmet, and I watched as red and purple boils marred their face and neck. They scratched their skin and violently began to take off the rest of their armor as the boils exploded with green pus. When black liquid began to sprout from their mouth, nose, and ears, and they began to choke, a thrill rose within me.

Good.

The feeling of punishing was intoxicating. I called on more Darkness, pooling at my feet. The air changed then and became tense, as if every atom was holding its breath.

The three people attacking Demira halted and began looking around, as if sensing a change in the fight.

I looked to Cylas, who kept transforming into fire, wind, and various objects to escape the soldier attacking him. Cylas would not kill. Cylas did not like death, and I knew the deaths in his past weighed heavily on him.

When his attacker lunged and nicked him, my anger grew and I called on my Black Fire sword.

Cylas would not kill.

But *I* would.

"Renna," Aeroth warned.

"Yes?" I replied, moving toward Cylas with my sword.

Aeroth followed. "You have called on and used Darkness. Three times. I know what it does."

"*And?*" I barked.

"I know you have this handled, but is this what you want to do?"

A dark feeling spread over me, making my heart race and mix with a heady dose of satisfaction.

I looked to Aeroth.

"Would you stop me?"

Aeroth lowered his chin, his eyes boring into mine. "Will I need to?"

In the next breath, a spear flew at my shield. I bent my knees slightly, grounding my feet down as the impact reverberated through my body like a tremble.

The magic in me thrashed in fury.

I looked to my left and saw a mercenary with a cocky look staring at me. From his position and arm, I knew he had thrown the spear.

"You want to show off with a few shadows?" he yelled. "You're a coward fighting with magic," he gritted out.

Did they not know what the shadows around me were?

The fury inside me grew, and the Darkness began to pour from me, forcing my shield to expand to accommodate it.

Cylas and his aggressor stopped and looked at me.

"Who are you?" Aeroth demanded of the assailants.

"They look like exiled mercenaries to me," Cylas spat. "Scavenging what they can from people visiting Elinoor. *Pathetic.*"

One of the people by Demira grabbed her in that moment and held her to them against their chest with a dagger at her throat.

"Let her go! You have no idea what you're up against."

The man who had launched a spear at me spoke.

"*Up against?*" He threw his head back and laughed. "You're traveling with a god who cannot even kill." He spat on the ground and glared at Cylas.

Did the man have a death wish?

Cylas fisted his hands, and green-colored magic appeared in his palms, but before he could attack, a hovertror appeared out of nowhere and raced toward Aeroth.

My body rolled with nausea as the hovertror guns fired and rapid flashes of ammunition blasted through the air toward Aeroth.

The thought of Aeroth being injured made my anger rise to a frenzy, and that was all it took.

The Darkness exploded from me, shooting at the rider. I watched as it consumed and eviscerated the rider, its flying contraption, and the ammunition.

Ashes fell to the ground.

"May your soul know no peace," I said to the ashes.

I spun around and launched Darkness at Cylas's attacker, slicing his neck straight through.

Blood gushed from his neck and marred the ground with his blood before the head and body began to evaporate into black ash.

The rest of the attackers began to run, and I willed my Darkness to form a circumference around the area.

"And then there were three," I called out to the remaining soldiers huddled together.

"Let us go!" a female attacker yelled at me. She took off her sleek helmet to reveal her blonde hair plastered to her skin from sweat.

A laugh bubbled from me as I saw how fearful they were.

Aeroth approached me. Wrath rolled inside me as I recalled how he would have been injured.

"Strongborn."

"What?" I snapped, feeling my anger rise. "You said I had this handled."

He frowned and narrowed his eyes. "Do you?" he asked and crossed his arms.

"*Renna*," Cylas said, approaching on my other side. "I cannot condone this. You're using dark magic." He shook his head.

"I never asked you to approve of me."

"It corrupts the soul," Cylas countered. "I watched Am-Re descend into something irredeemable over time from his extended usage of Darkness."

Aeroth stepped in front of me.

"Darling," he said, tilting his chin down.

My eyes widened at the sudden endearment. It felt so out of place coming from him, but at the same time, it felt like he had been calling me darling for years.

"I know what it's like to lose control," he said. "Take a deep breath. There is a different way to go about this."

I pointed at the attackers with my fingers, and they jumped back. Someone shrieked.

"So what do you want me to do?" I demanded.

Aeroth tilted his head side to side with raised eyebrows. "Maybe not gruesomely kill them?" he suggested.

"Or kill them *at all*?" Cylas added.

I looked to Demira, who stood silent, now safe inside the camp dome. She simply stared at me, her face expressionless.

"What should I do instead? Question them?" I asked Aeroth.

A tight smile appeared on Aeroth's lips. "A wonderful thought." He gestured to the wide-eyed attackers with his palm. "Care to start?"

I sighed and walked toward them.

"Who are you?" I yelled.

"There is a bounty out for a traveling group with three women," one of the women responded quickly. "We're mercenaries from Konah and happen to be on Elinoor."

I looked to Aeroth, who regarded me silently, his face devoid of expression.

I turned to face the woman.

"So you just attacked us because we happen to have three women in our group?" I asked. "Seems ridiculous."

"With all due respect," the woman began. "A video and photographic ad was issued, and you three look exactly like the ad."

"Who called in the bounty?" Aeroth walked to stand next to me.

"Sethos, The Ahtar of Vasarys."

My stomach turned. Sethos was relentless when he was after something. That was clear when he caged me in Daya to prevent me from alerting the gods of his attack. He also made his displeasure with me clear when he sent mages to attack Elrle's craft.

Sethos was furious with me, but his actions were extreme. Illogical. There was no reason for him to want to capture Demira and Illona. Their magic posed no threat to him. The only explanation I could think of was how deeply my father's magic had taken hold of him.

I shivered.

I knew if the mercenaries captured me, Sethos would likely

keep me caged someplace far from the battlefield. I probably wouldn't even have an opportunity to speak with him.

"You need to leave," I gritted out to the woman.

She laughed, the cold, shrill sound filling the air. "The bounty is great," the woman challenged, shaking her head. "I'm not leaving here without you three."

"And how much is your life worth?" Aeroth asked.

"We're a network of mercenaries," she replied smugly. "We already notified our group leader. It doesn't matter if you kill us. Our star craft is stationed by the lake with a tracking device, it recorded our arrival on Elinoor."

My heart raced.

My Darkness could kill these mercenaries. It could also destroy something as large as a star craft. I recalled the fight in the woods of Daya, where Sethos and I encountered the band of criminals and the small star craft my Darkness destroyed.

"We're not going anywhere," Aeroth growled.

The woman narrowed her eyes at me. "Taking one of them would be enough."

"And now you've said the wrong thing," Cylas gritted out and stepped forward, green magic at his palms, a silver godlike glow outlining his body.

"Others will come," the woman fired back.

The blood in my veins continued to race, and I began to sweat, my palms turning clammy.

"*Breathe,*" Aeroth's voice was gentle next to me.

I shook my head, and my eyes dilated.

I wouldn't be taken. I wouldn't allow my sisters to be taken. Would I kill all the soldiers?

This is what Sethos had warned me in the woods of Daya. Would I be ready to kill when the time came?

I had already killed the others.

And it had felt good.

I looked to Cylas, who regarded me with wide eyes, and then to Aeroth. He visibly gulped and reached a hand out toward me.

"I know you're scared . . ." he began. "Think this through."

I shook my head once, and my vision glassed over.

"I'm sorry," I whispered as my body trembled with power.

I screamed as I willed my Darkness to cover the mercenaries in a wave. The shadows emerged from me like tentacles of smoke to the ground, crawling and clawing in a flurry toward the soldiers. They didn't have time to run; the dark shadows eviscerated them whole, turning them into nothing but black ash. I moved my body to the rest of the fallen mercenaries and willed my Darkness to swallow them.

The smell of burning skin was overwhelming, and I doubled over when it was done.

As the black ash of the soldier remains swirled around us in the breeze, some landed on my clothes, causing my stomach to twist. I vomited.

The moment I lost my focus, the wall of Darkness around us fell, and my protective shield vanished.

Aeroth was at my side, holding my body as it shook while I vomited.

My father killed. Sethos killed.

And here I was.

A murderer like them.

I pushed Aeroth off me and wiped my mouth when I was done. I moved to get away from him. I could hear Cylas walking toward me, calling my name, but I ignored him.

I was disgusting.

It was one thing to kill a nonliving robot. It was another to kill a living, breathing being.

Did the people I killed have children? Had they been raised in a loving family that would never see them again?

"Renna," Illona called, and I turned. Demira and Illona ran

toward us and crossed the runes. Illona's eyes were on me, kind and worried.

Self-hatred at seeing a reaction I did not feel worthy of moved through me like a wave. I didn't deserve her kindness.

"Strongborn," Aeroth said. He lowered his chin. "It's going to be okay."

I shook my head and looked down at my hands. They were trembling. I clasped them together to keep them still.

I looked up to the sky and around us. More mercenaries would come.

I had to ensure we were all safe.

Without thinking twice, even though I knew I would regret depleting my magic further, I waved my hand, opened a portal to the lake, and stepped through.

Portaling was an ability I had mastered with Sethos. The sensation of portaling was like being ripped into a million effervescent bubbles. Through practice, it became a painless experience as the body learned to relax and not fight the process. Somehow, even though my body was in pieces and I did not possess ears or eyes, I could hear swooshing sounds and see an explosion of colors. I was everywhere at once, being carried to where I had set my intention.

When it was over and my body had reassembled, the portal spat me out. I stumbled forward, landing next to the lake.

A gray and black star craft was stationed next to the lake on the same bank where Aeroth and I had been before. Someone had to have seen us and reported us.

Was someone watching again?

Aeroth portaled next to me and walked to stand in front of me. His fiery burgundy eyes were practically garnet.

"Have you come to berate me?" I said to him, wanting my voice to sound stronger than I felt.

Aeroth clenched his jaw and stared at me. "I will berate you when you endanger yourself."

I lifted my chin. "Yell at me," I gritted out and took a step toward him. "Tell me I did wrong."

He frowned. "What is done is done."

I shook my head and held up my hands. "I killed. I—" My voice broke. "I killed them."

Aeroth crossed his arms. "They would have died by your hand or mine. They would not have left us alone. You and your sisters need to stay safe."

I felt like my hands were pulsing, so I rushed to the lake and dipped them in the cool water. I scrubbed at them as tears poured from me. If only I could wash away the smell of burned skin that seemed to settle inside my lungs.

I washed my arms and waded farther into the lake. I needed to be clean.

Would I ever be ready for battle? How did one make peace with their first kill? Would I remember the faces of the soldiers for the rest of my life? The shock and awe in their expressions as the Darkness consumed them?

I bent down in the water and let the lake cover me up to my chest as I furiously scrubbed my entire self with a large pebble from the lake floor.

I heard Aeroth enter the lake and was thankful for his silence as he stood next to me while I scrubbed my body and cried.

When my arms and hands got tired, I sat back and let the water come up to my chin.

I wanted nothing more than to submerge my whole body and hold my breath to see if the self-hatred and disgust would stop. If the fear of becoming like my father would simply halt.

"Be grateful you killed for love," Aeroth said, staring off into the distance.

His words made me pause.

"Love?" I asked, incredulous.

"You killed to protect your sisters and everyone in our group," Aeroth said, his eyes now on me.

I wanted to tell him I didn't love any of them—except perhaps Cylas, as one of my closest friends. But everyone else was a stranger.

"Part of me was excited to kill," I told Aeroth. "And now I feel like I'll never get their faces out of my mind."

"You won't."

I sniffed. "You don't mince words."

"I thought you valued honesty."

I stayed silent.

"You don't have to feel love for someone in the familiar or romantic sense to do acts of love for them," he continued. "You knew the mercenaries meant us harm. You killed to keep us safe. That is an act of love."

I looked away from him. "And in battle?" I asked. "When I'm faced with a decision of whether to use my Darkness or not? I don't want to be like Am-Re."

"You will remember this day and will weigh your options."

Aeroth looked to the sky, and I wondered whether he was thinking of the other mercenaries that would surely come for us.

"I don't know how to feel."

"You will grieve for a time," he said. "Death changes a person. Allow your body to feel what it needs to feel."

I scoffed. "Does it get easier?"

He frowned and looked down to the water. "No."

There was that honesty. In a way, I was glad he wasn't offering me a hug or flowery words, telling me everything would get better.

"So what's next for me?" I asked.

Aeroth looked down to me and uncrossed his arms, extending a hand to me.

"You getting out of this lake to start."

I took his hand, and he pulled me up. I was soaked and frigid as the water began to cool on my clothes and skin.

"There is a spell for drying your clothes," he said with a tight smile. "I'm sure Demira can show you."

I nodded. "Thanks."

Aeroth nodded back and looked at the mercenary star craft.

"We need to get rid of it," I said to him.

"Yes. It may have a location tracker, which is not good." He glanced my way. "Do you want to do the honors?" he asked.

His response caught me off guard. "I just told you how deeply these deaths affected me."

"And yet you have Darkness still. The power is not going anywhere, Renna."

I looked down at my hands.

"If you use your magic with the intention of keeping others safe, you will never be like your father."

I looked up at him. His words were so different from Sethos, who urged me to use magic to control and gain respect.

"I will sit with you all night and talk with you about what you are feeling," Aeroth said. "I will help you make sense of all the thoughts crossing your mind. But right now, we evacuated a star craft that was attacked by mercenaries. We were tracked to Elinoor. And we were just attacked. I can assure you there are more mercenaries on the way. You will be pursued along with your sisters. Relentlessly. They will not stop." He shook his head. "The star craft needs to be destroyed."

I nodded. I knew he was right.

"Aren't you afraid I'll corrupt my soul?" I asked him, recalling Cylas's words.

Aeroth studied my eyes for a moment. "I'll never allow that to happen," he said, his voice soft. "That I vow."

"Honesty," I remarked.

"My best quality."

A small smile formed on my lips.

Aeroth gestured to the star craft. "Do your worst, Strongborn."

I looked to the star craft and let the dark magic inside me erupt.

17

SETHOS

I was in a dark room.

Water.

I needed water.

I moved my hands, but they were in chains.

I was naked.

How long had I been in here?

I tried to move my body around but found my ankles shackled too. I tried to scream but found my vocal cords weak. And then, from the corner of the room, keys rattled and a door opened.

And then I heard his voice.

"Oh good. You are awake," Am-Re said.

A sick feeling overcame me.

"Will you refuse to portal to Renna again?" Am-Re sneered.

I remained silent as my body anticipated the pain.

"I told you then and I will remind you now," Am-Re began. "Renna will never be yours. You defy my command to portal to her."

Tears streamed from my eyes as I thought about how much I had hurt her.

"I will break you until I can force your mind to portal to her, boy. And I don't give a fuck what law of the universe I will be breaking."

"*No,*" I croaked, the words painful. Am-Re was silent for a moment.

"Well, then," he chuckled, "let's practice my favorite game, shall we?" Am-Re asked.

At his words, the memories came back to me.

After I had shifted and left Vasarys for Taria, Am-Re had caught up to me in transit . . .

"Shift," Am-Re ordered.

I shook my head. He had brought me to this room and forced me to transform into his dretani over and over again. Once I had shifted form so many times, I lost consciousness.

"Fuck you," I whispered.

"I said *shift*!"

His magic shot me in the chest, and my body began to tremble as the beast inside me won over.

18

RENNA

I was warm. So splendidly warm compared to the cold in Elinoor.

I nestled further into the cocoon around me.

When the cocoon rumbled a chuckle, I opened one eye.

I was floating through the woods . . . I opened both eyes and looked up at my source of heat.

Aeroth.

As if I had called him, he looked down at me, and a corner of his lips lifted. I was in his arms as he walked. An animal fur of some kind covered me.

You passed out after you destroyed the star craft, Strongborn, Aeroth spoke to me through the bond.

I was embarrassed. Passing out after using a lot of Darkness happened often.

I don't mind holding you, by the way. You haven't snored and it's been quite pleasant not hearing you scold me.

I narrowed my eyes and opened my mouth to fire off a response but Aeroth shook his head slightly.

He silently gestured ahead, a smirk on his face as if something funny was happening next to us. I frowned and turned my head to my left to see Cylas and Illona walking side by side.

Arguing.

"Please," Cylas drawled. "Continue to explain how being a glorified necromancer and the ability to reanimate the dead are necessary gifts. We already have Lerrick for that."

"I don't just bring back the dead, *god*," Illona evenly snapped back. "Golden Fire does much more than that."

Cylas was silent for a moment, his eyes intent on Illona as if he was shocked by her sharp response. Illona was quiet and sweet, and her losing her temper was strange even for me to witness. Demira was the one who was quick to anger—not Illona.

"*What?*" she asked Cylas.

Cylas shook his head and murmured something I could not catch.

"And stop casually mentioning the God of the Dead's name," Illona whispered angrily. "Do you want to summon him?"

"You mean *Lerrick*?" Cylas chuckled. "Your sense of importance is inflated, princess. Lerrick won't show up."

"I know the legends. Keep saying his name and he might!"

"Lerrick, the God of the Dead or the God of the After, won't show up when *I* say his name." Cylas leaned in and whispered loudly. "He kind of hates me. We have different goals. Me being the God of Creation and he of Death does not bode well when we're in the same room."

Illona crossed her arms. "I find it hard to believe someone would have any problems with *you*. You're a perfectly pleasant person."

"Not a person. God, sweetheart. I am a *god*."

Illona stuck her finger in Cylas's face and began to tell him off for his condescending tone and calling her sweetheart.

I chuckled to myself, and Aeroth's chest moved as he tried to suppress a laugh.

"Do you want to walk?" he asked me.

Although using that much Darkness had been draining, I was not injured. As comfortable as I was in Aeroth's arms, I knew I could walk.

"Yes," I answered.

Aeroth set me down and my body instantly missed his warmth. I felt like a hypocrite. I was still nursing emotional wounds from Sethos, and now I was craving the body of another.

But Aeroth is your mate . . . my brain reminded me. *Perhaps the pull you feel toward him is purely biological. You could not have predicted this.*

I took the fur blanket Aeroth offered me, wrapping it around my body as we walked a bit further back from the group.

"Where are we headed?" I asked as we strode side by side.

"When you destroyed the mercenary star craft, Cylas scoured the immediate woods around the lake to find anyone else who may have reported us or seen us when we destroyed the craft."

"And did he?"

Aeroth shook his head. "No. But he did find a secluded part of the woods near a cliff where we will be staying as we make our way to find the caves. We will have to be more careful as we move around Elinoor, since we expect the other mercenaries to show up."

I pursed my lips as I thought of Cylas's powers. "If he is the God of the Planets, why doesn't he know where the caves are?"

As if Cylas had heard my question, he was at my side in the next breath.

"Elinoor is nothing *but* caves, Ren baby."

Aeroth scoffed and shook his head.

Cylas ignored him and continued.

"While we can find entrances to any cave underneath, not all of them are inhabited. And the cave system below is extensive and spans the entire planet. There are hundreds of cities underneath with structures carved from stone as tall as the mortal ones you are used to."

"Also, there are mercenaries looking for you and your sisters," Aeroth added.

"Correct," Cylas agreed. "I'd rather we not go knock on every cave entrance. People will do anything for money. They may speak to the mercenaries of our movements."

"Are you saying we're safer on the surface of Elinoor? With mercenaries landing here?" I shook my head. "You can't be serious."

"We will hide for two days by the foot of a cliff known to have a fatal drop. No one goes there," Cylas said. "In the meantime, I will speak to the sprites here. I used to be involved with the Queen of the Forest Sprites . . . here's hoping she only remembers the good days we shared."

"You don't sound confident," Aeroth deadpanned. "I'm assuming you did not end things amicably with the lady in question?"

Cylas rolled his eyes. "It depends on who is telling the story."

I crossed my arms. "And while you look for the sprites, where will we hide? Another camp?"

Cylas smiled. "Leave that up to me."

"How far is the foot of the cliff?" I asked.

Cylas gestured ahead of him with a wide sweep of his arm. All of a sudden, the dense forest opened up to reveal a clearing with a massive waterfall. Water pounded violently against the various boulders lining a massive pool. Black, thorny vines curled around the bottom, surrounded by slick moss.

I understood now why the cliff was fatal—the waterfall led to a gruesome death.

I shivered as I watched the water crash onto the thorns.

Demira turned to face us, and her eyes narrowed on Cylas. "I didn't take you as someone who enjoyed violence. The thorns say otherwise."

"They're not thorns. They are the remnant of a tree giantess. It used to be a nice pool before with water nymphs," he gestured to the sharp wood extending several feet high from the water, "before the giantess threw herself off the cliff due to a lost love. It was quite gruesome."

Illona went to the pool and bent down to touch the water.

"The energy of many souls dwells here." Illona looked to Cylas. "People throw themselves to their deaths from the cliff?"

"Yes," Cylas shifted uncomfortably. "None come by this cliff or pool unless they need to."

The horror of hearing this was the resting place of people who found no other alternative made my chest hurt.

"You couldn't have picked a better place?" I asked him.

"I promised to ensure your safety, did I not?" He shook his head. "People stay away from here. We need the seclusion."

"Renna," Illona said. "If it helps, the souls don't dwell in this space." She gestured around us. "There are energetic imprints from the souls here, but not the soul itself."

"You can sense that?" I asked Illona.

Illona turned her face to look at me over her shoulder. She nodded. "With Golden Fire, I am able to bring back living beings on the brink of death. I can sense the spirit in all things." She turned her head back to the water. "Even in nature, I could tell you the age and impending death of any nearby plants or animals."

Her magic sounded complementary to Cylas's magic and purpose. Cylas detested death, and Illona could keep his creations from that dying . . .

"Perhaps you should work alongside Cylas," I told her. "Both of your purpose is life."

Cylas cleared his throat and walked a short distance from the group. We all watched as he stood with his hands on his hips, looking up at the trees surrounding the plunge pool.

"What is he doing?" Demira asked.

Cylas bent down to the forest floor.

While kneeling, he raised his hands up so that they were parallel to each other, and a sphere of green magic appeared.

The sphere glowed with various shades of green, the colors shooting around the sphere like falling stars. The sphere seemed to pulse slightly, much like a beating heart.

Cylas moved his hands away from the sphere and took a step back.

The ball began to descend until it made contact with the ground and disappeared, melding with the dark brown soil.

I looked to Aeroth, who frowned at the spot on the ground as we waited for something to happen.

Then the trees began to move.

Illona jumped as a tree root under her feet shifted, twisting into a spiral shape while the bushes and fallen leaves came together to form stairs. Fallen branches levitated on the ground, forming handrails to the stairs that were now materializing in a spiral shape.

I glanced back at Cylas, who had a hand under his chin with a wicked smile, his green eyes sparkling.

Impressed? he mouthed to me and winked. I laughed and looked back to the creation happening before our eyes.

Three more tree trunks began to twist around, and I realized they looked like columns to the entrance of a palace, with the spiraling staircase in the middle.

The tall canopies above us began to shake and move and creak. We ducked as vines and branches swooped toward us, moving this way and that. Through the foliage at the top, I could make out walls made from tight-woven branches. The trees then rearranged so the lower branches covered the magic that was occurring above.

When the trees stopped moving and the night became quiet again, small glowing orbs of gold lined the stairs before us, as if beckoning us to ascend into the trees.

Illona walked to the stairs, her face tilted up in a wide smile as she looked around.

I turned to the left and noticed how intently Cylas watched her. When she turned to face him, he cleared his throat and his smile was gone.

"This is incredible, Cylas," Illona breathed. All traces of her tense words with Cylas were gone.

He nodded.

Demira rolled her eyes and murmured something under her breath about the structure being a glorified tree house and moved to the stairs, pulling Illona to climb up.

Cylas clenched his jaw as he watched them go, then turned to Aeroth and I.

"The tree house awaits," he said, forcing a smile.

"Don't sell yourself short," Aeroth said, tilting his chin down. "It's a tree mansion." I suppressed a laugh, and Cylas shook his head and climbed the stairs.

Aeroth turned to me and gestured to the stairs with his palm.

"Shall we?" he asked. I nodded and walked toward the stairs.

The ground changed from soil to leaves and moss, patted down to form the illusion of tiled flooring. I moved my hand to the polished handrail made from branches. When my foot came down onto the first step, the stair felt somehow springy yet sturdy. If I wanted to, I imagined I could almost bound up the stairs from the bounce under my step.

The staircase spiraled several times toward the canopy. In the middle of the staircase were more golden spheres of light resembling a chandelier of sorts, casting a warm glow.

As we climbed, I moved to the center of the staircase to examine the spheres. They were full of tiny glowing bugs flying in a circle. Their wings gave off a vibration that sounded almost like humming or music.

"This is beautiful," I whispered. When Aeroth didn't answer, I turned to find him smiling slightly.

"Let's keep going up, Strongborn," he said and continued up the stairs.

I followed, and we climbed in silence.

When we reached the last step, my jaw dropped.

The stairs had delivered us to what could only be described as a great hall. The branches and leaves that made the walls reached up to form a ceiling, with several arches decorated by more of the glowing chandeliers.

Even though the walls didn't have any windows, they did have several glowing lights shaped in the form of arched windows. I walked toward the closest arched faux window and saw the glowing came from more bugs like the ones in the orbs. The bugs were dormant, but their bodies still gave off an ethereal light made up of all the colors ever imaginable. Together, they almost formed a stained-glass-window effect.

"And does my lady approve?" Cylas asked.

I looked up, and he had his arms crossed with a lazy smile.

"It's definitely larger than a tree house." I laughed. "Won't this structure get us noticed?"

"Not when you command flora," he quipped. "The trees, vines, and flowers created not only this," he looked up and gestured around him, "but also hid its creation. If anyone should walk past, they will only see dense forest trees."

"And if we leave this place?" I asked. "Won't we get lost trying to find it?"

Cylas shook his head and lightly tapped the tip of my nose. "I have infused magic in the flora to remember the essence of each one of you here. It will reveal itself to you should you step outside. Come," Cylas said, extending his arm to me. "I'll show you around."

I looked back to Aeroth, who stood with his arms crossed, his facial expression unreadable.

"I trust you'll be fine on your own?" Cylas asked him and grabbed my hand to place it around his extended arm. "I'm going to give my girl the tour."

I lifted my eyebrows and swung my head to Cylas.

"*Your* girl?" I asked.

"Renna and I will stay together," Aeroth said and squared his shoulders. "She's my obligation."

The word obligation cut through me. Aeroth had already called the bond inconvenient. He clearly regretted meeting me, and being someone's obligation was humiliating.

"Both of you are speaking as if I'm not in the room," I said. "Which is extremely rude."

"Cylas?"

The three of us turned to find Illona standing in the hallway.

"You have a visitor," she said.

Cylas frowned. "I'm busy," he said before adding, "and besides, *no one* knows we are here. The flora is enchanted."

A glowing orb of greens and cool blues that looked like flames emerged behind Illona.

My first instinct was to step back because I had never seen an orb like that before, but Illona's calm demeanor made me stay put. I flexed my hands, ready to call my Black Fire in case a threat emerged.

The orb continued past Illona and moved toward Cylas, Aeroth, and I.

I was the closest to the orb, and I braced myself as it approached. Aeroth was at my side instantly, sword withdrawn.

The glowing ball of green and blue fire halted, and in a flash of white light, the orb expanded until it resembled a large oval. Then a young woman stepped out.

I blinked as I took her in.

She wasn't just a woman; she was one of the most beautiful women I had ever seen. Her skin was light blue, speckled with glowing greens and golds. Her hair was a deep green, laced with red. Her tresses almost looked like vines and extended to the ground like a veil. Light pink flowers dotted her hair, matching the light, sheer fabric that covered her body.

I averted my eyes from where her dress revealed the most intimate parts of her. Out of curiosity, I glanced at Aeroth, and his eyes were fixed on her face, never once traveling downwards.

Not that I would care.

The woman extended her arm to her side, and a long staff that looked like a tree branch and topped with a brilliant yellow glowing crystal came into her hand. She settled it on the ground, and the crystal glowed.

The woman looked at Aeroth and I with mischievous green eyes and a knowing smile.

"You could be fun," she said to him, giving him a once-over.

Aeroth frowned and shifted on his feet.

"Your Majesty," Cylas said behind us.

Her eyes flickered from Aeroth's groin to Cylas, narrowing at the god.

"It seems ages ago you and I were lovers, God of Creation," she said with a clipped tone.

Cylas cleared his throat and came to stand on the other side of me.

"Ah, but the God of Creation and of the Flora and Fauna is ever the lover to the Queen of the Forest Sprites."

My heart raced at hearing her title. Cylas was counting on her to help us find the Metidon riders.

She gripped her staff tighter, her smile cold.

"Is that so?" she asked, tilting her head.

Cylas bowed.

The goddess continued. "I seem to remember a cold bed and subsequent news that you had married Ukara, Goddess of War. Is that how you leave all your lovers?"

Cylas lifted his head to look at her. "I never wanted to leave you. But I was young and had an obligation to my enclave."

Aeroth scoffed under his breath.

"You knew what we had and its nature, Divica."

"Did I?" She laughed loudly, her eyes crazed.

The yellow crystal on Divica's staff began to glow into an almost blinding light, and Cylas stepped up to her.

"Let's discuss this elsewhere," he said to her and placed a hand on her shoulder. "It's been many years, and we owe each other a conversation. I recall we were friends first."

Divica narrowed her eyes and shrugged his hand off. "You contacted the forest sprites, seeking an audience with me. Seeking my help. After all this time, you *finally* seek me out, asking for a favor. I owe you *nothing*."

"Divica—"

"You left me. I was alone."

"Divica," Cylas said gently. "I am sorry for the pain I caused you. Please," he placed a hand on her shoulder again, "allow me to apologize."

"*Why?*"

"Because the young man from our last night still lives inside me, and he misses you."

A look passed between both of them, and her face softened before she cast her eyes downward and nodded once.

Cylas stepped closer to her, brushing a hand across her jaw before looking at me.

"The tour will wait," he said, wrapping an arm around Divica's waist. "Although I'm sure you can find your way around. The structure has four levels. My room is on this floor. Your room is on the fourth floor." He winked. "It has the best view."

I wasn't sure what to say, so I simply nodded. I felt like my words would somehow break the spell between Cylas and Divica. Her longing for him was palpable, and the pain at their outcome made me melancholy for my own love. That, and my inability to find someone I could trust romantically.

Although I did not know the exact details of Cylas's past with Divica, I knew how much Cylas put his heart on the line. His lighthearted demeanor was merely a façade for a man who loved and cared deeply. After being hurt from his relationship with Divica and his divorce from Ukara, I could understand why he hid his true personality from most. It was hard to be vulnerable.

Cylas turned with Divica to walk down the corridor past Illona. She seemed tense, her eyes fixed in front of her, not even blinking when they walked past.

I sensed Cylas hesitate in his step when he almost brushed against Illona. It seemed like he was about to say something to her, but thought better of it. Instead, he continued walking with Divica.

When Cylas and Divica turned down the corridor, Illona almost sagged.

"Illona?" I asked gently.

She kept her eyes fixed ahead and spoke, her voice almost hollow. "I'm headed up to my room. It's on the second floor. If you see Demira on your way up, tell her I do not want to be disturbed."

Illona turned on her heels and walked down the corridor toward the stairs, disappearing from view.

Aeroth and I stood in silence for a few moments before I spoke.

"Aeroth, it's becoming more and more complicated to be together at all times during the day. Being in the forest and having to use the bathroom while you stood by . . ." I shook my head. "I need to do basic hygiene, and I cannot have you stand beside me. And be your obligation. We need to exchange blood."

"You are not an obligation."

I laughed bitterly and shook my head. "Right."

"This has not been easy, Renna. I never meant for you to interpret it that way."

I narrowed my eyes. "Well, you don't have to be offensive."

"I don't—" He paused and closed his eyes and pinched the bridge of his nose. "I . . . I'm sorry. I feel like I can't do anything right. I promise, I'm trying to make this work."

A heavy sigh settled in my chest. Sethos often apologized and always managed to say the right things to appease me. And like an idiot, I trusted him blindly.

I would not be made a fool again.

"When I called the bond inconvenient," Aeroth tried again, "it's because my job is not easy. I cannot die for the reasons I explained. And the sudden duty of caring for a mate while I oversee the entire Astral Plane and my kingdom and my family is . . . intimidating." He paused. "But *you* yourself are not an inconvenience. You are not an obligation. I should never have said that. This situation is an inconvenience."

I pursed my lips.

"It is my obligation to ensure you are not in pain—*ever*. That is what I meant, and I understand based on my past words, and perhaps actions, why you interpreted the word differently. I take full responsibility for that. I am sorry."

I wanted to believe him. But at the end of the day, he was a stranger. I didn't truly know him.

"Let's exchange blood," I said. "I need some time apart."

Aeroth sighed and nodded. "We will need someplace private, as drinking blood straight from a person can be a bit overwhelming."

I didn't care how overwhelming it could be. I just wanted distance from him.

"Then let's head up to the fourth floor to my room," I said and began to walk down the hallway with Aeroth in tow.

19

RENNA

The stairs leading to the fourth floor were spiral-shaped with transparent glass-like steps and vines intertwined with red glowing flowers for handrails.

Like the stairs leading up to what I now referred to in my head as the tree mansion, there was a beautiful chandelier of golden orbs in the middle of the spiral staircase inside.

The second-floor landing revealed lush trees and tall grass. Vines of black dahlias covered the ceiling, giving off a sensual aroma. Small glowing orbs lined the walls, creating a soft glow. At the end of the hallway stood a single purple door, which I guessed was Illona's room.

I wondered if she was okay and if she would be open to talking with me. Her demeanor a few moments before seemed odd.

Aeroth and I continued up to the third floor, and when we approached the landing, I almost laughed.

The floor here, which I could only assume was Demira's floor, was covered with glowing blue moss. Giant carnivorous plants lined the walls. The ceiling was also blue and glowed with some sort of moving magic that resembled shadows and water. A black door was at the end of the hallway. This floor nearly screamed danger, one I did not want to step foot in. I suspected Cylas wanted Demira to feel the same fear.

But when we arrived to the fourth floor, I gasped.

Beautiful arched windows with glowing gold orbs lined several windows, which revealed the tree canopy that surrounded us and a view of the waterfall. Green leaves covered the ground, woven together like tile. The ceiling had strings of the golden orbs that made the space feel warm and inviting.

A lone green door stood at the end, and Aeroth and I walked toward it.

The room was beautiful, with the same illusion of tiled flooring, woven walls, and the same arched windows I had seen on the outside. The windows were covered with white translucent drapes that moved with a soft breeze.

The bed on the far end of the room was covered in silky, emerald-colored sheets, vines framing it on each corner, making it look like a four-poster bed. Like the windows, there was a translucent drape that framed the top. Additional drapes gathered at each post, and it appeared they could be drawn around the bed for privacy.

I had never seen a more beautiful bed in my life.

To the left of the bed, against the far wall, was a shallow pool of water, one big enough for several people. A door to the left of the pool likely led to the bathroom or closet, and I almost sobbed with relief. Using the bathroom in the forest was something I never wanted to repeat.

I cleared my throat.

"I need to use the bathroom," I stated. "Can you stand outside the door?"

Aeroth nodded, and we both walked to the door. When I opened it, I was relieved to find a toilet, sink, and shower. I closed the door behind me and was glad for the door briefly separating me from Aeroth.

He was too much.

Too large.

Too tall.

Too imposing.

I leaned on the sink counter and looked at my reflection in the oval mirror hanging above the sink.

It was exhausting to be on edge all the time around Aeroth. Always trying to catch him in a lie, trying to decipher what his facial expressions were saying, trying to interpret his tone. His laugh. His posture.

I squeezed my eyes shut.

Would this be my life? Deeply distrusting everyone around me? Crippled by paranoia?

Taking Aeroth's blood to establish separation for as long as possible was what I needed to get clarity on everything.

I turned on the faucet and splashed water on my face, and my skin instantly cooled. I was finally able to take a full breath, as if my head was clearing from the rush of confusing emotions that resulted from being next to Aeroth.

After I was done, I used the bathroom, thrilled that the separation pain had not kicked in. Before I left the bathroom, I looked at the shower at the far end of the bathroom. It was so inviting . . .

I longed for a shower and wondered when I would be able to have one. I was sweaty and tired and would be going into my second night without being able to wash myself. Using Darkness also exhausted me, and I wanted nothing more than to relax. I recalled the pool in my room, but the shower was here now, and Aeroth could stay on the other side of the door.

I took a deep breath.

No time like the present.

I took my clothes off as I walked to the shower. *No separation pain yet.*

The smooth beige stones and the bench inside greeted me. As I turned the water on and adjusted the temperature, a knock gently rattled the door.

"Everything alright in there?" Aeroth asked.

"Yes!" I said and stepped inside. "Just hopping in the shower quickly."

Suddenly, a pang of pain shot through my temples, and I closed my eyes.

No.

I could do this.

This wasn't just a shower. This had to do with me claiming my freedom and autonomy.

I stepped under the spray, covered my face with my hands, and let the water run down my body. My muscles sagged in relief, and I lowered my body on the bench to sit under the water.

Another shot of pain moved through me, and I yelped.

"Renna?" Aeroth called, knocking again.

"I'm alright!" I yelled shakily. "It's the bond pain."

"Yes, I know. I feel it too."

"I'll be right out."

"I don't like hearing you in pain, Renna."

I didn't either. I hated this so much.

I knew the smart thing was to get out of the shower and rejoin Aeroth. But running toward him felt like giving up the small amount of control I had in this situation.

And hadn't he called me stubborn already?

I opened my eyes and stood up slowly, stepping toward the various jars placed on a shower ledge next to the shower head.

I opened a jar that looked like either body soap or shampoo and smelled like lavender. After pouring a healthy dollop into my hand, I lathered my body and hair with the concoction.

As I massaged my head, the movement elicited more pain, and black dots began to form in my vision. Within moments, pain rammed through me like a bolt of lightning, and I doubled over. My feet slipped on the soap on the ground, and I tumbled down, my hip hitting the bottom of the shower. Between the impact from the fall, the soap in my eyes, and the separation pain spreading all over my body, I couldn't help but cry out.

"Renna?"

I began to sob from anger, frustration, and pain. The tears welling in my eyes mixed with the soap, stinging badly, which only increased my crying.

"*I'm fine!*" I replied, sounding anything but fine. "Everything is fine."

"Everything is not fine. I'm coming in. I'm sorry."

"*No!*"

Aeroth came into the bathroom, and I scrambled to sit up from my pathetic position on the ground, covering myself as best as I could with one arm across my chest and a hand covering my crotch. I squinted as he moved toward me.

"I'm not looking anywhere I shouldn't, Renna," Aeroth said. He came into the shower to sit with me under the water, pulling me into his lap. My arms were still secure in all the places that mattered.

"You're getting all wet—"

Aeroth ignored my comment and began to wipe the soap from my hair and eyes. I was too stunned to even protest. His armor had disappeared, and he wore a black long-sleeve shirt with strange ribbing and long black pants with the same type of material. I could only guess this was what he wore under his armor.

His touch wasn't lewd; it was more about helping me. I was shocked that I didn't feel the obvious horror and embarrassment I thought I would.

When I was able to fully open my eyes, Aeroth found my gaze.

The water was still running above us, making his black hair stick to his face and cheekbones. I followed the water droplets, trailing down to his lips.

"I think you can turn the water off now," I whispered and looked back into his eyes. "I'm sorry."

Aeroth shifted, extended his long arm up, and behind him to turn off the water.

Silence settled between us, and I averted my eyes; I was afraid his gaze would consume me. It felt like flames beckoning me to fly closer to his light.

"Where do you hurt?" he asked. "You fell."

I nodded and looked down at the right side of my hip, which had turned red and was likely to bruise.

"May I touch your hip?" he asked.

I laughed at the ridiculous question since he was already touching me. "Now you ask? Look at us."

"I'm sorry," he said quickly and began to move from under me. "You cried out and I was also in pain, and all I could think about was the need to get to you."

"I know," I replied. "I should have gone to you when I first felt pain, but I didn't want to."

Aeroth gently lifted me off his lap and stood, grabbing a towel from the shelves next to the shower. He draped it around me and turned around to give me some privacy.

I wobbled up to stand, wrapping the towel around me, wincing as my hip throbbed.

"I don't blame you," he said. "Not wanting to come to me."

I didn't respond because I had said all I needed to say on the matter, but it felt good to know he didn't hate me for rejecting the bond.

He continued. "You wanting to maintain some form of control

and autonomy is expected. I respect you too much to judge you on that."

"Thank you." I paused and quickly added, "I think we need to exchange blood. *Now.*"

Aeroth inclined his head slightly and asked, "May I turn around?"

"Yes."

Aeroth turned and crossed his arms. "I understand you want to get this out of the way—"

"This cannot continue, Aeroth. I want to be able to do basic things without you."

He put his palms out. "And I'm not saying no—"

"So we're not leaving this bathroom until we exchange blood," I demanded, looking down at my towel. "I'd rather not get my clothes stained with blood either. And you've already seen me naked, so I don't care that I'm in a towel."

"I didn't gawk at you—"

My heart began to gallop. "Universities on Andora have communal showers. I learned to get comfortable with nudity," I continued, my voice coming out quicker. "So I can get past this incident—"

"Renna—"

"But I cannot be dependent on you—"

"*And I understand that*—"

"And I refuse to pause my life—"

"Renna—"

"What?!" I yelled. My chest was heaving.

Aeroth approached me. "You are spiraling. Take a deep breath."

I nodded and tried to breathe, but my breath caught in my chest.

"Deep breaths . . ."

I tried again, and my breathing began to even out.

“I’m not refusing your request,” Aeroth began, “but I do want to make you aware of what will happen when you drink my blood and it passes your lips.”

I nodded.

“The blood transfusion was a direct intravenous procedure. You likely felt nothing as my blood entered your system.”

I shook my head. “I felt more awake than ever before,” I admitted. “Like I was in the middle of something that was exhilarating. Colors were unexpectedly brighter. There was a glow to everything.”

“This will be different. When my blood passes your lips and touches your tongue, you may become . . .” he paused and scratched his neck, “*aroused*.”

My mouth formed an *O*, and I blinked.

“I would rather be honest with you now.”

“Are you just assuming I find you attractive?” I said and crossed my arms. I knew I could have control over my senses. “I’m not going to fling myself on you.”

“It’s just what happens with Naaviri blood. It has nothing to do with whether you find me physical pleasing.”

“Aeroth, I was just naked on your lap—”

He squinted his eyes. “I know.”

“And I didn’t throw myself at you.”

“*Right.*”

“So arousal won’t be an issue. I’ll be fine.”

He raised his eyebrows. “I want to be transparent and honest with you. Arousal *is* a side effect—”

“And I’m an adult who can control myself.” I inclined my head. “As can you, I’m sure.”

“I am very old and have drank the blood of many people—”

I threw my head back and stared at the ceiling. “Why is this relevant?”

"Because regardless of how long I have been alive, I still get aroused when feeding off a person."

"Sounds like a personal problem."

He stared at me for a long time, and patience began to gnaw at me.

"I don't have all day, Aeroth. I'm tired and I want to sleep. I would like to be alone. I can't do any of that while you are next to me. So let's get started."

My chest heaved getting the words out. But how else was I expected to react? Surprisingly, Aeroth did not fight back. The fire behind my words fell flat, and a small gnawing feeling of regret rose inside me at being so abrasive.

Aeroth nodded. "Understood." He looked around the bathroom. "Due to our height differences, we would need to sit down."

I looked at the shower floor, but Aeroth spoke. "I'm not sitting on stone again," he said. "Can you sit on the sink?"

I glanced at the sink and the wide counterspace and nodded. "Sure." I looked at his clothes, which were soaked. "What about your clothes? Won't you be uncomfortable?"

He looked down at himself. "Don't worry about them," he said in an amused tone before looking up at me and making a face. "But thank you for your concern."

I frowned. "What is that face expression for?"

I almost berated myself for analyzing everything about him.

"Your concern for my well-being is surprising, seeing as you deeply despise me."

My chest tightened.

"I'm sorry," I grumbled. "For my tone and mood since you've met me. This has not been easy."

He nodded. "I know. Just know whatever you are feeling, I probably feel as well."

I looked down at my hands. "Yes."

The space felt lighter, and I was able to breathe a little easier.

"Renna," he began, and I looked up. "The bond cannot be dissolved unless one of us dies, and even in death, we would follow the other. There will be moments when we exchange blood that are less than comfortable—*like now*." He lifted his eyebrows and lowered his chin. "Unless you would rather me take my shirt off?" he teased.

I didn't blame his attempt at humor. One could either try and find the humor in our state of dress or hide in the corner from embarrassment.

My mind began to form images of what his bare chest would look like.

I swallowed.

Keep him at a distance, my brain reminded me. *Maintain a cordial but polite, pleasant distance.*

"Keep your clothes on," I replied. "Let's not make this more awkward than it needs to be."

Taking charge, I walked past him to the sink and tried to awkwardly push myself up, but I struggled with the tightly wrapped towel. Aeroth moved to my side, and with one quick movement, he lifted me up, propping me on the edge of the counter.

The towel bunched up to my mid thighs, and I pressed my legs together.

Aeroth then stood before me, just to the side to avoid my legs.

"Right," he began. "We tried this once before."

"*Unsuccessfully,*" I added. The medic mages had come into the room while we had awkwardly tried to exchange blood.

"Correct." He moved his right hand to my neck, and I shivered as he moved the wet strands plastered on my skin to my back. I kept my gaze straight ahead, not knowing where to look. How was one supposed to act in situations like this?

His warning that I could become aroused rang in my ears, giving me even more cause to remain rigid.

"My saliva has a numbing effect, so you will not feel my fangs pierce your skin," he stated.

I nodded, still keeping my eyes away from him.

"Renna?"

"Yes?"

"Can you look at me?"

I laughed nervously. "Is it necessary? Can't you just get on with it?"

Were there women who just launched themselves into a situation like this? To have a Naaviri pierce their skin and drink their blood like it was nothing?

"I would like to keep explaining this to you to ensure you understand."

I slid my eyes to him, and he tilted his head.

"Are you afraid?" he asked.

"I'm not sure what I feel," I admitted. "Or what I'm supposed to feel in a situation like this."

He bowed his head in agreement. "That's understandable. This is new for you. I can tell you once I pierce your skin, you will start to feel the same sensations you felt during the blood transfusion. You may hear your heartbeat in your ears, and it will speed up. It's all normal."

It was my turn to nod. "How long will it last?"

He ran his hand over his chin as if in thought, and I watched it scrape along his stubble. His hands were beautifully large and deeply tanned, with veins running over his knuckles. His fingers were long and thick.

"I'm not sure. When I drink blood, I do it to survive. And for pleasure. But never with the goal to maintain distance from someone." He dropped his hand, pulling me out of my trance.

"Drinking blood is pleasurable, Renna. You will feel like you are in a haze. Many call the experience like being in a crimson dream."

"Crimson?"

"When you feed, your vision will turn a shade of red. And colors will become more vibrant. Time may feel like it's moving slower. Like you are in a haze or dream."

A trickle of curiosity entered my mind then. "This seems extremely intimate. And I know perhaps you were partially joking about having other partners . . . but I guess I would be upset if I was in a committed relationship and my significant other was doing this with another."

He frowned.

"Will your other partner or partners be upset you are doing this?" I asked.

Aeroth shook his head. "There is nobody else."

Oh.

I tilted my head. "But I thought you said—"

He laughed.

"I was playing off your statements, Renna. But no. There is nobody else. I don't have hundreds of women waiting for me back in my kingdom. Not even one."

I nodded.

"And even if there was," he added, "you are my mate. Any other partner of mine would have to get accustomed to our new situation."

I wanted to ask so many questions about what our arrangement would look like. Would he eventually take on a partner? It was only logical . . . Would I eventually want to find someone else?

I knew there would be a time to ask these questions, but this was not it. I wanted to sleep and be ready for the next day. If we had to abruptly leave with Divica in the morning, I wanted to be ready.

"Back to your earlier question," Aeroth said. "I won't drink a lot of your blood. If you get uncomfortable or want me to stop, tell me."

"Alright. And what about me drinking from you?"

"I will make a small incision on my neck, and you can feed from there."

Feed.

The sound of the word reverberated through my spine and settled low in my core. The only thing I could do was nod as no words to respond came to mind.

"Let's . . . *er*," Aeroth frowned. "Begin."

I focused straight ahead as Aeroth moved closer and lowered his mouth to my neck. Panic rolled inside me, and my anxiety began to unfurl.

"*Wait!*" I said and moved slightly back.

Aeroth paused.

"My anxiety," I told him. "I have an issue with anticipating things. I like to know exactly what will occur—"

"Would you like me to explain in more detail? I was trying to do that earlier."

I shook my head. "No. Can I go first?"

"As you wish." Aeroth's instant agreement was calming.

He pulled aside the neck of his shirt, placing his pointer finger on his skin. Red magic emanated from his finger, and a small incision appeared.

I winced as I saw the blood ooze on the surface of his skin. He leaned down and placed both hands on either side of me on the counter so his neck was easily accessible.

"Drink," he said.

I hovered toward him, my eyes on the cut in his neck.

I can do this.

I got closer still and placed my hands on his shoulders. He

tensed under my touch, and I wondered if he was as nervous as I was.

"Renna," Aeroth murmured. "Drink."

I slightly nodded and lowered my face to his skin. The usual metallic smell of blood was there, but also something different. Clover?

Without thinking, the tip of my tongue darted out to the slit to experimentally taste him. His blood tasted like dark honey and something deeper I could not place.

I licked him again, and Aeroth tensed even more.

I might have heard him gasp, but I was so focused on his blood I wasn't sure.

"Renna," he whispered hoarsely.

I took a deep breath, lowered my lips to him, and sucked.

Adrenaline rushed through my system, as if overwriting every cell and forcing the blood to shoot through my body, rising to the surface and making my skin sensitive. My vision turned crimson and everything around me glowed. Colors exploded. My nostrils opened more as if inhaling for the first time in my life, and the smell of him, of deep musk and the scent of oud, penetrated my lungs.

I inadvertently pressed my body tighter against him and looped my hands under his shoulders to bring him closer to me as I drank. At some point, I felt Aeroth's hands move to my waist to hold me there, as if helping me drink, and I almost sagged in his arms as the rest of my body draped on his upper body.

My breasts became heavy, begging to be cupped and pulled and sucked, and I felt like my skin was on fire from want.

This arousal was . . .

Suddenly, my mouth was dragged away from the euphoria, and his teeth pierced my skin. I cried out from the intrusion, but there was no pain.

Only want.

And in those moments, reasoning was not a factor as my arms wrapped around his neck and head to hold him to me. His lips sucked and sucked, each pull making my body vibrate as if it was made for him alone, ready to give him anything he wanted.

In many ways, my body *was* made for him and this moment.

Aeroth's hands went around my backside at some point so I could wrap my legs around his waist as he took from me while standing. My body sang with relief as I pressed myself against him. Thoughts of everything in my past melted away, and my mind became quiet.

There was no past.

No future.

Only this.

Only him.

My skin tingled. *More.* I wanted so much more—

And then it was over.

He pulled away from me, and we stared at each other, heaving, our chests rising and falling in sync. His eyes were wild, deep, almost glowing red.

A trail of my blood, which was black due to my magic, dripped from the side of his lips, and I wanted to lean forward and lick it.

Aeroth ran a thumb across my lips, as if to clean me, his eyes intent on my mouth.

"I don't know how long this will help the separation bond," he said with an almost groggy voice.

I nodded. He hadn't ever fed from someone with that in mind. I knew we would figure it out eventually.

He leaned down and ran his nose along the puncture wounds on my neck, and he licked them intently. The mumbling effect of his saliva made my sore neck feel like nothing had happened at all.

I shivered as Aeroth moved his nose up along the back of my ear, nuzzling into my hair. "You smell lovely," he whispered.

I bit my lip to stifle a moan as my body longed to have him drink from me again.

My mind slowly came to, and I knew two things. One: Exchanging blood was not unpleasant. Two: While there was no escaping the feelings of arousal I had because of it, I still had to create distance. I needed to continue establishing a boundary.

Moving slightly backward, I lowered my chin to look at the ground, my face and skin in full blush. Aeroth also moved away, and once we were fully separated, I felt the absence of warmth and a longing in my chest.

In my attempt to further create a boundary, I cleared my throat and said, "Thank you. I will finish getting ready for bed and then sleep."

Aeroth blinked and then nodded. "Of course."

I almost asked if Cylas had created a room for Aeroth, but thought better of it. If Cylas hadn't, which would be something I could see Cylas doing out of spite, I would feel compelled to ask him to stay in my room. That was the opposite of setting distance.

He is a grown man, my brain reminded me. *Let him figure it out.*

Right.

"Well . . ." I pushed my hair behind my ears. "I will see you tomorrow morning?"

"Let's hope the exchange lasts that long. There is no way to know."

I laughed nervously. "Right."

"Do I have your permission to enter your room if the separation pain occurs?"

"Yes."

I blinked as my vision slowly returned to normal, as if indeed I was waking up from a dream.

A thought occurred to me. "Can we carry each other's blood somehow?"

He tilted his head. "What do you mean?"

"Like in a vial. For emergencies, to keep separation pain at bay."

"While it seems like a great idea, the magic from the Astral mixed in my blood makes it so that outside of the Astral Plane, when exposed to air, my blood evaporates and breaks down fairly quickly. Any storage of my blood would need to be kept in the Astral Plane or under watch by medic mages trained by my kingdom who know how to deal with my kind of blood."

"Oh."

A stilted silence settled between us and Aeroth exited the bathroom.

I followed and sat on my bed as I processed the feeding and what our dynamic would be.

"I'm sorry, Renna."

I nodded. I was trying everything I could to work through The Settling.

"I will give you some space," Aeroth said. "I will go to my kingdom and check on everything."

I glanced at him. "Of course."

"And then travel to see Khellios and the rest of the fae monarchs to get an update."

"Alright."

"I know I said I wouldn't leave you while you were here, but I feel confident in Cylas's enchantment of this place." He looked around the room. "I should be back fairly quickly."

I clasped my hands in front of me. "I'll be here."

20

AEROTH

She was intoxicating.

And *not* what I needed.

I traveled through the Astral Plane to my kingdom of Eniraath, landing in the gardens behind my palace. Renna was getting under my skin, and I had a mission to get her off my mind.

Perhaps I should take my government council's advice seriously and agree to meet with the women they had selected for prospective queen consorts.

I stood still in the silent garden outside, listening to the sound of silver-lined moths, native to Eniraath, flying around, their wings making music. Eniraath was suspended on a flat rock in the Astral Plane, full of life and enchanted vegetation, but forever enveloped in darkness. Distant stars bathed it in light that often resembled moonlight, while brilliant cosmic dust of oranges and magentas reminded me of the light just before dawn. Should a mortal gaze upon our skies, they would say our kingdom was in a state of constant twilight.

But there were no mortals here.

Eniraath was made up of the people of the Astral. We were

the guardians of the Astral Plane, and my family had ruled since Source created a universe. The Astral Plane served all seven universes, and my kingdom lay somewhere in between all of them, existing in a place without time.

Although the Melodar Elves, the inhabitants of Eniraath, lived in a land separate from other civilizations and could never leave, Source infused the land with magic. The land was designed so that the Melodar Elves, who protected the plane, could self-sustain without the outside world. Fauna and crops grew as they did on any planet, and water flowed down waterfalls that emptied to the nothingness of space.

The sound of the creek that ran through the gardens bubbled in the night, and inside the palace, I could hear musicians play music. They often played for my family and Eniraath's government conclave during the dinner hours.

The people here lived and died in Eniraath, their bellies full and hearts content. We had no war, no conflicts. The peace in Eniraath mirrored the silence and stillness of deep sleep.

It was home.

But as my eyes turned to the glimmering glass and white limestone palace, which had been erected by Source when the first Melodar Elf breathed air, a sharp pain shot through me, throwing me off balance.

It settled in the hollow of my chest and began to spread through my limbs until my body ached. My brows gathered at the sensation, but even moving my forehead worsened the pain.

I found a nearby stone bench and sat down. The sound of footsteps on the pea pebbles grew nearer, and I knew who it was before she spoke.

"Aeroth?" a female with a familiar melodic voice spoke.

I swallowed as my mind raced with the reason for the pain.

This isn't separation pain.

I grunted a greeting and closed my eyes, taking a deep breath.

"What's wrong?" she asked, sitting next to me. "Why are you here?"

"Nothing is the matter," I replied and took another deep breath before looking to my sister. "Nice to see you too."

She sat next to me, reaching a hand out to move the hair from my face to feel my forehead, but I gently swatted her away.

"You don't have a fever . . ." she said, confused. "Look at me, please."

Knowing better than to refuse her, I looked up at a pair of burgundy eyes, much like my own.

Like our mother's.

"Cressida. I will be alright. I'm exhausted."

"Don't *Cressida* me," she replied, narrowing her eyes. "You look almost pale. We weren't expecting you for a few days."

"I wanted to come back to say hello," I said, trying to catch my breath.

"Let's go inside," Cressida stated, pulling me up. "You could have sent word you were coming home early. Are you hungry? We just finished dinner, but I'll have the cook warm something up for you," she offered as we walked toward the palace, completely unaware of the turmoil raging inside me.

I was hungry—just not for food.

The violent ailment that riddled my body made me crave one thing only.

Blood.

My hand reached for the ring that hung around my neck. The cool metal calmed me.

"Perhaps you're exhausted from a big confrontation with this Sethos character?" Cressida asked. "The last I heard from you, he was going to attack the land of the celestial gods."

"Not yet," I managed. "We're still planning for his attack."

Cressida stopped walking and faced me. "So why are you

exhausted? You don't look well. What were you doing before this?"

My mind raced to Renna.

Bloodlust was an unfortunate trait that ran through my lineage. Among Naaviri, bloodlust was seen as a deep affliction of the mind. It was a trait my mother had not disclosed to my father when they married.

One passed along to me.

One that deemed me as a liability by my father and that I tried to bury far inside me so I could instill confidence in my people to prove everyone wrong and show my mother's illness had somehow skipped me.

Luckily Cressida never showed signs.

How ironic that Naaviri, who needed blood to live, could be affected by bloodlust.

I thought I was in the clear after the last time . . .

Isidra's face flashed through my mind, and I closed my eyes.

She had looked so pale before she died.

"It's been a long day. I just need to lie down," I said.

Cressida chuckled. "Tough luck. You should have come back slightly later. Your first minister and our family are just starting dessert. Henrik is home as well."

The guilt at hearing the name of Isidra's son made me want to scream. I dropped the pendant from my hands, feeling guilt claw its way toward my heart.

I stopped walking and closed my eyes, taking another deep breath.

I could control this urge.

Naaviri, who suffered from bloodlust, often experienced extreme wrath coupled with concurrent feeding.

I prided myself in remaining calm at all times—I had to, as ruler of the Astral Plane and the number of souls I oversaw.

But between the search for Renna, finding her hurt in Daya,

learning she was my mate, topped off by feeding from her, it was apparently too much.

"You need to tell me what's wrong," Cressida pressed. "Henrik will pester you about this. He's more of a mother hen than a son to you sometimes."

The last moments of Isidra's life flashed before my eyes. The look in her eyes haunted me. Would Henrik ever forgive me if he knew? I was not worthy of being a father figure to him.

I took one last deep breath, bringing my mind to a calm and controlled state, and the red clutches of bloodlust began to subside.

Cressida would not understand bloodlust symptoms. Even though our mother had suffered from bloodlust, she had done so while Cressida was still in her womb. And then, when she was a child, I had been sent off by our father to fight in the Galactic Wars.

"I feel better already," I said, forcing a smile.

I knew I could not visit Khellios and the rest of the monarchs in this state. That visit would need to wait. Sethos was not expected to attack for several more days as he traveled with his army.

I would travel right back to Elinoor after this visit.

As we reached the glass doors that led to the dining hall overlooking the gardens, I clenched my fists and forced myself to stand straight. People expected a king in all the ways. Only Cressida and Henrik had seen me at my most vulnerable.

Cressida opened the doors, and cheers greeted me. The dining room, like the rest of the palace, was crafted from translucent crystals, and even though the large chandelier in the middle of the room cast a bright light, the vibrant colors of space and the stars that surrounded us trickled into the room, bathing it in pinks, reds, yellows, and blues. The palace of Eniraath was unlike any palace owned by the fae.

My first minister walked toward Cressida and me with a welcoming smile. I forced a smile back, trying not to let my emotions get out of control.

I noticed the minister carried two clear goblets of red wine.

My breath caught at the sight, my mouth watering as I pictured blood instead.

I cleared my throat and focused on the minister's face.

"Aeroth," he greeted once he stood before us. "In good tidings, how do the monarchs fare? The gods? Is the Sethos matter resolved?"

My eyes involuntarily dropped to the artery in his neck.

No. His blood would not do.

There was only one I craved at this moment.

My eyes slid back up, and I took the offered wine.

"Tolon," I greeted him and patted him on the back. I steered him in the direction of the dining table and discreetly set the wine down on a side table. Tolon was like a family member to me and had counseled me since youth.

I looked to the rest of the dinner guests. My six other governmental council members sat at the twenty-person table. My aunt Erina and her wife also dined with their two children.

They all urged me to sit, asking questions about the status of the campaign. I filled them in as best as possible about preparing for Sethos's attack on Taria and his abduction of one of Am-Re's daughters. I omitted the fact that the daughter was my mate and that I had just left her in Elinoor.

"You were just the person we were discussing before you arrived," Aunt Erina said cheerily.

"Where is your wine?" Tolon asked me. He snapped his finger at a servant and waved his hand for a goblet.

I shook my head. "I am alright—"

"Nonsense," Tolon said gayly as the servant set down a new goblet in front of me.

My jaw clenched as I looked at the red wine.

My aunt spoke again. "Aeroth, we have been compiling a list—"

Cressida spoke up. "Erina, don't start." Cressida laughed at my aunt. "You know he won't do it."

I looked to my aunt, who rolled her eyes and waved a hand.

"Aeroth is reasonable. You hate being regent, Cressida."

"What are you all discussing?" I asked.

Tolon cleared his throat and chuckled. "See, that's why I gave you the wine. To make you more amenable."

I frowned and lifted my eyebrow.

"You must marry, Aeroth," he said. "The state of this conflict with Sethos and Am-Re." He shook his head and paused. "If the campaign is not successful, their powers will grow."

He didn't have to reference my death for me to understand what he was getting at. My government had been pestering me for years about the topic of marriage, and each time it came up, I quickly brushed it away.

But now?

My death would set off a chaotic chain of events for the stability of the Astral Plane and Eniraath.

The room grew silent, and all eyes looked to me, waiting for my reaction. Every marriage I had seen growing up, besides my aunt's, had been a disaster. Seeing my mother abused daily by my father had cemented in me an aversion to marriage, even though I knew it was inevitable.

What would marriage be like for me?

My mind immediately went to Renna. I would be around her my whole life . . .

Perhaps in another life, our circumstances would be different and she would not despise our bond. I wondered what marriage to her would be like . . .

I shook my head, attempting to clear the thoughts from my

mind. I needed another to focus my attention on. Perhaps with a spouse, my craving for Renna would fade.

"Who do you have in mind for me to wed?" I asked.

The occupants in the room immediately sat straighter. Faces lit up in excitement.

Tolon pursed his lips. "We don't have anyone in mind at the moment," he said quickly. "But we have to begin the process to search for a candidate."

"I agree."

Several gasps filled the room.

Tolon patted my back with a chuckle. "I knew you'd come around," he said cheerfully, as Aunt Enira clapped.

Cressida leaned in close. "You don't have to do this because of me," she whispered while the rest of the room broke out in animated conversation.

A smile I did not feel formed on my lips. "It's time I settled down, Cressi."

She lifted her eyebrows and touched my forehead. "Are you sure you're alright?" She chuckled.

Suddenly, the dining room doors burst open and Henrik stormed in. His child-sized black armor, cape, and sword gleamed as he ran toward the table with his fencing master chasing after him.

"You're home!" Henrik said, tossing his arms around my neck in a hug.

"Hello, Henrik," I said and kissed the top of his head and straightened him. "You just came in from practice, I assume. No dinner for you today?" I looked at his approaching fencing teacher with a frown.

My aunt whispered loudly how I would be a natural with a wife and children of my own.

The fencing master bowed when he reached my side. "Your Majesty, young Henrik insisted on training late into the day.

Dinner was supplied to him at the armory, but he refused. He ran here as soon as the servants made known you were home."

"Thank you," I said to the teacher.

Henrik was not a blood relative, but I had raised him as my own. I was the only family he ever knew.

I hoped his mother Isidra was proud of me.

"Will you take me with you on the campaign?" Henrik asked. "I've been practicing."

"*Henrik,*" Cressida said with a motherly tone. "You know war is not for children."

"I am not a child!" Henrik protested. "I am twelve."

"Hardly a man either," I said and felt a twinge of separation pain begin to settle into my muscles. I massaged my temples. I needed to leave.

"You were fifteen when you went off to fight," Henrik said with narrowed eyes. "You will keep me safe."

His words made me freeze.

Tolon chuckled. "Aeroth brought us glory in the Galactic Wars," he said. "He left home a child and came back a man of twenty."

"I am almost fifteen," Henrik argued back.

Cressida laughed. "Not for a while. Did you not just say you are twelve?"

Henrik looked at me. "Please take me with you. Nothing bad will happen if I fight alongside you."

As if my brain mocked me, flashes of Isidra's bloody body and her screams as she went into labor in that filthy war camp besieged me, and I tensed.

Thoughts of losing Henrik to the conflict with Sethos flooded my mind. I began to see red dots, and my gums started to ache.

"Your Aunt Cressida is right," I said and began to move to the doors leading to the gardens. "You are too young."

Henrik yelled in displeasure, and with a swift movement,

Henrik's elbow knocked the goblet of wine and my eyes shot to the red liquid at the table as if mocking me.

I gently moved Henrik out of the way and stood. My muscles began to stiffen under my skin, tensing as more predatory instincts started to take over.

I needed to calm my mind to quell the feelings of bloodlust.

I can do this.

"I must leave you all once more," I said to the room.

Tolon stood. "I will ensure your government knows of the latest updates and that you are in good health. We'll begin preparations as we finally search for a consort."

I nodded, fighting a wince as my muscles started to throb.

"We will select the very best fae candidates," he added.

I forced a smile. "Right."

Cressida stood and spoke. "You speak of females like cattle, Tolon. I don't like it."

Tolon bowed his head. "I apologize, Princess Cressida. It's just that the matter of choosing a suitable candidate is not to be taken lightly. This choice will result in the next heir. The next queen must be beyond reproach." He said the last words while looking at the ground.

My mind flashed to my mother and her unsuitability.

I didn't say anything, and Cressida also did not take offense. We knew best of all the problems my mother had brought to the monarchy, and to Tolon's lifelong commitment to the throne.

"In that case, I will help with the search," Cressida stated. "I know my brother best."

Tolon bowed his head in agreement, and I turned around to walk away.

"Before you go," Aunt Enira said. "Have you met Am-Re's daughter?"

I stilled and turned around slowly.

"I'm sorry?" I asked, not knowing where the question was going.

"The one you said was abducted by Sethos."

I cleared my throat and looked down at the red wine stain on the table, slowly growing.

My mouth watered.

"Yes. I helped rescue her."

"*Well?*" she asked. "Is she beautiful? Surely a person would not risk a war for any woman."

She was right. Renna was not just any woman.

And she was beautiful.

"She is of divine blood," continued Enira. She looked to Tolon. "To have the next heir in possession of that kind of divine magic would be remarkable—"

Tolon spoke quickly. "We are looking for *suitable* candidates," Tolon reminded Enira. "The daughter of the God of Darkness, Chaos, and Ruin, who is likely addled like her father, is *not* suitable."

Tolon calling Renna addled made my blood boil. The skin around my eyes tightened, and I could feel my spine begin to curve and nails lengthen.

"Do *not* call her addled," I spat.

The room fell into silence, and all eyes blinked at me in confusion.

My eyes went back to the spilled wine.

My canines grew.

"*Aeroth*?" Cressida whispered and began to look all over my body with concern. I shook my head and opened the Astral.

Within moments, I was gone.

21

RENNA

The separation pain split through me like lightning, and I shot up in bed.

My room was empty, and I could hear thunder outside. The dense canopies made it hard to see the rain, but I could hear it.

"Shit," I murmured and swung my legs out of bed. I wasn't sure if Aeroth had returned to Elinoor or if he was still away.

Another pang of throbbing pain gripped me, and I recoiled back into bed.

More thunder.

Renna, Aeroth's voice rang out in my mind.

When another wave of pain hit, tears sprang from my eyes. I gripped the bedcovers and pulled them over my head as if that would help. Through the covers, I saw a flash of light fill the room, and I knew Aeroth had arrived.

The pain began to dissipate.

I pulled the bedcovers off to find Aeroth standing off to the side. I blinked to bring him into focus.

"*Aeroth*?" I asked and sat up.

He remained still without answering. I called his name again.

"Are you alright?" he asked, his voice rough and dry.

"I am now."

His voice came out like a croak. "I'm sorry I am the cause of your pain."

His tone took me aback.

"You were in pain too . . ." I sat forward. "Are *you* alright?"

"I . . ." He looked down at the floor.

I moved to stand, but he put a hand up to stop my efforts.

"Don't come any closer." His tone was clipped.

I stilled.

"I'm not myself," he added.

I frowned and put my palms up. "I don't understand."

I observed his posture. He seemed tense and he was not standing straight, as was his usual imposing posture. His hands were at his sides, and I could have sworn his fingernails were longer than I remembered . . .

Lightning filled the night, and within moments, thunder rang out, making the structure quake.

I shivered.

"Where is the Goddess of Rain when you need to make this rain stop?" I said out loud, looking at the window. A tense silence settled between us, and I didn't know what else to say.

"The gods have so many limited powers they're basically useless," he said.

A small grin formed on my lips at his surprising comment, and I looked back to him. Was he trying to make a joke?

I placed my hands on my hips. "You're no better than a god," I added. "You only drink blood. Pretty mediocre ability."

He grunted, eyes still on the ground, but a smile tugged on the corner of his mouth.

"You don't seem to complain when my blood is inside you."

My heart stopped as his words wove into my core. I blushed.

"No," I whispered, the response almost automatic as thoughts of pleasure spread like warm honey inside me, coiling into all my sensitive places. Aeroth's eyes rose, locking on the base of my neck, and my heart began to race.

"Are you alright?" I asked again, gentler this time.

His eyes met mine, but he did not answer.

My body tingled with awareness as his gaze traveled down my body. "Will you drink from me again?" I whispered, my throat parched.

"*No,*" he said almost angrily.

I blinked. "*No?*"

He shook his head.

"I'm here," he replied. "That is enough."

Something was wrong. My mind ran to dark places, remembering all the times Sethos had lied to me.

"What's wrong?" I asked. He stared at me for a long time.

"You and I are bound for life, Renna."

I frowned. "Yes, I know."

"And I refuse to share a life with you, no matter how it may look, without honesty."

I bit my lip. "*Go on.*"

"I have . . ." He paused, took a deep breath, and exhaled. "I have something to tell you."

I stilled.

"My family is plagued by an illness unique to Naaviri. It's called bloodlust. My mother had bloodlust, and the affliction comes from her."

The term sounded like a person driven by a need for blood. Dangerous, even. I moved back slightly.

"And I don't want to hurt you," he said. "That is why I would rather not feed from you again today."

"How would you hurt me?"

"You must know I have controlled bloodlust for the better part of three of your centuries," he began. "Bloodlust only affected me once when I was a young man and sent off to war. It's brought on by the threatening of one's kin. Extreme emotions of fury or wrath, combined with feeding, exacerbate it."

I shivered.

"Do you have bloodlust now?" I asked.

"No. Not yet. I am experiencing symptoms."

"*Here?*" I asked. I pointed to my chest. "With *me*?"

"Yes."

I frowned. "But I am not your kin."

His jaw tensed as our eyes locked. "But you are my mate. My body recognizes you as mine."

I blinked several times, taking in his words. This wasn't a declaration during a moment of passion where he declared me as his, or during an argument where he was stating a possessive claim.

His words were a primal claiming. From the bond's perspective, we belonged to each other. His body recognized me as his kin. His to protect. Defend.

And because of all of that, I had triggered his bloodlust.

I didn't know what to say.

"Meeting you," he continued, "has been something I never imagined for myself, and now you are under constant threat."

"But I am safe now," I said. "With *you*. Shouldn't the symptoms recede?"

He shook his head. "The threats against your life and the injuries I have seen on your body will not leave my mind. I am in a constant state of alert. My body will not relax."

I gulped. "I don't understand bloodlust. Explain it to me. Maybe I can help you."

He closed his eyes and remained still.

"I don't want to hurt you," he said through clenched teeth. "I am grasping at the threads of my sanity, fighting against the need to feed."

There was no reason for him to feed from me now that we were together. But I also could not ignore that drinking blood was a part of who he was. I had asked him to not feed from anyone else. Was he not getting enough blood to sustain him?

"Does drinking blood help you remain calm during these symptoms?"

He opened his eyes. "Drinking blood does bring me calm. But don't offer," he said. His eyes were hard. "I know what you will say."

I crossed my arms. "You are incredibly stubborn!"

"As are you."

I lifted my eyebrows. "I'm a problem solver, Aeroth—"

"I'm not a problem to be solved."

"But this bloodlust is. And now it's my issue too." I moved the collar of my shirt and tilted my head to the side, offering my neck. "*Drink*, Aeroth."

22

RENNA

Aeroth remained still, looking almost horrified.

"Why aren't you moving?" I asked him, still holding the neck of my shirt to the side.

"I—" he began and paused.

"Just drink, Aeroth."

Aeroth closed his eyes.

"*Aeroth,*" I prompted again.

He opened his eyes, shook his head, and began to pace. "Offering blood . . . That's not something you say to a Naaviri with a bloodlust affliction. I could kill you."

I took a deep breath. There were two ways I could react to Aeroth right now. One, life had taught me that the men I cared the most about tended to physically hurt me. It would be natural for me to keep moving far away from Aeroth.

But I was not going to run from my problems—not anymore. I built my life on coming up with solutions, and this was no different.

The second option, to stand my ground and look at danger in the face, knowing that Aeroth could never kill me. That actually gave me a twisted sense of comfort. I was powerful. I could call on Darkness in a heartbeat and kill him.

"Well I can kill *you*," I said to him, lifting my chin.

Aeroth stopped pacing, and a small smile appeared on his lips.

"You threaten the King of the Astral like it's nothing."

"And? Should you be given preferential treatment if you mistreat me? Or threaten my life?"

He lifted his eyebrow. "If you killed me, you would die as well."

I shrugged. "Then don't hurt me."

He remained silent. I continued.

"I won't think twice if you hurt me. I will end your life."

He tilted his head. "At the expense of yours?"

"You clearly are not a woman. I'm tired of being mistreated. And honestly, I would rather kill a man than allow him to treat me like I'm expendable, even if it means ending my own life."

Aeroth looked down to the floor.

"If you really think you are a danger to me," I told him, "then drink my blood just so you can create some distance between us."

That seemed to snap Aeroth out of whatever cloud of hesitation he was in.

He chuckled. "You are like a queen, expecting your commands to be followed."

A smile tugged at the corner of my lips. "It feels good to command power."

He tilted his head. "Is that what you think you are doing?"

I mirrored his head movement. "*Yes.*"

I was at my back on the bed in an instant, with Aeroth lying on top of me. His body stretched the length of me, arms caging me in as if I were prey.

Despite the position I was in, I was not scared.

Instead . . . being underneath him felt, well, thrilling because I knew he could not kill me. For once in my life, I felt like someone's equal. I felt formidable. Powerful.

"*You don't command me,*" he growled.

I smiled. "Oh, but I do. You can't kill me. So *yes* . . . I do command you."

Aeroth growled once more, and his face lowered to mine. My chest rumbled against his as I laughed quietly.

"Why are you laughing?" he asked.

"Because for years, powerful men have lorded over me and dictated my life. And now . . . here I am."

He lowered his nose to my jawline, and I shivered.

"Here you are," he murmured.

I swallowed.

"Here you are lying beneath me." His voice was husky and sent waves of anticipation through my body.

"*Yes.*"

"Thinking *you* command *me*."

The air felt electric with emotions, and my chest grew tight as I became more aware of how my body fit under his. I closed my eyes and inhaled his essence. Deep musk and oud filled my lungs, and I almost moaned, my body automatically melting under him.

He must have noticed because he stilled and moved off me. He sat at the foot of my bed. I frowned and sat up.

"Did I do something wrong?" I asked, curling my knees up to my chin.

He turned his head slightly to look at me, and a sad smile met me. "You have done nothing wrong. None of this is your fault."

I leaned my head on my knees. "Isn't it my fault?" I asked. "Your body recognizes me as your kin. My safety was threatened. Your bloodlust was triggered. And now you are struggling. Seems pretty obvious to me that I am at fault."

Aeroth turned fully to face me. "And is it my fault you can't even go to the bathroom on your own if we don't do a blood exchange? Do you think I don't blame myself for your lack of privacy?"

I looked away.

"Let's not start the blame game, Renna. We will get nowhere."

I moved from my spot on the bed and sat next to him.

"Tell me about your bloodlust," I told him.

23

RENNA

Aeroth looked straight ahead and was silent for a time, so I waited.

He shook his head. "I wanted to die after I realized I had killed people I knew. I was a monster."

He called himself a monster, yet the man who sat next to me had been more honest and kind than any other man I had met.

"What happened last time? It will help me understand you."

He laughed bitterly. "You shouldn't want to understand me, Renna."

I touched his arm, and he looked at me.

"I want to," I said. "Our lives are connected now. I have a right to know."

"Once you know, you will hate me for it. To be chained to a man like me." He paused and shook his head. "I'm sorry."

"How old were you when bloodlust first happened?"

Aeroth closed his eyes and began to speak. "Eighteen." He stood and crossed his arms as he looked out toward the window. "My father sent me off to fight in the Galactic Wars as punishment and so I could have military training."

"How did the bloodlust start?"

"I met a woman while at one of the war camps . . ." His voice trailed off, and he was quiet for a moment. "Her name was Isidra. She was a former prisoner of war, and I fell in love with her. I had been away from home fighting for almost two years, and Isidra's kindness and warmth became home to me. She was pregnant when I met her and wanted nothing to do with love. Her husband had been killed, and she was in mourning. And so I waited for her to heal from her heartbreak. And as months passed, she and I became close. She could only offer me friendship, but I didn't care—I worshipped the ground she walked on. I hoped one day she would see me as more than a friend, and I was willing to wait. I was young and idolized her. She was the sun."

My heart ached as I anticipated his next words.

"The camp I was in was led by a demon known as Leviathan. He is one of the seven princes of the Infernus. He taught me everything I knew about combat. Leviathan had many enemies, and one night, the camp was attacked. There were many deaths, and the women in the camp were raped. I saw the men as Isidra was . . ." He shook his head. "She was still pregnant."

I covered my mouth and stood. I walked to stand in front of him at the foot of the bed.

"You don't have to share if—"

Aeroth locked eyes with me.

"I loved her. And I lost control in a rage. The bloodlust began to emerge then. I became like a beast, thirsting for blood. I was like a machine and killed the enemy soldiers in the camp. In my madness, I forgot about Isidra, who was bleeding out. The attacks on her body brought on immediate labor."

I shook my head.

"She died because of me. I did not think to stop avenging her. I didn't realize what was happening. She needed me to stop. I killed her. My actions killed her."

I grabbed his arms. "You did not kill her. You were trying to avenge her. You—"

"She lived long enough to give birth that same night. She handed me her child, Henrik, and I realized I needed to ensure he was truly safe and kill all our enemies. And so my bloodlust fully emerged. I left him to go kill. I'm a monster, Renna. How could she have trusted *me*?"

"Does the child live?"

"Yes!" He shrugged off my hands and covered his face. "The women in the camp cared for the babe. I could not."

"Where did you go?"

"Initially, I don't remember. My bloodlust lasted for weeks. I killed many. I would suck their bodies dry of blood. Bloodlust always makes me crave blood beyond reason. My war general eventually captured and restrained me. He had never had to capture a Naaviri before."

I frowned. "But how could they have restrained you? You are the King of the Astral, able to travel anywhere with a snap of a finger."

Aeroth locked eyes with me.

"I was not a king then. I was a prince. One must ascend to the Astral throne to bend time and space and travel through the Astral Plane."

"I see."

"When one succumbs to bloodlust, the brain narrows down to basic instincts. I usually don't remember who I am or the identity of those around me. If I succumbed now, I would not be able to summon the mental ability to Astral travel or portal."

"What happened after you were captured?"

"My war general brought me a young woman who . . ." He frowned and looked away. "She volunteered to offer her blood to me to keep me satiated. I was restricted to only feeding from her until I only craved her blood. When my body eventually had its fill of her blood, and it registered everyone I loved was safe, the bloodlust receded."

I ran my hands through my hair. The news of Aeroth's affliction had my mind reeling.

"What are some of the symptoms I should be looking out for?" I asked.

"My eye color will be one of the first signs. The red in them will fade to dark brown or black."

He paused and took another deep breath. His hands trembled in the low light.

He continued. "In a full bloodlust episode, a Naaviri resembles more of a beast. So my body will begin to morph into something you will eventually not recognize. My back will curve as my spine rearranges. My nails will elongate. My fangs will be more prominent. When the symptoms become more severe, I will shun the daylight."

I nodded, and then I noticed the sharp points of his nails. His curved posture. His fangs. His tense body, likely due to the constant looming threats from Sethos and Am-Re.

How much more until he descended further into his symptoms and bloodlust overtook him?

"We need to address this *now*," I said.

Aeroth shook his head. "You make it sound so simple."

"Isn't it?" I crossed my arms. "Feed from me," I repeated. "I'm willing."

"Being next to you will have to be enough," he growled. "I will force my body to relax."

His eyes narrowed to slits and darted to my neck.

My heart raced, and I clasped my hands together, feeling unsure.

"Is my blood not enough to satisfy your needs?" I whispered.

His gaze met mine. "You know nothing of my needs," he murmured as his eyes darted to my lips.

My heart raced, and fear began to stir inside me. Like a shadow, he moved swiftly, standing very close, our chests almost touching.

Out of instinct, I began to backtrack. "And what are they?" I asked, hoping my voice didn't give away the confusion knotting in the pit of my stomach.

"*You.* I desire you," Aeroth said and was in front of me in the blink of an eye. "My body craves you. I cannot stay away."

A low fire began to stir inside me at his words, and despite the danger surrounding him, my nipples hardened.

"Yes." My voice came out like a whisper.

Aeroth gained eye contact with me, furrowing his brow.

"*Yes?*" he gritted. "You should be running from me."

"At least you aren't repulsed by a woman you're effectively stuck with for the rest of your life. A woman who can help you."

His eyes dropped to my lips again.

"I want you, Renna Strongborn," he whispered. "I want your blood to be a part of me until I don't know where you end and I begin. I crave you with everything I am."

I blinked.

"My need for you—" He shook his head. "It scares me, Renna."

Aeroth brought his hands to my neck and pulled our bodies close. His nose almost touched mine, and my nipples brushed his chest through my shirt.

"I crave your blood like the air I need to breathe. When you are inside me," he growled, "when your life and essence invades my system, I feel like I need to cling to you to live."

Our lips were so close now. My body swayed toward his.

"Aeroth—"

"I want to drink from you and not stop," he murmured.

"But you would kill me," I breathed. "And die in the process."

One of his thumbs brushed my lips. "To die while in heaven—"

"Did you ever drink from Isidra?" My question snapped him out of whatever haze he was in.

"No."

"If drinking blood is pleasurable and you loved her—"

"She was pregnant. I would never take blood from a woman who is nourishing life."

I nodded, not knowing what to say, and he dropped his hands from me and stepped back.

"*Fuck!*" he said and ran his hands through his hair.

"Aeroth, we can work together to help you—"

"No!" he yelled and spun from me to pace the room.

I put my palms up. "You clearly need help, and my blood can calm you. Besides, we need to exchange blood to stop the separation pain. We cannot stay glued at the hip."

He faced me. "I will not drink from you."

My heart sank. I didn't want to be by him all hours of the day. I loved my independence— I had lived alone since the age of eighteen, when I left my foster apartment for university. I had friends on campus, but I liked living alone. The only true friend I had on campus, Helena, had never been my roommate either.

To now have a roommate—a stranger at that—as an adult?

I hated this situation.

"So we're stuck?" I asked him.

He crossed his arms. "Other fae species don't have the advantage of exchanging blood to pause separation pain. They remain together for the duration of The Settling year. We can get through this period."

I covered my face.

"This can't be happening," I murmured.

"I will not risk your safety."

"What about my privacy?" I yelled and threw my hands down.

"Didn't you mention the guilt you felt a few moments ago? Do you think I enjoyed you standing by me as I pissed in the fucking forest? That I enjoy not being able to shower without you in the same room?"

"You said communal showers were—"

"*That's not the point!*" I screamed. "I didn't care about you coming into the bathroom earlier because of how terrible I felt. But I expected that to be *one time.*" I pointed my finger at him. "Now this will be a daily occurrence. I can't live like this, Aeroth."

"I'm sorry—"

"And sleeping?" I gestured to the bed. "Will we sleep together?"

"You will sleep," he replied. "I will remain awake."

"Doing *what*?" I yelled. "Waiting for me to wake up? That's incredibly disturbing. I didn't choose this!"

"Neither did I!"

"And I'm giving you an opportunity to help you through this fear! You got through it once, you can do it again—"

"And I'm telling you I don't trust myself. I don't feel comfortable taking that risk!"

"Being around me at all times is a violation of my boundaries."

"And by you forcing me to drink blood, when I have been consistently telling you I do not want to, *you* are violating *mine.*"

Our chests were heaving as we stared at each other.

I didn't want to look at him.

I hated him.

I hated us.

I spun and climbed on the bed, cursing under my breath.

"What are you doing?" he asked.

I stopped to look at him.

"What the fuck does it look like?" I snapped. "I'm tired. I've just been told I am physically stuck with a man not of my choosing for all hours of the day. One who ultimately will likely kill the person I am trying to save. I don't want to think. I want to close my eyes, and sleep, and pretend none of this is happening."

He remained silent as I arranged the bedcovers around me. Once I was lying down, I looked to him.

"*Well?*" I growled. "Are you going to stand there all night?"

"And where am I supposed to go?"

I laughed. "Clearly not out of my room. You're stuck here, *remember*?"

His eyes narrowed, and he moved to the side of my bed where I was and sat on the floor.

"For fucks sake, Aeroth, get in the fucking bed."

"Fuck off."

Fury stewed in me. "And have you complained all morning about how sore your body is from sitting on the floor all night?"

He did not respond.

"I hate you," I whispered.

Aeroth rose and was suddenly leaning over me, his arms caging me in. "And make no mistake that I hate you as well," he grated.

I lifted my chin. "Well at least we know how we feel about each other."

He laughed bitterly.

"You are so fucking difficult," I said.

"And you have control issues. You have that in common with Khellios."

I rolled my eyes. "You are a child."

"*And I am your king.*"

My breath caught in my throat.

"Might I remind you I am the ruler of the Astral Plane, king of Eniraath."

"And we are not there," I spat.

"But you are my mate. And therefore, under my jurisdiction at all times. *My subject.*"

My eyes darkened. "*How dare you—*"

"And whether you like it or not, I am your king."

"Fuck you."

"And you will *not*," he brought his face close to mine, "talk to me in that matter. Have some respect."

I pushed my face up to meet his, not wanting to cower even in the position I was in. "Respect is earned. I don't give a fuck who you are."

"Have I not tried to lead this relationship with respect?" he growled. "I have been honest. I told you who I was as soon as I knew. I am putting your safety *first*—"

"Get off me."

Aeroth pushed off and stood. He pinched the bridge of his nose with his fingers and closed his eyes.

"I'm trying," he said in a low tone. "I'm trying, Renna."

Something in my chest tightened, and I felt like crying.

I could not be the only mate who felt like they'd been denied their freedom. I had fought for everything in my life, with the belief I had the power to change my fortune if I worked hard enough. Now with Aeroth as my mate, I was shackled in a state of suspension, not knowing what was next for me.

I also felt incredibly selfish for demanding Aeroth drink my blood. But what could I do? What would another person do in my place? I was not the type of woman who allowed things to happen to me. I could not be passive in my own life.

"I'm sorry," I said.

"For what?"

"That I have to ask you to do something you are not comfortable doing. But I don't know how else to solve this."

He dropped his hand and opened his eyes.

"There is no right way to handle this," he said.

I hugged my pillow. "We have two problems, Aeroth. Your bloodlust symptoms and this separation pain. My blood would solve both things, but you refuse to take my blood. There must be a solution to dealing with this separation. How do people in your kingdom deal with mate bonds?"

He shrugged and sat on the bed. "There are no mates in Eniraath, as Source never assigns mates within their own species. That, and citizens in Eniraath do not leave the kingdom. But I have met mates in other places. I have never asked anyone what they did during The Settling period, as I never planned to meet my own mate. Before I met you, I spent most of my time in my non-corporal form watching over souls in the Astral."

I closed my eyes and sighed, trying to think of a solution to at least one of the two problems we faced. If blood could pacify his bloodlust symptoms, maybe he needed to drink blood from someone else.

I found him staring off into the distance.

"You need to find another," I told him.

He glanced my way with a frown and raised eyebrows. "Excuse me?"

I sat forward. "If you're afraid that you'll hurt me if you drink too much of my blood, then perhaps you need to find someone who won't inspire those feelings."

"What are you saying? I thought you didn't want me to drink blood from others?"

"Do you have a better solution? What will happen if you don't drink blood at all?"

He turned and looked forward. "Naaviri need to feed regularly or we become unwell."

Panic began to set in. "*Unwell?*"

He looked up to the ceiling. "Aren't you disgusted by me already?" He shook his head. "I've brought chaos into your life."

I scrambled to sit beside him. "*How* unwell?"

"We can become rabid if we go without blood."

I wanted to scream. "Then you clearly need to drink blood! If not mine, then someone else's. Can't you see that?"

He looked at me for a long while.

"I'm in the process of finding someone."

His words, although they should have relieved me, took me aback. A dull ache began to form in my chest.

"Oh" was all I managed.

He nodded. "I need a wife."

I blinked at his words.

"I've told you of the responsibility I have to ensure my line continues. I need to marry. I will ensure my wife understands the need for me to feed from her before she agrees to marry me. If I can ensure your safety and I can get enough blood from another source, I think that will solve our problems."

"Right." My voice sounded bitter and harsh. I knew how intimate drinking blood could be, and the thought of him potentially drinking from me as a married man made me sick.

"What's wrong?" he asked, studying my face.

"Once you find her—you cannot drink from me."

He shook his head. "You are correct. I will never be unfaithful to my wife."

I nodded. This was not how I envisioned our conversation going.

"When do you plan to marry?"

He stood and walked to the window. When he spoke, his voice was dry, emotionless. "I visited Eniraath this evening. I instructed my government to find me a wife."

I looked down at my hands, and my chest felt heavier.

Why did I care what he did?

I wondered if my reaction was purely biological because of our bond. If his body recognized me as his enough to trigger bloodlust symptoms, could my body also feel the same? Was the idea of him being with someone else troubling because my body didn't want to share him? The bond was designed for companionship and procreation, after all.

I shook my thoughts from my head and moved back to my pillow and slid inside the covers.

Aeroth walked to the other side of the bed in silence and began to take off his cape, unclasping the gauntlets on his forearms. Was he getting ready to join me in bed?

Why was my heart racing?

I didn't want him by me, but he wasn't taking my blood and we needed each other.

"You're getting into bed." My statement sounded foolish, even to me.

He paused. "Did you not tell me to?"

My eyebrows lifted. "I—er. *Yes.*"

He pursed his lips and continued to take off his armor. "Well then?"

I thought of any excuse. "I thought I couldn't tell you what to do. You're a 'king.'"

He paused and looked at me. We stared at each other for several moments. I felt so awkward.

"How soon will you get married?" I asked.

"Hopefully as soon as possible, so we can get out of this nightmare. And I need to leave an heir in case anything happens to me."

In case he died.

In case I died.

I didn't respond as I began to arrange a wall of pillows between us. Thankfully, Aeroth did not protest.

"Just so you know," he began, "I always sleep on my left."

I lifted my eyebrow and looked up at him. The comment was so unexpected that I didn't know what to say.

He gestured to the left side of the bed.

I narrowed my eyes. "Not anymore. I'm not moving."

He snorted a laugh. "I see."

To further send a clear message, I turned around and gave him my back.

"Night," I said. "Don't kill me."

"Good night, Strongborn. I truly would not be able to."

I smiled to myself for some idiotic reason and closed my eyes. My interactions with Aeroth were like nothing I had experienced before. How could we go from yelling to sly jokes in a few moments?

I felt him settle into bed, and my pulse quickened as I became hyperaware of being in the same bed as him.

"I'm going to take off my shirt, by the way," he said.

I held my breath.

"I sleep naked," he continued. "But for you, I won't."

"Please don't," I said, looking back at him.

He laughed.

"How do you feel?" I asked. "About your bloodlust symptoms, I mean."

Aeroth shifted. "I feel okay right now."

I nodded. "That is good to hear."

"Yes."

The conversation was taking another awkward turn, so I shifted around again. Aeroth didn't answer for a long time, and I wondered if he had gone to sleep. I was halfway to closing my eyes when he spoke.

"I know this is difficult—to sleep next to me. I am imagining what my sister would feel like if she was forced to sleep next to a stranger, and I am angry that you have to go through this. Just know that you are my mate, and hurting you would be like hurting myself. I will always put your needs first. I will always keep you safe. Regardless of how you feel about the mate bond, my loyalty is to you. By design. And by choice."

"Thank you," I whispered, my voice breaking. "I'm sorry for how all this has played out."

Aeroth was silent for a few moments. "I know. Me too."

More silence ensued, but this time, some of the uncomfortable tension was gone.

"Can I ask you a question?" I asked with a yawn.

"Always."

"Your body remains next to mine when I sleep, correct? To prevent the separation pain?"

"Yes."

"Then where does your mind go when you sleep? You are King of the Astral Plane. Does your soul detach and go to your kingdom?"

"Not always. When I sleep beside you, my soul remains in my body to ensure I can be conscious for any immediate threats."

"Interesting."

"It's a good question."

I smiled.

"Night."

"Good night, Renna."

24

RENNA

I woke to the sound of Aeroth's soft snores.

It was like I had stepped into a new reality.

Aeroth had kept his promise. I was safe, and I knew deep down I never truly doubted my safety around him because he was honest. And because I had the means to protect myself.

I smiled sadly. In an ideal world, perhaps Aeroth would be the type of man and partner I would have been happy with. What were the chances that after so much pain, someone like Aeroth would come into my life? I wasn't looking for him.

But I was looking for someone like him.

I moved to my right and lifted a pillow that was between us and stole a glance at Aeroth.

My eyes widened and my heart raced.

He was sleeping on his back, the covers lowered to his hips, his face turned from me. My mouth watered as my eyes traveled to each dip and curve of his tanned body until I got to his abs that rose and fell with each breath.

He was the most beautiful man I had ever seen.

Aeroth shifted, and his left arm moved to cover his face. My eyes traveled farther south as he shifted slightly, stretching his legs.

When a very particular part of his anatomy began to tent the sheet, a deep red wave of embarrassment burned my cheeks. I rolled back and lowered myself onto my pillow, mouth open in shock.

I had not seen anything, but I was certain whatever had risen in that lower half of his body was the biggest "member" I had ever seen or would see in my lifetime.

Aeroth shifted some more and groaned. I held my breath and clapped a hand over my mouth.

"Gasps of fear are not usually the response I get, Strongborn."

I squeezed my eyes shut from embarrassment.

"You're awake?" I asked, my voice high.

"Would I be speaking if I was not? You were moving a lot."

"*Sorry . . .*"

Aeroth moved again, and when I felt his shadow on me, I opened one eye and saw him staring down at me over the wall of pillows. His burgundy eyes were hooded, and I felt captive in his gaze.

Desire. Aeroth looked at me like he desired me.

Heavens help any woman at the receiving end of Aeroth's gaze.

I squeezed my thighs together as I felt my body respond to his bare torso.

"It wasn't fear," I said, my voice breathier. "You said I gasped in fear."

"You threw yourself on your pillow and squealed." His eyes were daring as if they begged me to engage in whatever game he was playing.

Dangerous.

"I was . . ." I cleared my throat and pushed my hair behind my ears. "Making sure you were still there."

He smirked.

"Like you, I have been told I also snore," he deadpanned. "You must have heard me?"

Aeroth gazed at me for a long time and pursed his lips slightly, as if he was more amused than peeved.

"Were you startled?" he asked.

"Uh," I tried to school my face into neutrality.

You likely have the biggest cock I have ever seen.

"Yes . . ." I replied cautiously.

He nodded. "Well, it can't be worse than *your* snoring. You snore like a bear."

A laughed escaped me, and then I remembered sharing the same conversation with Sethos. My heart ached and I sat up.

I felt Aeroth move off the bed. "Did I say something wrong?"

I shook my head and pushed to stand.

"I clearly said something wrong."

"No."

Aeroth was in front of me then, analyzing my face. "I hate when women do this. Tell me what's going on."

"I doubt you want to know."

He sighed. "How old are you, Renna?"

"Almost twenty-eight."

"The typical fae lives about two thousand years."

"And?"

"You are fae and a demi-god. You will likely live over two thousand years. Members of my family live to be about four thousand years old. That is a long lifespan to be around each other and a very long time to not be honest with one another. Tell me what's wrong."

I hugged my arms and looked away as I spoke.

"Sethos told me once I snored like a bear. Your comment just made me remember him and the moments we shared."

Aeroth was silent for what seemed like an eternity. "I see," he said after a while. "He was right."

I looked to Aeroth and found him smiling.

"You care about him a lot," he added.

I nodded. I had told him so, a few times before. However, this conversation was different. I was not begging Aeroth to let Sethos live.

"I know that bothers you," I said.

Aeroth crossed his arms. "It doesn't bother me that you care about him. It bothers me that he threw away your affections and mistreated you. It bothers me that I saw you on the floor of the fucking forest in Daya, battered and weak. Crying. Scared. In a fucking cell."

A shiver ran down my spine. He continued.

"Seeing you in a cell reminded me of my mother and how my father locked her away. How she begged to be let out. My father didn't care about her health or pregnancy when she carried my sister and left her for dead. Just like Sethos didn't care about you and left you for dead."

I looked down to the floor. "He said he did it because he cared about me."

Aeroth cursed.

"He wanted me to see the reasoning in his ways," I said. "He hoped I would change my mind—"

"Through abuse and *coercion*?" His voice was raised now.

"I . . ." I shook my head. "I don't want to think back on that night."

Aeroth closed his eyes and sighed. "I understand." He opened his eyes. "I'm sorry my comment triggered that memory."

I nodded.

"I have to ask," he said carefully. "And I ask that you tell me the truth . . ."

I frowned. "Go on."

"I saw the way he left you on the forest floor. I have to wonder how far his abuse extended. Did he ever force himself on you?"

"No."

"Are you sure?" His voice was like a growl. "You need to tell me right now, Renna, because if I find out later that he did—"

I lifted my chin. "He did not. My physical involvement with Sethos was my choice."

Aeroth's lips pursed slightly. "Was it really your choice if you were manipulated?"

Rage boiled inside me, and my skin grew hot. "You don't get to pick at my experiences to fit some narrative of what you think happened!"

He remained silent.

"Stay out of it."

He nodded once.

I didn't want to think about the intimacy I shared with Sethos. To try and unpack the moments I spent with him with the degree of his betrayal was too much to process.

"If we're going to spend every fucking hour of the day together," I began, "then you need to know the topic of my sex life with Sethos is a hard boundary."

He clenched his jaw. "Understood."

I rubbed the back of my neck and took a deep breath. "I would love to walk away in this moment and have a little piece of privacy to just sit with these feelings." I paused and closed my eyes. "But seeing as I cannot do that, I'm going to pretend this conversation never happened. And I want you to change topics, because that is what I need to stay sane."

"We should join everyone downstairs," he said, and I opened my eyes. "I hear them congregating. Perhaps Divica has some good news."

"You can hear that far?"

He nodded. "Naaviri have good hearing as we are designed to hunt prey."

I recalled how he'd heard the attackers in Elinoor's forest.

"I don't trust Divica," I said.

"Neither do I. However, Cylas trusted her many times last night."

I gasped, and my eyes widened. Did he mean what I thought he meant?

"You—" I paused. "You heard him and Divica?"

He nodded. "I would imagine your sister Illona might have heard them as well, seeing as her room is one floor above his."

My mouth formed an *O*.

"Illona has been raging to Demira all morning. I tried to tune out her words, but I know she is not happy. I believe she has feelings for Cylas."

I shook my head. Cylas was a complicated man to unravel. There was only so much of him he showed others.

"We should go down," I said.

WE WANDERED down to the main level of the tree mansion to find Demira, Cylas, and Divica arguing. Illona sat on a nearby couch with her arms folded, looking forward with a hard expression on her face.

"What's going on?" I asked.

Divica laughed while looking at me. "*You!*"

Her eyes were wild. and the glow around her brightened.

I stood my ground with my palms ready to call my magic.

"Me, *what*?" I snapped.

Divica launched herself at me, and Cylas rushed in front of her to block her from me.

"Tell her!" Divica yelled. "She is the cause of it all!"

"These are my forests too, Divica," Cylas argued.

"And yet you are not *bothered* by the loss of life!" she cried out.

Demira stepped forward with her arms crossed. "And if you'd stopped fucking each other for two seconds last night," she yelled at both of them, "we'd know where the fuck the Metidon rider descendants were. And perhaps found the beasts and rode to the planets to help! Metidons, as you know, breathe *ice*."

Illona shot up from her seat and began to storm out of the room.

"What's going on, Cylas?" I asked again.

Cylas spun to face me and opened his mouth, but nothing came out, as if he could not form the words.

"Speak," Aeroth commanded.

Cylas slid his eyes to Aeroth and glared before he looked back to me.

"Three planets burn," Cylas said to the room.

My eyes widened.

"Khellios summoned me, and I left briefly for Taria," he began slowly. "When I arrived, he shared the news. Sethos sent mages to three different minor planets. They set fire to each one. They are engulfed in flames. No survivors left."

My jaw dropped.

"Three *planets*?" I asked, my voice barely a whisper.

Cylas nodded with a pained look in his eyes.

"Sethos somehow knows you are with me. He is taking revenge out on my planets. Different gods have been scrambling to put out the fires and aid Berion."

"Who is Berion?" I asked.

"He is the God of Fire," Cylas answered. "And Illona's half brother."

I looked to Demira, who rolled her eyes. "He's a shit person from what I hear. You will find no love from Illona toward him based on what we know."

Cylas looked to Demira and Illona in confusion. "You don't care for him? This is news to me." I didn't understand Cylas's comment to my sisters, and I continued with the matter at hand.

"How is Khellios?" I asked Cylas.

"He's furious that Taria now has fewer gods to protect it, since so many scrambled to help."

Divica launched herself at me once more, and Cylas held her back. "This is all your fault!" she screamed.

Aeroth was at my side in an instant to pull me back and placed himself in front of me. But I didn't need a man to save me.

"No!" I said and walked out from behind Aeroth to face Divica. "I did not cause the fires," I gritted out.

"Yet your involvement with your past lover is the cause for all of this!" she spat. "He searches for you."

"That's unfair, Divica," Cylas said. "And you know it."

"And what of the many forest sprites that died as a result of the fires? The mages trapped life inside the forests. They could not escape," she screeched. "What of them?! Is that fair?"

My heart sank. She looked at me, her gaze filled with dark hatred.

"How can I make this better?" I asked, my eyes watering. "Please tell me."

Demira spoke up, directing her question to Divica. "Do you know where the Metidon rider descendants are?"

"She does," Cylas answered. "It's one of the things you promised to tell me this morning, was it not, dearest?"

"You proved useful last night," she gritted out at him. "But the tables have turned. The damage is too great. Why should I help you now?" Divica snapped.

Cylas almost recoiled at her words.

Demira walked up to her. "Because you are not the only one with a bone to pick with Sethos. Renna is not the enemy," she said and looked at me briefly. "Sethos is. My father is."

Divica narrowed her eyes and looked me up and down.

"And I can promise you," Demira continued, "if you help us, I will personally ensure to bring honor to the sprites you have lost."

"And how will you do that?" Divica snarled.

"Ride with us," Demira offered. "I told you of my vision. There were many Metidons flying into Taria in my vision."

Divica scoffed.

"We will destroy the mages who set fire to the planets. And deal with Sethos and my father," Demira pressed.

"You have too much confidence, witch," Divica barked. "You are no warrior queen."

Demira lifted her chin. "I am heir to the throne of Vasarys. Sethos abandoned our lands to wage war. I *am* the queen. And I will ride into battle."

Divica slid her eyes to me.

"Aren't you older?" she mocked. "Isn't the throne yours?"

"Demira was born to rule," I said with as much strength as I could convey. I didn't need to make an enemy of Demira when she was my way into Taria. And I truly never wanted to rule.

I looked to Demira, who remained expressionless.

"In fact," I added, "she is the one leading this search for the Metidons, and I defer to her leadership once we find them. I will ride alongside her into Taria."

Divica pursed her lips and looked between Demira and I.

"And your lover, Sethos?" Divica seethed. "We all know about him. Most of the galaxies do at this point. We now know he searches for the woman who slighted him," she said and spat on the floor.

I blinked at the shame it caused. Humiliation surged from deep within me.

"I wonder how Sethos would react if he knew you smelled of

him." She pointed to Aeroth. "Moved on rather quickly. Or perhaps you are simply a whore."

Aeroth was in front of me in the next breath, facing Divica.

His voice was so low it was practically a growl. "Insult Renna again, and I will personally drain your blood until you are on the brink of death, then throw your physical body into the Astral Plane so it may freeze and shatter."

My breath caught in my throat.

Was that what happened when a person's physical body instead of their soul entered the Astral Plane?

"You dare speak to me when you currently stand in my forest?" Divica hissed. "I will set my sprites on Renna, I swear it! And they shall rip her apart the moment you turn your fucking head."

Aeroth clenched his fists until I could hear his knuckles crack.

"You won't live that long," Aeroth growled.

He stalked toward her, and I remembered his bloodlust. I grabbed Aeroth's arm and saw his eyes were glowing fire red. He looked like a killer.

"Aeroth," I whispered. "She's not worth it."

Aeroth's brow furrowed, and he looked down at me and then at my arm. He looked like he was in a daze.

"Please," I begged.

Aeroth swallowed a lump in his throat.

"Come with me," I urged and began to pull him from the room.

Divica laughed. "The great King of the Astral," Divica mocked. "Led by a mere girl."

"No," he spat. "A woman. And my mate."

Divica broke out in maniacal laughter. "This just gets better. You forgot to add *slut*."

Aeroth moved toward her again, but I placed myself in front of him and faced Divica.

"Says the woman who was married and fucking another person," I seethed and looked to Cylas and back up to her. "Did your husband know you were fucking Cylas? You took offense to Cylas even bringing him up yesterday. Did you confess your sins to him on his deathbed? You're no better than me. I know your type. You shame women for their sexuality. And that makes you worse."

Divica blinked.

I called on my Black Fire, conjured a dagger, and pointed it at Divica.

"Insult me again," I growled, "and you won't have to deal with Aeroth." I took a step forward. "You will deal with *me*. Cylas and Demira can tell you how I deal with bullies."

I looked to Demira, who had a small smile on her face as she looked to me. Her reaction, perhaps pride, emboldened me.

I looked to Divica once more. "You'll find the remnants of the bullies I burned not too far from here. Their ashes are all that's left."

Divica's jaw dropped. I extended my dagger.

"Consider yourself warned."

I recalled my Black Fire. "Tell Demira and Cylas where the descendant riders are."

Divica grimaced.

"If you don't, and more people die," I said, tilting my head and stepping closer to her so we were almost face-to-face, "I will hold *you* personally responsible for the death of others."

Divica's eyes widened.

"And although Aeroth promised you a certain type of death that I would not wish on anybody, it will be merciful compared to the way I will have Darkness tear you apart," I said in a low tone. "I will flay your skin. And rip you apart limb to limb until you burn from the inside out until your body combusts."

Divica looked to Cylas, enraged.

"Renna," Cylas warned, his voice devoid of any emotion. "That's enough."

I saw deep hurt in his eyes, and I almost wanted to further threaten Divica for how she referred to Cylas as a sexual object, but he shook his head and I kept my lips shut.

I clenched my jaw and backed away.

I found Demira's eyes again, and she had a wicked grin on her face as if she wanted to clap. She nodded once to me, and I nodded back.

I then turned to face Aeroth, whose eyes were still a fiery red.

"Come," I said and dragged him from the room.

25

RENNA

"Where are we going?" Aeroth asked once we had left the room.

We turned the corner into a hallway with an open archway at the end that led outdoors. I could see a wooden bridge at the end, high among the trees.

"Outdoors," I replied and kept pulling him along.

As we approached the bridge, Aeroth took the lead and stepped onto the bridge first. The little daylight on Elinoor bathed Aeroth in a soft glow, making him look ethereal.

He turned to extend his hand to me to help me cross.

"Are you okay?" I asked, looking him over.

He was visibly shaking, his fists curled.

"I had to pull you from the room," I admitted. "I knew your anger was growing. I didn't know what could have happened. I felt like you could have snapped at any moment—"

"She threatened you. I should have ripped her apart for talking to you that way."

"And I'm assuming desiccating people's corpses and ripping them apart is not your usual go-to?"

"And you?" he asked, lifting an eyebrow. "You seemed comfortable issuing threats with Darkness."

"I grew up on people threatening my life. What I said was nothing."

His rage seemed to increase at my words, and I wanted to kick myself.

"What do you need right now, Aeroth? Tell me how to help you."

His eyes drifted down to my lips and up to my eyes. My heart began to race, thinking of what his blood did to me.

Aeroth looked away from me, and his jaw clenched.

"I hate that I want you," he murmured and shook his head. "I feel anger, and all I can do is focus on the memory of how your blood feels inside me."

I swallowed.

"Should we go back inside?" I asked and then added, "to my room?"

Aeroth laughed and ran a hand over his face. "In close proximity to your bed? You're offering yourself to me like a lamb. You realize this?"

Images of Aeroth's naked torso on my bed flashed in my mind, and I shook my head to clear the image.

"Being by your side," he added, "is the greatest temptation I have ever known."

It was my turn to look away. His burgundy eyes were intense —I couldn't handle the emotions in them.

"I'm sorry," I said.

"Why are you apologizing?" His words did not come off as angry, but they were sharp and clipped. The familiar feeling of being a burden came back to me. I knew none of this was my fault, yet my heart felt like I was in the way.

I looked to him. "You refuse to drink my blood. You don't want to be alone. Yet I'm the one company you'd rather not have. What do we do?"

In that moment, we heard yelling inside. We looked back to the hallway that led outside and could hear Demira and Illona screaming at each other. I could not make out every word, but it sounded intense.

"Do you think they need help?" I asked and began biting my nails.

"No."

I wiped my head to look at him. "How do you know?"

"Because I caught a few words of what they're saying, and they do not need our help. Come," Aeroth said with a sigh. "I need to be distracted."

Holding my hand in his, he led me across the bridge, his footsteps purposeful.

The bridge felt stable and hard under my feet. It moved very little, which was great because, based on the height, a fall would be fatal.

"Strongborn?"

"Yes?" My voice came out higher than intended.

"Are you alright?"

"*Perfectly.*"

Aeroth quickened his pace, and soon we reached the end of the bridge. The landing was a wide tree branch with a wooden platform with barely enough room for two people and subsequent steps descending down around the tree in a spiral.

Aeroth spun to face me.

"Your heartbeat increased," he said. "Are you afraid of heights?"

My eyes widened. "You can hear that too?"

"Yes."

The implications of Aeroth's abilities took me aback. If he could hear my heart race, he would be able to pick apart my emotions. The lack of privacy was too much. I took my hand from his and crossed my arms.

"You didn't answer my question," he said.

"Maybe I don't want to answer it."

He raised an eyebrow. "And what is the matter now?"

I rolled my eyes. "You can hear my heart."

He lowered his chin and narrowed his eyes as if he could not comprehend.

"You can *hear* my heart, Aeroth."

"You saying the same sentence again does not provide clarity."

I shook my head and moved past him, starting to climb down the stairs rapidly.

"And you walking away provides even less clarity—"

I uncrossed my arms and spun on my heels to face him. He was two steps behind me.

"It's a lot, okay?" I said, my voice coming out strained. "Meeting you and learning of your abilities is too much. *And* you can speak to me in my mind because you're the Astral."

"That is not something I knew I could do. Speaking to souls is new for me."

"New or you never tried?"

"Does it matter? My job is to shepherd souls through the Astral. To keep them safe so they may return to their bodies. Not ask them about their lives. I do my job in silence."

"Well stay out of my mind. At least."

"And what if there is an emergency?"

I looked up to the sky but was met with a green canopy instead.

"We are at war, Renna. Speaking to you in that way is vital. And you know I have not abused that ability."

I pursed my lips. He was right. He wasn't having conversations with me in my mind. The times he had spoken to me were when he was trying to find me because of separation pain.

"Can you at least explain why you are bothered?" he asked.

"I thought if I exchanged blood with you, I could have some sort of privacy. But I don't. You hearing my heart means you can guess when I'm agitated. Or angry. Any number of emotions. It may seem insignificant to you, but it's an invasion of privacy."

"And you think I want that?" he said, stepping down one step.

I crossed my arms again.

"You think I enjoy hearing when people's hearts stop? When they have a heart attack? When your heartbeat races as you get ready to call Darkness, and I am powerless to know what will happen? If you will hurt yourself by exerting yourself too much? How your heart beats hard when this bond causes you separation pain?"

I blinked as his words settled in.

"It's not an ability that I'm ecstatic about, Renna."

I looked away, feeling embarrassed.

"It's a biological trait in every Naaviri, and I cannot make it go away. I am sorry that you are upset and that I am the one who puts you in so much distress."

"Are you going to guilt trip me now?" I snapped.

He frowned. "That's not what I'm doing."

Waves of emotion crashed inside me. And I was supposed to be helping him de-escalate his feelings of rage. I wanted to scream.

"I don't know how many more times I need to apologize—"

I put my hand up. "Just *stop*."

He nodded.

I closed my eyes and took a deep breath.

"We are going to find a quiet spot and sit down. We are going to be silent," I said. "No speaking. No talking—"

"Isn't that the same thing—"

I opened my eyes and narrowed them.

He had a small smile.

"I hope you don't prohibit breathing. That could be a problem for both of us. We could *die*," he teased.

I bit my cheek to prevent myself from smiling.

"We're going to sit side by side. You will stay out of my mind. You will calm down, or whatever you need to do to settle feelings of rage, so you don't go off killing people."

"How long are we doing this?" he asked.

"Until I say so. Is that a problem?"

"I just don't sit around. Kings aren't idle."

I gestured around. "Do you see a fucking castle? We are in the middle of a forest on a planet, trying to find the impossible. Plus, we are sort of stuck here for the moment while our search party loses their minds inside a tree mansion. Learn to relax."

"And *you* know how to relax?"

I wanted to respond with a smart comment, but he looked at me with hesitation, as if he was trying to find words to say.

"*What?*" I asked with a sigh.

"You got me thinking—"

"No." I shook my head. "I told you. We are not thinking. We are going to find someplace to sit. And we are going to sit in silence until Divica tells us where we are going."

"Come to Eniraath."

I blinked. "What?"

"There is a spot where I like to go and read. We can sit in silence there."

I frowned. "I thought you said you didn't just sit around."

"Reading is not just sitting around."

I rolled my eyes. "You want to leave *now*?"

"Why not?"

"We can't just leave, Aeroth. What if Divica tells Cylas the location of the caves and we are not here?"

He shook his head. "From what I can hear, they are arguing. There is nothing to share right now."

I crossed my arms. "What about Taria? Wouldn't you rather go there? What if Sethos or my father attacks?"

"Taria does not need me as of yet. I do not command armies, I leave that to the other fae monarchs who have militaries. Taria will need me in the thick of battle."

To deliver the final blow, my brain said.

I shivered. The way Aeroth spoke about battle and his role was so casual that it was chilling. He knew he was deadly, and his confidence was frightening.

"And," Aeroth added. "Cylas was just in Taria with Khellios. If something urgent had occurred in Taria, I would have been made aware."

"And if the other fae monarchs want to speak with you? Gods can be summoned. Can fae royalty be summoned in the same way?"

"No one summons me. My lineage has existed longer than that of any of the living fae monarchs. No one summons the rulers of the Astral Plane."

"Oh . . . So you are the most powerful fae monarch."

He smirked. "Is that a statement or a question?"

I lifted my chin. "You tell me."

He extended his hand. "Come to Eniraath."

26

AEROTH

Within seconds, we landed on a familiar, glittering white stone balcony.

The night was calm in Eniraath, but my pulse was racing. I had never portaled another person here before. Renna let go of my hand and gasped.

"Did the portal hurt you?" I asked and assessed her.

She shook her head and took a few steps away from me, her eyes wide as she took in where we were.

"No. I just—" She waved me off. "This is . . ." She covered her mouth. "Aeroth, this is like something out of a dream."

Atop the balcony, we had a perfect view of all the waterfalls, as far as the eye could see. Green life and vegetation dotted the spaces between the waterfalls in a series of hanging gardens with willow trees.

Although Eniraath had no sunlight, it was not suffused in night. It was not a kingdom of darkness. Rather, because the sky was dotted with stars and vivid colors from nearby nebulae, the glow of those celestial bodies bathed everything in vivid colors. The crystal buildings and waterfalls glowed with oranges and purples and blues.

I followed Renna's eyes to the side to the other towering structures, with various levels and balconies alit by floating lanterns casting a warm glow.

"This is . . ." She tried to find the words while my eyes roamed her profile—her long, graceful neck, her delectable collarbone. I longed to run my tongue over the grooves of her skin. My eyes continued their downward path to the heaviness of her breasts, the rounded mounds that made my pulse quicken. My gaze continued down to the rounded area of her belly and hips, and the way the fabric clung to her just so. She was all woman, and she made my mouth water.

My eyes then moved up to hers, and I smiled. Her mouth was lovely and full, and when she laughed I . . .

I wanted her.

But she doesn't want you, my brain reminded me.

"Home," I responded to her sentence as my eyes drifted lower still to her thighs and—

"Aeroth, this is beautiful."

Pride filled me hearing that she found my home beautiful.

She looked beautiful in it.

I clasped my hands behind my back. "My father's Ancestors were the first elves, a species of fae, created by Source and were gifted dominion over the Astral Plane. This land, or rather suspended dimension, was gifted by Source as well."

She moved to stand by the balcony railing and placed her hands on the banister. I joined her, watching as she gazed at the waterfalls and the hanging gardens that separated each one. Her eyes moved down to the bottom, where the waterfalls broke off into rivers that formed canals and encircled homes and public places. Small boats that ferried people around moved about, not knowing that the first woman I had ever portaled into Eniraath stood several feet above them.

"Can souls visiting the Astral come to Eniraath?"

"No. Eniraath is home only to the Melodar Elves, my father's people. They are born and die here without leaving. They know no war, only peace. Eniraath, like Taria, is protected by a shield that hides it from souls wandering the Astral."

"Are there other outsiders who come to visit?" She looked to me. "Like now?"

I nodded. "We have fae monarchs and their entourages that come and go for governmental affairs. Our government grants them entry, but visits are not common."

"And your people never want to leave?"

"We have everything they could ever want. Eniraath is its own society with an established government, laws, travel systems, universities—"

Her eyes grew. "*Universities?*"

I smiled. "Two."

She looked back at the scene below. Her voice was so low when she spoke that I had to lean in to hear her. "I miss my life back at university. I had purpose then."

We had spoken briefly about what our lives would look like after the bond settled, but never in detail. Besides, once the year was up and the mate bond settled, our proximity did not have to be what it was now. While we would have to remain within a certain distance from each other, it would allow her to lead a separate life.

She could settle here. Find her purpose. She could study. *Teach.* I would be able to give her a home where she could do with her time as she wished.

Housing was free in Eniraath, so she would never feel indebted to me. She would have to answer to no one but herself.

At the same time, I realized Renna settling in Eniraath would not be much of a choice because, as Eniraath's ruler, I could not leave this kingdom. She would have to settle here.

I gripped the banister tightly, hating that the choice was being taken from her.

The other alternative would be for blood exchanges so she could establish herself anywhere else in the seven universes.

I would let her go.

Of course I would.

All monarchs of the Astral Plane could bend reality and travel anywhere. I would be able to reach her.

My mind began to formulate ways in which I could ensure minimal discomfort if she settled far from here. Perhaps she would not want to see me regularly for blood exchanges and I would arrange for a blood bank with my blood and hire a medic mage to give her blood transfusions.

She wouldn't have to see me often if she did not wish it.

I wanted to tell her so many things, but it was not the time.

A thought occurred to me then: My rage and bloodlust symptoms had dwindled without the need to feed from her to satiate my needs. Her presence had been enough to calm me and bring me back to stasis.

Renna spun around then to look at the rest of the balcony, and she gasped.

I turned to look at the scene behind me.

"*Books* . . ." she breathed and took several steps toward the building we were in.

I chuckled. "Eniraath's library. Holds the largest collection of books in all fae kingdoms. Several stories high."

She rushed to the doorway leading to the interior, and I followed after her.

The inside of the library, all mahogany and browns and deep red plush carpets, met us. Eniraath's cylindrical library boasted rows of books kept behind polished, curved banisters, while the center of the space was hollow and held floating lanterns that descended to the first floor.

"This is like nothing at my university."

"I would imagine not."

"Is the library open to all?" She looked back to the balcony and the couches and throw pillows. "Can anyone come here to read?"

"Yes and no. The library is open to all. This is my private balcony. Perks of being the current ruler."

"You read?" she asked.

"I have to. Eniraath is closed off to the world. I cannot be an efficient ruler without knowing the history of other peoples and governments."

She tilted her head. "I meant for fun. Do you read anything for fun?"

"The study of why the Great Migration occurred is not fun?" I teased. "Is learning how the supernatural world was revealed to humans at large on planet Earth and the subsequent governmental scramble to establish new human and supernatural laws not interesting?"

She laughed.

"I meant, do you read fiction? I like romance, for example."

"Ah." I turned around and walked to the coffee table surrounded by the couches and picked up a book. "I am reading this book currently."

I handed her a green hardback book.

She opened it. "It's a diary? Wait, these dates and entries . . ." She ran her hands over the pages. "Some of these say year 2037 . . ." She turned a page. "2267 . . . then 1918?" She turned another page. "1509?" She looked up at me. "This doesn't make sense."

"It's a diary from Earth. And her name was Annephine Pranais."

"What is it about?"

"She was a human who lived through the Great Migration.

She helped the Naaviri population on Earth evacuate. Quite the heroine for my kind."

"And the various dates?"

I smiled and took the book. "You will have to wait until I'm done so you can read it for yourself."

"Is there romance?"

"*Quite.*" I chuckled. "Annephine is rather descriptive."

"Well now I'm curious." She pouted, and I wanted to lean down right there and kiss her.

But I wouldn't.

She doesn't want you.

At least she knew I desired her. I craved her. And although my body's physical reactions had a lot to do with the mate bond and the arousal effects of the blood, I was starting to *like* her.

I cleared my throat and placed the book back down on the table. When I walked back to her, Renna was leaning against the door frame that led into the library.

"I wish I could spend the entire day here," she said. "I feel like I could easily get lost here and forget the rest of the world exists."

"You are welcome to come here. I will enable the shield around Eniraath to allow you entry."

A smile that did not reach her eyes appeared, and she looked down to where her fingers were fidgeting.

"Perhaps after everything is done," she whispered.

I knew what she meant.

Everything with Sethos.

Her father.

The battle that loomed.

A feeling of unease gnawed at me.

I wanted to help Renna with every fiber of my being, and it was within my power to do so . . .

But she would never agree to it.

Renna was too stubborn. Too proud. Too independent. All qualities I liked in her.

Which is why I could not further rob her freedom.

I cleared my throat. "We should portal back."

She looked up at me. "Are you feeling better? How are your bloodlust symptoms?"

A smile tugged at the corner of my lips. "Does it look like I'm ready to commit murder?"

She graced me with another of her laughs. It lit up her entire face, and when she leaned her head back, my eyes dropped to her throat. My pulse raced thinking of the next time she would allow me to drink from her.

Divica's words and the manner in which she had spoken to Renna came back to me. No one shamed me for the partners and experiences I had. In fact, no one shamed men.

The fault was always with women and their sexuality.

No one dared speak to my sister in the manner in which Divica had spoken to Renna, and I knew it was because of who I was and the protection Cressida had.

No one would speak to Renna in that manner ever again.

"I'm sorry Divica said those things to you," I said. "None of what she said was true. I cannot support when women are disrespected."

Renna nodded. "I'd rather not talk about it."

"Understood."

Renna tilted her head to the side. "You surprise me."

I lifted my eyebrows. "Why?"

"Some men I have met treat women like sexual objects, always trying to whet their appetite. We are a means to an end. You're respectful and kind. You treat me like your equal."

I frowned. "Because you are my equal."

She gave me a soft smile. "Where did you learn how to treat women this way?"

My body tensed, and I had to walk away from her. I hated thinking about my father. The man I had killed. I walked to the balcony edge and gripped the handrail.

"We don't have to talk about it," she said and placed her hand on my shoulder. "I'm sorry if I upset you."

I settled my eyes on my people below and how calm and free they moved about their days. I knew I had made the right choice in killing my father. He had been a tyrant.

"My father was an unkind man," I told Renna. "He was a womanizer and treated the people around him like property."

"I know a thing or two about terrible fathers," she said in a soft voice. "I'm sorry you, too, had that experience." She dropped her hand from my shoulder, but out of instinct, I caught her hand and held it.

I marveled at how well our hands fit together. I looked to Renna and the warmness in her eyes and hesitant smile. I wanted to bask in her warmth like a feline stretching under sunlight. She was magnetic, and I found safety in her presence.

I wanted to share everything I was with her.

And so I continued. "He was not a physical abuser, at least not many times, but he resorted to emotional and psychological abuse. He liked to belittle people. To manipulate and humiliate others."

Renna nodded and looked across the landscape, as if her mind was recalling her own experiences.

"Sometimes," she said, "psychological abuse is far worse than physical blows. To get inside someone's head . . ."

I rubbed my thumb over the top of her hand. "I'm sorry."

She looked back at me and said, "I'm sorry too."

"My mother tried to take her life several times because she could not withstand my father's treatment. She tried to leave Eniraath to seek treatment for the abuse in a neighboring galaxy, but he denied it every time, threatening to banish her from ever seeing me again.

"My mother's lineage had some Ancestors with bloodlust, but she never showed signs. When my father began to abuse her during pregnancy and pose a threat to her unborn child, my sister Cressida, her bloodlust activated.

"In her last attempt to leave, she was pregnant with my sister. My father caught my mother and incarcerated her. He put her in solitary confinement. She went mad."

Renna grabbed my other hand from the handrail. I had been squeezing the rail so tightly that my knuckles were white. She took both my hands and rubbed her thumbs on the inside of my palms. I closed my eyes as her touch calmed me.

I continued. "Bloodlust gives a Naaviri heightened strength. She broke from her cell and killed several of the guards, even her maid. She almost killed me when I was alerted and went to try and help her. She hadn't recognized me in the haze of bloodlust."

My heart began to pound fast as I thought of me being a liability to Renna, of attacking her.

I pulled my hands back gently to not startle her, but Renna stopped my progress and laced her fingers with mine.

"It's okay," she said. "You are okay."

"Renna," I said, shaking my head. "You are afraid of being like your father. I am afraid of being a danger to you because of what I am."

"I'm not afraid of you," she said, her eyes going back and forth between mine.

I looked up to the sky as if I could find counsel there.

"What did your father do when your mother nearly killed you?" she asked.

I sighed. "Medics were eventually able to subdue her and put her in a coma long enough so she could be induced and give birth.

A coma is the only way to subdue a Naaviri in bloodlust, but the danger is catching a Naaviri and controlling them enough to initiate a coma." I paused, recalling those chaotic weeks, especially for a fifteen-year-old. "But whatever medicine the medics gave her was not enough. I was told my mother woke almost instantly and she was rabid. My father chained and starved her of blood. She became weak, and I knew he ordered her to be beaten daily. I knew he enjoyed her suffering. He would laugh about it and taunt me."

Renna moved her hands up to my biceps, her grip almost an embrace.

"Did you ever see her again?" she asked me.

I shook my head. "No. My father sent me to fight in the Galactic Wars shortly thereafter. He claimed my worry over my mother and my pleas to see her made me weak. When I was sent away, Father continued to deny my requests to see her, and I was ordered to remain at camp. I was told she died a few weeks after giving birth."

"Who told you of her death?"

"My aunt. She wrote to me with the news."

Renna squeezed my arms. "I am so sorry, Aeroth."

"I made a vow to never be like my father and mistreat women," I told her. "It's one of the codes I live by."

She smiled. "You would make your mother proud."

I shook my head. "She'd likely tell me to stay away from you. As much as possible, anyway. Naaviri with bloodlust are not safe around our kin."

"She sounds like a brave woman."

"She was."

"A brave woman who had to survive difficult situations for her children. She must have also known her own mind."

I opened my mouth to agree, but she cut me off.

"I, too, know my own mind," Renna said, her voice harder. "Don't tell me what is or is not good for me."

I blinked.

"I know you will not hurt me," Renna repeated.

"Renna—"

In that moment, she stepped up to me and her fingers covered my lips as if to keep me from talking. Her skin was soft and warm against my lips, and my own skin tingled at her touch.

"Don't," she said.

Then, as if she realized how close we stood and that she was touching me, she instantly dropped her hand and stepped away. Her skin turned a beautiful red and she looked away, and it took every control in me not to grab her hand and place it against me again.

I closed my eyes and rubbed a hand over my face.

I needed to focus.

"And if I feel like I am becoming a danger to you?" I asked. "If I feel like the bloodlust will overtake me? What then?"

"You need to tell me if it gets that bad."

I scoffed. "I doubt I would have the chance. I would become unrecognizable. I wouldn't know who you were."

"That's not true—"

"I will leave if it ever comes to that," I told her. "I will remove myself."

She frowned. "Don't say that."

"I'm being a realist, Renna. We have to prepare for that eventuality."

"So you'd just leave me?" Her voice was raised. "With no warning?"

I grew silent. I wasn't sure of the answer. We stared at each other for a long while.

"Portal to Eniraath should I ever go missing. My sister will know how to help you. I will make arrangements with her."

Renna moved away from me and crossed her arms, frustration lining her face.

"And what then? You will need to come down from your bloodlust. The last time, you had to feed off a volunteer to subside from bloodlust. You are not married yet. Will you need to find another willing participant in the interim?" she spat. "I'm sure you won't have any trouble finding a willing woman."

I studied her. Her face was flushed and her breathing was ragged, as if she was seething with fury.

Was she jealous?

The thought of her jealousy was partly thrilling, because it meant she felt something for me that went deeper than mere attraction. But I also did not want to play with her feelings. She needed to understand the severity of bloodlust.

I crossed my arms. "And what do you suggest I do?"

Her voice was calm. "If it gets to that point, feed from me."

I moved close to her so that our noses almost touched. "You have no idea what you are asking. Do you think I merely drank that woman's blood while I waited for my bloodlust to recede?"

Renna's blush turned darker. I licked my lips.

"I fucked her," I whispered. "I fucked her day and night. I turned her into my plaything. I played out all my fantasies and desires with her. And she begged me to fuck her. Every time." I looked at her lips. "That is what you are asking for."

Renna's eyes were wide, her pupils dilated. Her lips parted slightly.

"No matter how kind you think I am now," I told her, "I would not be able to offer you gentility in those moments. I wouldn't be making love to you. I would be fucking you and taking from you."

Renna swallowed, and my eyes moved to her throat. I resisted the urge to pull her to me and dive into the ecstasy that was her blood.

I curled my fists to keep myself in place.

I waited for her to respond, to say anything, but Renna remained silent.

"If that time comes," Renna said, her voice low, barely a whisper, "we will get through it together. We will find medics to help us. I know you will not hurt me. You can speak to me in my mind. Tell me when the bloodlust is emerging so that I am not left wondering where you are. Allow me to come to you and help."

I shook my head. "Did you hear nothing of what I said?"

Her eyes dropped to her hands, which were clasped. "Perhaps we should go back to my sisters," she said.

I grabbed her chin and lightly lifted it so her eyes faced mine. "Promise me you will come to Eniraath if I go missing."

"Don't leave me when you need help. There is strength in allowing others to help you."

"I may not have a choice."

"There is *always* a choice," she said with gritted teeth.

"Then we agree to disagree on what will happen when that time comes."

"*If* that time comes, then we can prevent it."

I turned from her and opened a portal and extended my hand. "Let's go back to your sisters. Hopefully Divica is gone by the time we arrive."

She put her palm in mine, but her touch was cold, the anger having dissipated the warmth from earlier.

"I don't like you sometimes," she murmured.

I couldn't help but smile. "Well that's a shame. Because I happen to like you a lot."

Her eyes flashed to mine, anger swirling there. "Don't try and make me smile," she snapped.

I couldn't help but grin. "You have a beautiful smile."

She rolled her eyes. "You're impossible. You're being dismissive, and it's making me hate you right now."

I stepped close and cupped her jaw in my palms.

"I want you to stay safe. Even if it's way from me," I whispered.

"The bloodlust is not something I want you to witness. I care too much for you."

"I care about you too, Aeroth," she grumbled.

Her response made my chest grow, and I grinned. She was an extraordinary woman. She was brave and fearless.

"I don't mean to be dismissive of how you feel. But bloodlust is something that afflicts *me*. I should get to decide how to deal with it. I'm sorry you feel differently."

She moved my hands from her jaw and sighed.

"Let's head back," she said, looking at the portal. "We will never get anywhere with this conversation."

"Of course," I said. I extended my hand to hers, and she took it. Together, we stepped through the portal.

27

DEMIRA

Illona seldom got angry.

She was the picture of grace and composure. The perfect princess, and if she wanted to, *queen*.

Which was why I did not recognize her now as she paced the room, cursing Cylas under her breath.

"He's an inconsiderate ass," she fumed as she fidgeted with her dress.

"He's a god, what did you expect?" I asked. I perched on the windowsill overlooking the forest below. "They care for none but themselves."

Cylas and Divica had engaged in a lengthy shouting match, and from what we could hear, now they had turned to other . . . pursuits.

I wanted to vomit.

"He knows we can hear him and *her*," Illona continued. "And yet he doesn't give a shit. I can't stand it!"

"Why are you so bothered by him?" I asked, rolling my eyes. "They deserve each other. So what?"

Illona's eyes bored into mine. "She's taking advantage of him. I could . . ." she seethed, and curled her fists. "I could . . ."

I narrowed my eyes. "You could what?"

Illona sat on her bed and lay on her back.

"Say it," I told her. "Let it out."

"I wish I could set a demon on her to haunt her for the rest of her days."

I laughed. "Illona, stop perpetuating the demon stereotype. They are not all bad. You know this." I shook my head and stood. I walked to her bed and lay down next to her so we were side by side. "What is this truly about? You never lose your temper like this. It's usually just me."

She chuckled. "And Renna. I heard her threaten Divica."

I rolled my eyes. "She doesn't count."

She turned to look at me. "She's our sister."

I lifted my eyebrow and turned my head to stare at the ceiling. "Not really."

"We share blood with her. Renna is not going anywhere, Demira. You better get used to it."

I groaned. Illona's ancestral gifts meant she always knew information I did not. Where I had visions of a distant future, Illona knew exactly what would happen because the Ancestors told her everything. Was Illona talking in general about Renna being a part of our family? Or was it that she would be in our everyday lives?

"I don't know how I should feel about Renna," I admitted.

Illona sat up and looked down at me. "She's been nothing but nice to me. She's suffered as much as us, Demira. Except she had no one growing up. At least we had each other."

Before Illona was born, I had Sethos to lean on. The elusive, adopted son who was kind to me when I was a child, but grew up to be a resentful man and cast me aside. Then, when I turned eighteen, Illona came along and I had become her sole caretaker after our father wanted nothing to do with her. After Illona's mother died in childbirth, her mother's family in the Elemental

Enclave wanted nothing to do with a child of Am-Re. I had fought to keep her when Am-Re considered sending her away. Sometimes I regretted having asked for Illona to remain with me because of the abuse we suffered.

"You have hated Renna for a long time, Demira. You need to let that hatred go."

Hating Renna for our circumstances was logical. She was someone to blame and direct my hate to when I couldn't fight back against our father when he lived. We thought she was dead—our father never told us he reincarnated her.

I never imagined I would ever meet her. The way she spoke to Divica, with rage and fire, I recognized within myself, made me oddly respect her.

I pursed my lips.

"I don't like when you get that look . . ." Illona sighed.

I frowned. "What look?"

Illona rolled her eyes. "The one where you are about to act impulsively. And I will no doubt have to clean up after you."

The image of Renna's unflinching demeanor when Divica threatened her made my blood begin to boil.

I always tried to prove to my father I was worthy of being his daughter. Even when he used to call us useless, I strived to prove I deserved his love and attention.

If Renna could stand up to Divica, I could too.

I sat up and swung my legs off the bed to stand.

Illona stood up. "What's going on?"

"Divica can play games with that idiot, but not with me."

I stormed out of Illona's room and descended the spiral stairs to the main level—toward Cylas's room.

"You cannot be serious," Illona said as she hurried behind me. "Don't tell me you're going in there!"

I looked back to her. "You're the one who had to endure an entire night of listening to him fuck her. Enough is enough."

Illona blushed.

I shuddered. "What the fuck is he doing to her? She sounds like a fucking animal squealing as it's being slaughtered. He cannot be that good."

Illona covered her mouth at my words, and her step almost faltered.

An uneasy feeling skirted over me about her reaction.

Did my sister feel something for Cylas?

I shook my head.

Nothing good would come from it, and it angered me that Illona might have feelings for someone like him.

That anger propelled forward until I reached the first floor and thundered to Cylas's door. I called my magic forth and willed Violet Fire to my palms. Heat shot through my veins and down to my palms as the magic appeared, the deep-violet flames a stark contrast to my pale skin.

With my magic, I forced the door open.

Divica shrieked, and Cylas cursed. A flurry of green and blue magic flashed before me, and I could see Divica in the corner of the room, righting her clothes.

Cylas sat on his bed, a black sheet covering the lower half of his body.

A deep scowl settled on his face.

"Are you quite finished?" I yelled at him. "How long does it take to fuck one person?"

A smirk formed on his lips as he settled his back against his headboard, quirking an eyebrow. "Are you here to find out?"

"How *dare* you!" Divica screamed, storming forward, her hair raised and staff pointed at me.

"Where are the Metidons riders?" I gritted out.

She laughed, and the cruel sound made me want to burn her. The Violet Fire at my palms jumped as if it knew. Illona touched my arm in warning.

"Unlike Cylas," I told Divica, "my body is not for sale. And I don't like to wait."

Divica turned to look at the man in question. "You're going to let her talk about you in that way?"

Cylas glared at me. A flash of hurt passed through his eyes but was gone instantly. "Leave."

"Leave *where*?" I narrowed my eyes. "There isn't a single place in this fucking tree house where we can't hear you fucking her."

"You have a colorful vocabulary."

"What do you want me to say? We've had enough. Illona can't even think!"

His face softened then, and his eyes slid to Illona, who was now at my side.

"Divica," he said, now looking at the sprite queen. His voice was calm. "We need to talk about the riders. We've dallied long enough."

"Dallied?" she yelled. "*Dallied?*"

Divica floated to Cylas and was a top him with the handle of her staff at his throat, pushing down. Cylas did not fight back and simply lay there.

"You are worthless," Divica gritted to him.

"*Cylas,*" Illona said, her voice like ice.

His eyes, now with tears, slid to hers.

"Why are you letting her do this to you? *Get up,*" she told him.

I looked to Illona, who had taken a step toward his bed. Her eyes were like a raging fire; she looked like she wanted to eviscerate Divica.

On second thought, I could subdue Divica with Alaric Chains . . .

Cylas then morphed into black sand, disappearing from under Divica, and materialized again across the room.

Divica shot up on the bed and stomped her feet, screaming

from what could only be frustration. I rolled my eyes at her childish display.

"You cannot be seriously attracted to him," I muttered to Illona.

Illona lowered her eyes.

Cylas cleared his throat, his eyes searching Illona's as if he had heard me and was seeing her for the first time.

Interesting.

"Divica," Cylas said again. His tone was harder. "Where are the rider descendants?"

Divica grimaced and hovered off the bed to the ground.

"I would have told you, but unfortunately your friend Demira pissed me off—"

"*Divica,*" Cylas said again, his tone now colder. "Where are they? This affects all of us! We cannot let Am-Re and Sethos go unchecked."

Divica smiled. "Am-Re was never my problem. He is *your* problem. Sethos doesn't affect my life."

Illona chuckled and shook her head. "See," she said, stepping close to Divica. "That is the problem with people like you. You refuse to speak or act on behalf of others in need simply because you don't consider their plight your issue. It makes you complicit in suffering."

Divica simmered at the accusation. "You are a sheltered young woman. A fucking princess. You know nothing of ruling. If I get involved and help you, then I put my people at risk." Divica crossed her arms. "Am-Re is *not* my enemy. Neither is Sethos."

Illona shook her head slowly. "You were never going to tell us. You used Cylas."

Divica smiled sweetly and looked to him. "*And?* He used me. He left me to marry another."

"You are cruel and *vile*—"

Divica laughed at Illona. "And you are a waste of space. We all know your father didn't want you. Go kill yourself."

At her words, Illona shrank back in shame, and Cylas rushed toward her.

And then I lost control.

Within seconds, I conjured Alaric Chains and cuffed Divica's ankle. She screamed and sank to the ground as her body contorted. I grabbed her staff and pointed it at her jugular, pressing the crystal into her skin until blood started trickling in a steady stream down her neck.

"Where the fuck are the rider descendants?" I yelled. "What cave?"

Divica coughed and screamed, but she could not form words.

I threw her staff across the room and got on top of her, grabbing her by the shoulders to slam her back against the ground.

"Tell me!" I roared.

Divica coughed.

I slammed her body again. She had not lost consciousness yet, as she only had one cuff on her body. I had survived with two.

"*Where are they?*" I screamed.

"At the edge of the Russet Mountains—" she choked out.

I looked to Cylas. "Can you find them?"

"Yes," he said. "All but two mountains on Elinoor are covered in forest. The Russet Mountains are just rock and barren soil."

I took one step closer to Divica. "If you are lying—"

"Let her go," Cylas barked. "This type of torture is immoral. You should know."

"She disrespected Illona," I snapped. "Who was defending *you*. Did you do something about it?"

He clenched his jaw.

"I'm sorry." Divica's chest was heaving as she spoke to me. "I'm sorry, please don't kill me."

I looked down to Divica and spat at her, "You will never look at or speak to my sister ever again. *Do you understand?*"

Divica managed to nod.

Illona stepped up next to me and leaned down to place her hand on my shoulder. With a soft voice, she said, "Let her go."

I used Divica's chest to push up to stand, and she groaned under me in pain.

Good.

Once I stood, I waved my hand and willed the cuff around her leg to dissolve.

Divica lay still for a few moments before turning to her side and using her arms to cautiously push herself to sit. Her ankle had a black ring of burned skin. She did not look at any of us as tears ran down her face.

I walked across the room to retrieve her staff and threw it down at her. The staff clattered on the ground, and Divica looked up, her eyes wide.

"Leave," I gritted out. "And you better hope you never cross my path again."

Divica slowly looked down at her staff, as if she didn't want to touch it. As if it were an evil thing.

Divica's voice was low. "You should not have touched my staff, you stupid girl."

I blinked. "Take it with you. It's garbage. Like its owner."

She shook her head. "You have no idea what you have done."

Her words didn't make sense, but I did not care at the moment. "Did you not hear me?" I screamed and leaned down closer. "*Leave!*"

Divica whimpered, and in a flash, she was gone. Her staff was the only thing that remained.

I picked it up, and as I left, I threw it across the room, crashing against a mirror. The mirror fell, shattering into a million pieces.

28

RENNA

When Aeroth and I arrived back in Elinoor, we were met with screams.

Demira, Illona, and Cylas were engaged in a shouting match in the living room.

"We should have stayed behind," Aeroth murmured to me.

At that moment, Demira turned to us.

"Oh good," she said with an acidic tone. "Let's ask *them* what they think."

I frowned. "What are you talking about?"

Demira rolled her eyes, crossed her arms, and opened her mouth, but Cylas cut her off.

"We now know where the entrance of the cave is. I know the Russet Mountains. I created this planet."

My heart raced and I almost clapped, but Illona interjected.

"We have to walk there," she said.

Cylas glared at her. "We do not. Walking there will take two days. We can portal there and arrive in the blink of an eye."

Illona clenched her fists and looked to him. "And I've told you, we have to walk. That is what the Ancestors have said we must do."

"Why do we have to walk?" Aeroth asked. "Cylas is right, portaling will be easier."

"*Thank you!*" Cylas yelled. He looked to Illona. "You are worse than Livina."

Illona's eyes widened. "The Goddess of Fate?"

Cylas crossed his arms. "The very same. She refuses to expand on why things must be done a certain way."

She sighed but continued. "The Ancestors will not tell me why we have to walk to the cave, only that we must. We cannot portal there."

"I will walk with my sister," Demira said and moved to stand next to her. "If you don't like it, you can leave this mission, Cylas."

He laughed. "So that's how this is, then?" He shook his head. "You used me."

Demira tilted her head. "No. Divica used you."

Cylas's jaw dropped.

"But you knew that when you agreed to fuck Divica," she added. "We won't force you to follow us."

He shook his head. "This is madness. You know there are bounty hunters looking for you. Why take the risk?"

Divica took a step closer to Cylas. "Because I trust my sister. And if she tells me we have to walk there, we will walk there. We will defend ourselves. With or without you."

Cylas narrowed his eyes as he glared at her.

In that moment, I knew that I needed to take a stand. Aeroth clearly preferred to portal like Cylas, but I could not in good conscience leave Demira and Illona alone. They had brought me here after all, allowing me the chance to go to Taria. If I traveled with them, Aeroth would follow for added protection.

"I will go with Demira and Illona."

Everyone turned to look at me. Demira nodded in thanks. Illona smiled.

I smiled back. "Did the ancestor tell you I would be traveling with you?"

She looked between Aeroth and me and gave us a smug smile. "They did."

I did not know what to make of her comment, or her glances between Aeroth and me, but we had no time to waste.

"Cylas?" I asked him. "Are you coming with us?"

He rolled his eyes. "If I must. I told Khellios I would protect you, dutiful servant I am."

I chuckled.

Aeroth spoke up. "I, too, want to protect Renna, but I'm beginning to believe we need her to protect us. Khellios must have not seen her Darkness."

I looked up at him, and he smirked at me.

"Did the Ancestors tell you when we are supposed to leave to the caves?" Cylas asked Illona.

"When the first full moon descends on Elinoor."

Cylas frowned. "There are three moons on Elinoor. The first one is full tomorrow."

"Then we travel tomorrow," Demira stated. "Is that a problem?"

Cylas took a step toward Demira. "Do you normally put words in people's mouths?" he snapped.

"Are we going to have to witness this constant showdown every day?" Aeroth whispered to me. "I don't know how much more of this I can take."

I sighed. "Aeroth and I are going outside before night falls," I announced.

"We are?" he murmured to me.

"Yes," I answered loudly. "Aeroth and I saw a small courtyard before we came inside. We are going to work on drills with our weapons. If we get attacked on the way to the caves, I would like to be prepared."

"May I join you?" Illona asked.

I smiled. "Of course. What is your weapon of choice?"

She hugged her arms. "I have never fought before. I tend to stay away from weapons."

"I've tried teaching you countless times," Demira stated.

Illona nodded. "I know. I want to learn now."

"There won't be much time to teach you between now and nightfall," Aeroth said. "But I'm sure we can teach you the basics."

Illona's smile lit up the room. "I would love to learn what you can share."

"I'll come with," Demira said. "I rely more on magic than weapons, but it will be good to see."

I nodded. "The more, the merrier. Let's go."

Cylas spoke. "I will stay inside. I will probably sleep. Might as well get some sleep if we're going to be on the road."

Demira rolled her eyes. "Good. Being in bed seems to be the thing you excel at."

Cylas's jaw tensed. "I will be glad once this is all over so I may never cross paths with you again."

Demira smiled. "As will I."

I closed my eyes and massaged my temples.

"You okay?" Aeroth murmured and touched my arm.

"I don't know how much more of Demira and Cylas I can take either," I whispered back.

29

KHELLIOS

I looked out at the endless mountains of sand, a common sight on the desert planet of Nelar.

That and the rows of war camp tents.

Ukara's ghost army glittered in the distance as they worked on drills.

To my right, various gods from the Elemental and Spiritual enclave gathered in a ring to practice.

Shadows covered us for a brief moment, and I looked up. Three angels soared above us, surveying the land.

"This is quite the turnout."

I looked to my left at Elrie.

Her white, padded shirt was covered in sweat from practicing with her troops. Her chest heaved as she flashed me a smile, a sword in hand.

"You left the lists," she said, looking me over. "Did we bore you?"

"I'm anxious," I confided. "I needed to clear my head."

"You've seen battle before, Khel." She walked closer to me and put down her sword on a table with maps spread over it.

She was right, I had seen many battles in my life—many with

Am-Re. Am-Re had fought with Arios plenty of times. He'd also fought with us.

Gods liked to fight each other one-on-one. It was a cleaner fight. But this time, it was different. We had never dealt with the number of troops coming our way, plus they were enchanted.

We knew the troops included different supernaturals, which presented a whole new dynamic. For a god to attack a species could shift the balance of peace, and Sethos was forcing us to engage with mages, tree beings, and other creatures. It could set off retaliation by the people of the soldiers who were enchanted.

Memories of the Galactic Wars flashed through my mind, and my body tensed. Everyone fought everyone in those wars, especially as people came to their allies' defense.

It was carnage.

Destruction.

Years of it.

That was why the Galactic Federation wanted us to avoid war and had sent for the fae monarchs to deal with Sethos directly. But now, with Sethos coming our way, the conflict had escalated.

And Am-Re was back.

Reports had reached us of his presence in various parts of this universe and planets.

What was he doing?

Was he working with Sethos?

I shook my head. Sethos had told us he killed Am-Re. Nothing made sense.

"Talk to me," Elrie said, walking to stand in front of me. Her big blue eyes searched my face.

"I don't like that this conflict has escalated to this level. I'm afraid for your safety. I'm afraid that we have not been able to locate Sethos or his army as they travel."

Elrie nodded. "Hearing the God of Witchcraft talk last night about the dark magic involved to fuel Sethos's army is disturbing."

It was the night before the Spiritual Enclave arrived to our aid. In the enclave was Tekah, the Goddess of Witchcraft. Her assessment of the magic involved in controlling the army, in addition to Am-Re being back, had her baffled. A lone fae like Sethos should not be able to command the power he did. Even if he had absorbed Am-Re's magic when physically killing him, Am-Re's magic would not have been capable of such a feat.

And if Am-Re was back in some form or another, that meant Am-Re's magic was regenerating.

There was only so much magic to go around . . .

Something was very wrong.

"Khel," Elrie said and grabbed my arms.

I looked down at her.

"It will be alright," she said. "We have so much help. We will defeat Sethos."

"And Am-Re?"

Her lips formed a tight line. "Everything will be alright."

"The fae monarchs will focus on taking Sethos out to halt the battle. We have to trust the process."

"I don't want you hurt, Elrie."

She smiled and placed a palm on my jaw.

"My father is on his way," she reminded me. "With more troops. I am certain my father has told them their *only* task is to keep me alive. He won't let anything happen to me."

I covered her hand with mine.

"I won't let anything happen to you. You are too important to me."

She blushed and dropped her hand from me. She hugged her arms and spun around to look at the landscape.

"Did I say anything wrong?" I asked, now standing next to her.

"Words and just words." She shrugged. "It's the meaning we assign to them that matters."

I stood in front of her now and looked down. "I mean it, El." I searched her face. "I will keep you safe."

She shook her head and squared her shoulders.

"I want to be important to you," she said and stepped closer.

I swallowed.

"Elrie . . ."

She moved her eyes down my body, taking her time, and my body became tense at her perusal. My heart raced, threatening to shatter through the gold armor on my chest.

"Khel," she whispered, now looking at my lips. "Help me."

My lips became dry, and I ran my tongue over them.

Elrie and I had been dancing around each other for weeks. Between the excuse of trying to find Renna and the mourning process of letting her go, I'd put up a barrier between Elrie and I. But her boldness was slowly wearing me down.

"You need help?" I whispered, now also looking at her lips.

"*Yes,*" she said, almost like a plea.

Elrie spun around and gave me her back. The table with the maps was in front of her.

She turned her head to the side to look at me.

"My bindings," she said, her voice so soft. "Undo the laces for me. I cannot reach them..."

I swallowed and shook my head. Her bindings ensured her breasts remained bound during combat. It resembled a corset. If I undid her laces, it would slide off and she would only be in her undershirt that was almost see-through.

"Khel," she said again, her voice breathless. "I need you."

Her words ran straight down to my cock, and I felt my member stir.

I looked to the entrance of my tent. No one stood there.

Good.

I paused—why did I care who stood by us? It wasn't like I would do anything. I had not been with a woman in a long time. I had not even tried to bed Renna because I wanted to go slow. I wanted to be a gentleman.

But Elrie was now here. And she wanted me.

And I ached.

Elrie placed her hands on the table and arched her back. She looked over her shoulder back at me.

"My bindings, Khel."

I could only hold back so much.

My eyes zeroed in on Elrie's lips—the first lips I had kissed after Renna's passing, when I had stayed in her father's kingdom during my years as a mercenary.

I would never forget what kissing Elrie was like. And the guilt that flowed afterward for feeling like I had betrayed Renna's memory and that of our unborn child.

I blinked as my heart struggled with grief and the sudden urge to push it aside and focus on the woman before me now.

How did a man move on after he lost everything?

Was I unique in my grief process, or were there other men like me who felt undeserving to move on? I felt like I had one foot in my past and the other yearning to take a step forward.

I took a deep breath and tried to focus on Elrie.

She did not deserve me to give her anything but my full attention.

Elrie was putting everything on the line to pursue me, and I did not want to leave her disappointed.

And so I walked to her. And when her smile grew at my approach, I reached to undo her laces.

They were coarse to the touch as I began to undo them. I wondered what she wore underneath in that moment, and my cock twitched.

A growl emerged from me. "Face forward."

Elrie blushed and moved only her head in obedience.

I pulled at her laces hard so that her back landed flush against me.

Her grunts were soft as her body swayed back each time, her ass pushing against my cock.

Experiencing her move against me was tempting and erotic. I closed my eyes and recalled the encounter we shared in her father's kingdom. In her arms then, I had allowed myself to pretend I was not mourning for Renna.

Elrie had approached me during a banquet held in my honor. She and various other women in her father's court had donned masks and put on a dance. When she approached me, I did not know it was her. But even then, in the back of my mind, I fantasized it was her. She was the most beautiful woman in her father's court.

And so when the masked woman approached me, I pictured it was Elrie with her legs wrapped around mine.

Her body had been open for me . . .

Wet.

Slick.

Warm.

Quivering.

Tight around my fingers.

Pulsing.

Wanting.

Her walls hugging my fingers so that she was pushing me out.

Crying out.

I hadn't known it was her. Not until a few months ago when she confessed.

My mind swirled to the present.

The woman I had fantasized about.

Here in the flesh.

"Elrie," I groaned and dropped my hands from the laces.

She whimpered in disappointment, but when my hands rested beside hers on the table, my body caging her in, pressing her down, she moaned.

"Khel," she moaned. "The tent. Others will see."

I moved my head down to the back of her neck and kissed her there.

I called my magic and willed the tent flaps to close. In moments, we were surrounded in darkness.

"Khel," she moaned. "I want you."

I nodded against her head. "I know."

"*I ache, Khel,*" she whispered, her voice ragged with her breaths. She pushed back against me, and my cock stirred.

I squeezed my eyes and grabbed her hands on the table. I would always remember it was Elrie who had made me forget Renna all those years ago.

And now Renna and I had no future, and Elrie was here again.

It would be so easy to rush into whatever this was with Elrie.

But Elrie meant more to me than a quick fuck.

She deserved to be worshipped.

And not for me to think about another woman.

She pressed herself against me, and I tightened my hands around hers.

Gods.

"I need you to do something for me." My voice was low as I leaned above her, my chest on her back.

Elrie arched more under me. "Yes?"

My lips tingled as they brushed her ear.

"Come to me after each practice so that I may undo your bindings. Fully."

She moaned.

"Can you do that for me?" I asked. I moved my hands down to her hips and squeezed.

She nodded.

"Use your words."

"*Yes, Khel.*"

As I rose off her, I kissed the back of her head.

"Good."

Gods this woman.

"You will drive me to the edge, Elrie."

She turned her head to the side and cast me a wicked look. "That's the point." She smirked.

"Your troops will wonder where you are."

She stood and turned to face me.

"Perhaps," she said softly as she placed her hands on my chest. "I am right where I am meant to be."

30

RENNA

I sat against the wall with my eyes closed, the sounds of Aeroth bathing in the tub next to me.

We had trained for the entire evening with Demira and Illona before we all decided to rest for the night. When we arrived back in my room and I told Aeroth I needed to shower, he accompanied me to the bathroom and stood with his back to me while I showered. Despite Aeroth insisting I could take my time, my shower was lightning fast.

Aeroth had opted for a bath, and because I didn't want to stand and wait for him, I opted to sit beside the tub.

As the heat from the bath filled the room and wrapped itself around my skin, my muscles relaxed even more than when I was in the shower. I tried hard to not doze off.

"Has anyone told you that you take the longest baths?" I asked, shifting so I could stretch my legs in front of me. "I would expect this from a woman."

Aeroth huffed, and I could hear water stir. "How do you know this is my longest bath?"

I shook my head. "Zero consideration for others," I said under my breath.

"I told you to take a longer shower," he said, groaning.

I stilled. Aeroth's sounds drove down into my core, and I tried hard to concentrate on something else. *Anything*.

"Besides," he said with a long, low sigh, "since this tub is big enough for multiple people, I can stretch comfortably. Makes it hard to leave."

There was a silence, and my entire body flushed with self-consciousness as I recalled Aeroth's body that morning.

"Are you hot?" he asked.

"*Why?*"

It sounded like he moved in the water, and when he spoke, he was right next to me.

"You're flushed," he murmured.

Before I could respond, his wet hand was at my brow and he placed the back of his hand to my forehead.

I stayed still as his touch remained there, my heart racing.

"No fever." His voice was like a caress.

When he removed his hand, water droplets fell down my face.

"I'm wet now," I said, wiping my face with the back of my black long-sleeve shirt.

In that moment, I made the mistake of looking down at him. He was on the edge of the tub, so close to me. His large, tanned arms rested on the lip of the tub. The size of them next to my thighs made him look like a giant, and I remembered what it had felt like to lie under him and how he enveloped my body like a blanket.

His eyes bored into mine with an intensity that made my slick drip from my core. My chest tightened with something like longing.

"I'm not sorry," he murmured.

I shook my head to clear my mind and looked away. If I longed for Aeroth, it was the safety he provided-nothing more. It was natural to feel drawn to someone who provided a true haven after everything, right?

The fact that he was attractive, had told me he craved me, and that he made my heart gallop meant nothing. I pushed to stand and gave him my back.

"I want to lay down. Can you hurry?" I asked.

"Sure," he said, and I heard him emerge from the tub.

I remembered his towel was on his side of the bed, and that I would see him walk past me to grab it. Seeing him fully naked would fracture the composure I was trying to maintain. I quickly strode over to grab his towel so I could give it to him with my eyes closed, but when I reached out, our hands touched.

My skin prickled with awareness, and my core pulsed.

I swallowed and kept my eyes on the bed to avoid seeing the rest of his body.

Aeroth took the towel, and I could hear him arranging it around his waist.

I could understand why Source designed mate couples to remain together for one year during The Settling. The intimacy, even if not wanted, was unavoidable.

And my body was on fire.

I moved onto the bed to get space from him and crossed over the barrier of pillows onto my side. Within the blink of an eye, his hands were wrapped around my waist, and he hoisted me up in his arms.

"*Hey!*" I yelled and thrashed in his arms.

His body was so warm, and his muscles were so firm. My mouth watered.

I looked up at him, and a wide grin flashed across his mouth, his pearly white canines peeking out from his lip.

"*Put me down!*"

"That is my side of the bed now," he said with a head tilt.

"I was just going to cross onto my side!" I said with a huff.

He lifted an eyebrow and tossed me in the air onto my side.

I scrambled to sit up. "I'm not a sack of food to be tossed like that!"

He laughed and removed the towel from around his waist to dry his hair, and I squeezed my eyes shut and lay down.

"Your communal showers must have been terrible for you," Aeroth said with humor laced in his tone.

"Why do you say that?"

"You dislike nudity."

I laughed. "I don't dislike nudity."

"Oh really?"

I crossed my arms.

"Open your eyes, Renna."

My throat dried up. "I will not," I answered and cleared my throat.

"And why is that?"

"Because."

He chuckled. "Because what?"

"Because I'm setting a respectful boundary. You don't affect me."

I felt the bed dip from his side.

"I see."

I didn't respond.

"You're still flushed."

"Do you always say what is on your mind?" I snapped and opened my eyes to look at the ceiling.

"And what's wrong with that? I thought you would find the honesty refreshing."

I rolled my eyes. "Keep your thoughts to yourself."

"I don't want to."

My breath froze as his words reverberated inside me.

"Good night, Renna."

My breath came out in small huffs as the tension in my core throbbed. I shifted to press my thighs together.

"Good night," I whispered.

A thought came to me then. "You're clothed, right?"

He laughed.

"Why would I do that?"

My jaw dropped.

"To deprive your peeking in the morning seems cruel. Maybe this time you'll get a better look."

I covered my face with my hands and rolled onto my stomach. I wished the mattress would swallow me in that moment.

He laughed, and I felt the bed shift again.

"Do you typically sleep like that?" he asked. "Can you breathe?"

"Go away."

"My words seem to affect you."

"They don't."

"Don't suffocate, okay?" he teased.

I bit the inside of my cheek to prevent a smile. "I feel like suffocating when I think of your face."

"*Ah, yes.* You hate me. Good night, Renna."

When I felt the bed shift again and heard his breath even out, I moved into a more comfortable position and hugged the blankets closed as I willed myself to sleep.

31

RENNA

"Renna . . ." a voice whispered.

I was cold.

The warmth of my bedroom was gone, and I opened my eyes to find myself on a cold, rough stone floor.

My body was sore, and I blinked several times, disoriented.

The air was hazy, and a low fog spread through the ground while a strange glow filled the sky, basking everything in an eerie gray light.

"Aeroth?" I asked groggily and pushed to sit, continuing to look around.

My heart rate began to speed up.

I was in a garden with high hedges that extended high up to the sky. This was a garden I had been in multiple times before.

The labyrinth from my nightmares. I knew I was dreaming.

My body trembled, knowing how the dream would unfold, and I slowly stood.

I needed to wake up.

A movement to my right made me jump and I squealed, but there was nothing but hedges. My frosted breath came out in puffs of air.

After having this dream multiple times, I knew I would walk forward to step onto the pebbled path in front of me. I would enter the labyrinth and run around and around until my father's whistle would begin to echo through the hedges. Until I crouched to the floor and begged for the sound to stop.

I would run next and feel footsteps close at my heels, but no matter how many times I would spin around, I would not be able to see anything but dissipating shadows.

My father was the hunter.

And I was his sport.

Run, little girl, his voice would taunt in this nightmare.

Run.

Run like the little daughter of a whore you are.

His favorite slur to hurl at me when he raged.

Just let me put my hands on you, you shit, let me find you, and I will beat you until you wish you were never born.

I will fuck you up until my hand bleeds.

Do you remember when you screamed at me to leave your home when you were a teenager?

I hit you across the face and you saw black.

I dragged you to the couch then . . .

And got on top of you . . .

Straddled you so you could not escape . . .

And put my hands around your neck and squeezed.

Do you remember how you clawed for me to let you go?

I was drunk too.

But I remember every second of it.

And no one will ever know . . .

No one will ever believe you.

Who will you tell?

Who will believe you?

A sob caught in my throat at remembering my father's words that would surely echo in this dream like they always did.

I clenched my fists. Could one change dreams? I had never tried or had the consciousness inside of a dream to ask that question. Why this dream?

Screams broke out.

My breathing stopped and my hands flew to my mouth, and I listened. The sounds of a whip rang out like echoes while a male sobbed.

Not any male.

Sethos.

No.

More screams from inside the labyrinth.

I didn't want to enter it.

I didn't want to hurt.

"Renna!" Sethos screamed.

A hysterical cry surged from me, and I crumbled to the ground, not knowing what to do.

"Renna!"

I covered my mouth to prevent myself from screaming back.

Was this a trap?

Was the dream urging me to enter the labyrinth and, at my hesitation, creating the sound of Sethos calling for me to urge me to complete the dream?

I curled into a ball as Sethos continued to scream. And then I heard my father.

"You fucked her, didn't you?" he screamed.

My breathing froze. More whipping ensued.

"That is why you will not fully submit to me!"

I shot up to stand.

Was this truly a dream?

"Your fucking magic controls this army and you refuse to submit to me!" my father screamed.

Screams of agony filled the air, the sounds he was making high-pitched as if an animal was being slaughtered.

I ran. Straight into the labyrinth.

To Sethos.

As the screams of Sethos and my father filled the air, I used their voices to guide me.

Right. Left. Left. Right.

Pebbles flew as I made jagged turns and spun in circles, at times trying to find their voices. It felt like I could never get close to them. I was always some distance away.

I prayed for Sethos's safety, but I needed his screams to guide me, and it became a sick mental game where I didn't know if I wanted to hear him or not.

Could there be a possibility that this was more than a dream? Had I somehow transported to this space? If so, was anyone aware I was gone?

"You sick son of a whore," my father seethed.

His voice was close now.

"You are a lowlife," he continued. "How dare you touch my daughter."

Sethos groaned.

"You don't care for her," Sethos said, his voice barely a whisper. "Let me go."

His words stunned me. I moved with cautious steps to the right, close to where the voices came from.

"You think your actions of killing my body would have no consequence?" my father cackled. "You are my property. As you have always been."

Silence ensued then, and I paused my movements. The silence seemed to stretch forever. Sethos whimpered, and his sobs were barely audible. My heart twisted for him.

Still, the voice of my father was absent.

Had he left?

I looked down at my hands. Could I call my Black Fire in a dream?

I had to try.

I erected my personal energetic shield and commanded Black Fire onto my palms and imagined a bow and arrow.

I enchanted the arrow with venom, took in a deep breath, and cocked it. My footsteps were light as I made my way to the end of the path that would then curve to the left.

I squeezed my eyes shut for a quick moment and then . . .

One.

Two.

Three!

I turned a sharp left and almost dropped my weapons.

As if he were in a visible dimension apart from the labyrinth, Sethos was surrounded by gray smoke in a large room of sorts. It was like looking into a window, getting a glimpse of where he was. He was chained and nude, his body bruised purple and blue. His head slung down, and his blood dripped onto the floor and caked in his silver hair. One of his legs looked twisted, as if it were dislocated.

Tears stung my eyes, and as if he could sense me, he looked up slowly and locked eyes with me. One was black and swollen, sealed shut.

The other wept blood.

"No," I whispered. "This can't be real . . ."

I had forgotten my father for a moment, but now I turned to survey the space. I began to lower my weapon, but one sharp look from Sethos made me tighten my grip instead.

I walked closer to the image of where he was.

"This is a dream . . ." I whispered.

"This is a nightmare," he said, as if answering me.

Could he hear me?

"How can I see you?" I demanded. "Where are you?"

Suddenly my father's voice filled the air.

"Shift," he ordered.

Sethos remained silent and squeezed his eyes shut.

"I said, shift!" my father screamed.

I could not see him, but I knew he was in whatever dimension Sethos was.

"Shift! Transform!"

"Fuck you!" Sethos screamed back and slung his head down.

And then, black electric magic hit Sethos's side and began to burn his skin. Sethos cried out as his pale skin turned bulbous and scaly.

I watched as his spine broke, morphing into something long and wretched. Then his legs rearranged and the Sethos I knew was gone. I backed up as he turned into the beast from my nightmares. The one who attacked me and urged me to let go.

I shook my head.

He was my father's dretani.

I stumbled backward, grateful Sethos was not in the labyrinth but in a separate place. The beast screeched a thunderous roar, and my body shook from the noise and I screamed.

A distant voice rang in my ears.

"Renna!" a voice urged. "Wake up!"

I awoke in Aeroth's arms, holding me as I thrashed against him.

"Easy, easy," he said, pressing the side of his face against my temple. "I have you. You are safe."

My body shuddered as I opened my eyes to find us together in the bed. He was propped against the headboard on my pillow—pillow fortress gone—and the top half of my body was gathered in his arms. I noticed he wore a short-sleeve shirt.

"You were having a nightmare," he said. "What did you dream of?"

"Sethos," I managed. "I dreamt my father torturing him."

Aeroth ran his hands through my hair. His touch was soothing, and I melted into his embrace, my muscles relaxing in the safety of his arms.

"I'm sorry," Aeroth whispered.

"I have to help him, Aeroth."

He nodded against me. "I know you do."

"Please don't kill him." I glanced up at Aeroth. "*Please,*"

Aeroth looked down at me and his right palm cupped my jaw. "I don't ever want to be the cause of your suffering, Renna."

I nodded.

"But if he begins to kill others or threatens your life or mine—"

"I know."

This conversation always went around in circles. There were a lot of possibilities. We wouldn't know what would happen until we saw Sethos.

Aeroth moved his hand from my jaw and shifted from under me, settling on his pillow. He lay facing me, and I lay down next to him.

"I wish I didn't feel so much," I confessed.

Aeroth remained silent, observing me like always.

"Don't ever feel bad for caring, Renna. I like that about you."

My eyes searched his face. His words gave me hope and broadened my understanding of Aeroth. He had a big heart, but responsibility weighed heavily on him. In that moment, I could not prevent my comparison of Aeroth to Sethos.

Sethos also had a duty, but his heart was limited. I had not truly allowed myself to reflect on the constant state of unrest I felt when I was with him. Not until now.

Being in Aeroth's presence, aside from the bickering, felt easy. I didn't feel a need to prove myself around Aeroth. He liked who I was. He did not demand I change.

"Close your eyes, Renna. Dawn is still a bit away. I'll guard your sleep."

I shook my head. "I'm afraid."

Aeroth shifted so he could look at me. "Why?"

"When I was in Daya, I knew my father could not portal to me. And now I am exposed. Am-Re or Sethos could portal to me at any moment."

"Your father could not portal to you because he doesn't know you as an adult. He interacted with you as a child. He would need to know your current essence to imagine you and open a successful portal."

"And Sethos?"

Aeroth frowned. "If he wanted to portal to you, he would have already."

I nodded. I wondered why Sethos hadn't come looking for me.

"But if Sethos comes, you will not be alone," Aeroth said, his voice hard.

I settled back on Aeroth's chest and allowed my racing heart to settle. I was so tired from being afraid all the time.

Aeroth's arms tightened on me.

"I will always protect you, Renna. You are mine to keep safe."

I closed my eyes, allowing my body to sink against his.

"Thank you," I said.

"For what?"

"For letting me feel safe."

Aeroth gave me a small kiss on the top of my head.

"Always."

32

RENNA

I awoke in Aeroth's arms.

And I remained very still as his chest moved softly under me, my cheek and hand both resting on his chest. He still slept, and I watched in wonder as rays of daylight filtered into the room, creating a golden glow.

How different this was to waking up alone, or with Sethos, in the gray world of Daya.

At the thought of being in Sethos's arms, sickly feelings of shame filled me. I hated myself for giving my body to Sethos.

I started to extract myself from Aeroth's body and he stirred. His burgundy eyes opening to find mine.

"Morning," I said.

"You slept well?" he asked, while stretching his arms.

I nodded and moved my hair behind my ear.

"Did you want to shower this morning?" he asked. "I don't know what conditions look like for the rest of our trip. This may be your last shower for several days."

The thought of being naked by Aeroth added to my shame as I thought back to my involvement with Sethos.

"What's wrong?" Aeroth asked. He sat up.

I opened my mouth, but he cut me off.

"And don't say '*nothing.*'"

Aeroth had said that we both deserved honesty—we were in a bond for life, after all. His honesty was jarring at times, but deep down, I knew I preferred that to being lied to.

I owed Aeroth the same level of honesty.

"Intimacy scares me," I said.

Aeroth's eyes roamed my face and he nodded. "Go on."

"I fell so easily for Sethos," I said, my voice a whisper. "Khellios told me I fell for a version of Sethos that never existed."

"And you are afraid I am not who I say I am?" Aeroth asked, his tone gentle.

How could I answer him in a way that could explain everything I felt inside?

"Renna," he shook his head. "I'm not trying to make you fall for me."

My chest felt tight at his words. "I know."

But I could fall for somebody like you.

I tried to take a deep breath.

"I could be engaged to be married soon," he added.

I swallowed the lump in my throat. "I feel like there is always the expectation of something behind any act of kindness," I admitted. "I'm on edge more often than I like to admit."

"Renna . . . we could be just friends."

I looked down to my hands.

"I know we disagree about the outcome of Sethos. And perhaps as time goes on, we can come to some sort of understanding of what needs to be done to ensure the safety of everyone."

"Yes . . ."

"But we keep saying that we hate each other."

I looked to Aeroth. I truly did not hate him. I wanted to,

because I wanted to blame someone. But deep down, I knew I hated the situation, not him.

"No. I just hate this situation, Aeroth."

"I know you do. Just remember, we have done nothing wrong. You said last night you feel safe with me."

I crossed my arms. "I do."

He nodded. "But I want more than that. I want you to trust me when I say I will not hurt you. That is a cornerstone of friendship."

I was hesitant to agree, since we were still practically strangers. But he had assured me he would never hurt me so many times.

Would another person in my position agree to trust someone so quickly?

"I believe your words . . ."

He tilted his head. "But not my intention?"

I clenched my jaw. "Why are you so forward?"

"How would you have me speak to you?"

I shook my head, not knowing how to respond.

The problem with Aeroth was that he forced me to look inward, at parts of myself that were too painful to deal with. I couldn't hide my feelings from myself when I was around him. It was unnerving.

I closed my eyes.

Would this friendship work?

"I'll think about it," I said.

"Said through gritted teeth."

I opened my eyes and saw the smirk on his lips.

"You're not an easy woman, Renna Strongborn."

"And you're not the first man to say that to me."

Instead of dismissing me, Aeroth threw his head back and laughed. His response caught me off guard, and I found myself biting my cheek to stop from smiling.

When he looked at me, I noticed his eyes were more brown than burgundy.

I frowned.

"What did I say now?" Aeroth sighed.

I shook my head. "Nothing, just your eyes." I leaned in. "Some of the red specks in them are gone."

Aeroth shifted uneasily.

I was used to supernatural eyes changing color when aroused or when angry. But I didn't think Aeroth was experiencing any of that at that moment.

"I haven't fed, Renna. That's why my eyes are darker."

Oh.

My eyes widened.

"I will be alright."

"No," I said, shaking my head. "You cannot starve yourself. We have too much to lose. You can't do this to yourself. Not now."

"Renna—"

"You refuse to drink my blood, so what is your plan? Could you drink blood from animals?"

He rubbed his nose and then leaned back on the headboard, crossing his arms before speaking. "Many Naaviri get blood from wherever it's available. Animals are not an exception. Some Naaviri enjoy animal blood."

My brows gathered. "But not you?"

Aeroth's eyes searched mine before speaking. "It's not animal blood I crave."

I swallowed and looked down at my hands, nervously playing with the bedcover on my lap.

"And now you're blushing again."

I lifted my eyebrow before answering. "And you're still being incredibly forward."

"So you've said."

I wondered in that moment what would happen if Aeroth had

my blood again. Did I run the risk of being hurt if he lost control and drank more than he should?

"You know what I find incredibly bothersome?" he asked.

I looked up at him. "I'm sure you'll tell me."

"Your face—"

I laughed. "*Wow*—"

"—is quite expressive. And I never know what to make of your facial expressions when you get quiet. It's like you're having entire conversations in your head, and I am left on the outside looking in, wondering what I missed."

"You speak like you've known me for years."

A smile tugged at his lips. "Haven't I? I was created to know you."

I felt my blush deepen. His words did something to me, because in a way, I felt like I had known him for a long time too.

"We are running out of options, Aeroth," I told him. "You need to make a choice."

Aeroth looked away from me then.

"I'm sorry for the way things are," I said.

He didn't respond or look at me.

"I won't force you to drink from me," I continued. "But know that if you want to, perhaps try and ration . . . Maybe take a little bit from me—"

He groaned. "Renna—"

"Just think on it," I urged.

"I try very hard not to."

33

RENNA

We walked for a long time, and even though I was used to physical exercise, I had to admit I regretted taking Illona's side instead of agreeing to portal. My thighs were sore, and my feet ached.

But when Demira conjured a two-person levitating carriage for her and Illona and offered to conjure one for me, I declined.

I knew I needed to get my body used to continuous movement for what was coming.

As Demira and Illona sped past us in their carriage, I walked between Cylas and Aeroth.

"Thank you for not being snippy with Demira today," I told Cylas.

He laughed bitterly. "The day isn't over."

As we moved through the forest, Cylas walked ahead of my sisters to scan the treeline, leaving Aeroth and I to walk alone.

When we weren't bickering, talking with Aeroth was surprisingly easy. I told him about my time at university and what the curriculum was like in a mortal university. He listened as I shared horror stories about teaching first-year students. He got angry when I told him Aramis had taken over my college, and the changes he implemented that affected my graduation. Conversation flowed between us and made time pass much faster than if we had remained silent.

We would take short breaks in small clearings deep in the trees, far away from any paths. Cylas enchanted the trees so some of the heavier brush surrounded us to block out any noise we created, and Demira conjured food for lunch. When night fell and we decided it was time to rest for the night, we chose a small meadow.

Demira called forth her magic to produce sleeping sacks, and Illona created a smokeless fire pit.

I felt useless as my sisters moved around the small camp, taking charge of the arrangements while Aeroth and I stood watching them work.

"I hate this," I said to Aeroth. "Not knowing how to help."

"They seem to have it covered," he said. "You shouldn't feel bad."

I crossed my arms. "This must feel normal for you, then."

He looked to me. "What?"

"You're a king. People do things for you."

He chuckled and looked to the sky. "Whatever you have to tell yourself, sweetheart."

I narrowed my eyes. "Don't call me that."

He crossed his arms and lifted an eyebrow. "I'm sorry, was that offensive?"

"You know it was," I replied.

"No less offensive than you assigning a false narrative to me."

I bit my cheek to keep from replying.

"You don't have to be useful or perform at every moment of your day," Aeroth said. "You are allowed to rest. To not be active."

Illona approached us.

"I was wondering," Illona said, looking between Aeroth and I with her hands clasped in front, "if we could all practice a bit with weapons again before we go to sleep tonight?"

"Of course," Aeroth replied at the same time that I said, "Yes."

Illona grinned. "Perhaps you could demonstrate first?" she asked us.

I pursed my lips. "You want me to fight *him*?"

She nodded.

Aeroth looked to me. "That was a rather interesting *inflection—*"

"I don't want to hurt him," I told her.

Aeroth laughed.

I looked to him. "*What?*"

"You wouldn't hurt me."

I frowned. "Why is that? I broke up the last fight with my Darkness."

"Could you have broken it up without it?"

My jaw dropped.

Illona chuckled, gesturing at the clearing in the middle of our campsite. "I trust this is big enough for a demonstration?"

Aeroth straightened and cracked his neck side to side, a wide grin spreading on his face.

Aeroth and I had tried to train together when we were at the tree mansion, but when everyone else joined in, we ended up giving pointers to Demira and Illona on how to use daggers and rapiers.

"We would be happy to demonstrate," he told Illona and looked to me. "Perhaps a fist fight?"

He had a point in not using weapons, especially with the limited space we had. "A fist fight would be lovely."

He chuckled.

Illona spun around to Demira and Cylas. "Aeroth and Renna are going to show us how to fend off an attack using hand-to-hand combat." She turned back to us and nodded. "Whenever you are ready."

Aeroth gestured to the center of the space. "Ladies first."

Once Illona sat next to Demira, I walked to the center of the camp and turned to face Aeroth. He backed up from me and bent his knees and squared his shoulders, shifting side to side on the balls of his feet.

He lifted an eyebrow. "You ready?"

"You realize you wouldn't stand a chance if I used magic," I said and crossed my arms.

"It sounds to me like you think I'm intimidating," he lobbed.

I smirked. "I don't think about you at all."

Aeroth charged, swinging his left fist toward me, and I dove under his aim just in time. I turned around to face him, my knees and arms bent, ready for another attack. Aeroth faked a punch twice, and I pivoted back both times on the balls of my feet. My eyes flashed to the ground, checking for rocks, a tree root, a weakness to help me. When I found none, I locked eyes with him.

He grinned then, and his confidence angered me. When he faked a punch again, as if provoking me, I swung my right arm, but he swiftly moved and spun behind me and kicked me in the back with his knee.

I stumbled forward, reaching out to steady myself, but I fell on my face.

Screaming in anger, I stood and turned to face him once more, my body squared up for another attack. I tried not to think about the soreness of my back or show that I was hurt. I would not give him the satisfaction.

"You're going to stand around all day?" he asked as we circled each other.

"You're the one who agreed to this."

Aeroth swung with his right fist and I parried his aim, but he pivoted and swung his left fist. I quickly dodged under his punch and thrust my right fist toward the left side of his face.

He was ready for my move and deflected my punch with his left arm and swung at my face with his right fist. On and on we went, blocking and parrying as if we were in a dance.

"Are you afraid to actually hit me?" Aeroth teased and winked.

"*Asshole,*" I gritted and jabbed twice with my right arm.

Aeroth pushed my last jab out of the way, grabbed my fist, and in a swift movement, spun around me and twisted my hand behind my back, where he held it. He then punched my lower back, right by my kidneys. The impact launched me forward, and I landed on my knees. I glanced back to him while grabbing the side of my back that was now pounding with pain.

He winked and put his palms up as if asking if I was through with the demonstration.

"You would hate me if I let you win," he said while pointing at me. "And you know it."

"I hate you nonetheless."

"Ah, yes. How could I forget?"

Aeroth leaned down and extended his hand to help me up. Grumbling, I took his hand, and he pulled me up.

Then a cloud of bats flew above, and his eyes shot up to the sky. I took my chance and barreled into him. My body crashed into his, grasping him around the waist and propelling forward.

He was all hard muscle, like a wall of stone, but since he'd been distracted, he stumbled backward. When his back hit a tree trunk, I almost scratched my face against the bark.

I laughed in triumph, but he pivoted and bent at the waist, wrapping one arm around my waist while he looped the other arm around one of my legs. He yanked me upward so that my legs were in the air and my back to his front. My head and arms dangled below me, and I screamed in frustration as he had me locked in place.

Trashing against him, I yelled, "Let me go!"

"*Try.*"

"This was the dinner and a show I didn't know I needed," Cylas quipped.

I wanted to curl up to reach his arms, but I didn't have the strength. I would have to work on my abdominal muscles.

"*Fuck!*" I yelled as Aeroth held onto me.

"Use every advantage you have," Aeroth told the group. "Keep your body moving. There is always an arm or leg you can grab to change the dynamic. *This*, however," he said and jangled me as if I were a sack of food, "was a very bad strategy on Renna's part. From this angle, she would not be able to free herself if she tried."

I cursed at him. "Put me down, you beast!"

"Are you certain?"

"*Aeroth!*"

He then let me go, and I fell to the ground. I groaned and rolled onto my back.

Aeroth dusted off his hands in a way that it sounded like a slow hand clap, and I looked at his face and saw the wicked tilt of his lips, as if he was challenging me to come at him. My aggression revved up, and I pushed off the ground to stand.

"C'mon, Strongborn," he said. "Fight back. I know you're angry."

A branch suddenly whipped out of nowhere toward Aeroth, and he turned to move out of the way, ducking and bending at the waist. I took the opportunity and hopped on his back, squeezing my arms around his neck in a rear naked choke to cut off airflow.

"A little distracted, are we?" I asked him, pressing my cheek against the side of his face.

He grunted as he tried to pry off my arms. I quickly wrapped my legs around his waist, locking my feet at the ankles.

"*You c-cheated,*" he managed.

"I don't think so," I gritted out and locked my ankles around him.

Cylas coughed. I looked to him and noticed a smug look on his face. I narrowed my eyes.

"*Cylas,*" I barked.

"Yes . . . ?" he asked.

Aeroth took the opportunity to pivot and grabbed my ankles, and the world rushed past me as we fell backward to the ground. Before I knew it, Aeroth pushed his body backward so I was pinned behind his back. I could not wiggle out from either side of him.

I held onto him as much as I could, but the impact of falling on my back, combined with bodyweight crushing me, was too much. I let go, gasping for air, when he rolled off me and stood. I coughed and sat up.

Aeroth looked to Cylas. "You cheated."

Cylas's eyes widened. "I don't know what you mean."

"The fucking bats, the abnormal branch."

Cylas looked side to side and shrugged. "We're in *nature*."

I caught my breath and stood, pointing at Cylas. "I wanted to win fair and square."

Cylas sauntered toward us. "Take your anger out on me," he said with a slow smile. He spread his arms out wide. "I'm right here, baby girl."

I saw red and charged at him, bending my waist to wrap my arms around his middle, and when I made contact, Cylas fell back.

The culprit had not been me but the fallen trunk he had been sitting on that made him trip.

"At last," he said with a laugh. "I always wondered what it would be like to have you on top of me. Fancy a ride?"

I tried to break free, but he bucked his hips and rolled us so that he landed on top of me, straddling my waist.

"My sweet Renna," he said with a devilish smile. "This is quite a treat indeed."

My chest heaved against Cylas's, and the slow perusal he gave me made my skin heat to a scorching red.

"Don't pretend you don't like how my body feels against yours," he murmured, looking at my lips.

How would anyone be immune to Cylas's charms?

"I want you," Cylas said in my ear.

"And I want you to get off," I snipped.

He reared his head back to laugh. "There is more than one way to interpret *that* statement. I am eager to know what you mean. And where."

"*Cylas.*"

Cylas gave me a peck on the cheek, then rolled to his side, pushing to stand. He held his hand out, pulling me to my feet. As I brushed the dust off, I couldn't help but notice Aeroth's glare flicking between me and Cylas. Aeroth was now sitting on a tree stump, leaning forward with his forearms resting on his thighs, hands clasped tightly.

"He hates this." Cylas smirked.

"Because you cheated."

Cylas snuck behind me, his lips brushing against my ear. "I doubt that's the cause of his scowl. This is more fun than riling Khellios up."

Cylas looked to me and winked.

Cylas and I moved off to the side to allow Demira and Illona to spar, and I sat down next to Aeroth.

"You look like you want to murder someone," I said to him,

my eyes on Demira and Illona, Cylas stepping in now and again to give them pointers.

"And why would that be?" Aeroth's tone was harsh.

"I'm sorry. Cylas likes to make a spectacle."

He huffed. "Cylas wants you."

I chuckled. "He wants everybody. That's who he is."

"I heard the way he spoke to you in your cabin inside Elrie's craft. His eyes follow you constantly, like a shadow."

"And that is a problem?" I asked and turned to look at him. "What is wrong with someone wanting me? You have no claim over me."

He glanced at me out of his peripheral before turning back to watch the sparring.

His dismissal of my comment angered me, and my body tensed.

I crossed my arms as I spoke. "You yourself said you could be engaged any day. That your government is looking for a wife for you. I would have to stand by your side and watch you interact with her," I pointed out.

He grunted. "It's a political marriage. I wouldn't return her feelings."

I laughed, and Aeroth glanced at me.

"Marrying is just a means to an end, Renna. I need an heir."

"That doesn't mean there won't be feelings involved. What if she finds you attractive? Do you want me to glare at her when she smiles at you? When she touches your arm to pull you in to say something private?"

He closed his eyes and massaged his temples.

"Stop being rude," I said to him and crossed my arms. I turned my face to look at my sisters.

"You're right," Aeroth said after a few moments, his tone lacking the anger from before. "I shouldn't care."

"No, you shouldn't."

Aeroth stood.

"Where are you going?" I asked.

"I want to wash off. I can hear a river or stream not too far from here." He looked down at me. "Come with me?"

I rolled my eyes. "Like I have a choice."

He shrugged.

"Lead the way," I said, gesturing to the forest.

We walked in silence, and soon Aeroth pointed to a winding creek. Large boulders surrounded the water's edge, providing some privacy. Aeroth tested the temperature of the water, and I walked to sit by the edge with my back to the water.

"You don't want to go in first?" he asked.

"I was going to ask Demira if she could conjure a shower," I stated.

"I don't think she should be using that much magic," Aeroth said. "If we are attacked, she will need her magic to be at its fullest to fight back."

"We won't get attacked."

"Does it hurt to be prepared regardless?"

I shrugged and Aeroth walked out of view, beginning to take off his clothes. Once he was behind a particularly large rock, I heard him curse as he entered the water.

"Cylas is terrible at fighting," Aeroth commented after a while.

"And you think you're better?"

"Absolutely," he said.

"You have a wildly inflated ego."

He laughed. "You do love to insult me."

"When you deserve it."

"Are you still angry with me?" he asked after a few moments.

I scoffed. "Yes. I wish I could hit you."

"Alright then. So fight me, Strongborn. Fair and square. No magic intervening this time."

His words made me pause. I shook my head.

"Don't mock me," I said to him. "You're just trying to make a point—"

"What?" He laughed. "Are you afraid I'll beat you without Cylas's help?"

I almost spun to face him. "You are *not* better than me."

I was lying. He *was* better than me, but I didn't want to admit that. I knew he had decades of experience in the military, and I'd seen him fight when the mercenaries attacked us.

"Then prove it," he urged.

"In your dreams."

Freezing cold water suddenly splashed my back, and I yelped, my jaw dropping open.

I spun to face him then.

"*Are you kidding me right now?*"

He grinned. "Come and fight me," he said.

My face reddened. He splashed me again, this time a heap of water drenching my entire front. I saw red and marched into the water fully dressed, but I wasn't ready for the large pebbles on the floor of the creek and I tripped slightly as my feet tried to find balance.

He looked at me with an infuriating smirk, and I launched myself at him, swinging at his face with my right arm.

Aeroth leaned back and ducked right.

"Now you refuse to fight me back?" I snapped. "*Coward.*"

He chuckled. "You're a very angry person."

I jabbed at him with my fist, and he parried with his right hand. I tried punching him again, and he blocked my blow once more. We continued back and forth until he splashed me in the face with water. The water went up my nose, and my sinuses felt like they were on fire. I closed my eyes for a brief moment and, despite the burn, bent my arms up in a ready position to strike. Suddenly, I felt Aeroth's arms behind me, and he pinned my arms down to the side of my body. He then hoisted me up in the air, his arms around my torso.

"How is this fair?" I yelled and thrashed against him as he held me, and with one quick swoop, he threw me above his left shoulder and launched me into the water.

As I scrambled to stand, I thought of my protective shield and how I did not erect it around Aeroth even as we were practicing. Had this been Sethos, he would have yelled at me or hurt me to teach me a lesson for not using it. Sethos taught by intimidation and pain. Aeroth taught me by taunting me to fight back but never by demeaning me. I enjoyed being around him.

"DON'T FIGHT IN WATER, STRONGBORN," Aeroth said as I stood before him, bending my arms at my elbows in a ready stance. "This is a terrible show."

I inched closer to him, and we began to circle each other.

"This is *not* a fair fight!"

"Says the person that is losing. Did you think this would be easy? That you would somehow be miraculously good at hand-to-hand combat? Use every advantage." He cocked his head to the side. "C'mon. You're angry. Strike me again."

I roared as I launched myself at him to knock him backward on his ass, and he simply moved out of the way and was behind me in an instant. He pulled my back against his chest, and my skin broke out in goosebumps as his mouth brushed the skin from my jaw and up my temple.

He squeezed me a bit tighter against him, and my stomach did a flip.

"Wasn't your mother a siren? You're supposed to be skilled in water."

Then I remembered that he was naked, and my heartbeat sped up.

"You're naked."

He lowered his lips to my ear. "You knew I was naked."

My breathing became ragged. "Aren't you a king? Is this kingly behavior?"

"Now you sound like my father." His tone was light, teasing.

"Well someone needs to remind you of your duty."

Aeroth moved his lips to the crook of my neck, where I felt his canines scrape my skin. "What is my duty, Renna?"

I felt like I was on the edge of a cliff. It was exhilarating to be in his arms.

"I like you like this..." he whispered against my skin. "Wet. Tight against me."

I closed my eyes and leaned back against him, reveling in being this close.

He moved a hand down toward my core.

"*Renna . . .*" His voice was like a groan.

"Yes?"

Aeroth suddenly tensed and abruptly let me go. Confused, I turned my head and saw him scanning the forest.

"What is it—"

Aeroth placed a finger on my lips. "We need to get out of the water. Someone is here," Aeroth whispered.

And then the screams began.

34

DEMIRA

Prepare for the worst. A motto I lived by daily.

And one I had sorely forgotten when mercenaries ambushed us.

The attack happened so fast, I didn't have time to conjure any weapon—not that I would truly know how to use one.

My gifts in magic were conjuring spells and objects. I could throw my magic, like purple fiery flames. But magic alone was never enough when it came to hand-to-hand combat.

The mercenaries were prepared. They knew who we were and took steps to protect themselves from magical attacks. One female mercenary had attacked Illona from behind, curling her arm around Illona's neck in a chokehold and bringing Illona's back against her front. The other hand holding Illona by the stomach shimmered with a translucent shield with glowing purple runes.

I knew the runes—they were used in protection spells. All of the mercenaries had the same shield.

"One move," the female mercenary said to me as she held onto Illona while the other soldiers circled us, "and you will regret it."

"Let her go," Cylas gritted, his body almost shaking with rage. His eyes were a vibrant emerald, and his skin seemed to glow from the bright, green vines that ran all over his body.

"We want no quarrel with you, god," the female mercenary said. "We merely want the girls." She looked around. "Where is the third?"

"No quarrel with me?" Cylas spat. "She is mine to protect. You are touching her. You and I certainly have a quarrel."

He took a step forward, and the female mercenary squeezed her hand tighter around Illona's neck. My sister whimpered.

I placed a hand on Cylas's arm.

"What is your plan?" I gritted out to Cylas under my breath. "You're going to fight the mercenary? Where are your godlike powers?"

Cylas blinked, and the fiery green in his eyes dimmed.

"Call on your powers," I demanded. "You don't need to fight them like a regular soldier. You are a *god*."

Cylas froze on the spot.

"*Kill them!*" I yelled to him.

Cylas's eyes turned dull, and his body stopped glowing. His jaw opened as if he was trying to find words to say.

"I—" He shook his head.

My heart plunged into my stomach with the realization that Cylas was of no help to us. He would not kill, just the same as he did not kill when we were attacked on our first night in Elinoor. Just like he did not kill in Isyos.

Cylas preferred peace.

The female mercenary laughed.

"We had it on good authority he would not attack," she said with a smug smile.

I called on Violet Fire and felt the warmth spread out from my chest, up my shoulders, and down to my palms. Two spheres of violet flames hovered above my open hands.

"Who sent you?" I asked.

"Sethos Malachi Physerion placed a bounty on your heads, and my crew *will* claim that money. The other half of our crew landed here," her eyes narrowed, "but we have not heard from them since." She tightened her hold on Illona, and tears began to spring from my sister's eyes as her face turned red. "There is no trace of their craft. *Nothing.*"

My body tensed, and I wanted to scream.

"We've been asking any being we encountered on the surface of Elinoor about your whereabouts. The Queen of the Forest Sprites sends her regards."

Cylas cursed.

The female mercenary looked around, repeating, "Where is the third?"

I didn't owe Renna my loyalty. I had no love for her. My life was a result of her death. My sadness and trauma were a direct result of her existence. And while I had expected Renna to be as hateful as my father because she shared his power, instead, Illona and I were met with a woman who had suffered as much as or more than we had. A woman who struggled as we did to find her place in the world. She hated our father and the burden his power caused.

The same power that could save us now.

"You want me?"

We all turned to the right.

Renna stood next to Aeroth.

The female mercenary laughed, delighted. "This may be easier than I'd hoped."

"Well I'm here. And we're not going anywhere," Renna said. And then Darkness rolled off her like a fiery ribbon, creating a large circular barrier around everyone.

My jaw dropped seeing how easy she could wield Darkness.

Renna stepped toward the barrier, the Darkness parting for her and Aeroth, who followed behind her. It sealed into a circle once more, raising behind them so high it came up waist-length.

The mercenaries looked around nervously.

Aeroth conjured an enormous black sword and extended it, his knees bent, as if he were ready to strike.

"Let Illona go," Renna said, her voice clear.

The female smirked and threw Illona down onto the ground. My sister coughed and whimpered as she rolled on the ground. I could do nothing but stand in place, afraid that if I moved, someone would strike.

"Did you kill them with this magic?" the mercenary gritted out to Renna. "Where is my crew?"

Renna tilted her face, and her irises darkened, turning almost black.

"You must not have looked hard enough," Renna said. Her voice was colder than I'd heard before. "You would have seen their ashes."

Silence settled on everyone like a heavy cloud.

The leader mercenary suddenly screamed a guttural cry and sprinted toward Renna.

Aeroth launched forward at the same time, and in one swoop, his sword slashed across the woman's neck—cutting her head clean off.

I froze as I watched the head roll, but the pause was momentary as chaos broke out and a full-blown attack commenced.

The mercenaries were armed with swords and cannon guns that shot out spheres of magic. I was not equipped to fight any of these people. All I could do was focus my energy and erect a shield.

Illona was at my side in moments, standing outside my shield and shooting magic at our foes. Illona was fearless, as I'd never seen her before. When a sphere of magic grazed her shoulder, I screamed.

Illona shot back stronger with a guttural cry, and fear settled deep in my bones. She would get killed. Quickly, I directed my magic to absorb her into the protective shield.

Illona spun to face me, her eyes lit with fury. "Let me fight!" she gritted out. "I can do this!"

She tried to break free from the shield, but I chanted a spell to prevent the shield from letting anyone leave.

"*Demira!*" she screamed.

"No, I cannot lose you," I told her. "You're my little sister. I have to protect you. We have never trained to fight like this, Illona."

As we argued, three mercenaries surged on us and began to hack at my shield. My body trembled as I kept my magic up, the hits like dull aches.

I watched beyond the shield as Aeroth and Renna fought side by side and envied their skill—especially Renna. She fought just as well, if not better than Aeroth, as she wielded a double-ended Black Fire spear.

I was skilled in magic, but I had only ever truly used it as a tool for witchcraft. In Vasarys, I had no need to fight off attacks of the physical battle type. My need to use magic had been to grant others boons as favors to win support so I could topple Sethos. I knew how to erect a protective shield but not how to fend off an attack of this sort.

I needed to train in defensive magic.

As my body shook with every blow, out of the corner of my eyes, I saw one of the mercenaries stake a gunfetror onto the ground. A gunfetror was a gun with high-voltage lasers that usually killed on impact.

Illona stilled as she saw the mercenary setting up the gun in our direction.

"Demira . . ." she whispered, her eyes wide.

But I never got to answer because the trees and forest vines around us animated, and the attackers were dragged by their feet high up into the trees, suspended in the air.

My jaw dropped as the vines made quick work of tying them up against the massive tree trunks, wrapping in elaborate knots. The attackers screamed, their faces turning red and purple from the pressure around their necks as the vines wove around their faces.

They were being suffocated to death.

And the cause of it all?

I looked down to find Cylas in the middle of where we had been attacked, his arms extended up and moving. His fingers shifted to-and-fro, as if directing the vines to their violent work.

"He's going to kill them," Illona breathed.

My brows furrowed. Cylas didn't like to kill. It wasn't in his nature.

So why now?

My answer came moments later as the struggling mercenaries' voices dimmed.

Cylas lowered his gaze, his eyes settling on Illona.

"You are safe," he said to her.

Illona's eyes grew wide, and she remained silent. I pulled back my protective shield.

"The forest will kill them," Cylas told us all, his eyes shifting to our group. "We should go."

We all nodded in unison, and all but me followed his lead.

Instead, I looked up. The female mercenary was halfway up on the canopy, her unseeing eyes focused on us. I shivered.

The stillness of the forest meant we were able to hear their headset radios. They were being paged, surely looking for them and asking for an update on our capture.

More would come for us. We would not be safe until we reached the rider descendant city.

I began to run behind my group, my heartbeat ricocheting inside my rib cage.

35

RENNA

I held Aeroth's hand for a long time as we hurried through the forest, following Cylas's lead to the Russet Mountains.

I could feel Aeroth's body tremble in shocks, as if he could barely contain his anger.

Our collective goal was to reach the caves as fast as possible. My personal goal was to get Aeroth as far away from chaos as possible. I could sense the amount of blood already spilled, coupled with the kills he would create, would set him off.

And we were so close.

"It will be okay," I kept whispering, knowing he could hear me. "It will be okay."

I glanced back to him and saw how dull his eyes looked. Where they were a faded red before, now they were more brown. I could not find a trace of red in them.

He had to feed.

"They hurt you," he gritted out.

"Everyone was hurt," I stated. "It will be okay."

"But they hurt *you*."

My mind thought of Isidra and how much seeing me wrestle

my attacker affected him. I knew how much he was holding back to not plunge into bloodlust.

I squeezed his hand. "I'm here with you. *Safe.*"

"You should have let me kill them."

"The trees will do that," I reminded him.

"*Not good enough,*" he growled.

I halted and faced him.

"You need to feed," I told him. "From me."

His eyes widened.

"Aeroth." I gripped his arms. "Listen to me. You are barely holding on. Your eyes are brown. You're pale. You are not okay."

"Renna—"

"My blood will nourish you and calm these feelings of danger. If you don't feed and we encounter another skirmish—"

"*I will kill them all—*"

I narrowed my eyes. "And set off your bloodlust. Aeroth, you would be putting all of us in danger."

"Never—"

"You would be putting *me* in danger."

Cylas approached. "We need to keep moving," he urged.

I shook my head. "Aeroth is unwell."

"What's wrong with you?" Cylas asked him.

Aeroth remained silent.

"You keep moving forward to the caves," I told Cylas. "We will come to you."

"How will you find us?" he asked.

How did one find a god?

"What's your sigil?" I asked.

Cylas lifted his eyebrow. "No blood summons this time, Renna," he warned. I knew he was referring to me summoning Khellios months ago.

"I had no choice in the matter last time," I reminded him.

He frowned and knelt on the ground. Magic emanated from

his hands, and he pointed a finger at the soil. In an instant, his pointer finger began drawing.

A vertical zigzag line appeared. It looked like the number three with a half circle arching horizontally through it. At the bottom of the zigzag, he drew a small circle.

"Draw it anywhere," he said, "and I will come get you both."

I nodded. "Keep my sisters safe," I said to him.

He nodded back and took off.

"Where do you want to do this?" I asked Aeroth once we were alone.

He was silent as he looked at me.

"Aeroth," I growled and pushed his chest. "You need to feed. What will happen in Taria if battle does occur and you're around spilled blood?"

He shook his head.

"You need some blood to sustain yourself so you don't lose control," I told him. "This is no longer an option."

He closed his eyes.

"And I'm sorry to be so forceful on this—"

"We need to go off path," he muttered. "The mercenaries have tracking devices, and I'm certain Sethos's mages will follow right behind us this time."

This was progress. "Okay. Where?"

"Come with me," he said and grabbed my hand.

It all happened so fast.

One moment I was standing by him, and the next he was leading me through the forest at lightning speed, as if we were the wind itself. The forest blurred as we weaved around trees and moved across streams. We zipped through a field with grass as tall as my waist and emerged back in the forest until we stopped at a copse of trees.

My chest rose and fell in heaves as I tried to catch my breath.

I opened my mouth to speak, but I never had the chance.

Aeroth pinned my body against the trunk of a tree, and his lips grazed the crook of my neck. His forearms caged me in, bracing himself on the trunk behind me.

"You are infuriating," he said with a growl and moved his hand behind my shirt to unzip my top. He shrugged me out of my long sleeve shirt and flung it away from us. I was left in a black tank top.

He ran his canines over my flesh, and I whimpered.

"I *shouldn't* be feeding from you."

His tongue darted out and lapped at the base of my neck and shoulder. I almost bucked at the sensation.

It didn't mean anything. His saliva had a numbing effect. This was part of the feeding.

"But," he murmured, moving his lips over my skin as he spoke, "I think you crave me feeding from you as much as I crave the taste of you."

Yes.

"Are you aroused, Renna?" He pressed his body against mine.

I could feel the hardness of his chest and the stirring of his cock.

I cleared my throat.

"As I recall, arousal happens with any Naaviri feeding," I pointed out.

He smiled against my skin. "So you are aroused."

I shrugged. "Any other Naaviri could elicit the same response," I assured him.

"Is that right?" he whispered.

I nodded and lifted my chin. "My reaction to you is not unique."

His eyes dropped to my lips.

"Any other Naaviri could cause the same response in me," I repeated.

Aeroth brought his face so close to mine that our noses touched.

"Unfortunately for you," he said, "no other will drink from you but me."

I laughed. "Don't flatter yourself."

He tilted his head and growled. "I do like a challenge."

I shrugged and picked a piece of invisible lint off his shoulder. "Now that I know how pleasurable this feels, maybe I will find myself another Naaviri—"

He lurched forward, and his canines pierced my skin. I screamed.

He took one pull of my blood, and my body buckled into his. He came up for air.

"*Count,*" he growled, fingers digging into my waist. "Count to six and then tell me to stop."

"*Yes.*"

I never wanted him to stop.

Aeroth moved his arms fully around me, and in one quick swoop, he lifted me up, gripping my ass, forcing me to wrap my legs around him.

Every pull felt like bliss, and if I closed my eyes, I could almost visualize streams of gold ribbons moving toward where he fed from me.

"Count!"

"*One.*"

One of Aeroth's hands moved from my ass to the side of my torso.

"*Two.*"

He grunted as his hips moved in a slow rhythm against me. I moaned as his movements hit my throbbing core.

"*Three.*"

The hand on my torso moved down to the hem of my shirt, and he began to play with the skin there.

"*Four,*" I whimpered.

He moved his lips off my wound and carefully lapped around the rest of my throat again. I closed my eyes, a million colors bursting in my vision, my skin aflame, making my nipples hard.

"No one will ever drink from you but me, Renna," he growled. "That is a promise."

"Five."

His mouth went back to the wound, and he continued to drink.

"You don't command my body," I gritted out.

The hand at the hem of my shirt moved up my skin and brushed at the underside of my breast. I wondered how my breast would feel in his palm . . .

I pushed my chest toward him, my body desperate for his touch.

"But your body begs me to," he whispered.

Yes.

These weren't my true thoughts and feelings—it was the effects of the feeding.

"*Six.*"

Aeroth let me go in an instant, and I sagged against the tree trunk.

He was backed up on another tree, facing me. Our chests moved in sync, rising and falling.

"Are you alright?" he asked.

I was breathless. "Yes ..."

"I didn't want to stop."

Aeroth moved his eyes from mine and looked at my neck. His eyes were hooded and he moved to my lips next.

"But you did," I reminded him.

The corners of his mouth shimmered with my black blood. I walked toward him, closing the distance between us. I brushed my thumb on the corners of his lips, my warm blood smearing across the skin.

Aeroth's eyes followed my thumb as I moved back, and his hand shot out to halt me.

He leaned down, securing his grip around my wrist, and brought my thumb to his lips. When he popped my thumb into his mouth and sucked, a shiver rolled through my spine.

How many more moments like this would we share in our lifetime? He would always be Naaviri. He would always need to feed.

Would he be the only one to take from me, as he promised?

Aeroth released my thumb with a pop and moved slowly toward me, his eyes on my neck. He began to walk us back to the tree.

"*Aeroth,*" I whispered as we moved.

He gently pushed me back against the trunk. My core throbbed, and my fingers flexed with the need to wrap my hands around his neck to pull him in further. I wanted more but . . .

I swallowed. "I think that's enough for today. We should get back. We need to summon Cylas."

"Let me clean you . . ." he said, his lips now against my neck.

Yes. And no.

What did I want?

"Aeroth, we set a limit. *I counted* . . ."

I closed my eyes as his tongue ran over my wound. I let my neck drop to the side as he laved at me, the eroticism of it all making my pussy throb.

"Aeroth," I pressed. "I don't think this is a good idea."

"I crave you," he whispered. "Gods how I crave you."

My nipples tightened painfully. "Aeroth, this is too much—"

"I know."

"Stop."

At the word, Aeroth stopped and lifted his head. He blinked

as if a haze had lifted. He shook his head side to side and squeezed his eyes shut, retreating off me.

"I'm sorry," he said after a few moments.

It hadn't been just him. I'd wanted his attention too.

He looked away from me.

"I hate this," he muttered.

"I'm sorry—"

"Don't apologize." His voice was hard. "You haven't done anything wrong."

I leaned my head back against the trunk. I hated how much my body responded to him, but at the same time, I knew I craved him too.

"I wish I had never met you," he said.

I steeled my heart to not let his words affect me. I knew he didn't mean to be hurtful. Meeting each other had complicated everything. He was stating the truth.

And I felt terrible.

"Aeroth, look at me."

He turned his head, and his eyes moved back and forth between mine. "I just don't want to hurt you like *he* did," he whispered.

My heart slowed down. "Like Sethos," I stated.

"You are mine to watch over and care for, Renna. No matter if this bond is romantic or not, I owe you a duty of care. But I didn't want to stop feeding from you."

"You are stronger than you know," I told him.

"This time," he said, pulling me closer. "I can't lie to you," he purred, looking down at my lips. "I won't lie and tell you I'm unaffected by you. By the feel of you—"

"There's that honesty," I teased, my skin flushed.

He grinned. "Wouldn't you rather me tell you how I feel when I taste you?"

"My body and blood are not unique, Aeroth. Don't blind

yourself. This is just your nature." None of this was real. It was the effect of the feeding.

He shook his head, bringing up his thumb to my lips and opening my mouth slowly.

"Drink from me," he urged, cutting a small wound in his neck with his other hand. "Let me feed you."

I gulped.

Aeroth wrapped a hand around my jaw and lifted my head up to face him.

"Feeding you in return, servicing you, giving you my blood, is in my nature too," he whispered.

My body buzzed, anticipating the feeding.

Didn't I want to establish a physical distance?

"Feeding is like a dream," I whispered and moved my fingers to his lips, still wet with my blood. "It's like a haze. A high."

He stepped closer to me.

"Then don't wake up."

My chest tightened.

I had to feed from him to ensure I could be separated from him. This was a means to an end. But I knew how much his blood affected me in turn.

"Can you count?" I asked.

"As you wish," he said with a lazy smile.

Bracing my hands on his arms, I leaned forward to the cut in his neck. I swiped my tongue against the opening, and Aeroth tensed under me. His blood felt like an explosion of colors and sounds on my tongue, and the world became more vibrant.

I inhaled the scent of his skin and almost moaned. Aeroth hauled me up to him once more, and I wrapped my legs around him.

"Now open those pretty lips and take me in."

My head nodded of its own accord. The need to drink his blood overwhelmed my systems. Nothing else mattered.

I moved closer to him. My body trembled with need and obsession for him. I felt like I was floating in an altered state.

"Take me, Renna."

I whimpered as his words echoed in my core and began to drink, letting the pleasure of his blood consume me.

He moaned.

"My greedy girl," he whispered.

Both of his hands moved to my hips that were slowly undulating against him.

"Shall I take you away like this when we come together?" he said, groaning.

"*Hmmm?*"

"So that only I can know how you move against me when I'm inside you?"

My clit throbbed, and I pushed myself even closer.

He grunted.

This was madness. But I didn't care. I wanted. He was letting me.

And I was taking.

Aeroth moved his right hand to grip my neck and keep me locked on his neck.

"Yes," he groaned. "*T-that's it,*" he whispered.

I needed to be touched.

"Renna . . ."

"Mmmm," I responded.

I continued to grind my pussy against his pelvis, urging the sensations of bliss inside me.

So much for not wanting emotional intimacy.

But there was no escaping Aeroth and who we were to each other. And in that moment of lust-filled haze, I allowed myself to accept that he would remain in my life in one way or another.

I moaned.

Time seemed to go on forever as I took him in until his gentle hands stroked my hair, coaxing me to stop.

"We have to get back," he whispered and squeezed my body in an embrace.

It took everything in me to part my mouth from his skin, but he was right.

This was just a feeding. And the dream had stopped. I had to wake up from the haze of him.

"Will it always be like this, Aeroth?" I asked, as he held my face in his palms.

His smile was almost sad as he searched my eyes.

"It's not within my power to decide," he whispered.

What did he mean by that?

Was he referring to his future wife and her objection to this level of closeness between us? I wouldn't blame her, and I would never get in the way. I was not the type of woman to ruin another's relationship.

Or was he referring to the likelihood of us surviving the battle that loomed?

I closed my eyes.

It didn't matter.

"I understand," I lied.

"I don't know if you truly do."

I unwrapped my body from his, and he set me down, dropped his hands.

A thought occurred to me.

"Did you count?" I asked. Feeding from him felt longer than he had fed from me.

When he did not respond, I looked to him.

His eyes were on me.

"No."

"You should have."

He shook his head. "I should do a lot of things around you. But reason leaves me every time."

I became self-conscious then. Did he regret us coming together the way we did during feedings?

"Right," I replied and hugged my arms. I looked to the ground, feeling awkward. I wondered if drinking blood from someone would ever feel normal.

"You are uncomfortable?" he asked.

I looked up. I didn't know what to say.

"Aren't you?" I asked, deflecting with a question.

He cleared his throat. "At least we don't find each other repulsive. Makes this all the more bearable."

I laughed to myself. It was like he was saying I was barely tolerable. His words immediately dampened my mood, so I bent to the ground and drew Cylas's sigil to summon him.

Aeroth knelt next to me.

"I meant that as a joke, you know." His eyes searched my face.

A tight, forced smile formed on my lips.

"Of course." I stood. "I feel the same."

Aeroth looked at me as if he was trying to figure me out, still staring when Cylas arrived.

36

RENNA

Some of the red had returned to Aeroth's eyes by the time Cylas arrived to retrieve us. I was glad he had decided to finally feed. I tried to push the selfish thought from my mind that it pleased me when he fed from me and focused on setting some distance between us.

Luckily, everyone seemed exhausted, so no one offered conversation to pass the time.

In the caves, every echo, drop of water, and phantom wind kept us on alert, and we were all running on no sleep.

Thanks to Illona's magic, she created torches for us to light the path forward. However, despite her magic and abilities, the Ancestors would not share the direct path to the city. It was incredibly frustrating to all, most of all to Illona, who scowled as we walked, muttering angrily to herself or perhaps those beyond the veil.

And so, exploring the cave and learning where to go took a long time. We had no clear route and merely advanced on instinct. At times, we encountered forks in the road, and Cylas would leave the group to explore potential dead ends before venturing back and telling us which was the best way to go.

The process took hours. And the air became colder with every passing moment.

Demira conjured us animal furs to wear to stay warm as we walked. Illona infused more magic into the torches to increase warmth.

Despite the hours we spent walking, we spoke very little to each other. Being in a strange setting and straining our ears to hear anything that could be a danger ensured we only spoke when necessary.

For me, the silence was a relief as I tried to sort through my feelings for Aeroth.

Every once in a while, he would turn back to see me and give me a once-over, not in an overt way, but as if he was assessing my overall health.

When he would turn back to walk, my eyes would drop to his body, and I would remember how it felt to be pressed against him. How hard his muscles felt on top of me. The span of his back, his thick thighs, and strong arms, and my mind would get lost in remembering the moments we shared.

Being with Aeroth . . . It felt like a blissful eternity when I was wrapped in his arms, exchanging blood, and submitting to the haze that came from feeding from him. It put my body in a dreamlike, altered state. It was addicting.

At the same time, I knew how wrong it was for me to think about Aeroth that way, because I was determined not to get emotionally attached. I knew now how futile that desire had been. How could someone sharing that kind of physical intimacy not become attached?

My skin flushed, and I was grateful for the warm furs so I could blame the heat on them instead of my racing thoughts about Aeroth.

As if I had conjured him, he stepped in front of me, placing a hand on my arm, and I jumped. "We're stopping here," he said.

I looked around and saw everyone else staring at me several paces behind me. They all looked at me like I was crazy.

"Oh." I could feel my skin heat up even more. "Sorry."

"Don't apologize," Aeroth said.

"We called your name a few times," Demira said. "Are you alright?"

I cleared my throat and looked to the ground. "Yes."

Aeroth's hand slowly dropped from my arm. I was hyperaware of how his fingers trailed down my forearm, his attention finally pulled away when Illona asked him a question—one I had not heard because I was focusing on his touch.

My breathing was all I could hear. And my mind replaying the sound of him moaning against my skin.

Take me, Renna, he'd said.

My core clenched.

"I will set up a perimeter against the stone," Demira called, and I focused on her words to draw me out of my mental spiral.

"I can help," I told her and moved toward her.

When the separation pain started to pull at my temples, I stopped moving and closed my eyes. My fists clenched, and I took a deep breath.

Aeroth was at my side almost immediately and placed his hand at the small of my back.

The pain subsided.

"I will help as well," he told Demira.

I was grateful he did not mention the separation pain in front of her. I didn't want anyone's pity or to be treated differently.

We worked in silence as we followed Demira's instructions to find hand-sized stones, which we lined up in a half circle beginning and ending at the cave wall.

Our hands brushed a few times when we would reach for the same stones. And each time my stomach somersaulted with giddy energy.

If Aeroth felt the same when our hands brushed, he didn't show it. His face was stoic. As we placed the final stones in the arrangement Demira indicated, he spoke.

"How are you really?" he asked.

"I'm alright," I said with a shrug.

"Your skin looked red earlier. Are you feeling hot? Or sick?"

"Just *stop*," I said, my tone angry.

Instantly I hated myself for being so rude. He had no idea what was going on inside my head. He asked because he cared.

This constant internal struggle was wearing me out, and I had no one to talk to about it. I felt isolated, just like I did with Sethos in Daya.

"What's wrong?" he asked.

"I'm just tired." I was more mentally tired than physically, but he didn't need to know that.

"Then I'm glad we are stopping to rest."

I groaned internally. He was too agreeable.

And what's wrong with someone treating you nicely? my mind quipped. *Not every man will treat you like Sethos did.*

I rolled my eyes at my thought.

"What have I said?" he asked.

I froze. He saw my eye roll.

"I didn't roll my eyes at you," I murmured so that the others wouldn't hear.

"Don't lie to me," he said and gently grabbed my arm and pulled me from the group so we could have privacy but could still see them.

"Please talk to me," Aeroth said.

"I'm sorry." I looked up at him. "By default, I keep thinking you'll turn into a terrible person. It's exhausting."

He remained silent for a few moments, observing me.

"Renna." He shook his head and put his palms up. "I keep telling you I am trying my hardest to not hurt you. And I keep telling you, despite the circumstances of our bond, I would like to be your friend."

"I know," I replied quietly.

"I do not hurt friends."

I bit my nails. I realized he was likely referring to hurting me during feedings or because of his bloodlust.

"That's not what I'm referring to," I said quietly. "I think . . ." I paused. "When we feed . . ."

I didn't know how to phrase my thoughts.

"When we come together and feed," I tried again, "it's hard to not let my mind pretend like we are more than . . ." I shook my head. "I'm afraid of feeling too much. I am afraid of that kind of hurt."

He was silent for a long time.

"I will never hurt you in that way, Renna," he said. He studied me. "You must know that although you may feel a certain way during feedings, anything romantic between us . . ." He trailed off, shaking his head. "We've just met."

Hearing him say the words made me feel foolish.

"And despite how beautiful you are, and how much I," he leaned down so that his cheek brushed against mine, "*crave you . . .*"

I swallowed hard and felt his exhale across my skin.

"The feedings are just feedings. Let them be what they are," he said.

I nodded slowly, feeling stupid. So very stupid.

"So just let this be what it is?" I asked.

He tilted his head to the side.

"Isn't that what you want?" he asked me, almost cautious.

I looked down at my hands. I had been the one who didn't want to get emotionally attached. And he had just told me to not dwell too much on what happened during the feedings.

I nodded. He was right. What we had was more. We came

together during feedings like lovers, and I never wanted to be parted from him. But after, when I didn't have the haze of his blood enveloping me, my insecurities and fears rushed back, paralyzing me. And then we came together again. It was a never-ending cycle.

But the cycle was all self-created in my mind. This was not the same toxic cycle Sethos and I had been in, where he would hurt me—physically sometimes—and I would crawl back to him, hoping the next day would be better.

Aeroth was considerate. Kind. He wanted my friendship. Aeroth respected my magic.

And most of all—he was *realistic*.

He didn't expect me to want to be by his side simply because he was my mate.

Where Sethos had been possessive, Aeroth simply wanted to let me be.

In fact, he wanted me to pursue a life of my own after The Settling year was up.

"Renna," Aeroth said. "If this is too much for you, tell me. We can figure out a way to bring a medic mage for blood exchanges."

Aeroth had once said to me he craved me so much he wanted to live inside me. While I knew exchanging blood medically was what I *should* want, my need for him eclipsed all reason.

"I vowed to you, when I helped you escape Daya, that as long as there are stars in the sky, my word would be true. Tell me what you need and it's yours."

I lifted my eyebrows.

I needed him.

But I was so afraid.

"I vow to respect you," he said. "To consider you. Honor your needs. And be what you need me to be to make this year go smoother."

He took hold of my hands, and I bit the inside of my cheek to keep from crying. My emotions were erratic.

Aeroth continued. "I don't hurt my friends. I value and care for you—not just as my mate but as a person. Allow me the opportunity to show that your trust in me—*your friendship with me*—is not misplaced."

As if he had somehow lifted a great weight from my shoulders, I was finally able to take what felt like the first deep breath since we arrived in Elinoor.

I had a year with Aeroth side by side.

I could do this.

"Okay."

"Okay?" he asked and studied me, as if he wasn't sure he'd heard me.

"Yes. I agree to be your friend."

A lazy smile formed on his lips.

In that moment, Demira called us over, and we looked to see that the camp for the night was set up. Five sleep bags were set up inside the semi-circle perimeter.

"Shall we walk back?" he asked me.

"Yes."

After a few moments of walking, he spoke up again.

"As your friend, I have to tell you that the sleep bags Demira has conjured for the group will not be comfortable to sleep on."

I chuckled. "I don't think comfort is in anyone's mind. This is a makeshift camp."

"We could portal to Eniraath for the night . . ." he said.

I looked to him.

". . . and come back in a few hours," he finished.

"And leave everyone else?" I shook my head.

"I don't care about everyone else. I care about my back. And my bed is much more comfortable," he said.

I clenched my fists, pressing my nails to my palms to keep from thinking about mattresses and Aeroth's body.

"We're staying, Aeroth." I lowered my chin. "Out of solidarity. Your back will survive. As will mine."

We ate food conjured by both Demira and Illona, and everyone began to settle in for the night. Aeroth and I chose sleep bags next to each other, lying side by side.

Cylas glared at Aeroth and me the entire time, muttering to himself, and was short when responding to questions. Finally, Illona snapped. She got out of her sleep bag and stood, hands on her hips and eyes narrowed.

"Why don't you do us an honor and leave for a while?" she said to him.

Cylas got out of his sleep bag and also stood.

"Gladly," he replied. "This space suddenly feels too small."

"I don't give a shit." She lifted her chin. "We haven't slept for days, and I won't have you here shuffling about and cursing under your breath when we are trying to sleep."

"If you come back," Demira said from her sleep bag, not bothering to move, "the protection wards will let you back in. Don't wake us up."

He huffed something unintelligible and vanished into a portal. I watched as Illona stared at the spot where Cylas had been and shook her head.

"Lay down, Illona," Demira said gently. "Forget him. Truly, you will be better off."

Illona stood for a few more moments and then settled back down.

I turned to face Aeroth, greeted by heavy eyelids and a soft smile.

"Will you sleep this time or go to the Astral?" I asked in a hushed voice.

"The Astral Plane will be fine without me for a few more days.

As long as I stay alive and the Keepers that watch over it remain vigilant, everything will be fine."

I snuggled into my sleep bag and put my hand on the bottom of my cheek.

"Keepers?"

He nodded and yawned. "They are members of the royal family. They are the spares who did not get to rule, but who have the ability to travel in and out of the Astral Plane and Astral project at ease."

Interesting.

"But they don't have powers like you?" I asked.

He shook his head. "Only the ascended rulers are one with the Astral Plane itself. The Keepers serve the monarch and the Astral Plane."

Aeroth yawned again.

"Sleep," I said to him.

He nodded wordlessly and closed his eyes.

He looked so carefree with his eyes closed. I knew he did not need sleep, but I was glad he was allowing his body to rest.

I moved slightly closer to him and closed my eyes.

I could not help but notice the smile on my face as I drifted off to sleep.

37

RENNA

Lips moved against my neck, rousing me from sleep.

My body thrummed in response, and warmth spread through me in waves.

Aeroth.

I was facing away from him, with my back to his front. Even though our sleep bags separated us, we were almost spooning.

He brought his arm around me and pulled me to his chest. I closed my eyes and melted into his embrace. His tongue darted to my skin, lapping at my neck in silence, and I stifled a moan.

He moved his lips to my ear. “I could eat you right up,” he said.

I nodded almost automatically. There was no danger. We were not physically separated. This was pure desire. Aeroth merely wanted to feed from me for the pleasure of it. My core pulsed at the thought.

I could do this with him. This was just a feeding. An indulgence. A raw need.

And most importantly, I had finally convinced Aeroth to drink my blood after being in denial. I could not refuse him now.

Nor did I want to refuse him.

I opened my eyes, glancing at my sleeping sisters.

"Not here," I whispered to him.

"Agreed," he said.

In unison, trying to be as silent as possible, we got out of our sleep bags and left the perimeter. We carried two torches with us to light our path. Our steps were fast as we walked to the next passageway and turned a corner.

As soon as we were out of sight, Aeroth pushed me against the wall, and my arms and legs came around him as he held me by my ass.

He grunted as I squeezed my thighs against him, his lips rushing down to my skin again, almost frenzied. He alternated between licking, sucking, and raking his teeth against my neck.

Everything he did shot straight to my core, and I could not help but moan against his shoulder.

"Look at you. And I haven't even tasted you," he said. "I need to feed."

"Is that what this is?" I teased.

He nipped me hard, and I whimpered.

"Let me," he urged.

Anyone looking at Aeroth's large warrior body would assume he was a man who took with no permission. But he was just the opposite. Aeroth valued consent, and it only made him more endearing.

"Say yes," he said against my skin.

"Hmmm . . ." I said, pushing my body impossibly closer.

"Renna," he warned. "I need you."

His words undid me, and I bent my neck to the side.

"Bite me," I whispered.

He smiled against my skin.

"Make me feel," I urged and pulled the neck of my shirt to the side.

"Does me taking from you feel good?" he teased.

I nodded. He knew it did.

"*Yes.*"

"Would you like me to bite you on the neck?"

I didn't understand the question. I knew the other place he could bite me was my thigh.

"What are you suggesting?" I asked him, my body on fire.

"You asked me to make you feel good." He leaned down to nuzzle my neck. "There are other places I could feed from."

He ran a hand across my chest, his fingertips lightly teasing my nipples.

Did he mean he would drink from my breasts?

My core throbbed, and my slick dripped from me.

He pushed his forehead against mine, bringing our lips close. It took everything in me to not give in to the moment and kiss him.

What would kissing Aeroth feel like?

"I vowed to honor your needs. To consider you," he whispered. "Tell me where to feed."

My heart raced. I was breathless. I wanted the pleasure he promised, but . . .

I shook my head. "My neck," I urged him.

He smiled against my skin. "As you command," he said, and his canines pierced into me.

I opened my mouth and screamed silently.

We moved against each other in silence, my body rising and falling against his chest and torso, him urging me with one hand on my ass and the other on my back.

I never wanted the rush I felt in his arms to end, and when he pulled away, I almost grasped him to me to keep feeding.

Seeing my blood on his lips did something to me, and I leaned forward, licking my blood from the corners of his mouth. Aeroth stilled, holding his breath as I worked.

"Do you like how you taste?" he whispered.

I pulled away to look at him. My blood was not like his—that tasted almost like honey. To me, my blood tasted like metal. But I liked the taste of my blood on him.

"I like how I taste on you," I admitted.

He smiled wickedly, then set me down and took off his shirt.

My eyes roamed over his skin and the way the torchlight cast shadows on his tanned skin.

He grinned. "Like what you see?"

A shameless smile spread over my face, and my blush deepened even more. He created an incision on his neck and opened his arms out to me to pick me up.

I hesitated and looked to the ground.

"You would rather I sit?" he asked.

I nodded. "I'm tired. You did wake me up in the middle of the night. And don't pretend like the need was dire."

He chuckled and sat against the cave wall and looked up at me as if he was waiting. Immediately, I realized that him sitting on the ground meant I would have to straddle him.

I gulped.

"Oh, the need is dire, Strongborn. I tried to stay away from you." He shook his head.

"And now?"

"It is no longer an option."

I blushed.

"Come, Daughter of Darkness," he growled. "The Astral Night begs you come."

Yes.

He extended his hand to me, and my body moved toward him. When my hand touched his, he pulled me down, and my knees bracketed his hips, draping over either side of him.

"Drink." His voice was hoarse.

As soon as my lips touched his skin and his blood flowed through my system, I was lost. I welcomed the erotic haze of him to envelop me and make me forget who I was. Even if this moment with Aeroth was something passing.

38

RENNA

Nothing could have prepared me for seeing the rider descendant city.

Andora and the other two human planets were governed by technology. Vast skyscrapers flooded the landscape, creating dense concrete jungles, while levitating road markers indicated highways that zipped around buildings. Buildings were covered in glass. Even my modest studio dorm room had floor-to-ceiling windows.

On Andora, the city landscapes looked like a glittering, glass mirage against the sand.

In much the same way, the city before us also glittered. But instead of glass, it was carved into stone and precious metals encrusted the cavern walls.

As I looked around, I noticed how the oval windows of the various buildings were all tinted, so we could not see inside.

Illona pointed above us, and when I looked up, my jaw dropped.

A large, flat, glowing circle hovered above the city, providing artificial sunlight. The light must have been enchanted so our eyes did not hurt as we stared.

I followed the rays to see a luscious landscape on the ground level, designed in a polished and symmetrical pattern. Flower beds lined the buildings, and trees were planted along the pathway.

The streets were cobblestone, made from the cavern stone itself, only adding to the glittering splendor of this hidden city.

As my eyes drifted to the city below, I observed people walking around dressed in robes of various muted earthy colors, almost mimicking the shades found in the caverns. Oddly, all the women wore robes in various shades of red.

Unlike in Taria, where there were no children, people of all ages moved about the city.

The city was vibrant, bustling with activity, from the street vendor pushing his cart through the center plaza announcing his wares, to the merchants carrying rugs across town. A woman shepherded small children across the square while a nearby elderly couple entered a storefront.

"I would have never imagined a place like this," Illona said next to me.

Demira snorted at Illona's other side.

"*Really?*" she asked Illona. "I doubt that. Did the Ancestors not describe this place?"

I looked to Illona, who shook her head. "They tell me many things, but sometimes I either tune them out or they hold back. It's becoming incredibly frustrating. I do appreciate the general clues of events, but I wish I knew more details." She looked to me. "Like in changes and alliances about to occur."

I shifted on my feet and looked away from her. She reminded me of Livina with her ability to foresee the fate.

And like Livina, I had now learned that Illona could only reveal what she was allowed. No more and no less. I wondered if what she shared was governed by a code of honor with the dead she spoke with.

I doubted Livina would be a fan of someone sharing the future when she guarded fate so closely.

"No time like the present," Cylas said to us, gesturing to the city below. "Let's get to it, friends."

Illona rolled her eyes and moved past him to descend, Demira following her. Cylas stood back with his mouth ajar while Demira grimaced at him as she passed.

Cylas looked to me. "What did I do?" he asked, his palms up in the air.

I lowered my chin, my eyes narrowed. "Do you really need me to spell it out for you?"

"I saved you all in the forest," he said and crossed his arms.

Aeroth grumbled beside me.

I sighed. "Cylas, the truth is you haven't been the most pleasant to be around."

"That's an understatement," Aeroth murmured.

Cylas glared at him. "Perhaps the problem isn't me."

Aeroth had been nothing but pleasant and had done everything to help us and protect our journey.

I stepped forward. "And perhaps you should go down to the city, Cylas."

He stared at me in disbelief.

"You've chosen him," Cylas gritted out. "Haven't you?"

My eyebrows lifted. "What is that supposed to mean?" I snapped.

Cylas looked up to the caves and sighed. He closed his eyes for a brief second before looking at me.

"Nothing," he grimaced. "Nothing at all." Cylas spun on his heels and walked down to the city.

I knew Cylas disliked Aeroth because he was Naaviri. But now I wondered if my dynamic with Aeroth bothered him because he felt something more for me. I knew Cylas felt emotions deeply. He was a caring friend. He wanted to ensure people's safety. He traveled the galaxies to find me—something I could never repay him for.

But when it came to romantic relationships, Cylas was . . . well, Cylas. Everyone knew he had multiple partners and never seemed serious about any of them. As much as I was attracted to Cylas, I could never see myself with him long term.

Aeroth moved to stand beside me, both of us watching as the rest of our group descended the stairs.

"You don't have to defend me," Aeroth said.

I shrugged. "He was rude."

"I can take care of myself."

I looked to him. "Just because you can take care of yourself doesn't mean you have to."

His gaze turned to mine, and a small smile formed on his lips. "Well, I'm flattered. I don't remember the last time a woman defended my honor."

I nodded once.

"Thank you," he said and shifted on his feet. He crossed his arms and turned his face to look at the city. "That's a lot of fucking stairs. I have half a mind to portal right into their square."

I chuckled. "And cause panic? They've never met us before."

"Panic? You think so? Some are already noticing Demira and the rest. Can't you see them pointing? They look almost . . . *excited*."

I looked down at the plaza and saw some people gathered in clusters, pointing. Some vendors even pushed their carts to the foot of the stairs.

"I wonder how often they get visitors."

Aeroth clapped once. "Alright, I'm going to portal," he said. "Fuck these stairs."

"The mighty King of the Astral won't use the Astral Plane instead to travel? Portaling like a lazy option when you can just step through reality."

Aeroth turned to me and pursed his lips. "I can't travel through the Astral with you in your physical form. You will freeze to death. Hence, we will portal instead."

I smirked. "Maybe I can put more layers on to combat the cold?"

Aeroth's eyes scanned my body, and a lazy smile formed on his lips.

"What makes you think I want you in more layers?" he asked, quirking an eyebrow up.

My body broke out in a simmering heat, and I bit my inner cheek to keep from laughing nervously.

Aeroth opened a portal and reached his hand toward mine. His voice was low and dark like a caress when he spoke. "Come, Daughter of Darkness."

I wanted to place my hand in his and allow him to draw me into his arms, but I was still getting used to the growing intimacy between us, the craving I had for his blood . . . and him.

I looked down at the stairs.

"I'll take the stairs," I said quickly and walked in that direction.

Aeroth growled and, in the next moment, was gone through the portal.

My eyes focused on the plaza awaiting his arrival, and I laughed as a portal opened and saw him step through. He was instantly surrounded by people who seemed to want to get a good look.

I was grateful for the blood exchange we had done earlier, as it allowed me the freedom to be away from him for a time. Besides, I knew distance was healthy, because as each day and feeding passed, I wanted nothing more than to remain at his side.

I bit my lip, recalling how my hands moved down his abdomen the last time we fed from each other. My body tingled from the memory of his lips on my skin, and I felt like I was on fire. My core throbbed.

In that moment, Aeroth turned to look in my direction.

I turned pink.

I actually prefer you taking the stairs, Strongborn, his voice sounded in my head.

I almost tripped.

It allows me to look at you at leisure.

I recalled that Aeroth said he had exceptional hearing. So I spoke back in a normal tone.

"How's it going down there?" I asked, trying to change the subject. "The people seem to love you."

Did I ever tell you that you have exceptional legs?

I squeaked a nonsensical response.

He laughed.

You're beautiful, Renna.

"*Er* . . ." I cleared my throat, and a smile broke from my lips. "Thank you."

A man in long brown robes and a bald head approached Aeroth and began to engage him in conversation.

I continued down the stairs until I joined my sisters, Cylas, and Aeroth on the plaza.

After we greeted the citizens of the rider descendants city, Aeroth introduced us to the bald man who had approached him. The man's name was Wyleth, the senior elder of Elsbeth, city of the rider descendants. He ushered our group into a great hall they called the Aelderhall.

The Aelderhall was like the rest of the carved structures in Elsbeth—the exterior was a honey-brown color with bits of precious metals at the surface. It made the façade of the hall look resplendent against the daylight disc above us.

The inside of the structure also boasted the same earthy tones, and the furniture inside was also carved from stone. Chairs and couches filled the space, the plush, jeweled-tone cushions matching the rugs that sprawled throughout.

Overhead, the ceiling was several stories high. Metal chandeliers hung symmetrically in a row from the entrance to the end, where a raised dais stood with seven thrones.

The six other elders greeted us inside the hall with reserved excitement, unlike Wyleth and the rest of the citizens of the city, who had enthusiastically shaken our hands and draped flowers around our necks.

"Elsbeth is lucky to be visited by both a God and the King of the Astral in one day," Wyleth declared as he sat down in the middle throne on the raised dais.

The rest of the elders joined him, sitting in their respective thrones, their faces stoic.

"We're here too," Demira said, her arms now crossed. "Or are we invisible?"

Wyleth almost turned pink and cleared his throat. I wondered if he was wary that the daughters of Am-Re were in his city.

"Of course not . . ." Wyleth nodded, uneasily eyeing Demira. He coughed and asked a nearby attendant for wine.

Demira began. "Well then. We are here seeking—"

Aeroth cut her off.

"You have a beautiful city, Wyleth," Aeroth said, his voice smooth.

Demira grumbled and almost interrupted, but I saw Illona grab her hand and squeeze it.

Demira silenced.

Wyleth smiled at Aeroth. "We are happy you think so. This is our peaceful little corner of the universe."

"You certainly designed this city to be left alone," Aeroth said.

"After the Wars . . ." Wyleth shook his head. "I was a boy then, but our elders at the time set out to find a place where we could peacefully exist. No one ever pays attention to the planet of Elinoor." He looked to Demira. "We were a nomad people before the Wars and are now glad to have a steady home base."

"The Wars were hard on a great many people," Aeroth agreed.

Wyleth perched on the edge of his seat, his eyes wide on Aeroth. "You fought in them? The Galactic Wars?" He shook his head. "Of course you must have!"

"When the need for peace is great, we all must step up to protect it." Aeroth looked around. "I don't blame your Ancestors for settling here."

"Why have you come?" a female elder dressed in a bright red robe asked Aeroth. Her lips were pressed in a tight line.

Aeroth stepped closer to the dais.

"We come here seeking peace, like the one your Ancestors and I fought for. You may not be aware of the state of affairs in other parts, but war has begun."

An attendant approached the dais and handed Wyleth a golden goblet. Wyleth drank copiously before answering.

Wyleth sat back in his chair. "I presume you are here seeking our involvement in some manner in this war?" he asked. "We are in the midst of our equinox celebrations. This is really not the best time to start conducting business."

Cylas stepped up beside Aeroth. "Am-Re's successor, Sethos Physerion, attacked my enclave months ago."

The elders all gasped.

"Why?" an elder asked him.

I was grateful Cylas did not turn to face me or point me as the cause.

"Am-Re is Arios's twin brother. Am-Re has warred with us for eons, always seeking to absorb the powers of the enclave gods for himself. His successor, Sethos, recently came into power with the same agenda. Am-Re no longer holds a corporeal form, but is very much alive and in the background. While he is not as strong as he was before, his magic controls Sethos."

Wyleth frowned. "And how does that affect us?" he asked Cylas.

"If Am-Re and Sethos are successful in destroying my enclave and absorbing the powers of the gods, then they will have unmatched powers. The dynamic of the universes will shift. No god or supernatural will be safe. We need to stop them now."

The female elder spoke up again, leaning forward in her seat. "You have still not told us how that affects us. We are in Elinoor, a planet no one visits. And we are below ground. Am-Re would not come *here*. We have nothing to offer him."

"And," Wyleth added, "you have not told us how you expect us to help you." He gestured to himself and his elders. "Surely you can see we are not warriors." He nodded to Aeroth. "We live in peace. We do not want war."

An elder at the right end of the dais spoke. He frowned and rubbed his chin. "Forgive me for the brusque question, but what made you want to come here? Why seek us out?"

Demira moved to stand on the other side of Aeroth.

"I had a vision we had the Metidons on our side assisting us in the war," she said. "We come to ask for their help."

The elders all silenced, their faces contorted in horror.

The female elder spoke. "Is this a jest? You waste our time with this offensive question."

Aeroth cleared his throat. "Offensive?" he tilted his head. "Please enlighten me."

The female elder pointed at Demira. "Do you not know who she is? And what she's done?"

I looked to Illona in that moment, and she nodded for me to

go to Demira. Illona and I moved to stand beside her. Aeroth furrowed his brows.

"Done?" he asked and looked back to the elders. "Pardon me, but we've just arrived."

Wyleth stood. "It is no secret our people are the descendants of the riders who took the Metidons to the Wars. Our partnership with the great beasts came to be because we were both nomadic groups. When the Wars broke out, we had already forged loyalty and friendship with the Metidons, and they allowed us to fight with them."

Demira crossed her arms.

"I did not fight in the Wars," Demira interjected. "I have caused no offense. Your quarrel, perhaps, is with my father, in which case, I want nothing to do with him. Although I cannot renege on my birth, I can assure you I am nothing like him."

"Be that as it may," the female elder replied, "you are the last person the Metidons will want to see. You are quite infamous in our history."

Demira narrowed her eyes. "*Excuse me?*" she snapped.

Wyleth walked down the dais and stood in front of her.

"You married Corrigrant, King of the Tatuiyah Fae. Did you not?"

Demira paled.

"*Yes,*" she replied, her voice faint.

"And were you not at fault for his death on the night of your wedding? His son Oberon, now King Oberon, slayed his father, did he not?" Wyleth asked.

Demira lowered her head. "I . . ." Demira's voice was hoarse. "I didn't mean to—"

"Did you know the Metidons originally hail from Daya and the other lands of the Tatuiyah Fae?"

My heart sank.

Demira looked up at him.

"No." Her voice cracked.

"Did you know that after King Oberon slayed his father, his family fractured? He was deemed mad and his lands went wild. Criminals now live in them. The Metidons abandoned their homeland. They became nomads."

"Because of me," Demira whispered.

Wyleth lifted an eyebrow. "Oberon slayed his father. You did not. The Metidons, however, speak of your involvement in their history. You are the woman who seduced the young prince to kill his father."

Demira shook her head. "I didn't seduce him—"

"A likely story." The female elder chuckled and also stood. "I have heard enough!"

Demira turned red and shook her head. Her fists clenched and her jaw tightened. Illona placed a hand on her arm.

"Dee . . ." Illona whispered.

Demira shrugged her off.

"I was raped!" Demira told the room.

The elders stood in silence once more, their eyes blinking.

"Corrigrant raped me. Violated me. *Wounded me.* All on the night of our wedding. I was a young woman. So young. My father betrothed me to Corrigrant against my will."

"Demira," Illona whispered. "You don't have to share."

Demira continued, her voice loud and clear.

"Corrigrant's death was just for what he did to me. I am sorry for what transpired after. I will live with that night forever. But know this," she spat as she looked at the elders, "I never seduced Oberon. I never asked him to kill his father."

Another female elder spoke up then, her voice soft. "Then why did he do it? He went mad after. His family and lands were destroyed. Help us understand."

"Oberon killed his father because," Demira's voice broke, "Oberon is my mate."

A collective gasp filled the room.

Cylas whistled, and Illona slapped him on the back of the head.

"Oberon saw me after his father had . . ." Demira shook her head. "He found me crying. Wounded. We did not know we were mates, but when we touched hands as he helped me up, we knew . . ."

I looked to Aeroth and found his gaze. Our lives had changed from one touch as well.

"That night was a blur," Demira said. "I never saw Oberon again after. My father kept us apart."

I had so many questions for Demira, among them how she dealt with separation pain. The pain was excruciating. I felt sorrow for her, and I knew that my idea of who Demira was would have to change. She carried so much rage inside her. Her moods and actions had to be correlated to Corrigrant's actions and her separation from Oberon.

I wanted to hug her, but I doubted she would have wanted me to.

"I realize now what horrible circumstance I find myself in," Demira stated. "Having had a vision of the beasts that hate me. But I have clung to that vision for months. I know that riding into battle with them is what I must do."

The first female elder now stepped down from the dais and stood in front of Demira.

"You have given us much to think about this night." She looked to the rest of the elders.

"Where are the Metidons?" Demira asked. "May I speak to them and explain what happened?"

The woman looked uneasy, but Wyleth nodded to her.

"We are amongst friends," Wyleth told her. "We trust the God of the Planets and Aeroth, King of the Astral, will *not* allow the location of the Metidons to be divulged?"

Both Cylas and Aeroth nodded. Anger coursed through me as Wyleth acted as if my sisters and I were not in the room.

The elder woman spoke. "The Metidons are located outside these caves, in the lake you may have seen when you entered this cave system. There are underwater caverns, enchanted with oxygen pockets, where the Metidons reside. And no, we cannot give you access to the Metidons, as we, the elders, are their only contact with the world. You are a stranger."

Demira scoffed.

"*However,*" the elder woman continued, "the elders can confer whether we can petition them on your behalf."

"*When?*" Demira asked.

The woman laughed as if Demira's question was absurd. She crossed her arms. "We are in the middle of the equinox festivities!"

Demira frowned. "That is not an answer."

Wyleth spoke quickly. "Business is suspended until *after* the equinox."

Demira shook her head and paced the room. Illona joined her and murmured words to her.

"How long are your equinox festivities?" Aeroth asked.

"Fifteen days," Wyleth responded. "Today is the second day."

What if Sethos attacked within that time? We could not wait. I opened my mouth to speak, but Aeroth was in my mind.

Easy, Strongborn.

I turned my face to look at him, my eyes narrowed to slits.

I know you were about to tell them that waiting that long is not good enough. I know you are worried about Sethos attacking. However, the politics of this place are complex. Let this play out. We need to be on the good side of the Elsbeth elders so they lobby on our behalf.

I frowned and crossed my arms.

"Will you stay and join us for the celebrations?" Wyleth asked us.

Demira and Illona paused and looked at the rest of us. Demira's scowl and fiery eyes said it all: She would not partake. And I didn't blame her. She had just shared a traumatic experience that had shaped her. I would not want to celebrate either.

Cylas clapped once. "I always love a good party," he said, breaking the tension in the air.

I frowned at him.

Wyleth's face lit up, and he looked to the god. "We are honored by your presence. Our people have never met a god before, so I am sure they will be eager to serve."

Cylas snorted a laugh. "I don't need them to serve me. Just point me in the direction of your nearest tavern."

Wyleth smiled and looked to the rest of us.

"The equinox celebrations happen every two years for our people," he said. "We have bonfire gatherings and dancing for the adults, and for the children, we tell stories, sharing the history of our people. Food and drink overflow. People get married. Children are baptized in our faith at our temple. Homes get blessed. Animals are anointed."

"It's a celebration for all," the second female elder spoke, her eyes beaming. "We have a final bonfire on the tenth day where we thank Source with a ritual." She smiled. "With your presence here this year, it will be our most celebrated year to date."

"We hope you stay," Wyleth told us.

The first female elder spoke. "Oh, they must. A once-in-a-lifetime opportunity."

Something was off about their comments, but I couldn't pinpoint what it was. I shifted uncomfortably.

Cylas spoke. "A ritual?" he asked. "Sounds ominous."

The female elder turned almost as red as her clothing.

"Nothing of the sort. Merely a retelling of the history of our people and the Metidons."

Cylas frowned. "Are you certain we have to partake? Why is the ritual so important?"

Wyleth shook his head. "The ritual has become part of our shared history. The last time they were bothered without a ritual, they were violent. They attacked the past leaders. Lives were lost. They are not gentle beasts. They were very specific in requiring a ritual on the equinox whenever we petition them."

"Well then," Cylas sighed. "I guess we'll wait it out?" He turned to look at our group.

Demira glared at him while I shrugged. We had come all this way—we could not leave now.

The hall became quiet, and Wyleth stepped off the dais. He clapped Cylas on the shoulders. "Come. Enough serious talk. You have said you love a good party. Let us show you all the city and the festivities."

As Cylas walked from the hall with Wyleth, Demira and Illona remained in place.

"I'm sorry," I said to Demira.

Demira looked away from me and crossed her arms. "I don't want to talk about it."

I looked to Illona, who gave me a small smile. "Demira and I will stay behind," she said and hugged her around the shoulders. "Please," Illona said to Aeroth and I, "follow Cylas."

My brows gathered. "They're insensitive," I said to Illona with a hushed tone. "Celebrating with them is the last thing I want to do at this moment." I looked to Demira again. "Do you want us to keep you company?"

"No," she replied in a curt tone.

Illona rubbed Demira's back. "*Please,*" she said to Aeroth and I again. "You have trusted me this far. *Go.*" She gestured to Wyleth and Cylas, who were almost at the door. "Follow Cylas. We will stay behind."

I looked to Aeroth and Illona. "I don't feel like celebrating," I said to them.

Aeroth ignored my comment and spoke to Illona. "Where will you both be?" he asked them. "Do you need assistance?"

"Is anything the matter?" Wyleth called back to us from the Aelderhall entrance.

His question was tactless. Of course something was the matter. Demira was clearly upset. How could he not have empathy for a woman who has just shared a story like that?

Illona spoke up. "My sister does not feel well," she told Wyleth. "We require a room to rest and sleep."

Wyleth nodded, and he waved two attendants over to him and Cylas. He spoke to them quickly, and the attendants rushed to us. They bowed when they approached us and straightened to speak.

"Elder Wyleth has directed us to lead you to accommodations," the attendant said. "We have guest rooms above the Aelderhall. Please follow us."

Demira and Illona began to follow, but I grabbed Illona's hand and stopped her.

"Are you sure I should go?" I asked her. "I don't feel right leaving you after—"

"*Just go!*" Demira barked over her shoulder. "Save me pity theatrics."

My jaw opened, and I dropped Illona's hand.

Illona offered me an apologetic smile. "Trust me. We will be okay." She lowered her chin and looked intently into my eyes. "*You* need to follow Cylas." She lifted her eyebrow. "Do you understand?"

I nodded.

Illona looked to Aeroth with a knowing look. "We are meant to be here. Let us be gracious guests and enjoy. *Perhaps*," she paused and lifted her chin, "we can learn more of this city? How things work?"

Aeroth frowned slightly but nodded.

I knew there was more in her words. What had she meant?

Illona smiled and looked to the attendants. "Please lead the way to our room."

Aeroth and I watched Demira and Illona walk off.

"Shall we?" he asked and gestured to Cylas and Wyleth, who stood waiting at the entrance of the hall, looking expectantly at us.

"If I must," I gritted out, and we both walked to join them.

39

RENNA

Outside of the Aelderhall, an attendant approached us carrying a tray with goblets. Wyleth eagerly picked up the goblets and gave us each one.

"No celebration can start without wine," Wyleth added with a cunning smile to Cylas, Aeroth, and I. "Please try it."

Without hesitation, Cylas chugged his wine and set his empty goblet down on the tray.

"That's very good wine," Cylas agreed, then grabbed another goblet and drank again.

Aeroth took a polite sip of his wine and nodded in agreement.

I also drank the wine. It smelled like honey and tasted like a mixture of flowers and berries. It was too sweet for me.

"It's very floral," I commented with a smile, trying not to sound rude.

Wyleth smiled. "We make it for the equinox. But I must be frank," Wyleth said and leaned in toward us as if he was sharing a secret, lowering his voice, "the wine is potent stuff, please drink with caution."

"In that case," Cylas said and grabbed another goblet.

I muttered a curse under my breath. I wondered if Illona had foreseen Cylas's intoxication this night and asked me to follow him for that reason. Was he going to do something stupid that would jeopardize our time here?

Wyleth looked to Aeroth and I. "He is quite lively for a god." He chuckled.

Cylas raised his goblet. "That I am, old man." He lifted his eyebrow. "Please," Cylas gestured beyond the plaza, "show us your city."

Wyleth nodded enthusiastically and led us through the city. The street vendors from our arrival were there greeting us once more, and more citizens welcomed us to their city, thanking us for sharing the equinox with them. A little girl with red hair and purple flowers in her hair began to walk alongside me, holding her doll close. She grinned up at me.

I stopped walking and knelt in front of her. Our group and Wyleth stopped and turned to face us.

"Hello," I said to her. "How is your equinox?"

She lowered her chin with a small smile and looked up at me. I wondered if she was too shy to speak. My eyes lowered to her little doll. The doll had long black hair and wore a long red dress with yellow and orange swirling ribbons at the hem. The doll also had a red braided ribbon on her neck from where the little girl had been holding her. I watched as the doll's head almost wobbled on the edge of decapitation.

"Here," I said to her and gently grabbed her doll. I held the doll by its middle and handed it back to her. "Your doll may like it better if you hold her from here."

The girl smiled and took the doll from me.

A worried woman, who also had red hair and had facial features that resembled the little girl, came up to us from the crowd. She apologized for the girl having bothered us, picked her up, and took the girl away and into the crowd.

Aeroth came to stand next to me and offered me his hand so I could stand.

I took it, and we continued walking. As we walked deeper into the cave, the light that had greeted us began to fade as we descended into darker surroundings. Floating orbs cast a warm glow along the cave walls, highlighting the colorful decorations for the equinox. Everywhere we looked, we saw flower displays on trestle tables, and ribbons wrapped around lampposts with glowing orbs inside the lanterns.

Children in groups ran to-and-fro, laughing while caretakers scolded and walked behind them. Every so often, troupes of musicians played lively tunes and couples danced.

We approached what looked like another plaza, a large bonfire blazing in the middle of while another band of musicians sat nearby, playing merry music with flutes and string instruments.

Elsbeth was lively and enchanting, and the celebrations made you want to participate. I looked down at my wine and took another sip.

"This portion of our city is the only family-friendly section of our equinox celebrations," Wyleth said. "However, if you walk down this path," he pointed to a torch-lit path to our right, "you will see six other squares with bonfires lit throughout the cave system. Each area around the bonfires has a different atmosphere of celebration where adults can enjoy the festivities, and each other."

Cylas smirked. "I like it here," he said.

"If a lack of clothing does not disturb you, great god," Wyleth noted, his face flushed, "you will find the last two bonfires to your liking."

"Say no more!" Cylas winked and walked down the path without a glance back at us.

I moved after Cylas. "*Wait!*"

Cylas stopped and looked over his shoulder at me with a grin. "Well aren't you adventurous?" he said with a raised eyebrow.

I rolled my eyes and linked my arm around his.

"It's not what you think," I told him as he guided us down the cave system. "I'm just making sure you don't do anything stupid."

He laughed.

"And I'm still angry you have been rude to Aeroth," I told him.

Cylas groaned. "You can't be serious. He's *nothing*, Renna."

I frowned. "He's not nothing. Why do you dislike him so much?"

"Are you truly that oblivious?" he asked me, looking down.

I paused. We had reached the second bonfire. The area was filled with young adults and had an atmosphere of heavy drinking and boisterous laughter. Mugs overflowing with alcohol clinked. No robbed or cloaked people were to be found here. Instead, the women wore short, red dresses and the men had tunic shirts and long pants. It reminded me of a university tavern with young people enjoying each other's company.

I looked to Cylas. "What am I oblivious about?" I asked him.

"He wants you," Cylas seethed. He shook his head. "Can you not see that?"

I blushed. I knew Aeroth craved my blood. And it was no mistake how I affected him when we came together during feedings.

Just let the feedings be what they are, Aeroth had said.

I shrugged. "It's not what you think," I told Cylas.

"Is he feeding from you?" he asked with a disgusted look.

I took my arm back and crossed my arms.

"And if he is?" I asked.

Cylas stepped closer to me. "He's a Naaviri, Renna."

"*And?*"

"They use people as blood bags. I know the effects of drinking blood off of one. I had a lover who was Naaviri. I thought he loved me. But even I could never keep Hakeem satisfied. And I have full divine blood."

I shook my head. "I'm not Aeroth's lover."

"But isn't that how it feels?" Cylas prodded. "Just know you are nothing special to him. He *will* leave you."

I remained silent, realizing that Cylas had an extensive list of conquests, but it sounded like none of them had made him happy. At that moment, I felt incredibly sad for Cylas.

"I'm sorry that was your experience," I told him.

Cylas laughed bitterly. "Do you think Aeroth will stay true to you?" he said mockingly. "Is that why you defend him?"

I had asked Aeroth to not drink off another while he was with me. But I had also asked him to find another volunteer when he was to marry.

I looked around the cavern at the beautiful women with long legs and then looked down at my dirty combat boots and travel clothes. Would he find another person to feed from while we were here?

"Grow up," Cylas said to me. "It's better you realize now that Naaviri are filthy beings who will never care about your heart. Why do you entertain him?"

I hugged my arms. "We cannot be separated during The Settling," I told him. "Exchanging blood is a loophole. It allows us moments of freedom."

Cylas ran his hands through his hair. "*Is he forcing you?*" his tone was deadly.

I shook my head and looked down to the ground, a blush spreading through my skin. "No."

"Unbelievable," he said.

Cylas's words were hurtful, but I knew he could never understand the dynamic between Aeroth and I. What we had was too complex to explain.

"Do me a favor," Cylas said to me. "Don't ruin my night, alright? Just stay away. I don't want to see you two together."

My breath caught in my throat, and my chest tightened.

"Why are you being so cruel?" I asked him. "We're supposed to be friends."

Cylas stepped close to me so we were nose to nose.

"I don't want to be your *friend*," he whispered. "I've never wanted to be your friend."

I closed my eyes. "Cylas—"

"But you never give me a chance. No matter what I do for you. And you dare give a fucking Naaviri the time of day?"

"I didn't choose this, Cylas!" I said. "I'm trying to make the best of the situation."

Cylas moved his lips to my ear and slid his fingers through mine. "Then come with me. *Choose me.*"

A shiver ran down my spine, and I knew if the circumstances had been different, I would have chosen Cylas. I would have gone to the ends of the universe with him.

But I knew deep down Cylas was not for me.

I thought of the way Illona looked at him and how she worried over his well-being. Cylas deserved someone who looked at him the way Illona did.

Cylas stepped back slightly to look down at our joined hands.

"I've wanted you, Renna."

I nodded. "I know."

"I hated Khellios for taking you for himself when you first came to our enclave. I hate him for being a cause of your death."

"That's not fair," I told him. "And you know it."

He shook his head. "I always thought perhaps in time you'd choose me. That you'd see my patience. My—"

Cylas paused and looked to our left.

I followed his gaze.

Aeroth stood a few paces from us.

Cylas looked to me.

"I won't ask you again, Renna," Cylas said. "I am too proud."

I knew he was asking me to choose him again.

But I could not.

I disentangled our hands.

"I love you, Cylas. As a friend."

Cylas laughed, the sound bitter.

"You sure know how to deliver a killing blow," he said.

"I'm sorry—"

Cylas stepped back from me. "*Don't* follow me." His tone was hard.

I knew Illona had told me to follow him, so I wasn't sure what to do.

"Cylas," I called, "we can still keep each other company while we are here—"

"We will not." He looked to Aeroth and back to me. "At least allow a man his pride, Renna."

I shook my head. "We should stick together—"

"Ha!" Cylas said and crossed his arms. "You forget I know the haze of a Naaviri feeding," he snapped. "Spare me having to see you whining and begging him to fuck you."

I recoiled at his words. "Cylas—"

Aeroth stepped in front of my line of vision, blocking me from seeing Cylas.

"That's enough," Aeroth growled. "Don't talk to her that way."

"Fuck you," Cylas spat.

I pressed my forehead against Aeroth's back, just wanting the conversation to end. Nothing hurt more than when a friend deliberately wounded you.

I heard Cylas walk off farther into the cave at a furious pace.

Aeroth turned and gently held my arms. I could not look up at him. The entire conversation with Cylas left me unsettled.

"I'm sorry I intervened," Aeroth said. "I wanted to let you handle it, but I couldn't stand there and let him be cruel to you."

I nodded. "Thank you."

After a few moments of silence, Aeroth spoke again. "I'm sorry."

"For?" I asked him and looked up. Aeroth was looking into the bonfire.

"You are young and have so much to live for." Aeroth looked back at me. "And you have to remain at my side."

I sighed. "I don't think there is more to say about this. We are making the best of this situation."

I looked at the people around us laughing and conversing. They reminded me of my best friend Helena and her group of friends who enjoyed nights out at campus bars. Helena had always wanted me to join her. I had always declined because of the multiple jobs I had to juggle to pay for my tuition.

"You could go to him," Aeroth said.

My eyes snapped to Aeroth's. "*Cylas?*" I asked him.

Aeroth nodded.

"There is history there," Aeroth said and shrugged. "I can't . . ." Aeroth shook his head. "I won't prevent you from spending time with another if it makes you happy."

My palms became sweaty, and I blinked several times. Was this Aeroth's way of telling me that he would try and also seek someone else to spend time with?

"And what?" I asked. "You and I would come together only for feedings?"

"If that is what you wish."

No.

"I don't want Cylas," I told him.

Aeroth's gaze became intense, and I looked down to the ground.

"You could also find someone else to spend time with." I gestured to the crowd around us.

"I could."

My eyes flashed back to his.

Right.

Didn't I want emotional distance? This was my chance.

"You should," I said. "Maybe they have medics here that can help with a transfusion."

Aeroth remained silent and studied me, and I felt my skin flush under his scrutiny.

I lowered my eyes.

I felt too much. For him. For whatever this was.

"Let's keep walking, shall we?" I asked him. "Maybe we can keep an eye on Cylas from a distance."

Aeroth followed me in silence as we continued down the cave.

40

RENNA

Elsbeth's vast cave system and the city's architecture continued to amaze me.

We walked past restaurants and cafes with outdoor seating. The glow of the caves with the dim lighting created a romantic atmosphere, and there were many couples huddled close, enjoying food and drink together.

Aeroth moved closer to me, and our arms brushed once or twice, each time sending shivers down my spine. I tried to focus on locating Cylas, but he was nowhere to be found.

As we walked, people offered us goblet after goblet of wine. Minding Wyleth's warnings of its potency, I politely declined. Aeroth, however, drank frequently, and I tried to not worry about what effect the wine would have on him. I didn't deal well with belligerent, drunk people. It reminded me of my childhood with my foster mother and the painful memories there.

As Wyleth had told us, each bonfire area had people who were merrier, louder, and rowdier than the last. The dancing became bolder, more sensual, and at times, sexual.

At the fourth bonfire, my eyes widened as I saw two women and a man all kissing wildly on a bench. The women were opening the man's shirt and running their hands through his chest and farther down. One of the women straddled him while the other knelt behind her and began to unbuckle the man's pants.

When the man moaned, my body prickled with heat and my core pooled with lust in response, I quickened my pace.

After a few moments, we arrived at the fifth bonfire.

The people here were clothed in exquisite red lace and transparent red silks—leaving nothing to the imagination. The fabrics hung sensually, outlining every edge and curve of their bodies. I could do nothing but silently stare in awe and admire.

When Aeroth spoke up next to me, I was slightly startled as I had been lost in thought.

"You are free to go," he said to me. He took a sip of the goblet in his hand.

"Go? And leave you here?" I said, quirking an eyebrow up. I saw from the corner of my eye a group of giggling women eyeing us—or more specifically eyeing Aeroth.

"You frown?" Aeroth asked me. His tone was light. "Cheer up, Strongborn. This is a celebration."

I pursed my lips. "Right."

Aeroth looked to the group of women approaching us.

"Do you think we will ever find Cylas?" he asked.

"I'm sure he's at the last bonfire," I said, focused on the women. "*Obviously.*"

When Aeroth did not respond, I looked to him and found him looking down at me.

In that moment, the group of babbling women joined us and almost draped themselves on Aeroth.

One of the women who had an arm draped around Aeroth spoke. She had beautiful black hair and ice-blue eyes, her lips a ruby red. "We seldom have visitors of your type for the equinox." She smiled. "*Welcome.*"

"Thank you," Aeroth said to her. He kept his eyes on her face and not the rest of her body.

"You must all be hungry . . ." She licked her lips. "Thirsty? Come," she said and gestured to a large table with food.

Aeroth looked to me.

I lifted my eyebrows and grimaced at the women and him. "*Enjoy!*"

Aeroth shook his head and let the women lead him away. I clenched my jaw as I saw him jaunt off, not once turning to look at me. As if I were nonexistent.

But wasn't that what you wanted? my brain quipped.

"You are overdressed for this party," a woman said.

I turned to my right and saw a short blonde woman with purple streaks in her hair standing next to me. She was dressed much the same as the group of women leading Aeroth away.

I sighed and looked back to Aeroth. "It would seem I am," I told her.

"Elizabeta always gets the best men," she said, staring at the woman who had spoken to Aeroth. "She is the daughter of the cloth merchant here. Wealthy beyond your dreams. She is always the best dressed—especially for the equinox." The woman looked at my clothing and quirked up her eyebrow. "You sure are overdressed."

"I'm fine dressed as I am," I grumbled, looking down at my pants, long-sleeve shirt, and combat boots. "My clothes suffice."

"But to catch a man?" the woman asked me.

I rolled my eyes and looked at her. "I'm not trying to catch anyone."

She laughed. "Really?" She stepped closer to me. "You keep looking at him. Is he yours?"

I observed Aeroth and saw him almost stiffen, turning his head slightly in my direction.

He had impeccable hearing, didn't he?

Irritation fired through me at seeing the women flirt and flaunt themselves at him.

"No," I told the woman next to me. "He is not mine."

Aeroth chuckled to himself and completely gave me his back, allowing himself to be pulled into conversation by the women surrounding him, who were growing in numbers by each passing moment.

"I saw the way he looked at you," the woman said quietly. "That man desires you."

The fact that a stranger was commenting on my life irked me, but I stayed silent. I didn't feel like making enemies this late in the day.

"What brings you here?" she asked me.

I watched as Aeroth laughed heartily at whatever Elizabeta was telling him. She, in turn, blushed a beautiful pink, her nipples starting to darken and point.

A redheaded woman began to rub Aeroth's back.

Aeroth was free to bed anyone, as was I. We had no vows or promises between us. But when Elizabeta led Aeroth to a bonfire dance, my chest tightened.

He had not put up a fight and seemed to be genuinely enjoying himself.

Would he sleep with Elizabeta and then feed from me?

A gnarly feeling clawed its way around my heart.

Mine.

I was surprised at the sudden possessiveness. Was it the wine? The mate bond?

I needed to push away this feeling of ownership—fast. I needed to leave the bonfire.

I looked to the woman standing next to me and thought back on her question. "We are here seeking the Metidons," I told her.

Her eyes lit up.

"I wish you luck with that." She chuckled. "Maybe you being

here will coincide with a miracle. We petition them each year to work with us, and they decline our ritual every time."

I frowned. Despite her cheery nature, her words chilled me. The mention of the ritual again felt wrong.

"What is the ritual?" I asked.

The woman smiled. "Every year we sacrifice one criminal to the Metidons."

My mouth shaped into an *O*.

"Do you have a lot of crime in Elsbeth?" I asked her.

She laughed. "Gods, no." She shook her head. "This is a good city. We source our criminal sacrifice from Daya. Surely you have heard of it?"

I stilled.

Daya—the place I had spent months in with Sethos—was filled with fugitive criminal fae. The worst of murderers and crime lords resided there.

"I have heard of Daya," I told her.

She nodded. "We hang and then burn the criminal."

"I see."

"Every equinox, we do the sacrifice, and every time, the Metidons refuse to work with us." She shrugged. "It's quite tragic, really, when you consider our intertwined history with the beasts."

It was curious how casually she referred to the ritual, but I quickly remembered how I had used Darkness with no hesitation in the forest in self-defense. I also recalled my experience with Daya's criminals and how Sethos had urged me to kill three fae men for being murderers and arsonists.

Now, with the lives I had taken, I had no moral high ground to criticize Elsbeth's practices.

Thoughts of murder and Sethos, my time at Daya, and continuing to witness Aeroth dance with the women became too much. I needed to get away.

"What is your name?" I asked the woman next to me.

"Ada," she smiled.

"Ada, I need your help," I told her. "I need a place to rest. To sleep. I know there are guest rooms in the Aelderhall, but I'd rather not walk back on my own." The thought of walking through throngs of merrymaking did not seem appealing.

I knew I was taking a chance asking a stranger to help me find someplace to sleep, but besides the questionable elders, the people of Elsbeth were hospitable and friendly. I also did not feel like setting out to find my sisters, since asking to sleep in their room seemed to assume a close sisterly relationship, which we did not have.

And I knew that no matter where I ended up sleeping, I would be safe. Because eventually Aeroth would join me. The proximity bond would begin to pull at us sooner than later.

Ada nodded. "Of course." She looked to Aeroth, who was now being dragged by the women to pillows on the ground. I groaned inwardly and rolled my eyes.

"Will you be asking your man to join you?" Ada asked me, wagging her eyebrows. "I'd welcome him in my bed anytime."

"No," I told her. "He is his own keeper." I leaned down to her while keeping my eyes on Aeroth, hoping he could hear me. "And quite frankly, a pillow would be a more welcome sight than he."

I almost thought I saw Aeroth freeze for a moment at my words, but I blinked and it was like I had imagined it.

Ada laughed. "Good bedding can rival the presence of a man." She nodded. "But he's *quite* the man."

"And I'm quite tired."

Ada smiled. "There is a spare bedroom above the dressmaker's shop where I work. I manage the business and the building. It was vacated by our last seamstress, who recently got married."

"I'm not fussy," I told her. "I just need a warm place to sleep."

"Then follow me."

I nodded and let Ada lead the way to a six-story building, where dresses were advertised on the ground-floor storefront.

I STOOD in the small bedroom with Ada at my side. The bed was small but filled with luxurious silk bedding and multiple plush pillows, as I would have imagined a wealthy cloth merchant to furnish their spare bedrooms. An intricate rug covered most of the floor. A small fireplace was in the corner of the room with a nice-sized armchair in front of it. An attached bathroom and extra linens were at the end of the room.

The room was beautiful. But despite its beauty, the room felt lonely . . .

I was so used to Aeroth's presence that I found myself longing for him. I recalled how carefree he had been when I left the bonfire.

I cleared my throat. He surely wasn't longing for me.

"Thank you for this room," I told Ada.

She nodded. "I'm glad I was able to provide a place to rest your head. Stay as long as you need. Like I said, I manage this building, so please let me know if there's anything else you may need."

I smiled and remembered Aeroth. "Thank you for your help. If the man I came here with asks around for me and you happen to be there, please tell him where I am."

Ada blushed. "And you keep saying he's not yours . . . but you invite him to your room?" She giggled.

"It's complicated."

Ada sighed. "I'd take complicated with him any day."

I chuckled, and after a few more words, Ada left. Once alone, I locked the door of my bedroom and began to get ready for bed. Before I knew it, I was fast asleep.

41

RENNA

A knock woke me up.

I froze to see my surroundings and panicked. I quickly sat up and remembered I was in the bedroom in the dressmaker's building. My heart began to settle, and I fell back on the bed with a groan. I was still very tired. I had fallen asleep with my same clothes on and the lights still on.

I rubbed my eyes, recalling the night clothes I had seen in the linen closet. They were translucent like the outfits the women had worn at the bonfire, and I had opted to not wear them. I knew if Aeroth eventually joined me, the last thing I wanted was to dress in a way that would pass on the wrong message when I was trying hard to set distance.

"Renna?" Aeroth asked through the door. He pounded on the door. "I'm—" He hiccupped.

I groaned. He was intoxicated. Great.

"*Renna?*" he asked again and knocked once more.

"I heard you the first time," I said and sighed. I walked to the door and flung it open.

Aeroth almost stumbled in, but he held onto the door frame. He grinned.

I rolled my eyes and moved to the side. "Are you alone?" I asked, looking to the hallway outside the room.

"Er." He looked back to the hallway and then sauntered into the room. "I am."

"*Wonderful.*"

He stopped and turned to face me. "You're upset." He was swaying slightly.

I crossed my arms. "It's late." I narrowed my eyes. "And I hate drunks."

"You were too," he said with a pointed finger.

I laughed. "I was what? *Drinking?*" I put a finger up. "I'm not drunk."

He shrugged and continued to walk farther into the room.

"Wyleth warned us of the wine effects. I *barely* drank. Clearly," I waved my hand up and down at him, "you did not heed his warning."

"You get angry very easily," he said and sat down on the bed before flopping backward. He was too large for the bed, and his calves hung off the mattress.

I ground my teeth and closed the door to the room.

"Angry woman. *Angry,*" he mumbled to himself.

"So what am I supposed to do with you now?" I asked, putting my hands on my hips.

He raised his eyebrows as he looked down at me. "I have a few ideas."

I looked up to the ceiling. "You need to go back to the women you were with."

He shook his head. "We both know that's not what you really want, Renna."

His comment made my skin prickle with heat. I lifted my eyebrows. I wasn't going to let a drunkard start exposing my feelings.

"*Leave,*" I ground out.

"Gladly," he said, smiling, and closed his eyes.

I smiled, unexpectedly pleased that he changed his mind so quickly. That was easy enough.

"Let me drink from you and I'll leave," he said.

I scoffed.

I knew if I gave in, I would be swept into the allure of the feeding, even though I had agreed to merely be his friend. But after tonight, I wasn't so sure. If I were honest with myself, I hated seeing him surrounded by other women. I hated the ownership I felt over him and the way my brain labeled him as *mine* whenever I saw him. I loathed how my body wanted him, and yet my mind was always trying to decide whether I should enjoy the closeness of him or keep him at bay.

I wanted to scream.

"No," I answered him. "We will not exchange blood. Not in your state."

Eyes still closed, he shrugged. "Then I remain."

I growled and moved to the bed. "You can't sleep on this bed," I told him and pushed his shoulder, as if I had the strength to push a man of his build. He barely moved.

"I like this mattress," he said with an unbothered smile.

"Why are you being so difficult?" I asked him.

Aeroth merely sighed and began to softly snore.

I sat down on the bed. "Aeroth."

His snores were my only response.

"I said move!" I told him and tried to push him again.

Aeroth stirred and shifted slightly, and suddenly I had hope he was actually going to get off the bed. But he merely rolled over to lie on his stomach. He turned to face me, eyes closed.

I looked to the ceiling, imagining Source there. "You have got to be kidding me," I whispered to it. I leaned down to lift Aeroth's hair from his face.

He looked so serene in sleep, nothing like the killer he was. Or like the man who was afflicted by the burden of bloodlust.

I felt his hair in my fingers, smooth like silk. I sighed and moved his strands behind his ear.

My eyes traveled up to his eyelashes and marveled at how long and black they were. He was perfect. My gaze then trailed to his lips, which were full and naturally darker. I licked my lips. I wondered what it would be like to kiss him . . .

I shook my head.

"*Aeroth?*" I whispered. I was close to him now, my body leaning down alongside his right side.

He grunted in response.

"You need to move," I murmured. "We won't both fit on this bed."

With a sudden movement, his right arm came out and swooped me to him, pulling me to him, my back pressed to his chest.

I was so shocked, I merely squeaked.

Aeroth's breathing was steady behind me, and from his snores, I knew he had fallen back asleep.

Was he aware of what he was doing? When I had my nightmare in Cylas's forest structure, Aeroth had held me as I slept, and I understood that as a mode of providing comfort to someone who was scared.

But this?

He embraced me like a lover. And even though I could not fully feel his body because of his armor, this embrace was deeply intimate.

I had two options: sleep like this or move. I thought about the armor at my back and knew my body would rail against me in the morning. I had to move.

Carefully, I tried to remove his arm from around me but

quickly regretted it as he only tugged me closer, moving his arm to my waist.

I looked behind me over my shoulder. "I cannot sleep like this," I told him, not expecting him to hear me. "How can anyone sleep with armor like this?"

He opened a sleepy eye and looked at me.

"My lady doth protest too much," he said, his words slurred.

I narrowed my eyes. "I am not your lady. I cannot sleep next to you with this armor."

In an instant, Aeroth's armor was magically gone. He hadn't spoken or moved, his armor had simply vanished into thin air. He still wore his usual black long-sleeve shirt and black pants.

"So you can take off your armor in an instant, but choose to take it off by hand other times?" I asked. "You are a confusing man, Aeroth."

Aeroth nestled closer to my back, his arm and body now curled around me.

"*Hush,*" he slurred.

I looked forward and raised my eyebrows. "Don't tell me to *hush*."

More snores met me, and I knew that was the end of our conversation.

And so, whether it was the steady movement of his chest as he breathed against my back, or his soft snoring, or the warmness of his body, I was softly lulled to sleep.

And as I fell asleep, I could not help but think how right it felt being in his arms.

42

ILLONA

What good was magic if it was tied to the whims of the dead?

We had been in Elsbeth for two nights, and for two nights, the Ancestors had been in my ear whispering, "*Taria.*"

They would not be silenced even after my pleas.

I wanted to scream.

"I wish I could be freed from their voices," I said to Demira as I covered my face with a pillow. I was lying in bed inside the room we shared above the Aelderhall.

Demira sat next to me. "And I of this vision," Demira said. "What are the chances I would be guided to the beasts that hate me?"

I pushed the pillow aside and sat up. I felt even more guilty at leading our group to Elsbeth when its leaders had been callous and uncaring for our petition.

"I asked him again," Demira said. "I found Wyleth this morning and asked him to make an exemption and petition the Metidons."

I shook my head. Demira and I had also approached him in private the day before, and he refused to cooperate.

"He denied me," Demira said with a bitter chuckle. "Of course."

I frowned.

"Do you want to know what he said to me?" she asked and faced me. "That he would bring my petition to the Metidons on the *last day*."

We could not wait that long. The Ancestors were incessant in their murmurings to me about Taria. Their voices sounded like hurried pleas.

"Why the last day?" I asked her.

Demira shook her head. "He mentioned something about the ritual he shared with us on our first day here."

Ritual.

The word sent a sickly, ominous feeling down my spine.

Demira continued. "He was very adamant that we stay until the last day. He said to me he was sure their ritual would work this time, and the Metidons would be pleased and work with the rider descendants."

The hairs on my skin raised. There was something off about the elders. They made me uncomfortable.

"I don't like that man," I told her.

"I don't like him either. But the vision led us here." She looked down at her hands. "The Ancestors guided our way to Elsbeth. We are meant to be here. I have to trust that I am doing the right thing. That staying here until the last day of this equinox is what we must do."

Something felt off.

Whether it was the constant urgency around the word Taria, or how insistent Wyleth was about this ritual, something did not sit right.

I closed my eyes and cursed the dead who spoke in my ear. I wished they would share more of what I was supposed to do.

"So what should we do today?" Demira asked and stood.

"Wander the streets of this fucking city again?" She went to the only window in our room. It had bars, which were a unique decorative touch, but at least we were able to see the outside.

"We could try and join Renna and Aeroth again for a meal," I offered.

Like us, Renna and Aeroth were at a loss as to what to do as we were effectively waiting out our time in Elsbeth. We had seen Renna and Aeroth strolling the streets of the city the day before and had joined them for a meal.

Demira spun to face me. "Spare me their company, please."

I tilted my head. "Demira," I said and stood. "You need to stop being so hateful. Renna is nothing but kind to you. Aeroth too. What more do you want?"

Demira crossed her arms. "I want them to stop flaunting their mate bond in my face," she gritted out.

I sighed. I knew Demira was exaggerating. Although we knew Renna and Aeroth shared a room, they avoided physical contact and never made inappropriate comments.

"I see the way he looks at her when she's not looking. He looks at her like she is his whole world," Demira growled. "Makes me sick."

I rolled my eyes.

Taria.

Taria.

I closed my eyes.

It was starting again. The Ancestors speaking to me without context. I massaged my temples and got back to my conversation with Demira.

"Would you rather Renna be paired with a mate that makes her miserable and mistreats her?"

Demira stayed silent.

Taria.

It begins.

It begins.

Taria.

I stilled.

It begins?

I shot up to stand.

"What are you saying?" I asked the Ancestors out loud.

Demira approached me. "Who are you talking to?" she asked, studying my face.

It begins.

Taria.

It begins.

My heartbeat raced frantically in my chest.

"It begins? Tell me what you mean!" I yelled, covering my face with my hands. "I can't live like this! Tell me!"

Demira massaged my back and helped me sit. She sat next to me. "It's the Ancestors, isn't it? I hate that they won't leave you alone," she said.

I dropped my hands and looked at Demira.

"They're telling me '*It begins.*' They won't tell me what is beginning. They only keep repeating the word 'Taria.'"

Demira's eyes grew and she paled.

"It begins?" she asked me.

I nodded. "No other context."

Demira stood. "What if there is a battle about to happen?"

I began to wring my fingers. "I don't know . . ."

In that moment, I was transported to a desert, deposited unceremoniously like a pile of bones on the hot, sandy surface. I coughed as the sand filled my mouth, and my muscles ached from the impact of falling.

"Rise," a female said.

I looked up and covered my face from the hot, blinding sun.

A woman in a black shimmering cloak of shadows stood

before me. Her arms were crossed, and she wore a cold expression as she looked at me.

"Rise, Daughter of Chaos," she said.

I frowned and pushed to stand, my muscles protesting.

"What is this?" I asked her. "Who are you?"

A second figure cloaked in black moved to stand next to her, its hood pulled low so I could not see its face. When the figure spoke, its voice somehow echoed throughout the world.

"She is Livina, Goddess of Fate. *Kneel,*" it said.

My eyes grew and I trembled, lowering my eyes to the ground.

"I asked her to rise, not *kneel,*" Livina said to the figure. "Do not speak for me, Time."

The figure she had called Time remained silent.

"Rise, Illona," the goddess said to me.

I rose, unsure of what to say or where to look.

"You walk two paths, Daughter of Chaos," Livina said to me. "Your gift of Golden Fire makes you unique. Wielders of Golden Fire always walk the middle line between life and death. You can communicate with the dead."

I nodded.

"However," she said and walked toward me, "your situation bothers me."

She narrowed her eyes, and I stepped back.

"I am sorry if I have caused offense, Goddess," I said, my voice shaky.

"The Ancestors tell you too much. They share news that is not theirs to share. News of the future. Of Fate."

My heart raced. I never knew what the Ancestors told me was wrong. I assumed everyone with Golden Fire had the same experience.

"The dead are not allowed to speak to you about the future," she snapped. "They have crossed a line."

I looked down to the ground. "I'm sorry," I said, shaking my head. "I never knew—I never imagined that I was doing something wrong—"

"Not you," she gritted out. "*Them.*" She paused. "*You* have done nothing wrong."

A small shot of relief moved through my body.

"The dead never share details," I told her. "They speak in nonsensical ways, and I'm left to figure out their meaning. Sometimes I'm shown images in my mind's eye. Other times it's verbal communication."

"I am sure they speak to you in confusing ways so they do not directly violate the mandate to never give details about the future. You can be sure I will speak to Lerrick about this," she said.

I knew who Lerrick was—or rather I had read about him. Lerrick was the God of the Dead.

"I'm sorry," I said again. "How long have you known about them communicating with me?"

"Fairly recently." She looked to the cloaked figure standing beside her. "Time alerted me to changes in the timeline. He says there are people where they are not supposed to be. That the order of events has sped up."

I gasped. The figure next to her was Time? I never imagined Time could be personified into a physical being. I then thought of Aeroth being the Astral Plane itself and quickly adjusted my views.

"Today," Livina said, "something has changed. After the concerns from Time, I have started to keep a close eye on you. I have listened in on conversations. I have walked where you and your group have traveled and remained unseen. Moments ago, the Ancestors told you '*It begins.*'"

I nodded. "Yes, I don't know what that means."

She looked to the horizon as she spoke. "I cannot tell you what will happen exactly or when. I would be violating Source laws. I do, however, feel empathy for your situation. You have been tormented for many years by the dead and their messages. You were labeled as mad by the people in Vasarys. It's an injustice done unto you, and I will not have it. You are an incredibly strong woman to balance walking both lines of the living and the dead."

I blushed and looked down to my hands. What did one say to a god? *Thank you?*

No one had ever spoken to me like her. Others felt pity for my situation. But her? I felt like she could see me. She understood the burden of knowing about events to occur.

"I will grant you one boon," she said to me and looked to Time. When Time nodded, she looked back at me. "We cannot have the timeline shift again, so we must continue on its path."

"Alright?" I inquired.

"You asked the Ancestors what '*it begins*' means," Livina said. "I can tell you, without violating Source laws, that when you return to your room in Elsbeth, you are to approach Aeroth and Cylas. You will tell them you have spoken to me and that I command them to don their armor and go to Taria."

My heart felt like it was falling into my stomach. Demira had been right—perhaps battle was about to begin. Livina was warning us.

I covered my mouth with my hands. "I . . ." I shook my head. "I don't know what to say."

"You could say *thank you*," Time said.

Livina smiled at me, and she leaned down so we were face-to-face. "And remind Renna that I told her once that she and I would meet again. Ravens close in."

I frowned. Her words made no sense. "I don't understand."

Livina straightened. "You don't, but she will."

I quickly thought about the Metidons.

"And what about the Metidons?" I asked the goddess. "Will we be successful?"

Livina pursed her lips. "I cannot tell you the future."

"But I was guided all this way to Elsbeth," I pleaded. "Please help me."

"King Oberon has power to command the beasts," she said. "That is all I can say." She narrowed her eyes once more.

Demira would never agree to be in the vicinity of Oberon. I didn't even know where to find him. I was sure the Elders of Elsbeth also did not know where to locate him- hence the ritual every equinox. This was a disaster.

"Thank you, Goddess," I replied.

She smiled.

"*Now go,*" she said, and with a wave of her hand, I was catapulted backward from wherever I was and into my room.

43

RENNA

War had arrived in Taria.

I knew it with every fiber in my being as Illona shared her conversation with us. Livina had not confirmed battle had broken out, but why else would she, Aeroth, and Cylas need to don armor and go to Taria?

I believed Illona's news because I, too, had conversed with Livina in much the same way the first time I spoke to her.

Livina's warning about ravens closing in was only further confirmation that Illona was telling us the truth. No one else knew about my conversation with Livina.

Illona had come to us as Aeroth and I were getting ready to explore Elsbeth. After she left us to warn Cylas, Aeroth and I stood silently facing each other.

What would happen? Would Aeroth be harmed? Would Sethos kill him?

Would he be put in a position where he had to kill Sethos?

I thought back on how Aeroth had fought in the forest and knew he would be a hard man to catch weaving in and out of the Astral Plane. The thought elated me but also frightened me for Sethos.

I spoke first.

"I'm scared," I told him.

"I know," he replied and walked toward me and grabbed my hands. "I know you're scared for what will happen to Sethos. I promised you I would ensure you have the opportunity to speak to Sethos, and I vow I will do everything I can to make it happen."

I squeezed Aeroth's hands. "I'm scared for *you*."

My words seemed to catch Aeroth by surprise, and he lifted his eyebrows.

"Wouldn't you be glad to not see me?" he asked me.

I dropped his hands and crossed my arms. "How could you say that?" I asked him.

"Anything could happen, Renna," he said. "I could succumb to bloodlust. And I would choose to not come back to you and put you at risk."

I narrowed my eyes and moved toward him so that we were chest to chest. "Don't you dare leave me," I said to him.

"And if I die?" he asked.

"Then I die too," I answered. "And I'll still hate you for leaving me. And killing me in the process."

A small smile curved on his lips. "You care for me that much?"

I put my hands on my hips. "Don't flatter yourself," I told him. "What I feel for you is because of the mate bond. I have no choice."

Aeroth gently lifted my chin with his fingers.

"And what do you feel for me, Strongborn?"

I felt a red blush spread over my skin.

"Kindred . . ." I struggled with what to say. "Affection."

He chuckled. "*Kindred affection?*" he tilted his head. "What does that even mean?"

I moved my chin from his grasp and shrugged at my own

jumbled jargon. However, I knew in that moment one thing was true: I did feel affection for him.

I wanted to see him again.

"Come back to me, Aeroth," I gritted out. "I mean it."

"You don't command me," he taunted with a smirk.

I rolled my eyes. "Are you sure about that?" I growled.

"Angry woman," he said as he laughed. "You're bidding me goodbye to war, and the last things I hear from you are threats."

I lifted my chin. "I thought you liked me as I was."

He grinned. "I'll keep your lovely words close to my heart when I'm fighting the enemy."

At that, I sobered and looked away. If Sethos died, I would have failed.

"I will do what I can," Aeroth said to me as if reading my thoughts. "I vow to you."

I looked back at him and nodded. "Thank you," I replied.

Aeroth shifted on his feet uncomfortably. "I have to ask you for one parting gift," he said.

"Yes, anything."

"Your blood."

I nodded automatically. We had not exchanged blood these last few days since we spent every moment together. We would need each other's blood to separate.

My core vibrated with desire in anticipation of our feeding.

"Where would you like to be?" he asked me, and suddenly the question felt awkward. The thought of lying on my bed felt like too much of a temptation, as I knew I could get carried away in the haze that was the feeding. And he needed to leave.

I looked to the armchair next to the small fireplace in the room.

"Perhaps . . . we could sit?"

He looked to the armchair and nodded. "Yes."

We walked together in silence to the chair, and Aeroth sat first. When he held his arms out to me so I could sit on his lap, he picked me up and arranged me so I was straddling him.

From this position, we were almost face-to-face, and I shivered when his arms came around my waist with his fingers dangling just above my ass. I wanted him to hold me like this and stay, but I knew he had to go.

"Well then," I said quietly.

"Well then."

The moment felt electric, filled with a myriad of emotions I could not name.

"If I die," Aeroth said to me, "you will follow."

I nodded.

"The pain will be great once I die." He looked at me with a hard expression. "Don't prolong your suffering. I could not go to my death knowing you'll be in pain."

I knew he was asking me to take my life. Aeroth never wanted me to suffer.

"Alright," I whispered.

"You are the first thing I think about when I open my eyes each day. And the last," he murmured, looking at my lips.

I swayed toward him ever so slightly.

"You will be the last thing I think about when I close my eyes for the last time," he said.

I hugged him then. I rushed into his chest and squeezed.

"Don't say that," I said to him and squeezed him harder.

I breathed him in and the scent of oud. I wanted to bask in his scent.

"Let me drink from you," he said. "Please. I need you."

I moved back and looked to him. "Need? Or want?" I asked him.

He smirked.

"Both," he said, and in that moment, he leaned in and bit my neck.

I screamed as the pain spread through my muscle, but his saliva quickly numbed the area, and all I could focus on was a rush of exhilarating emotions and the feel of his body against me.

He rocked against me as he took from me. Deep pulls of my blood dragging moans from my lips, the sound filling the air.

I was loud as I whimpered, moving against him, seeking pressure on my pussy as I begged him to not stop.

And then his fingers moved from my waist to my core, and he paused his movements.

"Renna?" he asked, his voice hoarse.

I nodded against him. "*Please.*"

Aeroth moaned and began rubbing me just so over my pants. Driving me wild.

This was insanity. And I wanted to bask in it.

When I moved my hands to open the laces in my pants, he pulled his mouth from me.

Black streaks of my blood were on the corner of his mouth, and I leaned in and licked them.

He groaned and pressed my body against him more fully and shifted us so that I could feel his . . .

"Do you feel that?" he growled. He thrust against me, and the pressure his large member created against my core had me crying out.

"Yes," I whimpered.

"You do that to me. Every fucking day," he said. "I don't even have to touch you to grow hard from looking at you. You ask me whether I need or want you, and the answer is always both. My body needs you. My soul wants you. My mind craves you. My blood sings for you. I don't want to be parted from you."

His words made something inside of me shatter—perhaps

any reserve I had about him. We had no control over how we had come to be together in the first place, but in that moment, I was glad to know him. To be worshipped by someone like him. To be idolized.

My body needed him too. My soul wanted him just as much. My mind craved him beyond reason. And my blood sang for him too.

He thrust against me again.

"Come back to me," I told him in a plea. "*Promise me.*"

He nodded. "I vow to come back."

And then he pushed his shirt over his head and cut a sliver of skin on his neck.

I rushed to his wound and started to drink.

Colors tinted in red exploded behind my eyelids as I drank, clinging to him and letting him move against me, bucking so deliciously I had to move my mouth from his skin just to scream his name.

Aeroth unlaced my pants, and I gladly urged him as his fingers moved inside to the core of me.

I was molten with want.

When his fingers reached me and he began to touch me, I shivered and sobbed with relief. He urged me to continue drinking from him as he worked me.

I moved in a frenzy against him, and when his fingers slipped inside me, my climax built. I arched backward, unable to keep drinking from him.

Aeroth held me as I felt like I exploded in a million pieces; all the while his fingers never stopped—as if he was milking me until he captured every last drop of my pleasure in his hand.

I felt limp and boneless.

Aeroth kissed my forehead, and I felt him carry me to bed. Still in our feeding haze, I happily let him move me.

"Sleep," he whispered as he settled me on the bed. "I will come back to you."

I felt him drag the covers of the bed over my body, and I sighed in pleasure.

44

AEROTH

Cylas and I arrived almost simultaneously to the celestial dimension—he by portaling in and I by stepping through the Astral.

Despite somewhat of a cordiality toward me around Renna and her sisters, he ignored me completely here on his turf. I knew he felt more for Renna than what he led on, but we had bigger things to focus on in Taria.

It was easy to spot where the gods had set up camp by their luxurious golden tents with pennants and white carpets that contrasted with the sand around them.

My eyes zeroed in on the floor cushions where some soldiers lounged with other supernaturals, as if they could not notice the gray sky above them with turbulent black clouds filled with black and green electricity jabbing against the shield, trying to break through.

Were the gods simply overconfident in their battle abilities, or underestimating Sethos would not break in?

There could be only one explanation for the gods' behavior of treating the battlefield like a resort: They were in denial. That mentality would be fatal.

To my left, Cylas walked past me toward the most elaborate tent out of them all—a tall white tent with gold embroidered designs. Tall palm trees lined the walkway to the tent while a deep-purple carpet poured out from the entrance.

Two soldiers clad in gold who seemed to be spirits, as they did not appear wholly solid, stood at the entrance of the tent. They each held a golden spear.

They did not blink or move as Cylas walked past them to enter.

I followed.

As I walked toward the tent in Cylas's wake, I could not help but feel out of place. My armor was dark gray, and unlike some of the pristine metal plates worn by the soldiers around me, my armor had been worn for many years and seen battle. It bore marks and stains that would never leave it. They were a reminder to me of the loss of life I had seen and the responsibility I had to my people and to Source to stay alive.

My jaw clenched and chest tightened.

I need an heir.

As I walked to the tent, the two soldiers at the entry moved in sync and extended their spears toward me.

They advanced and hissed.

"Only gods may enter," the soldier to my left growled, the inside of its mouth entirely black, its teeth pointed.

Up close, I also could see their eyes were pure white, no pupils or irises in sight.

The spear ends had black magic floating like a small cloud at the tip and a foul odor like sulfur emanated from them.

Poison.

"Who is your master?" I asked.

"The One Who Commands Wars," the soldier gritted out. "The Goddess of War."

The tent flapped, and Ukara, Goddess of War, leaned out.

Her eyes widened when she saw me, and a surprised smile greeted me.

"Aeroth," she said quickly. She cleared her throat. "King of the Astral. Welcome."

I nodded in greeting. "Aeroth is fine, Ukara. It is good to see you."

She smiled and looked to the soldiers.

"Let him through. The King of the Astral has full passage throughout this camp."

The soldiers immediately retracted back with their spears and now stood once more like erect statues at the side of the tent entrance.

"Thank you," I said to her and stepped through.

The exterior of the tent was deceptive. The inside was all marble and had pavilion-style seating, far larger than what the tent looked like from the outside. A throne of gold sat to the left on a dais. The far right side of the tent was open to reveal a vast open field of desert where several soldiers performed military drills.

"The last time I saw you was during the Galactic Wars. My gods it's been too long," she said.

I nodded. I had met Ukara then, and even though I was young and far too intimidated to speak to the Goddess of War, one never forgot her.

"There are few men I respect," Ukara said. "You are one of them. You are fearless and yet honorable. Qualities I admire."

I gave her a polite smile. I didn't like to think about the Wars and the bloodlust.

"The fae monarchs have yet to arrive at camp. Do we still count on your support, Aeroth?"

I nodded. "The monarchs are currently residing in star fleets outside Delphinus Galaxy, waiting for battle to begin. The Galactic Federation was very specific that we were to only interfere during battle to apprehend Sethos and catch him at his weakest."

"And *kill him*," she added, her eyebrows raised.

I clenched my jaw, and my body tensed as I thought of what Renna would do if her plans were thwarted and Sethos was killed.

Thinking about her pain caused me pain.

"We were asked to deal with him," I said.

Ukara lowered her chin and bored her eyes into me. "And *you* specifically were asked to kill him. You are likely the only one who can do that, Aeroth. You know that."

I cleared my throat. "*Yes*," I replied.

"The Galactic Federation asked *you* to deliver the final blow. Because of your skills and your ability to use the Astral at will."

I shifted on my feet. I felt like a traitor to the Federation and the fae monarchs that were with me on the campaign. A discussion to capture and rehabilitate Sethos was never part of any discussion.

Yet I was willing to do it for Renna and the memory of the woman who had taught me about humanity so many years ago.

I was not willing to share my plans with anyone other than Renna. Cylas and her sisters knew Renna's goal. And they knew I could not part from her because of The Settling. Yet they did not know I planned to help her when the time came in battle. Those conversations between Renna and I were private. In confidence. And for now, I had to keep our plan to myself.

In the end, I knew I would lose the respect of my peers. The Federation. The gods. And on a deep level, I felt shame. Shame for not being who the monarchs, the Federation, and the god expected me to be.

I was respected for being loyal. Honorable. Just.

A person who kept his word.

That shame kept me from visiting the fleet where the other

monarchs resided because I did not want to lie to them. I could not sit with my peers and go over military strategy when I knew I would try and sequester Sethos for Renna in the heat of battle.

But you are being loyal, my conscience reminded me. *And keeping your word—to your mate.*

My mate.

The woman I craved beyond reason.

Who would cost me my reputation, because for her I would do anything.

Isn't loyalty to her all that matters?

"Aeroth? Is everything alright?" She shook her head and put her hand on my shoulder. "I apologize—I should have asked why you were here."

Grateful for the change in topic, I answered, "Am-Re's daughter Illona spoke to Livina, Goddess of Fate. Illona felt Cylas and I needed to come."

Ukara's brows gathered. "What did Illona say?"

I shook my head. "Only that we needed to come."

Ukara sighed, and she withdrew her hand and crossed her arms. "Livina never gives up her secrets. I can only imagine her reason for urging you to be here cannot be a good omen. I will go and make sure my troops are at the ready after I leave you."

"Yes. That may be for the best."

She nodded.

"This is impressive," I said to her as I looked around, my eyes drawn upward to the imposing chandelier that looked like miniature suns. They hurt the eyes if one stared too long.

"This is my father's tent," Ukara grumbled. "Far different than what we saw during the Galactic Wars."

I lowered my chin. "Yes. And I was under the leadership of the Prince of Envy then. His squadron rarely had a moment's rest to enjoy luxury like this."

The Galactic Wars had shown me the worst of death and

deprivation. Planets, races, and dimensions fought each other for control. Nowhere was safe.

Ukara nodded. "Then you know," she gestured to the tent around us, "that this luxury is folly. An allegory to poetic illusions of what war is."

I remained silent. I did not know the relationship between Ukara and Arios.

"My father has never seen true war," she said. "He has commanded others to fight for him as chief god."

"It's curious, then, that you are the Goddess of War."

She grimaced. "Isn't it? Perhaps Source was tired of men making idiotic decisions. Source likes to be ironic."

My brows gathered as I thought about the irony of my mate bond with Renna.

"Before I leave you, tell me: How is Renna?" she asked, her voice low. She stepped closer to me as if she was careful to not be overheard.

A moment of my lips on Renna's skin flashed through my mind.

I shifted on my feet and cleared my throat.

"She is well."

Ukara narrowed her eyes and leaned in. "You hesitated. *Why?*" Her question was like a knife, aggressive and to the point.

Goddess of War indeed.

"He hasn't told you?" a man said behind me.

I turned to find Cylas. His smile was cold as he zeroed his eyes on me.

"Told me *what*?" Ukara snapped.

I clenched my jaw and looked to Ukara. Cylas stepped closer to us and clapped me on the shoulder.

"Aeroth is Renna's mate. Can't say I don't envy him. Forced proximity and all."

Ukara's eyes widened and her jaw dropped.

"*What?*" someone else exclaimed.

We all looked to our right to see Khellios.

His golden eyes bore into me, as if he was trying to burn me with them.

"Tell me it is not true!" he screamed and charged at me.

As he advanced, I knew I had the option to disappear into the Astral and appear a few steps behind or even across the room.

But I was no coward, and I had nothing to run from.

"Yes. She is mine," I gritted out as Khellios gripped my armor by the chest.

The tent quieted as Khellios screamed expletives. "I trusted you with my thoughts, with my feelings as I told you what she meant to me!"

He pushed me, and I did not fight back. I knew Khellios had a long history with Renna and the memory of her. I knew how he tore the universe to search for her. His desperation. His anguish.

How he mourned the child he lost and the woman he loved.

I didn't know what I would do in his place if the roles were reversed now that I had spent time with Renna and gotten to know her.

And touch her and—

"When?" he screamed and charged at me again. He threw me against a pillar and gripped my armor once more. "When did you know?"

"Khellios, let me go," I said with as much calm as I could. I gripped his fingers and pried them off my armor.

"*Tell me!*"

Elrie ran toward us then and tried to pull Khellios apart from me.

"Enough!" she yelled. "*That is enough!*"

He allowed Elrie to stand between us as she gripped his chin and pulled his face down to her.

"I don't know what is going on, but this is *not* who you are, Khel!" she yelled. "Control yourself!"

Khellios's face contorted as if he were in deep pain, and Elrie released him. His back caved, and he staggered back. "He's—" He tried pointing to me, but his eyes became glassy and he shook his head.

Elrie looked to me, hand resting on her sword hilt, eyes fierce and narrowed, as if I had wronged Khellios.

In a way, I had.

But not by choice.

"He's," Khellios tried again, and Elrie looked to him. "He's Renna's mate."

Elrie glanced back at me. "I am not fae, but I know it's an important bond—"

"I've lost her, Elrie." Khellios's voice was a whisper, his voice breaking. "I've truly lost her."

"I did not know she was my mate, Khellios, until we came back from Daya. Me touching her to help her portal activated the mate bond. I truly did not know when you and I had spoken before she was found."

Elrie walked to Khellios and hugged him. He hugged her back and buried his face in her shoulder.

"I'm sorry, friend," I told him. "This bond is not by choice. I can assure you."

Khellios's face rose slowly, and his eyes met mine. Wrath raged in them.

"You can assure me?" He spat and moved from Elrie to walk to me. "Don't you *dare* make it sound like being by Renna's side is a burden."

"And what would you have me say?" I fired back. "That I'm joyous I found my mate and I'm about to go into battle where I very well may die and she will die thereafter?"

He froze.

"Our lives are interconnected now. Her life is mine and mine is hers. If I or she dies, the other follows." I closed my eyes and took a deep breath. "I would rather never have known her, to put her life at risk."

I opened my eyes, and a different expression met mine—fear.

"And how is she?" he asked.

I shook my head. "She hates this bond, Khellios. If that makes any difference."

He looked up to the ceiling and shook his head. "She would hate it. Renna has her own mind about how things should be."

His comment irked me.

"I'm glad she has her own mind," I spat.

Khellios looked to me, his face contorting in disgust. "You don't know her."

I crossed my arms. "I'm trying to get to know her, given the circumstances."

Khellios stepped up to me and shoved his finger in my chest. "If you hurt her—"

"She will kill me."

His eyes narrowed.

"She told me herself," I added, and a small chuckle left my lips. "With Darkness, I might add. Renna described my death in gruesome detail."

"*Good.*" Khellios and Cylas both answered in unison.

Khellios pushed further into me. "Will you force her to honor the mate bond and remain at your side?"

"We are doing what we can, Khellios. A mate bond requires us to remain together for the first year during The Settling. After that, Renna will be free to live her life as she chooses."

He looked up and down at me with disgust again. "So you reject her?"

I crossed my arms. "It's not up to me."

"What do you mean it's not up to you?"

"Renna is her own person. What she chooses to do after The Settling and with whom is up to her. I respect her as a person and her decisions."

He remained silent for a few moments, assessing me like a hawk.

"I see," he said at last.

Did he expect me to be controlling and demand she remain at my side? I wanted to explore more with Renna, but I would let her go.

"And where is she now?" he asked, looking around. "Does this period not require you both to remain together or risk physical pain?"

Going into detail about my dynamic with Renna felt like a violation. I did not have her consent on how much she wanted to share about our blood exchange with people at large. Exchanging blood was deeply personal due to its effects. In many ways, it was more intimate than sex. Khellios would know that, and as soon as he found out, this rage would intensify.

Cylas chuckled behind Khellios, and I shot him an icy glare. He immediately stopped laughing and looked down to the ground.

"Renna is safe," I said to Khellios. "We made arrangements."

Elrie stepped up next to him and placed a hand on his bicep. "Khel," she said softly. "Let's take a walk."

"This conversation is not over," Khellios said to me.

I tilted my head and pursed my lips.

"What more is there to say?"

He remained silent as if he did not expect me to question him.

"I told you what I needed to say about my bond, which was deeply personal." I straightened. "It's not up for discussion. There is no more to say."

Khellios narrowed his eyes at me.

"I need to ensure she is well taken care of—"

I lifted my chin and cut him off. "That is no longer your responsibility. She is mine to protect now."

He laughed bitterly.

"And quite frankly," I added, "Renna would argue her safety is her own concern—"

He shook his head. "She doesn't know what is best—"

I stepped up to him, my voice low as I spoke.

"I'm going to pretend you did not just insult her intelligence because you are clearly going through a lot. I respect your past experiences, and I am sorry for your pain. I thank you for looking for her. For wanting to care for her. But you are done. And this conversation is over."

He took a step toward me, and we were now nose to nose, his eyes fuming.

"You are no one," he gritted out.

A younger me would have challenged him to a fight, but I knew it was his pain talking. I looked to Elrie.

"Perhaps it's best you and Khellios take a walk."

"Come," Elrie said to him, wrapping her hand around his arm. "Please, Khel."

Khellios clenched his jaw, and after staring me down one last time as if I were vermin, he allowed Elrie to take him from the tent.

I stood in silence for a while until Ukara came to stand in front of me.

"A different man would have escalated the situation," she said.

"He's in pain, Ukara."

She nodded. "I know. Elrie has been doing him a world of good. But as he has reminded me, healing is not linear. He has good days and bad. Letting go of someone he had been mourning for as long as he had will take him time. He only found Renna this year."

"You are good for him too."

She smiled. "I'm his family," she said, patting my shoulder. "And from hearing you speak to Khellios, I know Renna will be safe with you. Eons on battlefields have taught me to judge people's character in a heartbeat. And I can tell you are an honorable man, Aeroth."

I opened my mouth to reply, but in that moment, to our right, across the desert landscape, a loud boom and flash broke through the barrier of Taria, and a black cloud shot to the ground, making the earth quake.

My hand shot to my sword.

When the smoke dissipated, a lone man stood, dressed in black with glowing silver hair.

"*Sethos,*" Ukara whispered.

45

AEROTH

The people inside the tent moved in a panic and began shouting.

No one was prepared for an attack.

"I'll get my army," Ukara said to me and Cylas. "Wait for me before you advance."

Cylas nodded to her. "I will inform Khellios."

He and Ukara left the tent, and I remained alone. I walked to the flap of the tent side overlooking the field where the voice was coming from.

Sethos stood unmoving, like a statue, as if he were staring at our camp. And then a dreadful voice filled the air, and a phantom wind moved around the tent.

"*Renna . . .*"

My body tensed.

I did not know what Sethos sounded like, but it had to be him calling for her.

"*Renna . . .*"

My fists clenched, and I unsheathed my sword.

"*Come out, come out, wherever you are . . .*"

His voice was sickly.

Taunting.

He meant to terrify her, expecting her to be in this camp.

I recalled Renna's bloody body on the floor in Daya. Her tears. Her pain. The hollow look in her eyes.

'*Wait for me,*' Ukara had said. '*Do not attack without me.*'

I shook my head.

Renna's abuser was across the battlefield. And despite my promises to her and knowing I vowed to help her speak with him, I never vowed to not injure him . . .

I took a step forward, leaving the tent behind, the sun drenching me, heating my armor, causing me to sweat. I shook with rage as I focused on Sethos, and my feet carried me to the edge of the camp.

How easily it would be to slip into the Astral and emerge in front of him, killing him before he spoke another word . . .

Renna's face flashed in my eyes, and I stopped.

I didn't want her hate. I wanted her respect.

All of a sudden, a blaze of gold shot across the desert from behind me toward Sethos. I narrowed my eyes to understand what it was.

It was Khellios.

"Fuck," I cursed under my breath.

I looked behind me for signs of Ukara, but there were none.

As the god camp scrambled to come to formation, I knew they would not assemble in time to join him. Perhaps no one had even noticed.

Elrie suddenly ran past me, her mercenaries hot at her feet.

"Khellios!" she screamed, her back heaving as she sobbed.

I ran toward her and grabbed her shoulders.

"He's gone—" she cried, her tears flowing down her face. Her body shook in my hands. "He's gone mad, Aeroth. He's going to get himself killed, I know it!"

In that moment, a bolt of navy blue lightning shot through the sky toward Sethos.

Elrie's eyes widened as she followed the bolt of lightning, and she shook her head.

Her voice trembled. "I-it's *Madera* . . ." she whispered. "Khellios's mother." She looked to her soldiers. "I'm going after both of them. Go to the craft and get me my hoverbike. *Now!*"

Her mercenaries scrambled into action.

"I'm going after him," she told me and shook my hold off. "Either he or his mother will get themselves killed. I can't allow that to happen."

I shook my head. "*You* will not go. *I* will go."

"No! You said it yourself—you cannot risk being killed. If you die and Renna follows, Khellios will never forgive me."

Elrie walked around me toward the field, but I grabbed her right arm to stop her.

"And you?" I demanded, stepping in front of her. "*You* matter to Khellios too."

She shook her head. "What he feels for me will never be the same—"

"You matter, Elrie," I said, shaking her slightly. "Never forget that. And I cannot stand by and watch you sacrifice yourself when I have a better chance to survive by using the Astral."

Ukara's army began to advance, and my heart raced. I had no doubt Ukara would attack, and I needed to hold this battle off until Renna had a chance to speak to Sethos. I promised her I would help her, and I could not fail her.

"I'm going," I told Elrie. "I will hold them off as much as I can."

She nodded.

"Tell Ukara to hold the line. I will bring Khellios and his mother back."

Without another word, I opened a doorway to the Astral and

stepped through. Moments later, I was steps away from Khellios, his mother, and Sethos.

Shouts met me as I stepped from the Astral to where they stood.

Sethos's eyes locked with mine, and I froze in place.

His eyes were so familiar . . .

Where had I seen those eyes before?

"Khellios," Madera pleaded, her hands on Khellios's left arm. "Son, *please*, think reasonably."

Khellios kept his gaze on Sethos. He extended his golden sword, and Sethos snapped his eyes to Khellios.

"*This ends right here,*" Khellios gritted out to him. "You and me."

Sethos ignored him and looked to me once more. "Who the fuck are you?"

I withdrew my sword and bent my knees, ready for him to strike.

"I'm the man that's picking up the pieces you left behind," I growled.

His grin stretched across his face, and his eyes blackened. He moved toward me in a cloud of black smoke.

"And what pieces might that be?"

"I retrieved Renna from Daya."

His face contorted in a rage. "So it is you who took her from me."

I stepped closer to him, the tip of my sword now almost to his chest. "She left you of her own accord."

He laughed, and lines of magic rose on his face, spreading like black thorns across his skin.

"Stand down, Sethos. Do not seek battle."

"Did she tell you to tell me that? To be *good*?" he sneered and spat on the ground. "She's quite sensitive."

I clenched my jaw and shook my head. "She believes you will have the sense to stop this course. I don't know why she bothers."

"Because Renna is *weak*," he barked. His voice was now deep, as if it were an entirely different person altogether.

My blood boiled from anger at hearing him speak about her in that manner after the relationship they shared. She had trusted him.

I stepped closer so my sword rested under his chin.

"Never say that again," I growled.

He laughed, unbothered by my words and the weapon.

How I wished to kill him.

"Do not think about her. Do not seek her out," I yelled.

He tilted his head and sneered, "And why do you care?"

I started to tell him she was my mate, but in one swift movement, Khellios charged at Sethos. Sethos tried to lean out of the way to miss the blow, but Khellios was too quick, striking him on the right side of his head with the pommel of his sword.

Sethos stumbled back, catching himself to keep from completely falling onto the ground. Khellios took advantage of Sethos's position, descending onto him in a bolt of golden light, pummeling his face to the ground. With each punch, the ground shook from the impact.

Madera screamed and rushed to Khellios. Hovering behind her son, pleading for him to stop and leave.

In the next breath, Sethos screamed, and one of the nearby desert trees ripped from the ground, catapulting into Khellios and knocking him a good distance away.

The trunk landed square on Khellios, drilling him deep into the sand, the impact creating a crater. Khellios could not be seen and was likely deep under the ground.

Had he died?

Madera shrieked, and blue and silver spheres of magic

sprouted from her palms. She charged at Sethos, her cries a mixture of anger and grief.

Sethos sprang up from the ground and landed several steps away from us, his face bloodied and swollen. One of his eyes was closed, and his nose looked askew.

A regular soldier would have relented, perhaps begged for mercy based on the injuries. But Sethos was no ordinary soldier. He had the power of Am-Re and I could only imagine that magic, and his thoughts of revenge propelled him to keep going.

Sethos was ready when Madera shot magic his way. As the spheres whizzed through the air toward him, he grunted and pushed his hands in front of him, palms facing the assault, and redirected the magic back to Madera.

Madera cursed and sharply dove to the right, missing the attack just in time. However, the movement cost her as the momentum she used threw her off balance, and she stumbled. I shot to her and caught her in my arms to prevent her from falling.

"You need to cease!" I told her. "Go search for Khellios. I will deal with Sethos—"

Madera violently pulled from my hold and pushed against my chest.

"Never tell a mother to not defend their child!" she spat, her face red with rage. "Do not take this from me! Did you ever love something so much that you would lay down your life for it?"

I blinked.

"*I love my son!*" she screamed. "It is my right to fight Sethos. You don't get to steal this from me!"

I thought of Isidra and how I avenged her assault and death. The satisfaction of killing in Isidra's name had felt just.

"It is my right!" Madera sobbed.

I stepped back, not knowing what to say.

"Do not interfere!" she spat. "I forbid it!"

Madera looked to Sethos now and squared off, firing more

magic his way. Shot after shot, Madera and Sethos battled one another. I knew Sethos was capable of hurting her, and I wondered why he didn't resort to more brutal methods to attack Madera.

It was like he was trying to tire her out by using her own magic against her.

"Fight back!" Madera yelled at Sethos. "Truly fight back!"

Sethos laughed, but mid laugh, his voice changed again to that darker voice.

"I fight what is a challenge," he mocked in that strange voice. "You are nothing, Madera."

Madera's eyes widened, and she lobbed another sphere his way. Sethos deflected her magic again with a chuckle. Madera ducked again, but instead of returning fire, she stood still for a moment and extended her hands to the sky, her eyes trained on Sethos.

A buzz spread through the land, and waves of electricity filled the air.

A bolt of navy, almost neon-blue lightning spread from Madera's center and surrounded her like ribbon. She lowered her arms, and two spheres of blue magic appeared in her palms.

"I will kill you," Madera gritted out.

Sethos smiled.

"Foolish last words," he crooned.

Madera screamed in fury, and her eyes turned white as she bolted toward him, the brightness of her powers making her look like a lightning bolt herself.

Sethos erected his protective shield just in time, and Madera crashed against it, her body bouncing off the shield slightly, but she pushed against the shield as if trying to break through it.

Sethos wasted no time and called forth Black Fire, conjuring a sword. With both hands on the grip, he thrust forward, piercing Madera's center.

Madera's mouth opened in shock as she looked down to find herself impaled. Sethos twisted the blade in a clockwise motion, releasing the sword from its hold in her body. Madera cried out, her magic visibly dimming.

And then Sethos did something I had never seen in my life.

He reached one hand into Madera's chest and pushed through her body and skin.

Her wails filled the air like an echo and then . . . silence.

I watched as Sethos pulled his hand back from her chest. In his palm lay a golden mass, like a sphere or a circle of light.

It pulsed like a heartbeat, but it was not a heart.

Sethos stepped back, tossing his sword to the side, and conjured a dagger in his other hand, piercing the source of light in its middle. Carving a deep gash, he pressed his fingers into the gap and ripped the sphere apart.

Madera slumped forward, her magic instantly gone.

And then I understood what I had just seen.

Sethos had killed Madera's soul.

He recalled his protective shield, and Madera fell back, Sethos's Black Fire sword in her still.

"*How apt.*" Sethos smiled as he walked toward Madera's body. He crouched down to where she lay. "Khellios is now an orphan."

When he reached for Madera again, fury rose inside me, and I slipped through the Astral, appearing at Sethos's back. I raised my sword up and swung it down to his shoulder.

My sword cut through his armor, and bone met my blade. I pulled my sword back toward me, knowing it would cause significant damage to his muscles and tendons. Sethos screamed and propelled forward, his body falling next to Madera's.

I had vowed not to kill him.

But I would take pleasure in hurting him.

I tossed my sword aside and picked him up, holding onto his breast plate by the arm holes.

"You don't deserve to live!" I spat and threw his body across the desert.

Sethos's body flew and crashed in a heap of armor and limbs. He groaned as he struggled to get up.

I knelt next to Madera's body as a pool of gold blood collected underneath her.

I could not save her.

And it was all my fault.

46

AEROTH

The ground began to shift, and the sand around the crater Khellios had descended into moved.

Within moments, Khellios shot up to the sky, his eyes surveying the land, and he froze, focused on his mother.

He screamed and descended, making the ground tremble. He hurried to his mother and gathered her limp body in his arms. The wails wrecking through Khellios broke me, and I scrambled farther back.

I failed.

I failed to save her.

Images of Isidra's body flooded my vision, and then my imagination conjured images of Renna also slain, her body convulsing as if she were losing her life.

Red dots blurred my eyesight.

My body trembled.

Bloodlust.

And then the first wave of separation pain shot through me.

I needed to leave this place. I could not have bloodlust emerge now.

"How does it feel?" Sethos screamed to Khellios, now walking toward the grieving god. Sethos held his bleeding arm up with his other hand to his middle.

"A life for a life," Sethos sneered. "*Tell me how it feels!*"

Khellios pressed his mother's body to his chest and wept, not looking up.

"*Get up!*" Sethos yelled to Khellios.

When Khellios would not move, Sethos charged at him with his fists up, and I lunged forward in Sethos's path to confuse him. When Sethos changed direction to hit me instead, I dove under his aim and spun behind him. I placed my foot on the small of his back and kicked with all might, sending him scrambling face-first.

Sethos cursed.

As Sethos clambered to stand, my vision blurred with more red dots, and I blinked several times. I was losing my vision fast, and slowly, shapes and bodies became more like shadows. I saw Sethos now in shadow form with a conjured sword.

My fangs elongated.

I straightened my body and conjured a Black Fire sword in my palm, holding my sword with both hands in front of me in the direction of where the shadow of Sethos stood.

Stay alive.

I could not die.

I would not.

I owed Renna that much.

She needed to live.

"You are a dead man," Sethos snarled in my direction.

I blinked and rubbed my eyes as if that would somehow help me see better.

I needed to leave, but I would not leave Khellios.

Sethos laughed. "*Has your vision gone?*" he mocked. "What a pity."

Suddenly sand was thrown at my face, and I yelled as sand stung my eyes.

"It's quite interesting," Sethos noted, his voice circling me, "that you should take such a protective stance when it comes to Renna."

More sand was thrown my way. I whipped around, trying to slash my sword toward Sethos, but he was too quick.

I wanted to shout Renna was my mate once more, but something stopped me. Perhaps a niggling intuition that knowledge would enrage him, make him want to cause Renna more harm in retaliation, or that he would use separation pain to lure her.

Like he had lured Renna to the gods.

The need for violence thrashed inside me, as if my emotions were in a cage begging to be let out. My tongue tingled with the promise of blood.

Sethos's blood.

Gushing warm blood.

I shook my head.

Bloodlust taking over meant I would not be able to portal or slip into the Astral. I would be forced to remain on Taria, and the increasing separation pain now moving in waves through my body would likely be a deadly combination.

I had never experienced bloodlust with separation pains.

Would the pain of being away from Renna make me angrier and more rabid?

Renna.

I took in a deep breath.

Renna.

Her presence calmed me.

Grounded me like I never knew another person could.

My vision cleared for the briefest instant as I thought of her, and in the next moment, I saw Sethos lung for me, sword raised. I blocked him with my sword and kicked him hard in the stomach.

Sethos faltered backward, and when he charged again, I swung my sword high, aiming for his neck, but he parried my blow with his sword and dove under my swing.

Then everything became shadowed again, and Sethos's sword hacked into my shoulder, slicing through armor, skin, and bone.

I screamed and dropped my sword, stumbling to my knees. Blood poured from my shoulder, and my nostrils flared with the smell.

My tongue prickled with anticipation of blood on my lips.

My bones cracked as the bloodlust transformation threatened to emerge.

Renna.

Focus on Renna.

Her smile.

The warmth of her hands.

Her laugh.

My vision slightly cleared again.

I directed my own healing magic to my shoulder and picked up my sword, holding it with my other hand. I pushed to stand, my knees bent and ready to strike.

Sethos, likely thinking I was beyond saving, charged toward me with a yell. I summoned the rest of the strength I had and lunged forward with my sword, swinging up and over in a high and low fake strike. Sethos jumped back, and our swords clashed as he blocked my low strike. I pushed against him and looped my leg around his and, with a hard shove, made him fall back to the ground. His head cracked hard on the ground.

Sethos yelled all sorts of curses as he pushed to stand, and I threw my sword to the ground.

"We are finished here," I told him. "*Leave.* You have done enough."

Sethos snarled and sprinted toward me. I stepped back to create distance as my vision was leaving me again, but he was too quick. Sethos punched me in the face, and the impact, combined with my loss of stability, had me falling on my back. He got on top of me, and I felt the edge of his sword at my jugular.

His shadow lowered, and I felt his breath on my face. "I will never stop until every single god from the Celestial Enclave is dead."

Sethos pressed the sword into my throat, and I conjured a dagger and jabbed it into his face.

Sethos roared as I pulled the dagger out, and I felt his blood pour onto my hands.

"My eye!" Sethos cried. "*My eye!*"

The smell made my canines expand.

No.

As I collapsed onto the ground, the yells of Ukara and Cylas came to me.

Breathe in.

Breath out.

The bones in my spine cracked as the bloodlust tried to claw its way into my body, holding me in its clutches. As it felt like darkness closed in around me, Ukara's voice was suddenly at my ear.

I could not completely make out her words, but it sounded like she was telling me I would be alright. That Sethos had portaled out of Taria. That medics were coming to assess my injuries.

I shook my head.

I didn't want them.

I needed Renna.

I wanted Renna.

And I had promised her I would come back to her.

I must have spoken my needs out loud, because Ukara spoke then.

"Then go to her," she said.

I barely nodded. And with what little energy I had left, I willed the Astral to open, slipping away to her.

47

SETHOS

My body slammed into the hard floor, and a pulling, violent pain clawed from my center, bruising my organs, moving my bones, burning my skin, and battering my energy as the pain fought its way out of my body.

The pain felt like a thousand shards of thick, jagged glass shooting through me from my back, fighting their way to exit my body from the front.

It was unbearable.

And now, my normal.

I curled onto my side, holding my face with both hands as blood gushed from my eye. I didn't bother to open the one I still had to see the dark force that possessed me, Am-Re, emerge from my chest and onto the ground before me.

He had the form of a man in shadow.

"*Imbecile!*" he roared. With a shot of magic, my body was thrown across the room, and the pain in my eye increased tenfold.

A sob wracked through me.

Two hands made of smoke grabbed me from my front and pulled me up.

"If I had known you were going to be soft in battle when I possessed you, I would have picked a different body," Am-Re gritted out. "*Useless scum.*"

I was slammed down on the floor.

"You should have died when your mother did, you *pathetic* excuse for a life!" his voice thundered. "How are we to fight with only one eye?"

As the blood covered my face and filled my mouth, I pushed to roll to my side to cough. Forcing myself to sit up, I opened my remaining eye to see the familiar black, grated floor, the flickering neon lighting, and various floors visible beneath me.

We were in Am-Re's mothership.

Gods did not need star crafts to travel, as they could travel through space with no problem. The body of a god was built for exposure to interstellar space.

But Am-Re was not whole. He had no body of his own and instead was made up of smoke and shadows. To survive, Am-Re had to possess the bodies of others, as his soul was so fractured it needed corporal support. His soul could barely withstand portaling while inside the body of another, so he had to limit how he moved about.

And so Am-Re was now traveling through space with a newly acquired fleet that could house his allies and the army I had enchanted.

Footsteps sounded to my right, and I knew Am-Re's star commanders had arrived.

Am-Re's Top Commander spoke. "Your Most High," the man said. "We heard you arrive. Shall we send for another host so you may be more comfortable?"

Am-Re growled.

"Bring him in," Am-Re sneered. "This one," Am-Re said, and I was sure he was referring to me, "has lost his fucking eye. I need an able-bodied man. Not some *cripple*."

Part of me was glad he was choosing to possess another body.

I wanted to die.

But I was too valuable as I still had Am-Re's magic inside me, melded into my fae body.

"Right away, Most High," his Top Commander replied.

I heard quick shuffling of feet as people were sent to do Am-Re bidding. I looked around the room to see who else was there. The muted lighting of the command room helped my good eye adjust quickly to everything else around me. Tall floor-to-ceiling glass encased the command room, making the stars and space appear to be at arm's reach.

Along the glass was the command center with chairs and controls to steer the craft. Several soldiers dressed in black sat steering the craft, not paying attention to us—perhaps too frightened to turn around to see what was happening.

Am-Re was a floating, elongated mass of shadows with no real shape. His Top Commander gleamed in black armor and a black cape, and continued his report.

"We have located your daughters, Most High," the Top Commander reported.

My heart raced.

"We had several reports," his commander continued, "but due to heavy casualties, we have not had a firm confirmation."

"And?" Am-Re roared.

"They are in Elinoor."

Elinoor? I frowned. The planet was deserted, a rocky landscape in Konah Universe.

"*Why?*" Am-Re demanded. "What is in Elinoor that would be so important?"

"We are uncertain," the commander replied. "We do know the god Cylas travels with them. As well as Aeroth, the King of the Astral."

Am-Re cursed.

"He was there in Taria," Am-Re spat.

Aeroth. At first, I could not place him. It had been years since I had last seen him.

The commander nodded. "We have sent in more reinforcements to scan the area for the group's exact location."

"Good," Am-Re replied.

My fists curled at the thought of him hurting Renna.

"By the way . . . how is our esteemed guest doing?"

"Your niece is conscious."

Am-Re chuckled. "Nera is weak like my brother. And now the bitch has no god powers."

The commander remained silent.

"Did you locate the man you found her with? Her lover?"

"No. He got away. We do know he was a Nephilim."

"We have some Nephilim contacts. Find out who he was. I don't want him bringing his people against us."

"Yes, Your Excellency."

"Bartering Nera with the Celestial Enclave will be an advantage."

"Absolutely. A most wise military strategy. Nera for your daughter Renna."

"Yes." Am-Re sighed. "It's been a trying day. I need a body. Bring in the host."

"Right away! Also . . . we do have a visitor for you outside the command room. One that may shed some light as to where your daughters may be located."

"Excellent! I want to meet them."

The commander bowed low and gestured to two guards who stood by the command doors to open them.

Am-Re's shadow moved to face the doors.

When the doors opened, a woman I had never seen before walked through. From where I crouched, I could tell her skin was blue and glowed green and gold in some places. Her dark green hair had threads of red that almost looked like vines.

"Divica," Am-Re said to the woman. "It's been ages since we last met! *Welcome.*"

48

RENNA

I was in my room in Elsbeth, curled up in bed, tears streaming down my face from the separation pain.

Everything seemed to hurt more than usual. My separation pain had never been this bad.

Where was Aeroth?

My mind raced. Aeroth had said when a mate died, the pain was unbearable . . . And this pain was excruciating.

Had he died?

I shook my head. I pictured Aeroth's face and the way his eyes always observed me quietly. Every time he had held me to offer comfort. The way he guarded my sleep.

I grabbed his side of the bed and crumpled the sheets in my fist. More than once, we had slept in each other's arms since arriving in Elsbeth.

Would I ever hold him again?

I thought of when his head reared back in laughter, when he didn't hold back at something funny I said. I imagined his eyes and how they pierced mine to the spot when he desired me, making my toes curl.

Please don't die.

And the fact was, I didn't want him to die for fear of my own life. Rather, I wanted him to live because I needed him.

How had I allowed someone to get under my skin in such a short amount of time?

Fast-burn would be the way I would describe our dynamic. There could be no other word to explain how rapidly we had built intimacy.

I knew the mate bond and blood exchange had a lot to do with it, but I could feel my chest expand whenever I thought about him. My heart raced with anticipation whenever he looked at me.

I truly cared for him.

Another wave of pain hit me, making my body contort, and I cried out.

Yes, I cared deeply about Aeroth. And I wanted to see him now to make sure he was okay.

A flash of light blasted through my room, and I screamed. Then, out of thin air, Aeroth fell hard onto the floor with a groan.

The pain in my body started to dissipate as I sprang from bed and raced to him.

"*Aeroth!*" I yelled, kneeling next to his body.

His *bleeding* body.

My heart sank into my stomach, and I wondered what was happening in Taria that would cause these injuries, but I didn't have time to think about anyone else.

The man in front of me whimpered in pain, and he was all I could focus on.

He was curled onto his side, his back to my front. I touched his shoulder gently.

"What's happened?" I asked him.

He breathed heavily, unable to answer me.

I got up and moved around him to kneel in front of him, and my eyes widened at the pool of blood under him.

"Who did this?" I asked.

He shook his head.

"Tell me how to help you!"

He coughed and squeezed his eyes. "Keep talking to me," he whispered.

I shook my head. "Talking doesn't help you. Your injury—"

"It will heal. My magic is already sewing me back up." He groaned in pain, and his words rushed out. "And being here with you, seeing and knowing you are safe, already makes me feel better."

"You need medical help."

"I just need you."

I narrowed my eyes. "And you are a terrible liar."

"You mean too honest?"

His voice had a small trail of humor to it, and I curled my fists. Of course he would find some sort of humor in this situation.

"Aeroth, there is so much blood. Your right shoulder is—"

"Ah, *that*."

"Yes, *that*!" I yelled. "*What happened*?"

He clenched his teeth and groaned.

"Compliments of your lover."

My breath paused.

Sethos.

"*You saw him?*" I asked, not even bothering to confirm whether it was he Aeroth spoke of.

He nodded.

I wanted to ask if Sethos was alive, but I knew Aeroth would have told me. And he promised he would not kill him before I had a chance to speak with him . . .

Rage unfurled inside of me at knowing Sethos had hurt Aeroth. Could I truly save Sethos? Guilt and shame flooded me once more for caring.

"It looks worse than it is," Aeroth said.

I leaned down to try and see where his wound was.

"He cut through bone and muscle," he told me. "My magic has already set the bones back. Mighty uncomfortable."

I knew Aeroth was in pain, but his teasing tone rankled me.

"And is that amusing to you?" I snapped. "I have been worrying about you and wondering—"

"You have been worrying for me?" From his tone, I knew he was surprised.

"Anyone with a shroud empathy would care and worry," I replied.

Aeroth smirked through closed eyes and said, "You care for me?"

My palms became sweaty, and my jaw opened as I thought of what to say. This didn't seem like the right time to divulge my feelings.

"I care for the outcome of this war," I said, my voice sounding unsure.

"*Ah,*" he said with a smile. "Yes, let's also not forget about that murderous ex of yours. He was very empathetic today, also caring about the outcome of the war."

"Aeroth, you are laying in a pool of your own blood and you have the *audacity* to make jokes?"

"There she is, my angry woman," he smirked through closed eyes. "Thank god I lived to hear you scold me for another day. Are you at least happy I made it back," another groan, "*alive*?"

His angry woman.

I almost smiled.

"I want to throttle you," I said, gritting my teeth to force my smile to not materialize. "You can't even open your eyes!"

I should not have said that because as soon as he opened his eyes and our gazes locked, I was swept into the storm there.

There was anger there, mixed with fear.

Longing.

Desire.

But worst of all, his eyes were almost black.

He needed to feed . . . It didn't make sense. We had exchanged blood before he left. His eyes should not be this dark.

"Your eyes . . . I don't understand . . ."

"Bloodlust." His chest heaved. "It threatened to overtake me."

I shook my head.

Aeroth was a seasoned warrior.

He had only ever succumbed to bloodlust when Isidra was killed.

"When my body wanted to give in to bloodlust, I kept thinking about you," he said. "You grounded me."

My heart raced.

"I thought about your voice . . ." he added.

Warmth spread through my body like waves, and my eyes became glassy. My body swayed toward him.

"You kept me from losing control." His voice was a whisper now.

I wanted to reach out and touch him, but I held back.

"What happened?" I asked again, my voice gentler. "And tell me fully this time."

"Sethos arrived at Taria, and Khellios engaged him in combat."

"Is Khellios . . ." I swallowed.

"He's alive."

A breath of relief swooshed through my lungs, and my body sagged.

"But that's not all. Khellios was injured and then Sethos attacked Khellios's—"

"Wait. Sethos . . . Is he?" I fidgeted with my shirt hem.

"Alive. The coward escaped as well. There is more news."

I didn't care in that moment. The top half of my body sank to the floor, and I covered my face with my hands. Anxiety moved through me like a wildfire, claiming my body rapidly. My chest felt like it was closing.

I tried to breathe, but my chest burned.

"Renna, we need to keep talking about what happened—"

"You must hate me," I said through my hands. "I'm so sorry."

Aeroth groaned, and I heard him begin to move. I shot up to help him, but instead I hit his chin with the top of my head.

I sank down to lie on my side, holding my head.

"*Ow!*" he said and sank back down on the ground.

"What were you doing?" I yelled.

"I was trying to comfort you!" he whimpered and squeezed his eyes shut. "I can never win with you, and it's not for lack of trying."

His words broke through my resolve to try and limit our intimacy to only feedings. Aeroth only ever tried to comfort me. He was everything good.

I recalled his words when he left.

You ask me whether I need or want you, and the answer is always both. My body needs you. My soul wants you. My mind craves you. My blood sings for you. I don't want to be parted from you.

I shifted next to him, my free hand cupping his face and thumb rubbing his chin. Aeroth had told me how he felt, and here I was, a coward unable to admit to him I cared about him.

"I'm sorry," I said as tears spilled from my eyes.

"Stop apologizing."

I shook my head. "*I can't.*"

He opened his eyes. We were so close now, lying side by side on the floor.

"Why are you apologizing?" he asked. "Aside from the obvious assault just now."

That humor again.

I rolled my eyes. "Why are you like this?"

He sighed. "Like what?"

"Positive! You look on the bright side. And now you're *chuckling*!"

"Would you rather I not be?" he asked and moved his good arm to push a hair from my forehead.

"You're injured because of me," I pointed out.

"I gave you my word, Renna."

"And your shoulder?"

"It's nearly healed."

The pool of blood under his shoulder was alarming. He looked down to where I was looking.

"I'm not bleeding anymore, Renna. My skin has been stitched back up. It's just internal muscle healing now."

More tears spilled from my eyes, and he wiped them away.

"Your healing magic is fast," I whispered.

He smiled. "I am thousands of years old."

As if that made his injury any better.

"Trust me. I wanted to kill him. But your wrath . . ." He shook his head. "I didn't want you to hate *me*. I know how important it is to you—"

"I would rather you scream and berate me," I confessed.

Aeroth moved closer to me.

"Why?"

I shook my head. "It feels normal to me. To be hit. Kicked. Screamed at . . ." I closed my eyes because looking into his face and his gentle eyes threatened to expose all my vulnerabilities.

He remained silent.

". . . to be punished," I finished.

Aeroth stilled under my hand. "Renna . . ."

My lips quivered.

"It's breaking me to see you like this," he murmured and cupped my face. "Let me help erase your pain."

His voice was low, like warm honey. My breath froze, and I slowly opened my eyes.

Aeroth's gaze was locked on me, and despite the dark color of his eyes, they were glittering with raw desire.

I swallowed.

"No one can do that," I whispered, my voice failing me. "The memories will always remain."

"Then create new memories with me," he murmured.

He didn't have to explain his meaning. I craved him as much as he craved me.

"I'm afraid, Aeroth."

"Of what?"

"Of being happy."

The fear of my happiness being ripped from me once more after Sethos was terrifying. He brought our foreheads together.

"Every time you feel sad. Or angry. Or when the memories get to be too much, tell me. And I will do whatever is in my power to help you."

Tears continued down my cheeks.

"I want to kiss you now," he whispered.

My eyebrows shot up.

"But you . . ." I cleared my throat and shook my head to clear my mind. There were more important things to do right now. "You need to feed."

"I do."

My brows furrowed. In one swift movement, Aeroth grabbed me by the waist, and I found myself straddling him. He grabbed my hands and placed them on his chest.

"Aeroth, your shoulder—"

"Is better."

"What are we doing—"

"Do you trust me?"

I nodded. After today? I trusted him implicitly.

"Then tell me what you need and trust me. Tell me to stop if it's too much."

My mind raced, trying to think of the million things he might do. Aeroth wanted to please me, that much was clear.

"What are you going to do?" I asked.

He extended a hand up to my cheek and pushed my hair behind my ear.

"I'm going to love you until the pain stops," he murmured.

My heart stopped. The gentleness in his voice and the way in which he held me, like I was the most precious thing in the world, broke me, and a sob left me.

"Don't cry," he said, his eyes watery.

"I can't help it," I whispered. I looked to his shoulder. "Aeroth, I don't want you to do anything that will injure your—"

"*Trust me,*" he growled.

I nodded.

"What do you need right now?" he asked me.

I swallowed. What did I need?

I needed for him to not be injured. I needed for this conflict with Sethos to not—

"*Strongborn.*"

I blinked again.

"You're thinking too much." He rubbed my back, and his hand traveled down to my ass, where it lingered and then back up to my back.

"I need a lot of things in this moment," I confessed. "My mind is scattered."

"What does your *body* need?"

I tilted my head.

"Well . . . what does *your* body need?"

He stared at me for a few moments before speaking.

"You," his voice rasped.

My core throbbed again, and I stifled a moan.

He moved both palms to my ass and squeezed.

"I want you, Renna. Gods, how I crave you beyond sanity."

A delicious shiver moved down my spine.

"I want everything. I need to lose myself in you," he whispered.

Wetness pooled from me, and I whimpered.

"That's what *I* want," he murmured. "That's what my body needs. That's what I *need*. But I will not take what is not freely given."

I wanted all of what he was offering very much, but he was giving me a choice. And I seldom had an opportunity to speak up when it came to matters like this.

I wet my lips before speaking.

"I want you to drink from me," I said, my voice sounding more confident than I felt.

"Where?" he asked.

My breasts were heavy and sensitive, and I longed for him to touch me there. They had always been a place on my body where I felt the most confident, and his suggestion before that I may enjoy being bitten there came back to mind.

"My breasts."

He groaned, and his hips moved under me.

"As you wish." He smirked.

I nodded.

"Take off your shirt," he said.

My hands trembled as they moved to do his bidding, but the anticipation made my movements quick.

"I want to see you," he said. "All of you."

I tugged my shirt off and began to take off my brassiere. Once my breasts were bare, I whimpered with need as his eyes settled on me. I felt my magic emanate from my chest and move to him to close the distance to his mouth.

"Touch me," I urged him.

I waited for him to do something, but his eyes were fixed on my sternum.

Where my tattoo of Khellios's sigil still existed.

His brows gathered. My skin flushed in shame, and I could not bring my eyes to look at him.

"Look at me," Aeroth growled.

I shook my head.

"*Renna,*" he said, his tone deadly. "Look at me."

I sat up and covered my chest with my arms, shaking my head.

"Who did that to you?" he growled.

Etara.

"It doesn't matter—"

"The fuck it does. That's Khellios's sigil. Did he brand you?" he gritted out. "Is that why you left with Sethos? To escape Khellios?"

My eyes widened and met Aeroth's gaze.

"*No!* Khellios would never."

"Then why the fuck do you have his sigil on your skin?" His hands were gentle as he pried my arms away.

"I didn't know it was his sigil on my skin," I explained and slowly pushed off him and stood. I hugged my arms. "A woman named Etara—"

Aeroth's expression darkened, and he quickly stood. "What did you say her name was?"

I frowned. "*Etara.* She was on my university campus. She was a tattoo artist and tattooed that on me."

Aeroth ran his hands through his hair. "Etara, if it's the same woman I am thinking of, is a criminal witch wanted for killing the Queen of the Kingdom of Nightmares. A fae realm. Her husband, the King, is in the campaign to kill Sethos."

My jaw dropped.

"What did Etara look like?" he asked.

I started to pull my shirt on from the embarrassment, wanting the ground to swallow me whole.

Aeroth stopped me, his hands still gentle on mine.

"Answer me."

"Etara had red hair. A prominent serpent tattoo on her face."

Aeroth cursed and looked up to the ceiling of the room.

"Do you know it is said she sought the protection of a fae named Sethos after she ran?" he asked me. "There have been sightings of them spending time together."

Blood drained from my face. Sethos had admitted to luring me and using me for a year to get the gods to notice me. Knowing Etara was connected to him was like the last piece of the puzzle fell into place.

That was how the gods knew where I was on Andora. I knew then Sethos and Etara had devised to use blood summons on me on purpose to lure Khellios. Like a fucking tracking device.

As if I were an object. An animal to be branded.

The full extent of how much Sethos had violated my body and freedom crashed down on me like a bucket of water.

I was in Aeroth's arms, and he crushed me to him as I began to cry.

"I have to kill him, Renna," he said against my hair and carried me to the bed. "I hope you know I have to kill Sethos."

I didn't reply and simply looked down at my tattoo. Aeroth gathered me up and set me down on the soft bed cover, sitting next to me.

I couldn't look at myself. "I want it off!" I gritted out and tried to buck out of Aeroth's arms so I could claw at my skin. "Both tattoos. Get them *off*! I feel disgusting!"

Aeroth restrained me. "Listen to me," he said.

I raised my eyes to his.

"These scars don't take away from your beauty." He looked down at my body. "I think you are beautiful the way you are."

"I don't feel beautiful at the moment."

"If you want them off," he told me, "I would have to use my

magic. Or perhaps you could do it. You would have to direct your magic to the lines of the tattoo to lift and dissolve the ink. It may be painful."

He looked down to the one on my side below my breast that spanned my torso.

"The lotus one will be more painful since it's so large."

In that moment, I knew my reunion with Sethos would not be the teary, pleading reunion I had envisioned. I wanted to rage at him.

I wanted to make him hurt. To be sorry for how he used me.

"I hate him," I whispered and stood.

Aeroth also stood. "I'm sorry that happened to you."

"I know."

He averted his eyes, head slumped down. "I knew how badly Sethos hurt you when I saw you in Daya. But this . . ." He shook his head, and his eyes darkened. "I will kill him," he gritted out.

More tears began to fall, and Aeroth was at my side instantly and wrapped his arms around me. I wanted to erase Sethos from my mind. I wanted to pretend he had not used my body to manipulate me.

"I don't want to cry," I said. "I feel weak."

"You're not weak, Renna Strongborn." He placed his chin on the top of my head. "You're trying to stop a war. You're not hiding from Sethos. You are actively seeking him out, knowing your father will also be there. You have more courage than you know."

I placed my cheek against his chest.

"What do you need from me in this moment?" he asked.

I wanted Aeroth to take me in his arms and kiss me.

To make me forget.

Was that a realistic response? To try and replace the touch of another as a form of healing?

"Make me feel beautiful, Aeroth."

He stilled.

"Make love to me."

"Renna . . ."

I locked eyes with him. "You asked me what I needed. I don't want to think of him."

"Sleeping with another to cover the memories of someone else is not a good idea."

His hesitation about what I was asking, although logical, wounded my pride.

"*Get out,*" I said and stepped back.

Aeroth held fast. "Renna—"

"I said get out."

"I can't."

I rolled my eyes and closed them. Of course. The fucking separation pain.

But he gently cupped my jaw, tilting my chin up.

"I won't leave because I don't want to leave you," he whispered. "I am afraid."

My eyes opened. He was hesitating. I wrapped my hands around his arms.

"What are you afraid of?"

He placed his forehead against mine.

"I'm afraid of crossing this line. From convincing myself that my reactions to tasting you are normal when I know I have never desired another as much as you. I know having full permission to touch you will change me."

My stomach dipped, and my core began to throb for him.

My nose was now brushing against his.

"And how will you be changed?" I murmured.

"I will want you for myself when I should stay away. Because if I claim you, I will never want to let you go. I will never want to marry because I know I would never be able to give you up. And if my bloodlust comes forth tomorrow or the next and I hurt you, I will not be able to live with myself."

I closed my eyes.

My body tingled with need, but he was right.

“So what do we do?” I asked him.

He kissed the top of my head.

“I don’t know,” he said.

I felt like a knife had cut me in half, and instead of recoiling and screaming at his rejection, I buried myself into him because a part of me knew venturing into something more with Aeroth would alter me as well.

“Then lay next to me,” I said. “Hold me.”

Aeroth smiled. “Always.”

49

RENNA

Someone was calling my name.

I opened my eyes slowly and tried to orient myself.

I was laying on my right side against Aeroth's bare chest. He was sound asleep with his left arm around my waist. We were under the covers, and I wanted to bury myself in the bed and against his body and stay there. I curled my body next to his and recalled the night before.

"*Renna?*" a soft voice called out to me.

I frowned and looked to the door in my room.

Someone had been knocking.

I sat up and held the bed blankets to my body.

"Renna, please. We need to talk to you."

It was Illona's voice.

Aeroth shifted next to me, and his arm came around me and folded me to him, cocooning us in the bed, his body spooning mine. He moved his left leg over my legs.

"*Aeroth,*" I whispered. "*It's Illona at the door.*"

"I heard." His lips were against my neck.

My body shivered.

"I should go check what she wants," I said.

"She wants to take you from my arms," he murmured, sleepily.

He ran his nose along my skin. I wanted to sink into his embrace.

"Technically they don't know that you're in here," I pointed out.

He smiled against my skin.

"Do you want to let them know?" he teased.

My eyes widened, and my skin prickled with embarrassment. Aeroth moved his hands from my waist up to my breasts and cupped me there.

I moaned softly and arched my back along his front.

"I love your body," he whispered and peppered small kisses along my shoulder and the crook of my neck.

He kissed me like he knew me. Like I was his.

My stomach did somersaults, my skin breaking out in goosebumps, and my—

"*Aeroth!*" I hissed. "We need to focus."

He traced one of his hands down my back and slid it across my waist toward my core. I still had my pants on, and he caressed me over the fabric with the lightest of touches, forcing a shiver from me.

"Focus," I whispered.

"I am," he teased and slid his hand into my pants. My underwear became wet with want, and I moaned into my pillow.

Illona knocked on the door again.

"I'm so sorry to bother you both," she said through the door. "*Please.* Cylas arrived from Taria with news."

Aeroth's hand stilled, and I squeezed my eyes shut as reality set in.

"I'm coming!" I called out to the door. "Just a minute."

Aeroth moved his lips to the crook of my neck, and his teeth grazed the skin there.

"Both of those statements are a lie," he said.

"How so?" I asked.

He moved his fingers back into my pants and slipped between my thighs. He began to strum my bundle of nerves that was swollen and ready for him.

"One," he said and licked my neck, "you are not *coming*."

Warmth moved in my body like waves.

"And two?" I breathed.

"I recently learned," he continued to massage me there, and I bit my lips to stop from crying out, "that if I brush you here just so . . ."

I moved against him as he sped up his rhythm.

"I can make you come in under a minute . . ." he whispered.

Yes.

His breathing sped up and he moaned. "Look at how you're coating my fingers . . ."

"Aeroth . . .c-come inside me—"

He moved his middle finger into me and I cried out softly into the pillow.

"That's it . . ." he urged, dipping his finger in and out slowly.

I thrusted against his hand and he added another finger.

"You like that?"

I nodded.

"Tell me how much you want this."

I whimpered and sobbed and rode his hand. "I want it."

Now both of his arms were around me and his right hand moved to my core while his left hand, the one that had been working me, moved to my left thigh to open me up and get better access.

He began to play with my lips there. "Feel how swollen you are. You're dripping."

I bucked from how sensitive my skin was.

"More," I begged and moved his left fingers inside me.

He spoke in my ear. "You're mine, do you hear me?"

I cried out as his fingers fucked me.

"You will always be mine, Strongborn. Even after the day you and I cease to exist—"

I began to climax and my slick squirted out creating a mess as I sobbed onto the pillow.

Illona knocked again.

My core clenched in aftershocks, my body tingling in waves. I wanted to remain in his arms, but I forced myself to move from him and sat up. Aeroth groaned.

Aeroth's fingers followed me, and he ran my wetness up and down my bare back.

"Be serious," I told him.

He sat up and kissed my back. "I'm not finished with you."

I glanced at him.

"We need to get up. You're not helping."

"I like touching you," he said, flashing me an innocent look as I got up from the bed and put on my shirt. He slapped my ass. "Is that so wrong?"

I grinned and walked to the door and looked back at him. He looked disheveled, and his hair was a mess.

"Put a shirt on or something."

"For what?" he asked, a lazy smile meeting me. "So that we can pretend I've been sitting here the whole time at arm's length *chatting*?"

I rolled my eyes and opened the door. Illona stood there, wringing her fingers.

"I'm so sorry," she said, looking from me to the inside of the room.

Aeroth was suddenly behind me, dressed.

I rolled my eyes.

"I'm sorry we kept you waiting," Aeroth said to her. "Please blame Renna."

My jaw dropped.

Illona smiled slightly, her cheeks flushed as she said, "Cylas wanted to come and wake you earlier. I stopped him from doing so."

"You should have let him," Aeroth said and placed an arm around me. "Perhaps he would have taken a hint."

I pinched the bridge of my nose. "*Aeroth.*"

Aeroth shrugged. "He hates me."

"He doesn't *hate* you." I looked to Illona. "Has something happened?"

"Khellios's mother was killed by Sethos," Aeroth said behind me.

I whipped my head to him. "*What?*"

"I tried to tell you last night."

I knew he was telling the truth. I had been so focused on Aeroth's well-being that I dismissed him telling me about Taria.

Illona spoke up. "As a result, the Spiritual Enclave has decided to not intervene in the conflict. They are afraid of the magic he wields and the desire to kill gods. They have withdrawn support to stand beside the Celestial Enclave to fight Am-Re and Sethos."

I looked back at Illona.

"That's not all," she said. "My brother . . ." She frowned and looked to the ground. "My *half brother*, Berion, God of Fire, has convinced more than half of the Elemental Enclave to also withdraw their support."

Blood drained from my face.

"Where is Cylas?" I asked.

"He and Demira are in the Aelderhall with Wyleth and other Elsbeth elders."

"I need to speak with Aeroth," I said to her. "We will be there in a moment."

She nodded. "I'll see you both there."

Once alone, I pulled Aeroth into the bedroom, closed the door, and faced him.

He put his hands up. "I can feel your anger, Strongborn. If you're going to shout at me for not telling you about Madera's death, know I tried to tell you last night. Multiple times. Even as we laid down to sleep."

I crossed my arms. He was right.

I was mad at myself, and I wanted to direct my frustration somewhere else.

"A simple 'Khellios's mother died' would have sufficed," I retorted.

Aeroth looked up to the ceiling.

"I really don't want to argue with you right now. And I didn't know she mattered that much to you. I'm sorry if you shared a close relationship with her—"

"I didn't," I retorted. Madera hated me. She threatened me when I first arrived in Taria.

"Then I don't understand."

"It's Khellios," I said. "I can't bear to know he's in pain. He's already suffered so much."

"You couldn't have done anything for his pain even if you knew last night."

He was right—I would have been in a hopeless frenzy not knowing how to help Khellios. I could not force the elders in Elsbeth to escort us any sooner to the Metidons. I would have had to wait, and it would have crushed my sanity.

"And you would have been more worried about Sethos and the repercussions against him for having killed Madera."

I closed my eyes.

Sethos.

His murder of Madera would have lasting consequences. Whereas Khellios and the gods did not mean to kill Sethos's mother in the attack on Isyos, Sethos had deliberately killed her.

The gods would not forgive him. And I might never have an opportunity to save him.

But did he want to be saved?

"But you are right. And I am sorry," Aeroth said. "I should have told you about Madera. I will never assume how you may feel about a situation. This is a learning point for me. I'm sorry."

I ran my hands over my face and massaged my temples. The situation with Sethos was going from bad to worse, annihilating any hope of redemption.

My heart was breaking for Khellios. And for Sethos, who was in pain from the death of his own mother. And now, with the news that the Celestial Enclave would be fighting on their own, absolute chaos and carnage would follow.

My lips trembled.

I had felt hopeless and weak while in Daya because I didn't know how to properly wield my powers. Now that I could control my magic, I felt strong in that area of my life.

But mentally?

The constant mental highs and lows were wearing me down. In truth, I had never felt more helpless than I did in that particular moment.

"Talk to me," Aeroth whispered. "I promised to help you."

I looked to him and saw the lines of worry on his face. He was already helping me to the best of his ability. Him not killing Sethos when he had an opportunity and getting injured in the process because of his promise to me was remarkable.

To have the level of power Aeroth had and to choose not to wield it out of loyalty to me when bloodlust was threatening to emerge?

My father and Sethos knew no limits to violence and rage.

Aeroth chose restraint—something I would never forget.

"Renna," he said. "Please tell me what you are thinking. You go quiet on me and I . . ." He shook his head and ran his hands through his hair.

I stepped up to him and placed my hands around his waist.

"I forgive you," I said to him.

He sighed, and his body almost sagged.

"You don't fully know the dynamic between Khellios and I." I looked to the ground in front of us. "His mother always hated me. She never believed I was good enough for her son. Preventing me from reuniting with Khellios in this lifetime was her biggest goal."

Aeroth tipped my chin up with his forefinger and settled his gaze on mine.

"You are good enough." His voice was firm and steady. "And you will never be anyone's regret. Nor mine. I don't regret helping you forget your pain and sadness." His voice dropped to a whisper then. "You are kind. Strong. Brave. You jump into a fight when gods know you should not."

I laughed, and he shook his head up to the ceiling.

"I worry about what will happen to you when battle comes."

My smile faded. "Others have worried about my role in battle," I said quietly. "Khellios and Sethos."

He frowned. "Khellios worries for you in battle because he cannot control you. Sethos worries for you because he is afraid of losing access to your magic."

Hearing each man's motive made my heart retreat into a hard shell.

"I worry about you, Renna, because I know you will be brilliant. I know you will not back down. And because of all of this, I worry about the effects of battle on your mind. I worry about the memories that will come back to you in the quiet hours. I cannot stop you from fighting, so I will respect your wishes and fight alongside you. I'm just afraid I won't be able to shield you from the horrors you will see."

"I don't want there to be war," I whispered.

"Nor I."

"If Khellios's enclave has no other support, what will happen?" I searched Aeroth's eyes. "The monarchs also have vowed to help—will their word be true?"

"The monarchs have vowed to intervene to deal with Sethos. We were tasked with killing him."

My body tensed, and I clenched my jaw to keep from reacting.

Aeroth continued. "Given his magic and my ability to weave in and out of the Astral, the monarchs and I decided I would issue the final blow."

I kept my gaze steady on his.

"However, we counted on the other two enclaves to help Arios and his gods to fight off the rest of Sethos and your father's army. The monarchs brought a small number of soldiers with them from their realms to assist, but we never planned on being the only support to the Celestial Enclave. My realm has no soldiers. I offered only myself on behalf of my people."

I expected his next words so clearly that him saying them did not surprise me.

"I expect the monarchs to withdraw their support once they understand this battle is well lost. Many will stay on and fight, but taking on Sethos and your father . . . Their army will be insurmountable."

I nodded. "We need support from other realms, or people, or . . ." I paused and closed my eyes. "I don't even know what I'm asking for. There must be others out there in this universe who have a vested interest in peace. Taria and its people cannot be left alone in this fight."

"I suspect Arios has gathered other allies to join him, but the withdrawal of two god enclaves will make current and potential allies nervous."

I covered my face with my palms.

"You speaking to Sethos to stop this may be the only chance we have to turn the tide."

I dropped my hands. "What?"

"If we can convince Sethos or even stall and capture him to draw him away from your father—if you are convinced it is his magic controlling Sethos—"

"Yes!"

"—then we may have a chance."

Hearing Aeroth finally voice what I had been saying for weeks made my heart slow to a steady beat. I no longer needed a person's validation to believe in myself, but I had begun to care for Aeroth in a way that his opinion mattered to me.

"We need the Metidons to agree to help us," I said.

Aeroth nodded. "Yes . . ." He pursed his lips. "I will do what I can to ensure that they do."

50

RENNA

Standing in front of my sisters, Cylas, and the Elsbeth elders in the Aelderhall felt like I had been strapped to a chair while cold ice was being poured over my skin.

We were in a never-ending nightmare.

Cylas recounted the tense meeting with Arios and Khellios, where representatives of both Elemental and Spiritual Enclaves withdrew their support. As Aeroth predicted, some of the allies in the camps at Taria began expressing doubts about succeeding in battle, and Arios was scrambling to maintain their support.

Nothing was working in Taria's favor, and my body felt ill with waves of nausea thinking of the hundreds of deaths that would follow.

And when I thought it could not get worse, the Elders of Elsbeth refused to petition the Metidons early. They would wait until the last day of the equinox.

"You are condemning us to death," Demira said to Wyleth. "Fighting has begun in Taria. Now is not the time to stall!"

"There is an order in which the Metidons are petitioned," Wyleth told her. "Do *not* presume to tell us what to do."

Demira cursed and spun around, beginning to pace.

Aeroth spoke up. "I have been to Taria. And believe me, without the other two enclaves to assist Arios's group, this will be carnage."

"Then let us hope the Metidons grant our petition," Wyleth said, his voice almost on edge. "The ritual will not fail this time."

Demira screamed and stormed from the room. Illona rushed after her, but I heard them shouting at each other and ran to them.

"And don't follow me!" Demira screamed at Illona as Demira walked away.

Illona stood alone, her eyes glassed over. She hugged herself. "I don't know how to help," Illona said to me once I reached her side. "I love her and I want to help her. I don't have the answers and it's killing me."

We were out of time, and we still had no resolution. Terror filled me as slow defeat settled into my bones, making the reality we were now faced with abundantly clear:

Sethos could attack at any moment, and no one would be able to stop him.

There would not be anyone to provide a moral anchor to help him or pull him from my father's grasp.

My body became so cold, and I shivered.

Cylas approached us.

"I'm sorry, Ren." He placed a hand on my shoulder. "I don't know what else to do. I cannot break the barrier to Taria. And even if I could, doing so would invite more of Sethos's allies to attack with a weakened barrier."

I shook my head. "There has to be another way. I refuse to give up on Demira's vision."

I would not sit by as battle raged on in Taria. I had been silent and controlled for so many years, trying to not be noticeable as I cowered in fear. I had felt abandoned when my father abused me and wished so many times someone would protect me. Now that I could protect others during battle, standing aside felt like a betrayal to myself.

Aeroth joined us, and I moved to hug him.

"I'm sorry," he said to me against my hair.

I looked up at him. "We can't give up, Aeroth," I told him.

He nodded.

"There is always a way," Illona said and looked to Aeroth. "Like a tree with many branches. There are always many options. Sometimes things play out like they are supposed to for the good of all. I trust you understand?"

I frowned and looked to Aeroth, who was frowning at Illona. Aeroth did not answer, and I thought it odd. What was he not telling me?

"I will go and find my sister," Illona said to the group. She looked to Aeroth once more. "The Ancestors trust you know what needs to be done."

As we watched her go, Cylas shook his head. "Why am I drawn to women who speak in riddles?" he said to himself, but loud enough so that I heard.

Illona's words gnawed at me. What had she meant, and why had she looked at Aeroth?

As if he heard my inner monologue, Aeroth looked to me.

"I need to speak with you," he said quietly and then looked at Cylas. "*Privately.*"

Cylas rolled his eyes and shook his head. I nodded and moved to walk with him. Once we were farther out on the plaza, Aeroth spoke.

"There is another way I can get you into Taria."

I stopped walking and blinked.

"*What?*"

Aeroth stopped walking and turned to face me.

"It may be best to not discuss it here," he said, looking around uneasily, his eyes always stern at anyone who would gawk at him.

"Is this what Illona was referring to in the hall?" I asked.

"Yes."

I crossed my arms.

"And where are we to discuss this?" I narrowed my eyes and took a step toward him. "Did you keep something from me?"

Aeroth's lips pursed, and he crossed his arms. "Not deliberately, *no*."

"I asked you not to lie to me." The grating words tasted bitter.

Aeroth took a step closer. "And once you hear my offer, you will understand why it's so ridiculous to even contemplate."

"So ridiculous you all of a sudden consider telling me after Illona brought it up?"

"You won't agree to it," he said. "I know this."

My eyes turned to slits.

"Try me."

"Let's portal to Eniraath from your bedroom. I don't want the others to know where we go. I'm starting to not trust the elders."

We left the others and headed to my bedroom, where Aeroth portaled us to a long corridor created of clear glass or some sort of crystal. Burgundy carpet lined the floor, and I was sure but for the plush and soft carpet beneath my feet, I would likely see space under me as well.

An orange nebula pulsing in the distance, the rays of the cosmic event filtered through the hall, filling it with golden-orange light. The effect was mesmerizing as the crystal that constructed the space seemed to shine like billions of translucent crystals where the light hit them.

As my eyes moved about the space, I noticed chandeliers made of the same crystal lining the tall arched ceiling above us, following the length of the corridor. The chandeliers were lit with glowing yellow spheres not unlike the ones I had seen at Cylas's forest creation.

"What is this place?" I asked.

It felt like I was in a daydream—the setting vaguely familiar yet a strange place. Had I dreamt this before?

"Home."

I looked to Aeroth, who was studying my face with caution, as if he was afraid I would bolt.

"You seem uneasy," I told him.

"I think you will hate this place after you hear what I need to say."

I frowned. "Why bring me here?"

"Come," he said and nodded toward the rest of the hallway before us. "There is something you need to see before I tell you anything else."

Feeling my anger rise at the possibility of being disappointed by a man I had grown to trust and was now growing to care for, I stood my ground.

"I asked you not to hurt me," I said to him.

Aeroth moved to stand right in front of me. "And I told you I would not. I also told you my word would be true."

I tilted my head. "Then why does it feel like you are about to tell me something that will cause me pain?"

He put his palm out for me to take. "Please," he said. "Come with me."

Worries of what he would tell me whirled inside me. I could only conclude he'd lied to me, like so many other men in my life.

"Aeroth," I said, feeling my voice break. "Don't hurt me."

He grabbed my hand and kissed it. "And I won't."

Reluctantly, I nodded and allowed him to lead me down the corridor.

The palace we were in—which I assumed was his palace—

was empty of any soul. We encountered no one as we walked, which struck me as odd.

Was he not king here? Did kings not have soldiers and hundreds of staff members ready at their beck and call?

"There is no one here," I whispered as we passed closed door after closed door, moving through different hallways and passing enormous halls that looked like sitting rooms with lavish golden furniture and ballrooms with gilded chairs lining the walls. There were platform items resembling human instruments, but they looked far more technologically advanced. I was sure guitars did not levitate on their own or have strings that looked like they were made out of water.

"It's just my sister and I here most days," he said as we walked. "Despite the size of this place, we don't require much help. My sister enjoys cooking with the chef to pass the time, and we hire staff to assist us for mealtimes to ensure my people have options for employment here, should they choose it. Other than that, the palace is enchanted and cleans itself."

I shivered.

"It feels lonely here, despite its beauty," I remarked.

"My father's sister, my aunt, and her wife and their children visit us for mealtimes. They make this place seem less lonely."

I thought of Isidra's son and where he resided, but did not want to bring him up in case that was a painful subject to Aeroth.

We remained silent as we walked, and when we turned a corner into a room with a pool, a crystallized tree with red leaves grew out of the middle of it, and I froze.

I had been here before.

My heartbeat pounded in my ears.

When had I been here, and how was that possible?

"*Aeroth,*" I said, my voice shaky as I drew my hand from his and hugged my middle.

He walked to the edge of the pool or pond and turned to face me.

"I've been here before . . ." I whispered, looking about the room. The rest of the room was constructed in the same crystal, and a soft pink light from some cosmic event warmed the room.

"Perhaps," Aeroth said, studying my face.

"Perhaps?" I asked him, my tone high. "What do you mean, perhaps? Why do I remember this place?"

"In the forest of Daya, when I spoke to you through the cell Sethos caged you in, I asked you to imagine a place of happiness. Imagine my surprise when you described this room."

I searched my mind for that conversation. I had been delirious.

Sure enough, words drifted back to me in pieces like echoes inside my mind.

"Where is your mind?" Aeroth had asked me as I tried to find magic inside me to break through Sethos's cell.

"I'm in space," I had whispered as my mind had drifted off.

"Where?"

"In a palace among the stars . . . The palace walls are made of crystal. I can see space anywhere I look . . ."

I opened my eyes to look at Aeroth as the memory continued playing in the back of my mind.

Aeroth's eyes were calm as he observed me.

My voice drifted back to me.

. . .

"THERE'S A TREE. It's made of the same crystal material. There are red leaves on it, and they fall beautifully . . . There is a pool of water at the base of the tree . . ."

I SEARCHED Aeroth's eyes as tears pricked at my eyes.

"WHY THERE, RENNA STRONGBORN?" Aeroth had asked me. "What do you feel?"

"It's peaceful here. Quiet . . . It feels like home."

HOME.

Aeroth's home.

"I don't understand . . ." I breathed. "Why would I describe your home?"

He shook his head. "Perhaps it's the bond. That would be the only thing that could explain why your mind created a connection to me. Mates sometimes have flashes of each other throughout their lives before they meet."

I recalled the medic mage from Elrie's craft explaining the concept to me. That conversation seemed like ages ago.

"Why didn't you say anything?" I demanded.

I now remembered I had seen a shadow of stars in my vision. A shadow of stars was how I had experienced Aeroth before I saw his corporal body.

"We were trying to escape," Aeroth explained. "There was no time to tell you that you were describing my home."

"What is the significance of this tree? Why would I think about it in particular?"

He studied my gaze before answering, as if he were almost cautious or afraid I would bolt.

"The tree binds a monarch of Eniraath to the Astral Plane."

I crossed my arms. His words did not make sense.

"Why am I here?" I asked.

"You called this your home, Renna. In that moment in Daya."

I tilted my head. "Just say what you need to say, Aeroth."

"I have another way for you to go to Taria."

I marched up to him. "All this time!" I yelled and pushed his chest. "*How?!*"

"Marry me."

I blinked as the words settled into my system.

"*What?*"

"Marry me, Renna."

"Have you lost your fucking mind?" I yelled and pushed his chest again. "You bring me here to mock me—"

"Rulers of the Astral bend time and space and are able to travel anywhere."

"I am no ruler of the Astral."

"You would be as my queen. Once you marry me, we will have an ascension ceremony. Your body and soul would be merged with the fibers of the Astral Plane itself. You would be able to bend reality and enter Taria."

I was speechless.

"Bending time and reality and traveling through the Astral Plane is different than Astral projection or traveling through a portal. The latter is done when your body remains in one place and your soul detaches for a time and travels. Your soul usually always returns to the body. Being an Astral ruler would mean your entire physical body and soul would travel together anywhere you wish."

I now knew why he had never shared this possibility.

It was one thing to share intimate moments while feeding. It was quite another to marry. To agree to marry Aeroth would end any freedom I could ever have, and all I ever talked about was my liberty.

He was right in assuming I would reject the idea.

"Don't you want children? A true marriage? *Love?*" I asked him. "Why throw all of that away on me?"

Aeroth shifted his weight and looked at the tree as he answered.

"I need heirs, Renna. I won't lie to you. And I never expected love from my spouse, as I expected my government to find me a wife. I never even expected to like her. I fully intended to respect her, but not enjoy her company."

I scoffed, and he looked at me. "Please continue with your passionate rendition of what marriage means to you."

"I like you, Renna." He stepped up to me. "I won't lie and tell you I love you because we have not known each other long. *I loved Isidra.*"

His words had a mixture of relief and a sharp sting. Relief because I did not have to push myself to feel love for someone I had recently met, and sting because I didn't know if any woman would compare to Isidra.

"I don't know if I have the capacity to love another like I did her. I also will not lie to you and tell you I will develop love for you like that over time," he confessed.

I nodded. "I respect that."

Honest to a fault.

"I can promise you to respect you. To continue caring for you. To build a companionship out of trust. And most importantly, to help you."

I would not be expected to love him. Without love, there would be no heartbreak.

"And children?" I asked. "I am not against being around children, but I never contemplated being a mother."

And I was young.

"I want to continue my studies, Aeroth," I added quickly. "I want to work. I want to be independent."

"I know—"

"And I don't know the first thing about being royalty. Sethos offered me Vasarys to co-rule. I turned him down. I don't want to rule. I am not made to be a ruler."

"So have your own house in Eniraath. I won't tie you to live beside me here." He gestured around us. "You can work at the universities in Eniraath. Study. Get degrees."

"As the queen?" I deadpanned. "Would that be allowed?"

"Eniraath is small, Renna. The people here know only peace. They won't care if you teach or study. Besides, the universities here were founded by the first queen of Eniraath. She came here from Earth and felt lost and lonely in Eniraath. Teaching allowed her to feel at peace."

I looked to the tree and wondered about the first queen. How had she arrived here?

"She was a lot like you," Aeroth said, as if he could read my mind.

"A lot like me, how?" I asked.

Aeroth's smile warmed me down to my toes. A look of pride crossed his face, and he pushed a stray hair behind my ear.

I felt my skin flush, and I cleared my throat.

"She was a professor on Earth," Aeroth said. "When she came here, she thought she was a mortal human and clung to her previous life as much as she could. Over time, she and the King fell in love. The universities were opened by the first King of the Astral as a gesture of love to her."

I could only assume that the queen had been happy.

But the thought of having children resurfaced.

"And children?" I asked again. "You need heirs."

"Yes." He nodded. "I need two legitimate heirs. Perhaps your want for me has faded after this conversation, and you never want me to touch you again. I would not ask you to be a true wife to me should you not wish it."

My body tensed thinking of birthing children.

I was not opposed to having my own one day. I had just never planned it or thought I would meet someone who would make me want children.

"If you never want me to touch you intimately," Aeroth continued, "I ask that you agree to insemination or that a surrogate here in Eniraath would carry our children."

"Why not impregnate another woman altogether?"

"The heirs of the Astral Plane have the Astral woven into their cells and being. Their composition enables the magic of the heir who ascends to the Astral throne. This only occurs when both parents have ascended to the Astral and become one with the Astral Plane. You will be one with the Astral when you ascend."

"But a surrogate?" I shook my head. "Would that not diminish the legitimacy of the heir who ascends? What will your government or your people say—"

"No. Surrogacy in my lineage has been done once before." He lowered his chin. "And as for what my people think, I don't give a damn what they think. They think what I tell them."

I tilted my head. "So you are a tyrant?"

"No." He stepped farther up to me. We were so close that I tipped my head back.

"I care for your comfort only." His eyes searched my face. "The people here and my government will accept any decision you make. You will not be questioned."

"Even if we live apart?"

His jaw tensed. "Even if we live apart."

"And what if you find someone else later down the road you are attracted to? Someone better suited?"

Or what if *I* found someone else later?

"You nor I would be able to have children with any other

person," Aeroth said. "Illegitimate children would be chaotic for the balance of the Astral Plane. Even if those children don't ascend to the status of a ruler, their ability to move about the Astral Plane and Astral project would be dangerous. Having an illegitimate heir with the ability to Astral travel with ease could be chaotic."

Because I never truly contemplated having children, I likely would not grieve my inability to have children with someone other than Aeroth.

Aeroth continued. "I only ask you to remain here in Eniraath while our children are small. Even if you never develop a maternal sense, it will be good for them to see you and know you."

I could not imagine abandoning children like my father abandoned me.

"I understand," I said.

I moved from him and paced the room.

"You mentioned you need heirs soon to protect your lineage." I looked to Aeroth. "How soon?"

"I was hoping to marry this year. My government is actively seeking a candidate."

I laughed and shook my head. "How *romantic*."

"There is no romance in this, Renna. But at least we will have honesty. And through our union, I will be able to help you change the tide of this war."

Aeroth was offering me the last opportunity to see Sethos and stop this war. No one else was coming to save Taria or help Sethos fight his inner demons.

"Is the ascension painful?" I asked while looking at the tree. "How does the tree help me ascend?"

"It's difficult to describe. I remember the feeling of being pulled in different directions. I remember being cold as the cosmos wove itself in me. In terms of *how*, a marriage ceremony will be held here and performed by a priest. You and I will drink each other's blood served in cups that will be mixed with bark and leaves from this tree. That will begin the process and ensure your body is familiar with the properties of the tree."

I wrinkled my nose over how unpleasant drinking bark and leaves sounded.

"The tree was created by Source as the first life form in the Astral Plane. It is older than my lineage and infused with the fibers of Source. It is magic at its most pure."

The thought of drinking something made of Source with that magnitude of power made me shiver. Aeroth came to me and took my hands.

"A day must pass before your body accepts the magic in your system to prepare you for the ascension. It's less painful that way."

I shook my head. "I don't want pain."

Aeroth kissed the tops of my hands. "I will do everything in my power to mitigate any pain."

"How long does the ascension take?"

"Two days," he said.

Two days was a lot sooner than waiting for the last day of the equinox.

Aeroth continued. "You will give up your blood to the tree, which is why the leaves are red. They are made up of the blood of the monarchs in my lineage. During this, you are put in a state of trance. The tree will enchant your blood, and at the right time, your body will receive blood again. When the enchanted blood enters your system, you will begin transforming."

Not being in control of my body riddled me with anxiety. "I don't like that."

"I will not leave your side. I swear to you."

I took my hands from his.

"What if Sethos attacks in two days?" I asked.

"I will prolong what I must to ensure you have time to speak with Sethos. Trust me."

I knew that I could trust him. He did not kill Sethos when he had the chance.

"We are friends foremost, Renna," Aeroth said. "We can be friends through this. Let me help you."

"This is life-altering, Aeroth."

He nodded. "I know."

I needed time to think about his proposal—or more specifically business proposal. This marriage was a pact of interests that had less to do with a marital union and was more of a transaction.

"Where in Eniraath would we marry?" I asked, fearing crowds coming to see the ceremony. On Andora, when government officials married from the Planetary Council, the occasions were big and drawn out, drawing crowds from all over.

"We will marry here in this room," he said. "Beside this tree."

I looked around the space and saw how simple it was. There were no pews. No altars. No religious symbols.

"Don't kings need public pomp and circumstance for marriage?" I asked.

"No. Only vain kings do."

"Will any people come to see the ceremony?"

He shook his head. "Not unless you want to. It can just be the priest and us."

I tried to take in a deep breath and exhaled as I processed all he had shared.

Aeroth lowered his chin. "Do you want a large marriage ceremony? I apologize if I am dismissing your dreams of what a marriage day would look like for you—"

"*No.*" I shook my head and continued to pace, wringing my hands. "Frankly, I never thought to marry. I was always told by my father that I would never find a man who would want me. Or tolerate me."

Aeroth remained silent, and I walked the room again. My faith in Demira's vision still held true, but Sethos had just arrived in Taria and I'd been handed the keys to a faster solution.

"What are you thinking?" Aeroth asked me. "We can wait out the equinox in Elsbeth. You don't have to do this."

I knew Sethos. He would not quit. His drive for vengeance knew no end. His attack on Khellios's mother would only embolden him. He had set out to kill all the gods in the Celestial Enclave, and he had easily eliminated one.

I also knew Khellios. He was a protector. He would not back down from an opportunity to kill Sethos on sight—especially after his mother's death.

And despite Aeroth promising he would do everything in his power to help me speak to Sethos and enact a plan to see if we could help him, Aeroth was not in Taria in this moment. Aeroth was here—with me.

What if Sethos attacked later today? Or tomorrow? What if the attack was unexpected and someone killed him before they alerted Aeroth?

I looked to the tree that would meld my body with the Astral. I saw the countless leaves turned red by the blood of Aeroth's lineage. Had Aeroth's Ancestors seen their decision to become one with the Astral as an easy choice? As an inevitable duty?

Duty.

I stopped pacing in front of the tree.

I had a duty to not give up on a soul I believed with all my heart was redeemable. My belief in my capacity to save Sethos from the magic that corrupted his heart was unshakable.

Because I knew that every soul was redeemable. Every soul had an opportunity to choose differently. To better their path.

I knew that speaking to Sethos would not be enough. Clearly, he was in a crazed state of mind as he had killed Madera.

To stop Sethos, we would have to capture him. Lure him like he lured me. And once captured, we would have to drain him of his magic. Sethos would likely hate me for the rest of his life, but at least I would keep him and others alive.

I turned to Aeroth, who studied me with gentle eyes.

Marriage to Aeroth would not be easy, as I would have to adjust to a new life by his side. But it would not be a bad life.

There was no love, but we were friends.

He cared for me, and I cared for him.

And wasn't friendship enough for some couples anyway?

"I'll do it," I told him.

Aeroth's eyebrows lifted.

"You'll do *what*?" he asked.

"I'll marry you."

Aeroth nodded once. "Yes," he replied, his tone dry. "Alright."

I felt so incredibly awkward at that moment.

"After we marry," I told him, "we need to return to Elsbeth to let everyone know I will be gone for two days for the ascension ceremony. They will wonder where we are."

Aeroth nodded. "I agree."

I took a deep breath and exhaled.

"Where do we begin?" I asked him.

Aeroth blinked several times as if trying to process my words. If he was trying to equally process the situation, I didn't blame him. We both needed grace in that moment.

"Ah, yes," he said as a matter of fact. "*Right.* We need a priest to perform this marriage ceremony."

Aeroth walked past me and opened an arched-shaped door I had not seen at the end of the room. He poked his head in and spoke to someone there, and I could not make out the words. After several moments and sudden excited sounds of responses from the inside of whatever room Aeroth was speaking into, Aeroth closed the door and joined me.

"The priests' quarters are located through that door," Aeroth explained. "The tree is used for other ceremonies, hence the proximity of the priests."

I nodded.

"Someone should be right out so we can get this over with," Aeroth said.

Aeroth's "get this over with" comment was exactly how I felt. This was not a celebration of a joining—at least not to me. This was me taking action out of duty, and I knew deep in the core of my being it was the right decision.

51

RENNA

I stood in silence, watching as an older priest with black wavy hair moved slowly in front of the tree.

The priest was dressed in a white robe with golden leaves embroidered in his tunic. A table with bowls had been set up beside the tree. As the priest moved, he placed pieces of bark in one bowl and leaves in another. He scooped water with a third bowl from the pool where the tree stood.

I allowed myself to become distracted with the priest's movements as I thought about my future—one I was mourning. I had to accept that any childish notions of a family I once had—of finding a man I loved and wanted to spend the rest of my life with—were not possible for me.

I pushed the thoughts of the children I would have with Aeroth from my mind. That was a subject I did not want to fully explore at the moment.

The only thing that provided comfort was the lives I would be saving. For the first time, my life would have meaning. *Purpose.*

I would be using my magic for the good of others rather than just myself. That alone would set me apart from my father. He served only himself. I vowed to never be like him, and my choice to help Sethos and Taria would set me apart—even if I did use my father's magic.

I watched as the priest moved his hands over the bowls and saw golden beams emerge from his palms.

The magic settled into the bowls, causing the bark, leaves, and water to lift into the air. They began to swirl together in sync, faster and faster, until the light of the magic grew so bright I had to look away.

Within moments, the light faded and I turned to look at the priest.

The bowls were gone, and on the table was a crystal goblet encrusted with red crystals. Red contents swirled slowly inside.

"My king," the priest spoke to Aeroth and extended his hand toward Aeroth. "Your hand?"

Aeroth stepped forward and gave the priest his hand.

The priest turned his hand over so Aeroth's palm faced up.

"With your permission, my king, I will make a small incision to ensure your blood mixes with the ceremony elixir," the priest said.

Aeroth nodded, and I watched the priest conjure a small dagger made of what looked like solid gold.

Looking at Aeroth's solemn face, I wondered if he was mourning for the marriage he hoped to have one day and what he was giving up.

He spoke of his sister fondly—I wondered if he longed for a loving family.

I would not be able to offer him love, but I would respect him and consider him—just how he was now considering me.

Aeroth's selflessness was something I wanted to emulate. He wasn't even asking me to sleep with him . . .

At the thought, my body became warm.

We had lust. At least there was that.

Friendship and lust.

It would have to be enough. We could do this.

I could do this.

I watched as Aeroth's blood dripped into the cup.

Once several drops of Aeroth's blood were mixed into the goblet contents, the priest let go of Aeroth's hand and looked to me.

"Your hand, miss?" the priest asked me.

I stood in place, taking it all in. I felt so cold suddenly.

Aeroth turned and grabbed my hands. He squeezed them.

"Are you okay?" he asked.

I nodded.

"It's just a lot," I said. "I feel like I'm floating. Like it's not my body."

"I understand," he responded. "There is still time to back out. Tell me what you want to do. You are in control here. I will do whatever you wish."

I looked at his face and studied the laugh lines at the corners of his eyes. I would get to see him age and watch those laugh lines deepen.

I was reminded of his kindness.

His friendliness.

The way he laughed.

He would be a good husband—even if in name only.

I could do this.

I had to.

"I will go through with this." My voice came out steady—more than I felt.

He tilted his head. "You're sure?"

"There is no other immediate option."

He shook his head once and looked down at our joined hands. "I'm sorry this has played out this way."

My chest let out a heavy sigh. "I know. I don't know how I'll be able to repay you for helping me this way."

A small smile appeared on his lips.

"All I ask is when we have children, please be kind to them. You don't have to spend a lot of time with them . . . We will have help in raising them. But when they see you . . . please . . ." He paused. "Please be kind. That is all."

My heart stopped, and I frowned. "You don't have to ask me that. Of course I will be kind." I stepped closer to him. "I'm sorry for anything you might have experienced in your childhood." I shook my head. "I'm not motherly by nature, but I will try my hardest to be a good parent. The love I did not receive as a child, I will give to them." I squeezed his hand. "I swear it."

He nodded and looked up at me. "Alright."

I nodded back. "Alright."

We stood in silence for a few moments, looking at each other.

I faced the priest.

"I'm ready," I told him and gave him my hand.

The priest looked to me and hesitated. "Are you here of your own volition?" he lowered his chin and looked to Aeroth before looking back at me. "I know my loyalty is to my king, but I sense your fear. Are you being coerced in any way?"

Aeroth cursed under his breath. "Apparently my people think I'm the type that forces women to marry me."

The priest narrowed his eyes at him. "My deep apologies, my king. However, this is a rather sudden development. We were made aware that your government was seeking a wife for you, my king. We did not know they had found one so soon, and no one is here from your government to witness—"

"They did not find her, Manuel," Aeroth told the priest, who apparently was named Manuel. "*I* found her. She is my mate. And I am not coercing her." Aeroth straightened. "And I don't need my government's permission to marry. Nor them to witness this union. *I am king.* And you are here as minister to witness. That is enough."

The priest's eyes grew. "Your mate? I see." The priest looked to me again. "You would be the third monarchal Astral union to come from a mate bond. It is rare and special that you have found each other and that it will result in marriage—*if* that is your true wish."

"Yes." I lifted my chin. "I freely choose to marry him."

The priest looked at me for a few more moments before he nodded. "*Very well.*"

The priest took my offered hand and made a small incision in the palm with the golden dagger.

I watched as drops of my blood splashed into the goblet.

The next few moments passed in a haze, and I felt like my soul detached from my body as I listened to the priest talk to Aeroth and I about marriage and the importance of love and respect. Of companionship and patience.

When the priest began to instruct us in the ceremony, my brain went into autopilot. I nodded when I was told to. I spoke when directed.

I was numb.

If asked later on, I would not remember speaking my vows.

But one thing I did remember was Aeroth's vows.

He said they were Naaviri vows:

Ever mine. Ever found. Ever bonded.

Despite the mental fog I was in, his words brought me to life, and warmth spread through me. I looked at our now-joined hands, and like when our hands first touched in Daya, an electrical current went through me. I gasped, and he did as well.

And before I was able to process that we were married, the priest bowed to us both and then knelt in front of each of us.

I didn't understand why he was kneeling in front of me, and I wanted to reach up to him to help him stand.

"May you live long and reign well, Your Majesty," the priest said to me.

My body froze.

I knew I had married Aeroth and that he was king, but somehow my brain was still catching up to the fact that I would be addressed like I was queen.

I looked to Aeroth, who smiled at me.

"And a good queen she shall be," Aeroth said.

My heart pounded as a million thoughts of what my future would exactly look like swirled in my head.

Then the priest stood. It was over, and Aeroth and I stood in silence.

And in that same silence, we portaled back to my room, and I sat on the ground against my bed, my back to the footboard. Aeroth sat on the armchair.

Neither of us spoke for what seemed like an eternity.

Had I truly married him?

I wondered what Aeroth felt, but I didn't have the mental capacity to speak or ask questions.

I knew we had to tell my sisters and Cylas what we had done, but my body would not move, or perhaps I didn't want to move.

I still felt like I was floating.

Disassociation.

At some point, Aeroth moved to sit next to me on the ground, and I placed my head on his shoulder. We must have sat like that a long time because I drifted off to sleep in that position.

And during the night, I found myself on my bed, covered with my bed blankets with Aeroth on top of the blankets next to me, sound asleep.

I moved my hand to hold his, and in sleep, he shifted to his side to curl his body around mine, holding me.

And with his warmth surrounding me, I drifted back to sleep.

52

RENNA

I always wondered what the first few hours of a bride's new life were like.

Although my wedding had not been a joyous occasion, I knew that having an immediate path forward was going to make everything better. My hope for a clear solution was strong now.

However, as Aeroth and I walked the streets of Elsbeth to tell my sisters and Cylas that we had wed and I would be in Elsbeth with Aeroth to undergo the ascension, all that hope I had built inside me was shattered.

Illona rushed to Aeroth and I. Demira was missing.

Aeroth pulled Illona and me into an alley of sorts on the side of the building for privacy.

"Where did you last see Demira?" I asked Illona.

Illona's eyes were streaked with tears, and she shook her head.

"After she stormed out of the Aelderhall and asked me to not follow her, I didn't see her again."

I wondered if Demira had gone to a tavern to drink her anger away or had fallen asleep someplace—or with someone. When I gently suggested those alternatives, Illona quickly shook her head.

"Demira can pretend to enjoy drinking when it suits her, but she hates alcohol. Our father was drunk often. She detests drinking," Illona shared. "As for her finding someone to spend time with, it's unlikely. She has been so affected by memories of Corrigrant that I don't think she would let another person touch her in that manner."

I nodded. I understood why Demira would be opposed to drinking—I, too, limited my contact with alcohol because of my childhood experiences. And it would make sense for Demira to shun physical contact after being triggered by sharing her memories.

Aeroth spoke. "Perhaps she is merely walking around the city like we are. Did she sleep in your room last night?"

Illona shook her head. "I have searched everywhere. She is not here. She did go to our room because she left her clothing there."

I frowned. "What do you mean?"

Illona ran her shaking hands over her face before speaking.

"Attendants arrived yesterday to leave us clothing for the upcoming final equinox day. They let us know that it is a custom for women here to wear red, and they gave us a red dress to each wear for that day."

The women in Elsbeth all wore various shades of red, so the request to don red for the final equinox day seemed harmless.

"I thought nothing of the dress delivery," Illona said. "We have over seven days left until the end of the equinox. As you can see," she looked down at her clothing, which was the same we had arrived in but had been cleaned, "I am still wearing my normal clothing."

"Yes?" I asked, confused as to where she was going with this line of thinking.

"Demira changed into the dress they left her," Illona continued. "Her clothing was left on her bed. Folded. Demira had no reason to change her clothing since the final day of the equinox is so far away. And she never folds her clothes. My sister is the messiest person in the entire universe."

Aeroth crossed his arms. "Do you think someone forced her to change?" he asked Illona.

Illona closed her eyes and shook her head. "I don't know."

"Or maybe," I added, "Demira is trying to fit in?"

Illona opened her eyes and frowned. "What do you mean?"

"Would it be possible that Demira was tired of waiting for the elders to contact the Metidons and she decided to look for the Metidons herself?" I asked. "The elders shared the location of the Metidons."

Aeroth rubbed his chin. "We did not see anyone outside the caves though. The only thing outside the caves is a lake."

"But why would she fold her clothes?" Illona asked. "And why not tell us?"

In that moment, Cylas walked past us and did a double take upon seeing us. He slowly backtracked and joined us in the alley.

"This is cozy," he said, lifting his eyebrows. "Who are we talking about?"

Illona rolled her eyes. "Save your humor and sarcasm for once!" she snapped.

Cylas took in Illona's tears and stepped closer.

"What happened?" he growled, looking at her up and down, as if assessing if she was injured. He narrowed his eyes, and green magic emanated from his palms. "Did someone hurt you?"

"Demira is gone," Illona answered, voice shaking.

Cylas looked to me. "How?"

I shook my head. "We don't know. Illona shared she hasn't seen her since yesterday when Demira stormed from the Aelderhall. She apparently went back to her shared room with Illona and changed into clothing provided by the elders."

"Were there signs of struggle or anything that would indicate she was taken forcibly?" Cylas asked Illona.

Illona took a deep breath and exhaled. When she spoke, her voice was steadier.

"No," she told Cylas. "The clothing she had been wearing when I last saw her was folded—something she never does. I just have this odd feeling like something is the matter—that something is about to occur—and I can't pinpoint it. The Ancestors are silent."

"Take me to your room, and I can help you begin the search again," Cylas told her.

Illona nodded.

"If the elders are behind this, I promise you I will make them answer," he told her.

"Thank you."

Aeroth crossed his arms and spoke. "Renna suggested perhaps Demira left of her own accord, dressing in the clothing given to her to fit in and look for the Metidons."

Cylas sighed and closed his eyes. "That would be an incredibly stupid thing for her to do."

Illona pushed his chest. "Don't call my sister stupid!"

Cylas opened his eyes. "I'm sorry."

Illona shook her head and looked up to the cave ceiling. "Can we go and search for her, please?" she asked.

I looked to Aeroth. We had planned to tell them of our marriage and the plans for me to ascend, but finding Demira seemed more important.

As if reading my mind, Aeroth looked to me.

We will tell them of us after we find Demira. Let's not detract attention from locating her. She couldn't have gone far.

I nodded but instantly had doubts about how fast we could

locate Demira. I needed to ascend to go to Taria.

"I will look for Demira in the Astral Plane," Aeroth told everyone. "Perhaps she fell asleep someplace or is intoxicated and her mind went up to the Astral."

"Or was drugged," Cylas added.

His words earned him a curse from Illona.

"Either way," Aeroth said, "if her mind is in the Astral, I will locate her and travel to her body."

"Thank you," Illona said.

Aeroth looked to me. I knew I would have to part from him. I was glad we exchanged blood during the marriage ritual to make our time apart easier.

"You cannot go with me into the Astral," he said. "Will you remain with Illona and Cylas?"

I nodded. "Yes. We will await any news from you."

Aeroth and I looked at each other as if we weren't sure how to say goodbye in front of my sister and Cylas.

Aeroth cleared his throat and nodded once. "Right," he said. "Well, I'll see you soon."

I pushed my hair behind my ear. "*Yes.*"

With a flash, Aeroth was gone.

Cylas, Illona, and I immediately sprang onto the streets of Elsbeth, heading to Illona and Demira's room.

I kept my eyes alert as I walked, my eyes scanning people, shop fronts, restaurant patios, and alleys between buildings.

As I observed my surroundings, one thing did catch my attention and made me pause more than once: little girls carrying dolls with long black hair and dressed in red dresses with yellow and orange swirling ribbons at the hem.

The dolls resembled the same doll I had seen the first day in Elsbeth.

Like that little girl I had encountered before, the little girls who walked past also pulled their dolls by a red braided ribbon on the neck.

A chilling feeling crept up my spine.

What had the dressmaker Ada shared that first day? That a murderer was hung and burned in the ritual for the equinox?

I could not help but think the red braid ribbon around the doll's neck resembled a noose and the orange and yellow ribbons at the hem of the dolls resembled fire.

Was a female murderer hung and burned?

I shivered.

As I walked behind Illona and Cylas, we strode by two boarded-up buildings that caught my attention. The buildings had a small sliver of space large enough for a person to fit through, and between the space, I could see flames at the rear of the buildings.

If the buildings were boarded up and potentially vacant, why would someone create a bonfire at the back?

Aeroth would want me to follow them so I could stay in a group. But Aeroth also trusted my judgment and my gut told me to investigate what was behind the buildings.

And so, I stopped following Illona and Cylas and let the crowd in the street swallow them until I could no longer see them.

53

RENNA

I moved hastily toward the gap of the two buildings and had to walk sideways in an almost shuffle to emerge on the other side.

As I got closer to the end, I could see more flames. They were located farther away than I anticipated, almost an entire level down. As I pushed my body through the opening, I frowned. The flames came from a large bonfire that expanded higher than any bonfire I had seen in my lifetime. If I were to estimate, the flames were as tall as a three-story building.

The area down around the bonfire was at least a twenty stories below—and deserted. Past the bonfire was a cavernous passageway that had glowing blue markings along the walls. The long passageway eventually curved away from my vantage point.

I hadn't seen any symbols or glowing patterns like that anywhere else in Elsbeth. And I got the feeling not everything was as it appeared to be.

A thought gnawed at me.

Demira was a woman who had been raised in a palace, and although she'd been abused by Am-Re, Demira was a princess. She was used to getting her way.

If Demira wanted to speak to the Metidons, she would not sit back and let others decide when it would happen. She and I were alike in that respect—we were women of action. We did not wait for others to solve our problems. I married Aeroth to ascend when the elders refused to help us. Demira likely went to look for the Metidons when she became tired of waiting for the end of the equinox.

But what if I was wrong?

The dolls I had seen around Elsbeth flashed back in my mind. The long black hair on the dolls made me uneasy.

Demira had long black hair.

She was tied to the murderer of Corrigrant.

She was blamed for the Metidons having to flee their homelands. And the ritual had to do with the history of the Metidons.

I shook my head. Despite the callousness of the elders, we had no reason to think they hated Demira enough to kill her.

Right?

Trusting my intuition, I descended the stone steps to the level below. I wanted to take a closer look at the symbols in the passageway.

My legs were aching by the time I got to the lower level, but I wasted no time in advancing toward the passageway.

I wondered if Illona and Cylas had noticed I was missing.

The atmosphere in the lower level was cold, despite the raging fire. I could see my breath as I walked, and I hugged my arms. A damp earthy smell also filled the area . . . as if there was water nearby.

I hurried to the passageway and stopped at the symbols.

My jaw dropped when I looked at the figures more closely.

There were depictions of oval-shaped star crafts carrying two people—hundreds of them. The star crafts hovered near each other and were drawn heading in the same direction.

I looked for more clues as to where the star crafts were. Were they drawn to show how the rider descendants arrived at Elinoor from space?

My brows furrowed when I saw small fish drawn into the stone.

The star crafts were underwater.

The Metidons were underwater.

Were the depictions telling a story of how to access the Metidons by star craft? Or were they leading the way?

The smell of water grew as I ran down the passageway, following the depictions.

As I raced down the passageway, with only the glowing wall markings lighting my way, I wondered if I would find Demira at the end.

With each step I took, I started to see small bubbles of water suspended in the air, and my heart began to pound, threatening to escape my body.

I knew I was close to something, as the air was charged with magic. It was more palpable the farther I ran, the magic almost clinging to my body, sending tingling sensations along my skin.

The magic was not malignant, as I knew what that felt like-sickly and heavy. Rather, the magic here was light and exhilarating, like a rush of water.

Water!

I covered my mouth and stopped.

In front of me was a glowing blue lake, and on its shore, dozens of shiny black crafts just like the ones depicted on the cavern walls. The crafts each had blue, oval domes at the top that curved down in the front, making the inside of the craft visible.

As I walked next to the crafts, I ran my fingers along the surface. The vehicles were cold and smooth to the touch, and the domes were made of something like glass.

A sharp, pop sound came from my right, and I froze.

A curse broke through the air.

"*Fuck!*"

I moved to my right past several crafts and saw a person dressed in red kneeling alongside a craft.

"Are you *fucking* kidding me right now?" Demira growled in a low tone.

"You're here?" was all I could manage.

Demira spun to face me and fell on her ass. She frowned.

"What do you want?" she snapped.

"I . . ." I crossed my arms. "Everyone is looking for you!"

Demira pushed to stand and dusted off her red dress.

"*I know.*" She spun around to face the craft she was standing next to. She pressed the side portion of the craft. Blue buttons appeared, glowing under the black surface.

"You *know*?" I asked her and scoffed. "Do you know how worried Illona is for you?"

"Spare me your theatrics, Renna."

I stepped toward her and grabbed her arm, spinning her around.

"What the fuck is your problem?!" I asked. "You knew we were searching for you, and you act like you don't care. What are you doing here anyway?"

She shrugged her arm from my grasp and narrowed her eyes.

"Well I'm sure you're not the only ones looking for me," she said. "Do you know what the rider equinox ritual *is*?" She raised her eyebrows.

I shook my head, but a feeling of dread spread through my body at her words.

"I overheard the people of Elsbeth talking about the upcoming ritual when I left the Aelderhall," she said. "The elders sacrifice a *female* murderer every equinox as a symbol of the woman responsible for the death of King Corrigrant. They blame that woman—me—for banishing the Metidons from the homeland. The ritual is meant to appease the beasts."

"Oh, Demira," I whispered. "I'm so sorry."

She laughed bitterly. "The children are given dolls to cast into the fire. Ones that resemble me."

My heart dropped into my stomach.

"And the elders have told us themselves are *so sure* the ritual will work this time," Demira scoffed. "I have no doubt they would have come for me."

The dark magic inside me, the one that relished my rage and chaos, lifted its head as if waking up. I curled my fists.

"I won't let them hurt you," I told her, my teeth clenched.

Demira sighed and spun around, focusing on the craft in front of her.

"So you're leaving?" I asked, walking to stand next to her.

I looked down into the craft through the blue glass dome and could see the two seats with multiple safety belts. There were also a multitude of buttons, a steering wheel in front of each seat, and five screens. All in all, it was an elaborate helm.

"I'm going to speak to these fucking beasts on my own. I *will* make them see reason. I'm not having someone else do the honors for me." She shook her head. "Besides, the elders will likely try to kill me first."

"How do you know the crafts will help you reach the Metidons?" I asked.

Demira looked to her right and pointed. My eyes followed her finger, and I gasped.

The cave wall depictions of the crafts traveling to the same place culminated in an arrival at huge caverns. Inside the caverns were large, feathered serpent beasts with wings. The beasts, who I was certain were Metidons, had no wings, and I wondered if their magic propelled them to fly.

Seeing the lake and crafts stationed at the shore made me completely forget the cave depictions, but it was clear that if the crafts were at the bank of the lake, and the Metidons were underwater, this was a location the elders likely used to access them. It would make sense that the elders would have found a way to reach the Metidons that did not involve them leaving their caves and trekking outside.

Suddenly newfound hope emerged through my chest. If Demira was successful in petitioning the Metidons, I would not need to ascend—I would not be tied to Aeroth for life.

"Are you coming with me?" Demira asked.

Once more, I was presented with an opportunity to make a life-altering choice for my future. And not needing Aeroth to solve my entry into Taria seemed like the better option.

"Yes," I told her. "*I absolutely am.*"

Demira gave me one curt nod and a semblance of a smile, then moved her fingers over the buttons that had appeared on the side of the craft, and the dome opened.

"Easy enough," she said, grinning.

"What were you struggling with before?" I asked her. "When I came over, you were hunched down under the craft."

Demira grabbed her skirts, and in one quick swoop, she slung a leg over into the craft.

"The crafts are tethered to a base," she said as she slung the other leg in, pointing to the other crafts around us. "I tried to dislodge it myself by pushing it, but ultimately had to use magic to unlock this one from its base."

I leaned down to see another craft next to us and noticed the base she was referring to.

"Are you sure your magic didn't damage it?" I asked her as I hoisted myself into the craft.

"Only one way to find out," she said, bending down to move the safety belts aside in one of the seats and sitting down in it.

I followed suit, and once seated, I looked around the craft. It was small enough to only accommodate two people. At the rear of the craft, there was enough storage space for a few luggage bags and other necessities.

Both the floor and the sleek helm in front of us were black, giving the inside a surprisingly modern look.

I buckled myself. "I'm assuming you know what you're doing?" I asked as she began to press buttons on the helm.

She raised her eyebrows. "No clue. We're just figuring it out as we go!"

On my far right was a button with a symbol for what looked like the dome of the craft. I pressed it, and the dome instantly closed.

"Illona is going to be so angry when she realizes what I'm doing," Demira said under her breath.

I chuckled, knowing she was right. "She was in bad shape trying to locate you. I'm supposed to be with her and Cylas now, trying to find you."

"And your precious mate?" Demira asked.

I wondered how angry Aeroth would be when he found out. He had stressed how dangerous the beasts could be. I also wondered how fast our blood exchange would last before the separation pain hit me. Normally, I would have expected to already be suffering from separation pain. I thought about the elixir Aeroth and I exchanged at the marriage ceremony in Eniraath and whether that was the cause of me not needing his blood so soon.

After Demira pressed a few more buttons, the craft roared to life, and dim lighting turned on around us along the floor. A holographic screen with a thin, blue honeycomb pattern appeared on the glass with the word 'Enterion' also in glowing blue.

A female voice spoke.

"Hello," the female said. *"This is Enterion Craft, your waterway traveling craft. Where do you wish to go?"*

Demira and I looked at each other, our eyes wide.

She looked at the screen, and her voice was almost hesitant when she spoke. "The Metidons," Demira said loudly.

The screen changed, and a photo of a beast that looked like the cave depiction appeared. The words 'Metidinus Orion' appeared next to the photo.

"*Is this your selection?*" the smooth female voice asked.

"I would assume that is their true name?" I whispered to Demira.

She nodded. "I believe so. A text in Vasarys referred to them simply as Metidons, but it would make sense that they have an official species name."

"*Is this your selection?*" the female voice repeated.

"Yes," Demira replied.

"*Do you wish to use auto-mapping mode or manual mode to arrive at your destination*?" the female voice inquired.

"Auto?" Demira asked. She looked to me, and I shrugged.

"*Auto-mapping mode activated. Route in place. Please use the control wheel to steer.*"

Demira buckled herself quickly and grabbed the wheel in front of her just before the craft shot up into the air in a sharp jolt.

"What the actual fuck!" Demira cursed.

I held onto the sides of my seat.

"Have you ever been on a craft like this before?" she asked me.

"No. I would have remembered something like this!"

"*Waterway detected,*" the female voice crooned. "*Scan of route completed. Destination ahead.*"

"Please don't crash . . ." Demira whispered. "I don't know what the fuck I'm doing."

"*Descending in 3 . . . 2 . . . 1 . . .*"

The craft sped forward and angled down toward the water.

I closed my eyes and could feel my fingers cramp, not

knowing what would happen. Would the craft shatter upon contact going this fast?

Demira and I both screamed as the craft plunged into the water at an insurmountable speed.

The craft raced through the water for several moments until it began to slow down and cruise. When I finally opened my eyes, I was left speechless by the underwater world around us.

The neon lake remained a bright, fluorescent color, and everything under the surface glowed, as if every sign of life was bioluminescent. The fish that swam past us shimmered in silvers and whites. The tall kelp and underwater trees were a luminescent green and blue that almost blended in with the color of the water itself.

A school of fish abruptly appeared in our way, and Demira exclaimed, her eyes wide, "What do I do?"

I grabbed the wheel in front of me and turned it to the right, barely missing the fish.

The craft continued onwards. As I held onto the wheel, I could feel the engine vibrate softly, and I wondered why I had never seen machinery like this on Andora. We had large star crafts that transported people around Andora and to the two neighboring human planets. We also had various vehicles for single-rider transport, such as hover bikes. I wondered whether the other two human planets with oceans and lakes had crafts like this.

As we sped through the water, Demira turned to me.

"I don't hate you, you know."

I glanced to her. "*Really?* That's hard to believe."

Demira looked forward. "Thank you for coming with me," she said softly.

I nodded. "I would have never left you to do this on your own. Your vision stated that I was to be with you. I believe in your vision."

Demira was silent for a few moments before speaking.

"Illona is not in my vision."

I frowned. "Are you sure? You and Illona are inseparable."

Demira nodded. "I have had that vision so many times, and each time I try to search for her. She is not there."

A shiver passed through my spine.

"She must arrive in Taria through a different way," Demira said to herself. "I just don't know *how*."

I thought of Cylas and Illona searching for Demira earlier. I wondered if Cylas would ultimately devise a way to help Illona reach Taria. That is, if Illona didn't try and strangle him first.

"Part of me thinks this is a fool's errand," Demira murmured. She shook her head. "I just knew I would hate myself for not trying."

"That's how I feel about Sethos. I have to try and save him. Sethos protected me when I was young. I cannot just leave him to be consumed by Am-Re's magic. He killed Am-Re for me when I was eighteen."

Demira chuckled grimly. "He didn't kill Father *thoroughly* though."

I nodded.

"Sethos would have saved all of us this trouble had he killed Father's soul like he destroyed his body." Demira sighed, the sound heavy.

A silence settled around Demira and I.

And that's when the separation pain emerged.

I winced and let go of the control wheel to massage my temples. The craft continued to move through the water on its path.

"What's the matter?" Demira asked, on alert.

I shook my head gently as the pain increased. "Separation pain," I gritted out. "*Fuck!*"

"Oh fuck," Demira murmured. "This is just what we needed."

I didn't answer but instead concentrated on my breathing.

"I wish I knew how to help you," Demira said.

I frowned. "You also have a mate. How did *you* solve separation pain?"

Demira hesitated for a few moments.

"I sold my soul, Renna."

My eyes widened, and for a flash, my pain was almost gone from the shock. Demira looked straight ahead.

"I sold my soul to a demon," Demira said again with a nod. "In exchange for my soul, the demon banished separation pain from Oberon and I."

I shook my head. "Can you ever get your soul back?"

"No."

"Does Oberon know?" I whispered.

"No." Her voice was hard. "And he never will."

A dull wave of pain spread through my body, and I whimpered. I closed my eyes.

"We have arrived," the female voice of the craft said, and the vehicle started to tilt upwards toward the surface.

I peeked one eye open and could see the surface of the water.

When we broke through, the craft floated for a few moments before the engine kicked in again and began to direct the craft to the shore.

Ahead of us lay the entrance to an enormous, reddish-brown stone cavern. I thought of the cavern depictions of the Metidons and how large they had appeared compared to the drawn crafts. The scale of the cavern's entrance was terrifying, given the potential beasts inside.

As the craft moved toward the shore, I became nauseous from the movement of the vehicle and the dull pain that was slowly growing. Any other time, the separation pain would have rapidly increased, but now I was sure the concoction I drank during the marriage ceremony had something to do with the more muted separation pain.

"Are you alright?" Demira asked me.

I nodded and groaned from the movement.

"I blocked the pain from my memory so long ago," Demira said. "I'm sorry this is happening."

I didn't answer and merely closed my eyes again.

"So what's the plan?" I asked her as I tried to take a deep breath.

"From the cavern drawings in Elsbeth, the Metidons should be inside that cavern. We asked the craft to lead us here."

"*Right.*"

"From here, the inside of the cavern looks pitch-black, but we will have to go in. I'll conjure torches, and we will enter."

"Alright," I said with clenched teeth as the pain increased in waves.

The craft reached the shore, and the dome of the craft opened.

"Wow," Demira said in awe.

I remained silent, not wanting to open my eyes.

"Renna, look up."

I tilted my head up and opened one eye.

Above the cavern was moving water. It resembled a lake, almost like a reflection. How was it possible we were breathing air and above us was another body of water?

"We must have traveled through an underwater lake," Demira murmured. "The real lake is above us—the one seen from the forest in Elinoor just outside the caves that led us to Elsbeth."

Demira unbuckled her safety belts and got out of the craft with a jump. She brushed off her dress and stood with her hands on her hips, looking up at the lake above us.

"The elders did say the Metidons were located in a cavern system inside the lake located just outside the Rustic Mountains,"

Demira said to herself before turning to me. "Can you feel the magic here?"

With a clenched jaw, I undid my safety belts and carefully stepped out of the craft onto gray gravel. I wobbled on the ground and placed a hand against the craft for support.

I let my body adjust to standing, feeling a sort of dull pressure around my body, like pulsing electricity. The air smelled like sage or some aromatic herb that I couldn't exactly place. The magic in the air was palpable, as if this place had many magical wards placed on it. Was the magic in place to keep the Metidons from leaving . . . or to keep people out?

"I feel something," I told Demira. "It's not a bad feeling."

Demira walked to my side.

"You look pale, Renna," Demira said. "Maybe you should wait here?"

"*No!* I can do this. I won't leave you. We're in this together. I am in your vision. I am meant to be here."

Demira said nothing further, and with the wave of her hand, Purple Fire appeared in her right palm. She conjured a torch just above her palm, grabbed it by the middle, and nodded.

"Let's go in," she said and began to walk.

I took a deep breath and joined by her side.

"Are you afraid?" I asked her.

Demira was silent for a few moments.

"Yes."

At least she was honest.

As we walked, I called forth Black Fire and conjured a bow in my right hand and a quiver full of arrows at my back. With my left hand, I pulled an arrow and nocked it, ensuring I was ready should we need to defend ourselves.

Suddenly we saw torches moving in the cavern.

I frowned.

Three figures holding torches seemed to be moving toward the cavern entrance—toward us.

I put a hand in front of Demira and paused her. I pulled back the arrow, ready to strike as we waited for the figures to emerge.

"*No,*" Demira whispered, her hands going to her mouth.

"Welcome!" a voice boomed, and I winced from the sound. The voice echoed off the cavern walls, hurting my ears.

My eyes widened when I saw him.

Sethos.

Divica to his left.

And a man I had never seen before to his right. The man had dark skin and eyes that glowed almost silver blue—much like Illona's.

"Welcome, welcome," the man next to Sethos repeated. "It is so lovely to meet my little sister's siblings. I feel like we are almost family."

The man extended his arms out mockingly as if in a hug. Divica chortled a laugh and crossed her arms.

"Berion," Demira gritted to the man who had spoken. "You being here with *him,*" she jutted her chin to Sethos, "does not surprise me."

"Did my sister come with you?" Berion asked, angling his head to look behind us.

"Stay away from her," Demira growled.

"You are both a disgrace," Divica said to us and spat on the floor. I noticed she still did not have her staff.

My eyes moved to Sethos, who stood quietly, his eyes assessing me. The blue that I had loved in his eyes was gone—they were pitch-black. I knew from experience when Sethos eyes changed to black that my father's magic had taken over.

"Sethos," I said to him.

Berion laughed.

"Is that any way to greet your love?" Berion said to me with mocking laughter.

"Sethos," I said to him. "This isn't you."

Divica growled and said to me, "How dare you address the Most High in that way. Bow, you insolent crossbreed!"

In that moment, Divica raised her hands and shot green and lilac magic spheres toward us. Swiftly, I lowered my bow and called my magic from my center and erected my protective shield. My body shook from the sudden rush of magic and growing separation pain. I screamed.

Divica's magic slammed into the shield, and my body trembled from the impact. The shield deflected her magic instantly, and it vanished in the air.

Sethos remained silent.

"Are you going to let them hurt us?" I yelled at him. "*Do something!*"

Sethos's hand started to shake violently, and he threw the torch to the ground. His arms fell to his sides, and his fists clenched. His face became red, and he began to froth at the mouth.

What was happening to him?

"*Sethos!*" I screamed.

His face shook side to side rapidly until his neck cracked. And then the voice of my father Am-Re spoke through him.

"At last," Am-Re's voice said. "My favorite daughter."

Sethos's lips contorted into an evil smile. Despite me clearly seeing Sethos standing before me, I knew I could not think of him as Sethos in that moment. This was pure Am-Re.

"The boy cares for you, I'll give you that," Am-Re said to me. "His feelings for you make it difficult to fully possess him. He is stubborn."

My eyes widened, and Am-Re chuckled.

"Oh yes, my child," Am-Re said. "I am inside Sethos's body.

But rest assured he's still in here, kicking and screaming your name."

Am-Re laughed.

"*Renna, Renna,*" Am-Re mocked. "*Help me, Renna. Forgive me, Renna.*" Am-Re shook his head. "How he screams for you. Pathetic."

"Let him go," I gritted out.

"Alas, I cannot, sweet one," Am-Re replied.

My stomach turned over at his endearment for me. I wanted to vomit.

"You have something of mine that does not belong to you," Am-Re said. "Give me back my powers. *Now.*"

I shook my head and winced.

The separation pain was now fully present, and I wanted to curl up into a ball on the ground. But I could not show them any vulnerability, so I ground my feet into the gravel and steeled my body against the pain.

"*No?*" Am-Re said, and he animated Sethos's body so his arms were crossed. "Don't you remember what happens when you don't follow directions?" Am-Re sneered. "There is no closet for you to hide in now, *girl.*"

Rage erupted from me then as years of pain and grief rose to the surface. I screamed as I released my arrow, and with a wave of Sethos's arm, the arrow was instantly deviated and fell to the ground.

Am-Re chuckled. "Is that *all* you can do?"

Sethos's arms raised, shooting out green and black electric magic at Demira and me.

The magic bounced off my protective shield, and my body absorbed the shock of the impact. I shrieked as I tried to stay standing and gripped the bow.

With a shaky breath, I called another arrow, and it appeared in my hand.

I couldn't give up.

I cocked the arrow.

And then Berion's magic shot out, pummeling my shield. I crumpled to my knees as I struggled to maintain the shield. The bow and arrow disappeared like smoke as I steadied my hands on the ground for balance.

Divica laughed, sending another wave of magic at us. I could not withstand the pressure of holding it up, sobbing as the separation pain and the effort became too much.

Renna? Aeroth spoke in my head, and my heart expanded for a brief moment.

I did not respond to him. I could not risk his life.

"You need to do something, Renna," Demira urged me. She knelt beside me and put an arm around me. "You need to use Darkness."

My heart raced. I had no qualms using Darkness against others. But this was Sethos's body I was facing. I didn't want to hurt him.

"Renna, our father has the power of Darkness. He is *not* using it. Perhaps he does not have access to it anymore."

Demira was right. I wondered if Am-Re possessing the body of another limited his full use of powers.

"If you don't use Darkness, we will die," Demira cried out. "*Please.*"

I looked to my left at Demira's pale face. Her eyes were wide, and tears flowed down her face.

"Don't let him win," she gritted out.

I had to use Darkness. I knew I had to. There was no other choice.

The memory of Sethos demanding I use Darkness to kill flashed back into my mind. I had not been able to kill then.

What good is this magic if you don't use it!? he had yelled. *Do not be weak in this moment!*

I didn't want to destroy Sethos's body, but I had to do something to stop his attack.

"Renna!" Demira cried as more magic shot toward us from Berion and Divica. She stepped in front of me and locked eyes with me. "Don't let Father win!"

With tears in my eyes, I nodded, and Demira moved to help me up. I wavered on my feet, but I closed my eyes, took a deep breath, calling forth Darkness. I let the rumbling dark magic move through my body like waves of thick smoke.

I could do this.

I opened my eyes and watched as Darkness flowed from my hands onto the floor like shadowy tentacles.

Am-Re, Berion, and Divica instantly recalled their magic, and the attacks stopped.

I looked to their faces and saw a mixture of panic and awe.

"I'm going to recall my shield to attack," I told Demira. "Prepare to erect your own."

"Yes!"

In an instant, my shield was down, and I summoned more Darkness to flow from me. I was in a pool of shadows and smoke. The magic surrounded me, awaiting my instruction.

"Well, well, well," Am-Re said. "I am glad to see my power of Darkness is alive and well. It will be even better when I drain it from you, whore." He spat at the ground before me.

Renna?! Aeroth screamed in my head. ***Where are you?***

Forgive me, I whispered back to Aeroth, speaking through our bond.

My Darkness shot out toward Sethos's body, Berion, and Divica.

And then screams erupted.

ACKNOWLEDGMENTS

Thank you to The Creator, my family, and the female authors who have come before me (especially Mary Shelley and Jane Austen).

AFTERWORD

Women Trying to Fix Men with Problematic Behaviors . . .

When I set out writing book 3 I wrote it from the background of having had a fantastic Criminal Law professor who was a big advocate for restorative justice for incarcerated individuals. In my own practice I also assisted a non-for-profit and created a transitional shelter for previously incarcerated youth and also aided another non-for-profit organization in constructing a workforce campus that served previously incarcerated individuals also trying to re-enter society. Restorative justice is about ensuring an individual is not a repeat offender through various rehabilitation methods. Although the term restorative justice does not fit into a fantasy world the way it does in real life, I wanted a character who believes someone can be helped by changing their company, improving their environment, and giving them tools to thrive.

In my book, Renna mentions the term restorative justice as a way to propose Sethos be given a second opportunity to mend his ways instead of being killed. She knows Sethos was failed by those who raised him and deeply traumatized by catastrophic and abusive events. She does not condone his actions and is aware Sethos cannot simply walk away free after she drains Am-Re's magic from him. She understands he will likely be tried by a tribunal and jailed. For her, Sethos atoning for his sins while living is better than death. Knowing Renna, she would be the type of character to visit Sethos's jail cell from time to time to speak to him and perhaps aid in his recovery with medic mages. It would be my hope medic mages would offer him some sort of psychiatric help and help him deal with the anger and hatred he has inside. If medic mages followed real-life restorative justice methods perhaps they would convince Khellios and Sethos to sit down and have a conversation about their shared experiences and how to move forward.

Even though Renna fights for Sethos, you may have noticed I made sure Renna never wants to go back to him romantically. Too often we are shown female characters, or perhaps see examples in our own lives, where women in DV scenarios feel tasked with 'changing' or 'fixing' abusive male partner behaviors so they can stay with them in toxic romantic relationships. I wanted to show my readers that while one can root for a romantic partner to change, and in some cases if it's safe provide them with the tools to better their lives (e.g. provide hotlines for addiction, suggest vising a therapist, staging an intervention with appropriate support) it may not always be healthy to go stay in a relationship with a person who hurt you in the past.

With all my appreciation,
Mina

A NOTE ABOUT AEROTH

In the afterword of *A God of Moonlight and Stardust* I explained how Sethos came to me in a dream when I was post partum. The first dream sequence Renna has of him in Book 1 is how I dreamt him. Her conversation with Sethos was almost verbatim the conversation I had with him.

Aeroth came to me in a similar way during a daydream during the time I was writing Book 1. He appeared to me cloaked in black stars as a moving, breathing, morphing, monolith fragment in space. I imagined myself suspended in space, like Renna was when she crossed from Taria to Daya in *An Heir of Darkness and Ruin*. Just how Aeroth morphs from space itself into a body and speaks to Renna in that scene, that is how Aeroth appeared to me. It was a terrifying thing to daydream and because of his imposing personality I knew he was going to play a major role in the series.

Aeroth being half vampire, or half Naaviri, is a tribute to my love of Dracula. My own pen name of Mina is after Mina Harker. I hope readers enjoy my own space-themed spin on vampire lore.

It was fun and sometimes heartbreaking learning Aeroth's backstory.

The King of the Astral Plane, or The King of Crimson Dreams, will always be one of my favorite MMCs. I am glad Aeroth entered my life when he did. He really is one big green flag.

A NOTE ABOUT METIDONS

As some readers may suspect Metidons are inspired by my own Mexican mythology and in particular Kukulkan. As a person from Mexico I personally connect the most and have roots with the Mayan civilization. I actively honor the Mayan gods as a way to keep my culture alive. I tend to only visit the Yucatan Peninsula when I am in Mexico as that region feels the most like home. My favorite ruins to visit are Uxmal which I recommend to every person visiting that region. As Kukulkan is one of my favorite gods it made sense to add a beast in my series like him. In my book the Metidons are different in that they are iridescent and breathe out ice. I like to think the Metidons would be a cousin to Kukulkan.

SERIES GLOSSARY

The glossary below is available for reference, but not required.

Source: The Creator of the seven universes and all life.

Universes

Konah Universe: one of seven universes created by Source.

Stallias Universe: one of seven universes created by Source.

Galaxies

Milky Way: A galaxy that is mostly abandoned, inhabited by lawless beings. The galaxy includes the planet Earth.

Andromeda: A galaxy rich with life, inhabited by humans from Planet Earth and supernatural beings. The galaxy includes the planet Andora.

Sirius: A small galaxy inhabited by supernaturals.

Delphinus: A galaxy inhabited by supernaturals and the Elemental Enclave. The galaxy includes the planet Moringa.

Arcturian: A small galaxy inhabited by supernaturals.

Stars

Eusera: Closest star outside of Vasarys.

Planets

Earth: An abandoned planet in the Milky Way galaxy. Humans left this planet during the Great Migration.

Andora: A human inhabited planet in Andromeda galaxy. The planet is inhabited with descendants from the Great Migration. Includes supernatural beings who hide their magic and pose as humans.

Isyos: An abandoned planet destroyed by the Celestial Enclave.

Moringa: A small planet inhabited by the Elemental Enclave in Delphinus galaxy.

Tirose-B9: A planet inhabited by Arcadians, home planet of Princess Elrie.

Elinoor: planet in Konah Universe. Inhabited by rider descendants of Metidons. Includes a dimension where Metidons are located.

Nelar: planet where the dimension of Taria was relocated.

Cities

New Xhor: An existing city on Andora.

Old Xhor: An old city on Andora currently in ruins. The ruins are an excavation site.

Elsbeth: A cave city inside Elinoor.

Dimensions

Taria: A dimension where the Celestial Enclave resides. The dimension is not visible to humans. The dimension includes the ghost souls of old priests and priestesses of the Celestial gods and living people with magical powers escaping persecution from the Planetary Council.

Daya: A dimension suspended in outer space habited by criminal fae.

Vasarys: A dimension inside a black hole and Am-Re's kingdom.

Astral Plane: An alternative reality available to souls during dreamtime, meditation, and when the brain is in an altered state.

Civilizations

Arcadians: An advanced civilization inhabiting planet Tirose-B9.

Melodar Elves: The first elves created by Source. The reside in the Astral Plane inside the Kingdom of Eniraath.

Supernaturals

Naaviri: A type of fae that drink blood, also known as vampires on planet Earth.

Elves: A type of fae.

Mages: A being who is trained to practice witchcraft as a profession.

Medic Mage: a humanoid being who is half robot and half person and practices medicine and witchcraft to heal others. Originates from the Arcturian Galaxy.

Beasts

Dretani: a beast assigned to a god. Used as a proxy to fight in wars on behalf of their god. In some instances a demi-god may have a dretani.

Metidon: a feathered winged flying serpent. The first beast created by Source.

Kings and Rulers

Arios: The chief god of the Celestial Enclave.

Istron: The chief god of the Elemental Enclave.

Merida: The witch ruler of Taria's Witch District.

King Miletak: A ruler from planet Tirose-B9. He is princess Elrie's father.

King Oberon: A reclusive king of the Tatuiyah.

King Aeroth: The king of the Astral Plane.

King Corrigrant: The murdered king of the Tatuiyah.

Wyleth: The leader of the Elders of Elsbeth.

Divica: Queen of the Forest Sprites.

God Enclaves

Celestial Enclave: The assembly of gods who oversee celestial bodies and related cosmic bodies and events.

Elemental Enclave: The assembly of gods who oversee the elements, fire, bodies of water, and weather events.

Spirit Enclave: The assembly of gods who guide the practice of witchcraft, oversee spirits, and supervise people's abilities in clairvoyance, clairaudience, clairsentience, claircognizance, and clairgustance.

Kingdoms

Tatuiyah: A fae kingdom led by reclusive king Oberon.

Kingdom of Nightmares: A fae kingdom of dreams and nightmares led by a king who mourns his dead wife.

Kingdom of Eniraath: A fae kingdom ruled by King and Queen of the Astral Plane. Located in the Astral Plane. Inhabited by the Melodar Elves.

Governments

Planetary Council: A human government formed during the Great Migration. The Council oversees the three human planets in the Andromeda galaxy.

Galactic Federation: A multi-universe governmental body that creates and enforces laws for supernatural beings.

The Council of Vasarys: A governmental body that oversees Vasarys.

Elders of Elsbeth: A council that oversees the day to day operations of the city of Elsbeth.

Events

Great Migration: Mass exodus of humans from Earth.

Night of a Thousand Tears: Term coined by Am-Re to describe the attack on Isyos by the Celestial Enclave.

Equinox Celebrations in Elsbeth: A yearly sacrificial ritual to appease the Metidons.

ABOUT THE AUTHOR

Mina B. Castillo, formerly writing as Mina Brower, is a Mexican-American and immigrant from Mexico who aims to inspire other immigrants to chase their dreams. Mina is a mother, wife, and author of the critically praised Daughters of Chaos Series.

Mina is an avid fan of science fiction and was obviously present during the Galactic Wars and likes to think she has a saved seat at Galactic Federation meetings. She attributes her love of science fiction after her grandfather became a writer in the genre late in his life.

When she's not writing under her pen name, Mina is a partner at her law firm and mentors female pre-law and law students.

During her free time you can find Mina either hiking, at a museum, on a cruise ship, or competing with her horse in hunter jumper.

Follow Mina on social media for book updates and also visit her website at https://www.authorminacastillo.com to sign up for her newsletter.

ALSO BY MINA B. CASTILLO

Daughters of Chaos Series

Book 1: A God of Moonlight and Stardust

Book 2: An Heir of Darkness and Ruin

Book 3: A King of Crimson Dreams

Book 4: Title to be revealed soon

Valdenbrook Stables Series

Contemporary sports romance about showjumping coming 2027.

www.ingramcontent.com/pod-product-compliance
Lightning Source LLC
Chambersburg PA
CBHW030536130726
48054CB00020B/62

* 9 7 9 8 9 9 1 2 4 8 2 7 3 *